The Girl on the Edge of Summer

Acclaim for J.M. Redmann's Micky Knight Series

Ill Will

Lambda Literary Award Winner

Foreword Magazine Honorable Mention

"*Ill Will* is fast-paced, well-plotted, and peopled with great characters. Redmann's dialogue is, as usual, marvelous. To top it off, you get an unexpected twist at the end. Please join me in hoping that book number eight is well underway."—*Lambda Literary Review*

"Ill Will is a solidly plotted, strongly character-driven mystery that is well paced."—*Mysterious Reviews*

Water Mark

Foreword Magazine Gold Medal Winner

Golden Crown Literary Award Winner

"*Water Mark* is a rich, deep novel filled with humor and pathos. Its exciting plot keeps the pages flying, while it shows that long after a front page story has ceased to exist, even in the back sections of the newspaper, it remains very real to those whose lives it touched. This is another great read from a fine author."—*Just About Write*

Death of a Dying Man

Lambda Literary Award Winner

"Like other books in the series, Redmann's pacing is sharp, her sense of place acute and her characters well crafted. The story has a definite edge, raising some discomfiting questions about the selfishly unsavory way some gay men and lesbians live their lives and what the consequences of that behavior can be. Redmann isn't all edge, however—she's got plenty of sass. Knight is funny, her relationship with Cordelia is believably long-term-lover sexy and little details of both the characters' lives and New Orleans give the atmosphere heft."—*Lambda Book Report*

Death of a Dying Man

"As the investigation continues and Micky's personal dramas rage, a big storm is brewing. Redmann, whose day job is with NOAIDS, gets the Hurricane Katrina evacuation just right—at times she brought tears to my eyes. An unsettled Micky searches for friends and does her work as she constantly grieves for her beloved city." —*New Orleans Times-Picayune*

The Intersection of Law and Desire

Lambda Literary Award Winner

San Francisco Chronicle Editor's Choice for the year

Profiled on *Fresh Air*, hosted by Terry Gross, and selected for book reviewer Maureen Corrigan's recommended holiday book list.

"Superbly crafted, multi-layered…One of the most hard-boiled and complex female detectives in print today."—*San Francisco Chronicle* (An Editor's Choice selection for 1995)

"Fine, hard-boiled tale-telling."—*Washington Post Book World*

"An edge-of-the-seat, action-packed New Orleans adventure… Micky Knight is a fast-moving, fearless, fascinating character…*The Intersection of Law and Desire* will win Redmann lots more fans." —*New Orleans Times-Picayune*

"Crackling with tension…an uncommonly rich book…Redmann has the making of a landmark series."—*Kirkus Review*

"Perceptive, sensitive prose; in-depth characterization; and pensive, wry wit add up to a memorable and compelling read."—*Library Journal*

"Powerful and page turning…A rip-roaring read, as randy as it is reflective…Micky Knight is a to-die-for creation…a Cajun firebrand with the proverbial quick wit, fast tongue, and heavy heart." —*Lambda Book Report*

Lost Daughters

"A sophisticated, funny, plot-driven, character-laden murder mystery set in New Orleans…as tightly plotted a page-turner as they come…One of the pleasures of *Lost Daughters* is its highly accurate portrayal of the real work of private detection—a standout accomplishment in the usually sloppily conjectured world of thriller-killer fiction. Redmann has a firm grasp of both the techniques and the emotions of real-life cases—in this instance, why people decide to search for their relatives, why people don't, what they fear finding and losing…and Knight is a competent, tightly wound, sardonic, passionate detective with a keen eye for detail and a spine made of steel."—*San Francisco Chronicle*

"Redmann's Micky Knight series just gets better…For finely delineated characters, unerring timing, and page-turning action, Redmann deserves the widest possible audience."—*Booklist*, starred review

"Like fine wine, J.M. Redmann's private eye has developed interesting depths and nuances with age…Redmann continues to write some of the fastest –moving action scenes in the business… In Lost Daughters, Redmann has found a winning combination of action and emotion that should attract new fans—both gay and straight—in droves."—*New Orleans Times Picayune*

"…tastefully sexy…"—*USA Today*

"An admirable, tough PI with an eye for detail and the courage, finally, to confront her own fear. Recommended."—*Library Journal*

By the Author

The Micky Knight Mystery Series:

Death by the Riverside

Deaths of Jocasta

The Intersection of Law and Desire

Lost Daughters

Death of a Dying Man

Water Mark

Ill Will

The Shoal of Time

The Girl on the Edge of Summer

Women of the Mean Streets: Lesbian Noir
edited with Greg Herren

Men of the Mean Streets: Gay Noir
edited with Greg Herren

Night Shadows: Queer Horror
edited with Greg Herren

As R. Jean Reid, the Nell McGraw mystery series

Roots of Murder

Perdition

The Girl on the Edge of Summer

by

J.M. Redmann

2017

THE GIRL ON THE EDGE OF SUMMER

ISBN 13: 978-1-62639-687-6

This Trade Paperback Original Is Published By
Bold Strokes Books, Inc.
P.O. Box 249
Valley Falls, NY 12185

First Edition: April 2017

Credits
Editors: Greg Herren and Stacia Seaman
Production Design: Stacia Seaman
Cover Design by Sheri (graphicartist2020@hotmail.com)

Acknowledgments

Sitting in front of a computer trying to make words turn into worlds is never easy. (Nor are the words ever as perfect as the vision we have in our heads.) There are moments when I come home from the day job and I'm tired and want nothing more than to turn my brain off, pour a glass of wine, and read a book instead of writing one. But in those moments, I remember the coterie of readers and writers, who keep me sane and focused. Yes, that would be you. Thank you.

My writer friends, all of us who struggle to get the words on the page amidst everything else life throws at us. Carsen, Ali, Anne, VK, 'Nathan, Jeffrey, Rob, Fay, Ellen, Greg, and I know I'm forgetting some of y'all. You keep me sane, or at least aren't bothered by my insanity.

I also need to thank the generous folks who have willingly supported my day job at NO/AIDS Task Force by donating because I used a name of their choosing in the book. The support is greatly appreciated, and it really helps me come up with names.

A big thank you to Greg Herren for his editorial brilliance and calmness, especially his Zen about deadlines.

Mr. Squeaky and Arnold because I'm a lesbian and we have to thank our cats. Also, Sammy and Ms. M, the rescue cats left homeless by the floods in the summer of 2016 who shared my house this fall and are now in their forever home thanks to Mary and Ginny.

My partner, Gillian, for all the joy in us both spending evenings at our respective computers working on our respective books. At least I don't have to footnote and index mine.

There are many people at my day job who keep me sane—or don't point out to me that I'm not—and are greatly understanding about the writing career. Noel, our CEO, Reg, our COO and my boss for his tireless leadership and letting me run off to do book things. My staff is great and makes my job easy enough that I have time to write—Narquis, Joey, Lauren, Allison, and all the members of the Prevention Department. I would love to be able to write full-time, but since I have to have a real job, I'm very lucky to have one of the best ones possible.

Also huge thanks to Rad for making Bold Strokes what it is. Ruth, Connie, Shelley, Sandy, Stacia, and Cindy for all their hard work behind the scenes, and everyone at BSB for being such a great and supportive publishing house.

To the City of New Orleans and all my friends here.
A fascinating, beautiful, maddening place and a glorious one to set mysteries in.

Chapter One

I cursed. Silently. I had to keep my face neutral, to look like I didn't regret the question I had just asked. But the words were out, and she would answer. And the answer would compel me to do something I desperately didn't want to do.

It had started out as a good day, cold—for us—but with clear sun after days of drizzle and clouds. Traffic was post–Mardi Gras light. Everyone was either crammed in the airport to leave or home sleeping it off, leaving the roads blessedly sane for a few days.

I'd even caught a coconut at Zulu, now proudly displayed on my mantel. I hadn't been exactly sober but maintained a pleasant buzz, enough to enjoy the insanity but not stumble into the gutter—as many other people were doing. I had seen Zulu in the non-tourist area up on Basin. You *could* pay me enough money to watch Mardi Gras on Canal Street, but it would have to be a lot. A whole lot. After a wander through the French Quarter to see all the costumes—and get a voodoo daiquiri to keep the buzz going—I'd come home. It had still been light out. For New Orleans, I was a good girl.

I'd taken it easy this week, used Ash Wednesday for a grocery run to replenish my bare larder. I live in an old neighborhood, close to the French Quarter, and once the parades start it's hard to get out and about. I don't quite recover from the tromping around—and to be honest, the mix of alcohols—as when I was younger. Thursday was a half day at the office, half day at home cooking the newly bought food. Friday I left early; it was Friday, after all. The work could wait until a real Monday, far from the toss of shiny beads.

And Monday, it was, one of bright sunshine, the light changing, stronger, more direct, a harbinger of spring, the renewal of what had gone in the winter. I'd come to my office around the usual time, before ten but safely after nine.

In a few days I'd be busy with everything that had been put aside to ride on a float, make a costume for a ball—or to have left town to get away from the madness.

I had done paperwork, billing, which I hate, but it's part of the job and the part that pays the cost of my existence. My standards are to never darken the door of a Laundromat again—this is New Orleans, I know enough weird characters without having to meet any at the dryer, thank you very much. So much nicer to have my own. At least I know where the dirt it's washing off came from.

There had been one message on my voice mail. I'd returned it, my phone call of the day, making this appointment with Mrs. Stevens—she called herself Mrs., so I followed suit. Mrs. Susie Stevens. Yes, Susie, not Susan. Deep South much? Our call had been brief; she said she wanted me to find someone, and I agreed to meet to talk about it.

She had arrived on time, a little early as if I were a doctor's office and there would be paperwork to fill out first. She was neatly dressed, a conservative navy blue blazer with matching skirt, crisp white blouse. Pearls, even, although they were small and looked more middle-class respectable than money. Sensible black leather pumps. Her hair was the brown it probably always had been, with a few blond highlights that were either from a long summer on the beach or a bottle. My money was on the latter. Mrs. Stevens didn't come across as a long time at the beach person. She was every inch the kind of woman I'd pass in a mall in Metairie—assuming I ever went to the mall or the suburbs—and not notice. Except for her face. No, not her face, but the emotions sculpted into it, sad, lost, her glance searching for a place to focus but finding nothing to compete with what she was seeing behind her eyes.

Her voice was low, soft; I had to strain at times to hear the words. "I need you to find someone for me. I don't know his name, but I know what he looks like and have some idea of places he might be."

"Why do you want to find him?"

Her eyes looked away, the rest of her face immobile as if she didn't dare move it. "He obtained—I don't know how—a picture of my daughter. She had her shirt off. He posted it online, sent it to all his friends." Her lips were tight, brittle, as if the words could break them.

"What do you want to do with him if you find him?"

Her answer was ready, as if she'd thought this through over and over again. Or rehearsed it. "Only what he did to my daughter. Post who and what he is to the online judge, jury and executioner."

Maybe it was true. A twitch at her eye, the tight lips, a mask, or so many emotions, the real one was lost.

I asked the logical next question. "Can I talk to your daughter?"

Her expression told me before the itch of memory recalled a newspaper story. A car found on River Road by the Bonnet Carré Spillway. The body of a young girl had washed up. A brief story; her life was brief, only seventeen years. No evidence of foul play. Trouble at school. Suicide.

I didn't want to take this case, and I knew I would. If I said no, Mrs. Stevens would find someone else to take her suburban money and ignore her grief. Maybe I thought I could talk her out of anything rash, keep her to her word of shaming him online. Maybe I thought I would be kinder, wiser than the next person she tried. Rationalization comes so easy.

"You can't talk to my daughter. She killed herself," the words a bare whisper as if they were shards of glass cutting her mouth on the way out.

"I'm very sorry. That is a hard loss." No mother should bury a child. But she knew that, and there were no words in the world that would make any difference. I didn't try. "Will it help?" I asked. "Finding him?"

"It'll help his next victim. The next girl he taunts and makes miserable."

She continued, her lips still pressed together as if each word cost her, "The police could do little. They claimed they didn't have the resources to hunt down some anonymous online person. Particularly for…" Then the words cost too much and she couldn't say them.

For someone who killed herself. It wasn't murder. Sad, a troubled teen, desperation long enough for her to take her parents' car, drive twenty minutes, and embrace the dark water.

Maybe she had even given him the picture. Girls still do stupid things for love. Or the first glimmer of attention they mistake for love. The police don't make arrests for crimes of the heart.

I agreed to take the case.

After she left, I wondered why I felt guilty because one more young girl had died. Or why I thought I had any business being involved. The everyday violence against women. Men kill each other for drugs or they're drunk and stupid, or drunk and angry, or feel they have to prove something. But women die because they're women. How many times have you skimmed the headlines, "a woman's body was found" or "a woman's nude body was discovered" and then a short blurb more on her death than her life.

Mrs. Susie Stevens hadn't given me much because she didn't have much. A lump of a boy, maybe a school mate, maybe not, had gotten a picture of her daughter, Tiffany, showing her breasts. There might have been other pictures, but that was the only one she knew about. The only one she wanted to know about.

I was to meet her tomorrow at her home in Old Metairie. She would let me have Tiffany's cell phone and computer.

I had the feeling she wanted someone to filter her daughter's life for her, to see the other pictures, read the naïve text messages and only pass on what a grieving mother could bear. She said all she wanted was his name and address. I doubted that. The twitching of her eyelids, the tightness of her lips said she wanted something beyond what life could give—to go back to the moment before Tiffany took the keys to the car, to grasp that one short, oh-so-short hour of time and wrench it off the path it had taken.

I took a deep breath, then another. Then prepared a case file. I wanted to jump back a few days, to the revels when my biggest concern was how to hold on to a coconut and still catch beads.

Time marches on and pain isn't ended by a parade, only buffered, a respite of color and motion with the blare of marching bands for a soundtrack. All I could do was help Mrs. Susie Stevens through the days, find a few tattered pieces of that thing they call closure. Or maybe if Tiffany had held out a little longer, the swirling colors, the thumping drums, the bright, sparking beads in the air could have caught her and held her in this life.

My high school years, I tried not to think of them. The parades saved me on occasion. I remember clearly, all too clearly, once thinking *I could just step in front of that truck and it would all end*. All the misery, the despair of knowing I was so far out of place—queer, taken in by family that didn't want me, olive skin and black curly hair, not a fair child of the suburbs, but a bastard bayou rat. It seemed there was no place in the world for me. Except at the parades, and later the gay end of the French Quarter. Looking at the truck, its gears grinding as it sped up, my foot on the curb. A step or two. But I was meeting my friends Ned and his hidden boyfriend at a parade, Thoth, uptown. I let the truck pass.

A few little threads, having someone else gay in my life, plans to meet up, had twined together, enough to keep me safely out of the road. Luck, mostly, things that would be minor were still enough to keep me holding to life. Ned, two years older, off to college after we'd doubled-dated in high school, the façade of Bryan and me and Misty and him, but once away from prying eyes, we switched. Misty was my first girlfriend, also two years older, also off to college, but she wasn't coming back, not here, not to me.

Ned had, and said *let's meet for Thoth*. That was enough; I couldn't let him down.

Tiffany had taken that step.

It's a case, do what you're hired to do, I told myself. I had no magic; I couldn't save the lost girls.

Instead, I set myself to the usual routines. First of all, check out Mrs. Susie Stevens. My gut said she was who she claimed, a suburban woman carrying a heavy sorrow, but it's always best to fact-check instinct. Most clients are who they say they are. Not all of them are forthcoming on their reasons for why they want to hire a private detective. Guilt, shame, they don't want to reveal everything—why their kid really left, the real reason they're looking for someone. Best to dig behind what they say. A few clients are out-and-out cons, trying to manipulate me into doing their dirty work. Those get shown the door. With no refund on the retainer.

What Susie Smith had left out was that she only had a tenuous claim to the Mrs. The divorce papers had been filed and Mr. Smith was living in the kind of apartment ones moves into in haste, a big complex out in Metairie, built in the oil boom of past decades. He worked in insurance. Susie kept the house. A big empty house, with an older son in college at LSU and her only other child dead.

She did volunteer work for a local hospital, was active in a gardening club, winning a prize for her roses. It seemed her husband's paycheck had been the one that bought the nice house in Metairie, paid the college tuition, and kept the family firmly in the upper middle class. I wondered how long Susie would be able to hold on to the house. She put a brittle façade on her crumbling life and didn't want me to know. She didn't deliberately lie; the truth was too acid to tell. Her life was spinning out of control—her son's leaving was the only expected and accepted loss. Children grow up. But her second child would never grow up, never leave for college, always be a brutally torn scar of blame, regret, and loss. Her husband? Ex-husband? Maybe their marriage was strong until this ripped it apart. Or maybe it was already crumbling and this was the end of the end.

Susie Stevens didn't need to spend time and money searching for the lout who'd posted her daughter's half-nude picture. She needed to get into therapy, move out of a now haunted house, and find a way to live the decades she still had of her life.

I considered calling her to say I couldn't take the case. But the rationalizations came back. She would find someone to do it. It was better she find someone like me.

Plus, I had to admit, I wanted to find the asshole. Nothing illegal, but he needed to sweat, and sweat long and hard. Maybe that was the other reason I shouldn't take this case. But I didn't think about that. Even I wouldn't believe my rationalizations.

Chapter Two

Brandon ignored her the first time she called his name. And the second.

It wasn't until she was standing in his bedroom door, shaking something at him, that he looked up at her. This was the first time he'd gotten to level four, and he didn't want to be interrupted.

"Can't you ever take care of your things? I found these behind the dryer; they've been stuffed there for God knows how long. These are the new jeans your grandmom brought you for Christmas."

"Sorry, I forgot," he mumbled, not looking at her.

"How could you forget? They stink!"

"Sorry," he mumbled again. "They musta got dirty behind the machine."

"This isn't dirt, this is dog s—poop. Weeks-old, hardened dog poop."

He almost laughed at her clumsy switch from saying "shit"—like he didn't know the word. Poop. "Poop" was a funny word. But laughing would only keep her tirade going.

"Sorry, Mom," he tried again. "I didn't realize I must have stepped in it. And then forgot."

"How do you forget a mess like this? Can you look at me?"

He paused the game first, then looked at her. Just long enough to meet her demand.

"Sorry, I forgot," he repeated, his hand still on the gaming control. "I won't do it again." There, that should be enough, it usually was. His hand moved to un-pause his game.

"Maybe you won't do it again if you have to clean them." She threw the jeans at him, landing on top of his laptop.

His hand jerked away from the foul smear. To get it off his computer, he had to carefully wad the jeans up to keep the dog shit in the middle. Just in time to hear the bloop-bloop-bloop of doom. Back to level five.

He hadn't expected his mother to do that. When he said he was sorry, that was usually enough to get her to let go of whatever she was nagging him about. Even if he didn't mean it. That was their bargain. He obeyed the rules—sort of, saying sorry when it seemed like that was what she wanted. Getting Bs, sometimes even As in things he liked, like biology. And she didn't harass him too much.

She's probably on the rag, he thought, repeating in his head one of the lines Kevin used when girls were stuck up. But he quickly banished the phrase; he didn't want to think about his mother and down there. That was too heretical, even for him.

He hadn't forgotten about the jeans, more ignored them day after day because he didn't want to think about them, about peeling the wet and stinking jeans off, hoping his mother wouldn't notice how late he'd come home, wouldn't ask questions he couldn't answer.

He found a plastic grocery bag, one he used to sneak forbidden snacks into his room, and put the wadded-up jeans into it, tightly tying the handles together. Maybe it would keep it from smelling up his room.

Then he went back to playing his computer game.

CHAPTER THREE

The weather held, bright and cheery, too nice by far for the errand I was on, going to Mrs. Susie Stevens' posh house in the suburbs to paw through her dead daughter's things.

I had to look up her location on the map—the one on my so-called smartphone. It wasn't smart enough to tell me not to take this case—or what to do about my love life, and that was the kind of smart that would have been truly useful, although speaking an address and having it tell you how to get there was kind of helpful. I know New Orleans proper, but for the suburbs I have something I call dyslexia of the chain stores. It all looks alike, so I'm never quite sure of where I am. Or if I should be there at all.

Mrs. Susie Stevens lived in a house off Metairie Road, the kind of street parents called a good place to raise kids, not knowing how wrong they could be. The houses here were originally built in the prosperity of the '50s and '60s. Most, like many of the women living in them, showed signs of having had work done to keep them attractive looking. Mrs. Stevens' house now took up most of the lot, the façade updated to matching red brick, with faux Georgian columns, a lawn clipped like a drill sergeant's head, tasteful landscaping on the borders, ordered like the sergeant's troops in neat rows and lines. No wonder Mrs. Stevens was so shattered; this house was one of order, a bulwark against the twists and turns and blind alleys life could take you on.

I sat in my car, ambivalent about pursuing this. Again, I ignored my instincts and let facts—the ones I was aware of—guide me. She would find someone else, and that someone else could be venal. Being involved gave me some control; walking away gave me none. And maybe that was it, no matter what my instincts told me; I couldn't just walk away.

I got out, striding up the perfectly weed-free walk, and rang the doorbell.

She answered as if she had been hovering at the door waiting. For anything to intrude into her shroud of grief. She managed a weak smile, but it didn't reach her eyes, the reflex action of a woman named Susie, not Susan, always polite.

The wan smile was the only greeting she managed. "Please come this way," she said as I entered her house.

It felt too empty, not a dog or cat or even parakeet to keep her company. As with the yard, it was as neat and clean as a house about to be shown by an owner desperate for a sale. Even the strong morning sun didn't reveal a mote of dust. I gave her the benefit of a doubt that this was grief, obsessively cleaning as if it could restore order to her life, that once there had been a family and people running messily through this house, leaving the usual trail of footprints, glasses left on tables, books half-read on a couch.

With no other words, she led me down a long hallway, with a large den running the length of one side and on the other first what was clearly a boy's room with football memorabilia and sports car pictures, then a bathroom, also too clean to have been used recently, and finally, a smaller room than her brother's, a room just as clearly a girl's, with pictures of boy bands—I had no idea who they were, except to be able to tell they were either in showbiz or gay. Or both. Her bedspread was pink, with white curtains dotted with pictures of pink roses that matched the bed. Clearly this orderly household allowed for no gender nonconformity.

You don't know that, I reminded myself. Maybe Tiffany and her brother were happy in their traditional choices. Cordelia used to say you're not really open minded if you don't accept people making choices you would never make. Like a pink bedroom. It didn't matter what Cordelia used to say, even if she was right. Cordelia was my…ex? Was that all that was left?

"Let me know if you need anything," Mrs. Stevens said at the door.

"What should I be looking for?" I stepped into the room.

She didn't follow; this room had too much grief. I turned back to her and the door, standing close enough that she could see only me and not the room. But she didn't look at me, only down at her clean floor.

"Whatever will help you…find justice," she said softly.

I won't find justice here, I wanted to say. Pure, shining justice was only available on TV or books or in the stories we tell ourselves. Real life was muddy and messy, with everyone telling their version of the truth so that nothing like one truth existed anymore. I might find a few facts, complicated bits of information that could fit into a truth she could live with. Maybe one she could call justice.

"I'll do what I can," I offered. "Do you know what her passwords were?"

She pointed to a small pink notepad. "They're supposed to be listed in there. We didn't let her have any accounts we couldn't monitor."

I doubted that. She wasn't likely to be sending racy pictures where her parents could see. "Supposed to" was as close as her mother was likely to admit to her daughter having had a life her parents didn't know about.

She repeated, "Let me know if you need anything," and without waiting for a reply, went back down the long hallway.

The computer and her phone would probably tell me more than anything else, but I paused to look around the room. Unlike the rest of the house, this room felt like someone lived here. School books piled on the desk, a note with a phone number jotted on it stuck under a clock. The obsessive cleanliness had stopped at this door. Mrs. Stevens, and presumably her husband, couldn't bear to erase the faint traces of their daughter, couldn't straighten the books on her desk, wash the pants hung over a chair in the corner, make the bed more neatly than the hurried pulling-up of the covers.

Interspersed with pictures of the boy bands were ones of her with her friends, attesting to the ever-present cameras we now lived our lives with, groups shots of her with several friends, the same shot, first serious, then less serious, then goofy and acting up. She had a wide smile, the perfect teeth of the middle class, shoulder-length brown hair, hazel eyes that even when she was smiling never seemed content and comfortable. Just the angst of adolescence? Or was she unsure of herself, hovering at the dreaded edge of acceptance and rejection by her peers? I looked again at the picture, searching for a clue to who she was, but it remained resolutely just a fraction of a second of her life, one safe enough to put on the walls of her room. There were additional pictures of a family trip to the beach, again, multiple shots, a happy family posed before emerald-blue waters, probably of the Florida coast around Pensacola. This time they were all smiling.

I turned away from their smiles.

I rarely looked at the few photos from that time in my life. Maybe

I had been smiling as well, hiding the pain, the fear. A split second of posing for the camera. My room had been radically different from Tiffany's, a thrown-together room in the garage of Aunt Greta's and Uncle Claude's home, barely enough room to stand up in even at the peak of the roof. Not a place I could invite friends to come hang out. But it was filled with books. I couldn't afford to buy many, but a constant stream from the library, both at school and the local one. Books—and parades—had saved me.

I took out my phone and took pictures of the pictures, of the room, of the pink bedspread. In a few weeks they would most likely just be more photos to delete, but it was easy to take a picture now in case it would ever come in handy.

I heard a vacuum cleaner start, as if this house needed to be even cleaner than it already was.

I sat at her desk, in a chair painted pink to match the pink roses and the bedspread, and opened the pink notebook. There were pages of various accounts and passwords, written in a neat, flowery script, with smiley faces over the Is. Computer geek I am not, but I can muddle through the basics. I checked the phone first.

I'm too old for this was my thought after attempting to translate text messages like "c u b4 shc," "r u go 2 wk." Maybe I was misreading, but most seemed to be about where to meet people and other exciting stuff like that. I scanned through the photos, but nothing that indicated where the half-naked picture had come from or been sent to. I put the phone down and opened up the computer. A quick glance at her browsing history told me she had other accounts than the ones listed in her pink notebook. I checked in the back of it, just in case she'd written them there. Several pages had been ripped out, leaving little tags of paper on the spiral wire. A quick look in her trash can told me she had been smart enough not to leave them there. Or she'd jotted down some note—schoolwork, a phone number—she wanted to take with her. I'd have to farm her laptop out if I wanted to gain access to those files—and make sure I warned the computer grannies of what they might find.

Since I was there and the vacuum was still going, I did a search of her room. Maybe the sheets with the secret passwords were hidden taped under her sock drawer.

I found a hoard of chocolate bars under her bras. Binge eater? Or just liked chocolate and wanted a stash her brother couldn't scarf down? I dumped them into my bag. Mrs. Stevens hadn't said it, but it seemed part of our bargain was for me be the one to forage through her daughter's life and filter what I passed on to her. Not deliberately hide, but unless the chocolate bars turned out to be important, she didn't need to worry her daughter had an eating disorder on so little evidence. Besides, it might be years before this room would be cleaned out. Stale, moldy chocolate wouldn't be a pleasant discovery.

That was the only secret her chest of drawers held, unless you counted one of her bras was a pushup bra in black lace, hidden behind her other demure white ones. Still, both it and the chocolate seemed almost innocent compared to what most adolescents were up to. No drugs or even booze as far as I could tell.

Nothing under the bed save dust bunnies. Under the mattress was only less than tidy sheet tucking. While she wasn't the neat freak her mother was—it may have been grief that pushed Mrs. Stevens into such obsession, but it wasn't likely she was a slob before—for a teenager, she wasn't bad.

But it wasn't my job to probe the family psychodrama. "Curiosity has killed much better cats than you," I muttered under my breath, far too quiet to be heard over the vacuum. I started to gather the computer and phone but then decided I might as well finish this pointless task and search the rest of the room.

Her bookcase was a disappointment, mostly in how few real books she had, shoved on a bottom shelf with the rest of it taken up with mementos of growing up, a trophy from a sixth-grade popularity contest, "most likely to make chicken soup for a sick friend"; with that as a category, probably every kid in the class got something. A signed picture from some boy from one of the boy bands, seashells from the family trip, albums of pictures, starting when she was six. But the pictures were the smiling ones. Its open shelves hid nothing, save how small her triumphs had been so far.

The closet held the usual assortment of trendy teenage clothing, bright colors and patterns, much of it on the pink side, most of it made to last for about a year. Nothing too indiscreet. Even the stylishly ripped jeans (were those still in? Or had they been out long enough to be in again?) would show less than seen on a typical beach. Maybe the bra was the one thing that hinted at the sexuality behind the smile.

On the second to top shelf, under a pile of sweaters, my hand ran over a large manila envelope. It had been pushed to the back as if to better hide it. But it was a hiding place meant only for those who would never look for anything hidden. Since I had to stretch to reach the top shelf, and I'm five-ten, I guessed that this was as high as Tiffany could go.

The vacuum stopped. There was a brief moment of silence, then it started up again in a more distant room.

I shook the contents of the envelope onto the bed. A flash drive, mercifully blue-gray, not pink, and several sheets of paper fell out.

I turned one of them over. I hadn't seen the picture yet, but my guess was this was a copy of it. If the young girl in it weren't dead, it would have been almost laughable in its naïve attempt to be a sophisticated, sexy adult. She had on too much makeup, as if smearing a bright red over her thin lips was all it took. She posed on the pink bed; the rose spread covered her from the waist down, one arm under her budding breasts as if trying to pump them up, the other stretched out with the phone to take the picture.

I wanted to grab her back into life and tell her this wasn't worth killing herself over. No one would think it more than a brief, and in a few years, easily forgotten moment of foolishness.

The photo was printed on cheap paper, the colors blurry. She didn't have a printer here in her room, so I wondered where she'd made this copy.

Then I looked at the back. There was a note in what was clearly not her handwriting. It said, "Hey, T, I like this pic of you. Why don't we meet up for more?"

No signature, of course.

The next sheet was the same photo. Its note said, "Nice tits. How bout a blow job? I've seen everything that matters."

The third and, I guessed, the final one said, "Hey, bitch, stop fucking around. Either put out or I send your titty shot to my list. U want to cunt tease, U get what U deserve. Three days to respond."

No date, but Tiffany had clearly responded.

I carefully put everything back into the envelope. My fingerprints would be on them, and Tiffany's as well, but I wanted to leave as few marks as possible.

If this was a crime. Yes, there was certainly an ugly threat there, but it seemed that he sent a picture she had sent to him to others. Was that a crime? The laws were slow to catch up to the technology. And even if they had, where did this fall? If she willingly sent the picture, where did that leave her?

The vacuum stopped again.

I put the envelope in my bag, hidden from view. I should show it to Mrs. Stevens, but I wanted more information—and to know what was on the flash drive—before having a discussion I suspected we'd both like to avoid.

I picked up the laptop, cell phone, and pink notebook, heading to where I'd last heard the vacuum cleaner.

She barely looked at me, as if ashamed she'd had to invite a stranger into her house, into her tragedy, to handle the messy cleanup, quickly agreeing to letting me take the computer and phone.

She followed me politely to the door, managing another fake smile as we said good-bye.

I didn't look back at the house, didn't want to see if she was still hovering at the door, quickly got in my car, deposited my bag and the items on the passenger seat, and pulled out.

As I drove away, I mentally made a list of the things I needed to do. Call my lawyer friend Danny and ask about laws on sexting, to see if there could be any legal action to take. Pass the phone and computer to the computer grannies—several older women who had discovered they could hack as well as the boys and computers were a job that could be done sitting down, in air-conditioned comfort, and they could make their own hours. I liked using them because they had both the tech savvy of the young guns and the wisdom and compassion that comes with age.

I focused on the concrete because I didn't want to think about the intangible. The tangible action steps I could control. But a young woman had died by her own hand because of a stupid mistake, a wrong turn in how to be an adult. She sent the picture to an ugly person, a brutish thug interested only in his sexual gratification. Why couldn't he have just masturbated? That was all it would be in any case. Tiffany Stevens was as much of a person to him as any blow-up doll would have been.

Traffic was kind on the way back to my office. Just as well; I was close to rage, and the road isn't a good place for it.

CHAPTER FOUR

I got back to my office shortly before noon and put in a call both to the grannies (since they weren't on the second floor in their not-often-used office) and to Danny. I had to settle for leaving a message for both.

Then I decided the turkey sandwich (on whole grain, mind you) wasn't an adequate lunch after this morning. To remain on the not-too-outrageously unhealthy, I settled on takeout from one of my favorite sushi places on Frenchmen Street. I needed the distraction, the movement, to concentrate on the mundane and important act of deciding what I wanted to eat. We get through our days one small decision/act at a time. Groceries, laundry, going from one place to another, nothing memorable, but there are times these buffers of normal and routine pull us through the days. Driving from my office, picking up the sushi, all worked for me, kept me from thinking about a young girl and her early death.

I doubted even the fierce vacuuming and superhuman cleanliness helped Mrs. Stevens.

I just decided I had ordered too much and could save some for dinner, when my downstairs buzzer rang.

I now own my office building. When I first moved in, as a renter, it was a down-at-heel working-class neighborhood. I had stayed, coming back after Katrina, probably because I was too bewildered and overwhelmed to do anything except return to what I knew. This area hadn't flooded, so it was easier for me to come back. About two years ago, my landlord decided he wanted to get out and offered me a reasonable enough deal that I said yes. It wasn't that I wanted to be a capitalistic bastard land baron, but I knew if he sold to someone else I'd either have to cough up a lot higher rent or be looking for someplace to move to in a rapidly gentrifying city. The only option was to buy.

It meant having two mortgages, one for my house and one here, but between a little hustling and being capitalistic bastard enough to rent the bottom floor to a coffee shop/café that was too chi-chi for me to patronize, I was able to make ends mostly meet.

The computer grannies had the second floor at a more-than-reasonable rent, but they were as likely to work from home as not. I had taken over the third floor. It had once been divided into two offices, but in a tear of renovation last year, I'd opened up the space, creating a proper, though mostly unused waiting area, a small conference room, a small separate office for when I worked with other people, and a decent-sized break room with a microwave, toaster oven, and full-size refrigerator. High on the hog.

There was a separate entrance for those of us on the upper floors, with discreet brass name plates, *M. Knight Detective Agency* and *Computer Solutions* for the grannies. Neither of us encouraged walk-in clientele, so I guessed the buzzer was either someone lost (how did tourists find themselves all the way down here—oh, right, gentrifying, and now the 'hood was hip enough for the coffee shop to be able to afford the rent I charged) or a friend with drop-in privileges. The former would be a quick distraction and the latter a welcome one.

I buzzed the downstairs door open, then sauntered to the landing outside my door where I could see down to the second floor, to wait just in case it was a lost tourist.

The man who came into view was too well dressed to be a tourist and no one I knew.

"Can I help you?" I asked as he rounded the stairs.

He was tall, handsome in a way straight women would probably like, brown hair just a tad shaggy, a clearly deliberate scruff of beard, strong, almost too big chin, but with a dimple that softened it, and wearing a suit that looked to be tailored especially for him. No tie, an open-collar white shirt, also expensive looking. I guessed either late thirties or early forties. The kind of man who expected life to open its doors to him.

He seemed surprised to see someone above him on the landing, but he showed little concern, instead came across as unworried he had anything to fear.

"I'm looking for the M. Knight Detective Agency," he said. He had a deep baritone voice, smooth with an accent I guessed to be somewhere from the northeast.

"Who sent you here? We don't usually take walk-ins," I said.

He continued up the stairs. I remained outside my office.

"Sorry," he said in a way that told me he wasn't. "I'm in a hurry, only in town a few days and needed to move things along. Scotty Bradley gave me your name. Said my case sounded fascinating, but he was about to leave for two weeks in the south of Italy."

Scotty was a PI I occasionally worked with, more occasionally met in French Quarter bars. I did recall him saying "ciao" the last time we talked and mentioning an upcoming journey. I'd check later. I knew Scotty was a decent enough sort that if this guy turned out to be a real asshole, he'd bring a nice bottle of Italian wine back for me.

The man joined me on the landing.

"How can I help you?" I said, still making no move to go back into my office. If this was a quick "sorry, can't do anything for you," there was no point in wasting more time and energy.

"And you are?"

He hadn't answered my question.

"I'd like to talk to someone in charge," he continued.

"You are."

"A woman. I like that."

"Does that matter to you?"

"Not really," he answered smoothly, "but it might be helpful in this case."

Much as I wanted to, I didn't sigh. If this guy turned out to be a serial killer of female private detectives, Scotty would have to learn to pick olives on the olive oil farms, because it wouldn't be safe for him to return to this side of the Atlantic.

"Why don't you come in and we can talk about it?" I said, stepping aside to let him enter before me. And avoid having my back to him.

"Thank you," he said with a smile. He'd won this round. Somehow I suspected that was exactly what he was thinking.

Still, the expensive suit meant money, and a paying client helped with the mortgages.

I ushered him into my office and even engaged in the usual pleasantries of offering coffee—he took his with a little cream, which got a fake apology from me that milk was all I had. Two percent milk at that, but I didn't go there.

I told him I was the M. Knight, even allowing the *M* was for *Michele*. Micky is for my friends, and he wasn't one and I doubted he would ever be one. His name was Douglas Townson.

Once we had sat down with a mug in front of each of us, I again asked my first question, "How can I help you?"

"I need you to solve a murder."

I left a long silence because you don't come to a private dick about a criminal case. There had to be more to this than his simple statement. However, he didn't fill the silence and clearly he wanted questions, so I obliged him. "What can I do that the police can't?"

"Are you interested?" he countered.

In whatever game you're playing? Not really. Again, he hadn't answered my question. But I didn't say that. "As I'm sure you know, the police should be contacted and will take the lead for any criminal investigation. It's only the TV detectives who don't work within the law. Any evidence of a crime, I will take to them."

"I doubt this one will interest them," he said.

"There is no statute of limitations on murder."

"True, but this one took place in 1906, so I feel if the police were going to solve it, they would have done so by now. My great-grandfather. Killed when he was thirty-nine years old. My grandfather was eight at the time. He lived just up the river near Baton Rouge, doing well in farming with sugar and cotton. We had to sell and my great-grandmother remarried, a merchant from New Jersey, who bought some of his cotton. It took the family a while to recover."

I cut in. "The best I could do is find a grave somewhere. Anyone old enough to kill in 1906 isn't around to put handcuffs on. And even that would be unlikely. If the police couldn't solve it then, the evidence is most likely long gone."

He waved his hands at me as if I was telling him information he already knew. "Oh, I realize that. I fully understand how quixotic this quest is. But I'm a hedge fund manager, and I make enough money to blow it on unlikely quests. I want to know whatever can be known. All I've heard are tales passed down from the previous generations, some of them clearly wildly untrue. I want to clear the air, or I'd like to at least get the official record. It's a tedious search; I could do it but I don't have the time. I can certainly make it worth your while."

That explained his confidence. Looks and money are more than enough to make people overrate themselves. I don't like all my clients, and if I could choose, I would leave all the asshole men out, but I rarely choose what cases to take on whether I like the client or not. This is a business. If I think I can help them and if what they're asking me to do is legal and I have the time and resources to take on their request, I usually say yes. There have been a few people I so disliked—or disliked what they were asking me to do—that I turned them down. But if I only accept cases from the decent people of the world, I might not have enough business to stay open. It's not usually the decent people who need my services anyway.

A murder case over a hundred years old; that seemed easy enough. A few records searches would be about the sum of it. There would be no witnesses left to interview. No, I didn't especially like Douglas Townson, but that hardly mattered.

I brought out a contract, named the most outrageous fee I thought I could get away with, and he signed it without blinking.

I led him through most of what he knew, admittedly not much, but enough for me to make a start. Great-grandfather was Frederick Townson. Frederick Kingsly Townson. Stabbed to death while on a buying trip to New Orleans from his estate outside the place we call Red Stick. No one was ever charged, and the family felt the police were incompetent or bribed, because for someone as important as Frederick Townson, the murderer should have been caught. No, he didn't out and out say that, but it oozed copiously between the lines. Most of the family repeatedly said he was a fine, upstanding gentleman, taken far too soon.

The wild stories—after a prompting question on my part—were that a great-aunt said he'd given his wife the pox. That would be syphilis. Ah, that was the worm in the wood. Douglas Townson was too proud to have any such scurrilous rumors floating around about a forebearer of his. He was really hiring me to clear his great-grandfather's name.

He was leaving tomorrow but left me his contact information, both his NYC apartment and the beach house on Long Island.

As he got up to leave (finally), he said, "You're here alone?"

My answer was, "Nope, I'm expecting one of my associates to be here any minute now. In fact, he's about fifteen minutes late. Former Saints linebacker, washed out with a knee injury and needed something interesting to do with his life." That took me to about fifty-five times I've told that lie.

He smiled again, not winning this one, and headed for the door. I told him they had great coffee downstairs, especially the sugar cane spice latte.

He thanked me for the tip.

I watched him as he went down the stairs, mostly to make sure he continued all the way down. I noticed signs of life for the computer grannies on the second floor, and I wanted him gone before I went down there.

I washed out our coffee cups; he'd barely drunk his—this was not cheap coffee—and then made a case file for him. That should be enough time for him to have ordered all the outrageously overpriced lattes he could possibly want.

I headed down to the grannies.

Jane and Timmy—sorry, Timothy were there. Jane is now the ringleader. When I first moved into this building, back when dinosaurs roamed the swamps, I shared the third floor with a woman named Sarah Clavish. At the time, she was old enough to be my grandmother, both prim and proper, and kind and generous. We were neighbors and we acted like it, feeding each other's cats, accepting packages, walking out together if it was dark. I made no bones about being lesbian—as I lived here in my office back then and she couldn't miss it—and she never wavered in her respect and politeness for me. Over time we became friends. She had been doing mail-order Cajun cookbooks, and once she started computerizing her business, discovered the possibilities of the tech world. She had started the computer grannies, pulling in a few of her friends, recruiting other older women who were willing to learn. Naturally I took my computer searches—and let's be honest, occasional hacking—to them. I hadn't become a private investigator to sit at a desk and stare at the computer screen, so I was happy to delegate those chores to them. Jane, known mostly by her handle LadyJane, had taken over running the business. In August of 2005, Sarah Clavish had gone down the river to try to convince her sister and brother-in-law to evacuate. He was confident they would be okay; he had a skiff in the backyard. They weren't. Only he made it to the boat.

The grannies had recently hired Timmy, Timothy, as their, yes, they used this title, Girl Friday. He had the goatee, trendy long sideburns, and enough of a coffee habit to help the coffee shop downstairs pay their rent, which paid my mortgage. He didn't know much about computers, but he looked the part and happily answered phones and talked to customers and consumed all the baked goods the grannies constantly brought in whenever they came by the office. He looked so young, I had trouble thinking of him as Timothy instead of Timmy.

I entered their office bringing the offerings of the computer, cell phone, jump drive, and pink notebook. Jane waved Timothy away to handle me herself. The reasonable rent I charged got me to the front of the line and the standard friend discount. Other than that, I paid them what they were worth.

"What have we here?" she asked as she led me to her office.

I told her about Tiffany's sad life, including that she might find nude pictures on the computer or phone. "You don't need to do a thorough search of everything. I'm trying to track down the identity of the jerk who threatened to send her photos around."

"What do you hope to accomplish?" she asked.

"I'm not sure," I admitted. "He might have broken the law by either threatening her or sending the pictures on. But my client wants to know. Plus, maybe a little—legal—harassment might make him think before he does it again."

"It was catcalls in my day, and at least you could walk away," she answered. "I'll see what we can do."

"Show me whatever you have. The unspoken part of this case is that the mother doesn't want to know everything, and I get to pick and choose what to tell her."

"The mother is the client?"

I nodded. Client confidentiality is important, but Jane was working on the case at this point, so was in the small need-to-know circle.

"Will knowing this do her any good?"

"I don't know. She thinks it will. I considered letting her find someone else to do this."

"Why didn't you?"

"I guess I felt this should be done by someone who cared that a young girl died."

"And that would be you?"

"Yeah. Me. I was a young girl once."

Jane nodded and then said, "So was I."

Timmy decided now was the time to interrupt to ask if we wanted coffee or tea. "A new chai tea, it's delish."

I took that as my cue to say I had to get back to my office.

Jane asked for regular coffee, black.

Chapter Five

Good timing. I made it back to my office just in time to catch the phone ringing. Caller ID told me it was Danny.

"Hey, Danno, what's up?"

"I don't know, you called me," she said easily.

"Yes, I did. But thought I'd be friendly before we got down to business."

"Friendly is good. I like friendly. How about trying that good pizza down by your office this evening?"

"Can't do tonight, how about Saturday?"

"Visiting Elly's parents, that won't work."

"How about the following Saturday, would that work?"

"Nope. Can't. Maybe the following weekend?"

"Maybe Sunday?"

"Can't, already booked. Let me check my calendar and come up with something." She continued, "Okay, so how about the business you wanted with me?"

"What do you know about sexting?"

"Don't do it. Not a good way to date."

"Not for me. This is a case I've taken on. Are there any Louisiana laws on sending out naked pictures?"

"Amazingly, Louisiana does have a law on the books. It can be considered child pornography, depending on the circumstances."

"How about if a young girl sends a picture of her bare breasts to the wrong boy and he threatens to send it on if she doesn't perform sexually for him?"

"Did he actually send the photo out?"

"Don't know for sure. Do know he threatened to, and he was the kind of lout who might go ahead and do it."

"Do you know the ages involved?"

"Don't know who the guy is, but she was seventeen."

"Was she seventeen before or after the photos were sent out?"

I did a quick scan of her case file. Her birthday was in late May, so unless this happened before last summer, she would have been seventeen. I told Danny as much.

"That complicates things," she said. "Seventeen is the cut-off. Louisiana considers anyone younger than seventeen to not be adult. But if she was seventeen and sent the photo out, then she would be considered an adult."

"And once you're an adult, half-naked pictures aren't considered kiddie porn."

"Pretty much," she confirmed.

I swore under my breath. "What about threatening to send the pictures out unless she had sex with him?"

Danny sighed. "Maybe, but the law considers them adults. Did she freely send the picture to him? Or did he some way steal it from her?"

"As far as I know, she sent it to him."

"I'd have to look at everything, but it might be a hard case to make. Unless he was over the top and it could be considered stalking."

I thought back to the three notes I'd seen. Only the presumed last one could really be considered threatening. That wouldn't qualify as stalking. He could easily claim he was angry and didn't mean it, that it was a one-off thing. I had to admit, "No, there seems to have been only one communication that threatened to do that."

"Is she afraid of him? Worried that he might do something?"

"At this point, no. She killed herself about five days ago. Her family wanted me to look into it."

"Oh…damn. That doesn't leave too many legal options, I'm afraid. The family might be able to sue in civil court, but a good lawyer will advise against it."

"Why?"

"Courts don't much like to get involved in affairs of the heart unless the law is clearly broken. It usually is a case of 'he said/she said,' and in this one, she's no longer around, so it'll be his version only. They could easily not win, it won't be cheap, and court cases can drag out for a long time, keeping the wounds open and bleeding."

"I'll pass that on, if it comes up."

Then Danny asked the question I was hoping she wouldn't ask. "What do they want you to do?"

I considered ducking the subject but figured a little legal advice couldn't hurt. "They want me to find out who the boy was she sent the photo to."

"What will they do with that information? You did ask, didn't you?"

"Of course I asked. I'm not going to help them blow his brains out. The reply I got was at most they would do to him what he did to her, expose him on the internet."

"I can't say he doesn't deserve it, but there are slander and libel laws—"

"If it's true, it's not libel," I cut in.

"Yes, but you have to be able to prove it's true, and remember what I said about court cases. He can decide to sue, he might win, and that's not a pretty picture. I'd suggest you use whatever influence you have to make them aware of the consequences of anything they might do."

"Don't worry, I will do what I can to make sure everything stays comfortably legal."

"Good to hear it. Check your calendar and let me know some possible free times for you." With that she hung up.

I mulled what she had told me. Life isn't fair, and it didn't seem like it would be fair anytime soon for Mrs. Susie Stevens.

I glanced at my watch. Time to leave this place.

The special at the coffee shop was "honey-roasted ghost pepper turkey on whole wheat croissants with organic tomatoes, arugula, and rosemary-garlic aioli." Leftover pizza sounded better.

Home. But the bra had to stay on. I was either insane or finally had entered the modern age and, at the rather insistent urging of my cousin Torbin, had agreed to try online dating. The reason I couldn't meet Danny was that tonight was D-day, so to speak. As I spat the mouthwash into the sink, I considered that perhaps a war metaphor wasn't the best way to view this. I had first suggested coffee, but she said she didn't drink coffee—not an auspicious start for a caffeine addict like myself, but I was trying to keep an open mind. We had settled on meeting for dinner; after all, she had pointed out, we had to eat. She had suggested a place uptown, not my favorite stomping grounds, but had offered to pick me up. I declined, claiming that I would be coming from running errands. Optimistic as I was trying to be, I was far too security conscious to let a stranger be my only transportation. She was coming from the 'burbs, me from downtown, so we'd agreed on a decent burger place around where St. Charles and Carrollton meet.

I looked at myself in the mirror. No hiding I was solidly into my forties, hair still mostly black but more than a few stands of gray, especially at the temples. I needed a haircut, but given that it was curly, a few fluffs and tucks hid how shaggy it was. Laugh lines at my eyes, faint yet, but they didn't go away even if I wasn't smiling. Still in pretty good shape, but that was now due to meeting my Russian personal trainer twice a week and spending a couple of hours on the elliptical and/or bike we had in the back spare bedroom. The elliptical had been a birthday present for Cordelia—that and roses, I'm not crazy—one she'd left when she moved out. Paying a lot more attention to what I ate, every burger had to be made up with two salads, those kinds of trade-offs I'd never considered when I was young and thought I was immortal. In other words, time and money were all that kept me from turning into a bloated couch potato middle-aged sloth.

I'd left my office a little early, but between stopping at home to spiffy up and the reality that I would have to slog through both rush-hour traffic and the road work maze of uptown, I had no time to linger.

Or think about whether or not this was a sensible thing to do.

I hated dating. When I was younger, it had been fun, meeting new women, new possibilities, living in the shining world of finding Ms. Right, not old enough or smart enough to realize they were all real people, just as real and flawed as I was. Now I knew how fragile love is, a miracle to find—that real person who is willing to take you and your imperfections and somehow find enough to love amongst them, and for whom you want to reciprocate.

Miracles are rare, and I suspected I'd already got mine and had squandered it.

I didn't want dating; I just wanted what I had back, someone I knew and trusted, sharing our lives, the mundane daily tasks, the beautiful moments when you noticed the light as it hit a hidden flower and could show it to her. Holding hands in the rain, making her laugh.

But that was gone, and the only slim possibility of getting it back was to go through this slog of frogs until I found one I wanted to kiss.

Even with the best of intentions to be on time, the traffic twists and turns—and drivers who seemed to have never ever seen an orange traffic cone before, so had to stop and contemplate it and pull up their navigation system to see if this really was the correct route and only then noticing the roadwork icon—slowed me down. I was about five minutes late when I drove up, and only reasonably smart parking—I didn't even bother looking for something close, but went to the next block over—kept it under ten before I made it in front of the restaurant, where we'd agreed to meet.

I had already rehearsed my apology, but no one resembled the picture I'd seen online, unless she'd transitioned to a he with a nose, chin, and face lift thrown in. A glance at my watch told me I was no more than nine minutes late. My phone confirmed that my watch was indeed right. I was both relieved and annoyed.

Maybe she got stuck in worse traffic. To be fair, I'd give her a few minutes.

I used my phone to make it look like I was doing important work, so important I had to stop right here on the street instead of looking like I was stuck waiting for someone who was clearly late.

After ten minutes, now twenty minutes after our agreed-on meeting time, the relief diminished and the annoyance started to take over. I pulled up the map of traffic on my phone—no major delays or accidents listed.

Five more minutes and I was out of here.

Four minutes and thirty-eight seconds later, someone tapped me—jabbed, really—on the shoulder.

"So, you must be Micky," she said. The photo I'd seen was at least ten years and thirty pounds out of date. She'd claimed to be in her mid-forties, but if that was true, she either had crappy genes or a career of digging ditches in the desert. Had to be mid-fifties. She had claimed to be five-four but could probably only make that in stilettos, which she wasn't wearing today, so her head was barely at my shoulder. Her hair was a frizzy brown, but with roots of gray showing, and she was wearing a pair of jeans that were so tight I didn't know how she breathed, a button-down cowboy shirt that wasn't giving her much breathing room either, and a black leather jacket that was obviously made for men, as it was too big in the shoulders and arms.

I get the vanity; yeah, I'd searched for the most flattering photo I could find. I don't get the deceit. You have to be honest if you want more than one date. One of my better traits is I'm not hung up on looks. A good brain and a reasonably sane temperament are more important.

"That would be me." I couldn't help it, I glanced at my watch.

"I've been watching you for the last ten minutes," she said.

"Why?" I asked. My real question was, "What the fuck?"

"Gotta check out what I'm getting into, you know. You should feel complimented; I usually give most of 'em at least fifteen minutes before deciding."

"You mean you deliberately leave people just waiting?"

"Oh, that's right; you said this was your first time doing this. No sense showing up if it's just going to be a waste of time."

"So if the woman doesn't pass your muster, you call and cancel?" I queried.

"I can pretty much tell in the first five minutes just by watching. Why add an extra few hours if I know it's a waste of time?"

I should have walked away then and told her I agreed with her. About the wasting of time, not the trickery of making a woman wait while she decided whether or not to bother keeping the date. I noticed she didn't answer my question, so I wondered if calling to cancel with an appropriate lie was part of the agenda.

We went in. We ate. She talked a lot. I listened more than I cared to. I had a beer and a second, considered a third but remembered the traffic maze driving home. Sobriety would be a necessity. I'd ordered a big cheeseburger and fries, since that would be the only compensation I would get for this evening. I heard about all the "losers" she had dated, about her previous five serious relationships, all of which seemed to have lasted no more than a year or two. I heard about how much she hated her job, something in insurance, and how stupid her coworkers and clients were. She asked a few questions. Did I like darts? When I said I didn't play, she told me about how much fun it was and how good a player she was and I really needed to learn. And…yawn.

I was so happy when the waitress put the bill on the table.

"Let me get it," she said and grabbed it. Then she ignored it for another forty-five minutes while she kept talking.

I finally managed to jump in when she took a breath to claim I had an early morning tomorrow and needed to get going.

It was another ten minutes before she paid the bill. She left a 5 percent tip. I waited until we were standing up, let her precede me, and while her back was turned stuffed a ten into the bill folder.

"I'm curious," I said when we got out to the sidewalk. "Where did you watch me from?" I had been off duty and not expecting it, but my professional pride was still annoyed I hadn't noticed anyone observing me.

She chortled—not an attractive sound—and pointed. For once, she didn't say anything.

"You hid behind the bush?" She hadn't. I would have noticed ten minutes or even five of that. But it was the most immediate object in her point direction.

"No, of course not." She chortled again. "See that beautiful piece of black machinery?"

"The motorcycle?"

"No, the H2."

I had no clue what she was talking about.

"Admit it, you've always wanted one. No one messes with me on the road."

A Hummer. Halfway down the block was a big, ugly gas-guzzling piece of shit. Politeness failed me. "Really? I thought those were only for men with extremely small penises."

"That shows what you know. C'mon, get in, I'll give you a ride. You have to admit, you're curious."

My fantasy car ride was an Aston Martin. So not a Hummer. I got back to my original question. "How much could you see from that distance?" She was parked a good half a long block away from where I had been standing.

"Binoculars. C'mon, I'll drive you to where you're parked. It's not safe after dark."

"I'm around back, it's not convenient from here."

"No problem, I can afford a few extra blocks of gas. And I need to make sure you're okay getting to your car." She smiled. It was about as attractive as her chortle. She grabbed my hand and started pulling me in the direction of her hulking vehicle.

I tried to take my hand back, but she just tightened her grasp and pulled harder. Inwardly I sighed. And fumed. I either had to fight her or go with her. I gave in and told myself if we didn't go directly to my car, I was jumping out at the next stop sign. At least I could get a look at her spy operation. I had a bit of morbid curiously there.

She didn't let go of my hand for the entire walk there. I kept my fingers limp and unresponsive so there could be no illusion we were holding hands.

At the vehicle—I can't call it either a car or truck—she finally let go. I had to stretch to get in. Her entrance was on the clumsy side of ungainly, like a cannonball in reverse, except for the mercy her seat didn't splash. As pretty a sight as her smile. As I had suspected, I've lived in apartments smaller than this thing. The interior was black leather, shiny chrome with a pair of boob beads hung around the rearview mirror. Charming.

I wrapped my left hand around my body to keep it as far as possible out of her reach.

"Listen to this engine roar!" she said as she turned the ignition.

The best I could do was a wan smile and resist asking why she wanted to drive something that sounded like a cement truck going up a steep hill. The radio was also blasting what I guessed was country music, although the variety that was more pop than anything else.

She was extolling all the wonders of the Hummer.

I asked, "How much do you spend every month on gas?"

"Too damn much!" was her answer. "Gas prices are crazy in this country."

I didn't argue. I doubted someone who drove something this big much cared about the nuances of energy policy. My only conversation was directions to my car. She had to take a long route, claiming she wouldn't fit down one of the streets. A turn and a turn and a turn and finally we were there.

I pointed to my car. She pulled into the only place she could, someone's driveway.

Somehow I managed a polite (barely) smile and said, "Thanks for the ride." I tried to open the door.

It was locked.

She reached out and grabbed my arm (the hand still hidden away), then clambered over halfway to my seat. "You are seriously one of the most sexy women I've dated in a long time. You have to be feeling it, too, right?"

I shoved myself against the door, scrabbling to find the unfamiliar lock. "Look, I'm sorry if you got the wrong—"

She was over the seat, on top of me planting a sloppy kiss on my unwilling lips.

Thank the cosmos for all those arm days at the gym. I had enough strength to push her back. I was about to drown in the slobber.

"No!" I said, almost like I was talking to a bad dog. The only way to refuse this woman was to be rude. Therefore, rude I was going to be. "Please get off me and let me out."

"C'mon, don't be shy." She shifted but didn't really move away. "We're adults, we can do this."

"Get the fuck off me and let me the fuck out." I didn't yell, instead used the coldest voice I could manage.

"What's wrong with you? I thought you said you liked women."

"Let me out of the car now."

"It's not a car, it's a Hummer, an H2."

"I don't give a damn what the fuck it is, let me out."

Finally, she slid back over to her seat. "Okay, you don't need to be rude about it."

The lock popped.

I got out without another word.

She roared off. So much for worrying about my safety.

I got in my car, hit the locks, and immediately took off, turning in the opposite direction from her. Personality disorder, narcissistic variety, came to mind. Most likely she'd roar back to the 'burbs, but I wanted to make sure my small, sensible, fuel-efficient (but with enough pep when I needed it) car stayed very far away from that big thing of hers. I couldn't be sure she wouldn't come back around the block to see if I hadn't changed my mind—and on finding I hadn't, take a fender off.

On the drive home I said every obscene thing I'd wanted to say to her for the entire evening. I don't call myself a model of sanity, sensibleness, and stability, but at least I'd managed one relationship of over a decade instead of burning through one every few years. I lobbed a few choice words at Torbin as well for suggesting this.

Instead of that third beer I really wanted—and fortunately didn't have—I poured myself a generous glass of the good Scotch when I got home. It was the only way I could begin to salvage this disastrous evening.

Chapter Six

I'm not sure what to do. He is nicer than I thought he'd be, after what the others said about him. Not pushy or stupid like the boys in school. He listens to me, asks about my day, not just talking about sports or hunting like the rest of them do. He took me out to a nice dinner last night, a real restaurant. He's the first one to ever do that. It felt nice, like I was who I wanted to be, not a kid stuck having to do what those so-called adults tell me to do.

Now he wants a picture. Me in the sexy bra he says he noticed the first day we met. That's normal boyfriend stuff, right? I took the pic, had to do it before babysitting. But I'm not sure I should send it.

Chapter Seven

Oh, hangover, there is not enough aspirin in the world for you. I went back to the bathroom and brushed my teeth for the second time this morning. I needed to obliterate the slop of her kiss from my mouth. Yeah, she'd tried a tongue, although it didn't get past my teeth.

As much as I didn't want to trudge into the office with this headache, it was probably better than staying here with nothing to distract me.

I filled the big travel mug with coffee. I'd make another pot when I got there. Aspirin and caffeine would be my spiritual guides for today.

The bright, sparkling sunny day didn't help the hangover.

When I got to the office, I closed the blinds. Usually I like a sunny day.

I made a pot of coffee while drinking what I'd brought in the travel mug.

Once I had a second cup in front of me, I sat at my desk, jogging my foggy brain to sort the day. I had hoped the computer and phone would be the quick route to finding the boy who'd threatened Tiffany. That might still work. I could be lazy and wait for their report.

I had jotted down some of the most-used phone numbers for Tiffany's phone before I gave it to the computer grannies. I could go through the tedious process of talking to them. The info from the phone and computer might, at best, give me Tiffany's side of the story. Maybe she led him on; maybe she'd done something to him that caused him to react this way. Much as we all want a clear truth with known villains and heroes, life is usually more complicated and murky. Or maybe he'd done this with other girls, and even if there was no actionable proof with Tiffany, the next girl might be under seventeen and the law would reach him.

I pondered my options. The only answer I came up with was that I probably needed food in addition to coffee.

I had promised myself that I would never darken the door of the downstairs coffee shop save to collect rent. I wanted—truly needed—the money to go one way. Admittedly by the time I drove someplace else and paid their price, I'd be saving no money, but it was the principle of the thing. Once I allowed myself to go there, the temptation of the praline bacon bagel with maple cream cheese might be too much to resist. I needed to be better than that. I didn't spend enough time at the gym as it was, and a quick jog to outrageous pastries was not in my best interest.

Sighing, I trotted down the steps and even eschewed my car, instead walking five blocks away to the next nearest coffee shop. I got a plain bagel with a blueberry croissant for dessert. Carbo loading cures hangovers, right?

Once back at my desk with another half a cup of coffee and most of the bagel in me, I again read over the case file looking for inspiration. It was one sheet so far, not very inspiring.

I started on the croissant. At least the blueberries were an excuse to call it not as terribly unhealthy as it could be.

Come on, Micky, I cajoled myself. *This isn't that complicated a case, save for how heartbreaking it is*. I find information and use it to create a path to the answer. I give my client the answers I've found and get on with my life.

The truth is I wanted to turn away from Mrs. Susie Stevens and her lost daughter Tiffany. I wanted her tragedy to be only a skimmed newspaper headline in my life, a page to be quickly turned. I didn't want to talk to the people who knew her for her short life. It would be a sad, grubby story, and no part of it would make things better for those left behind.

I pulled out the other case that had come my way, the murder in 1906. My hangover was improving, but not enough to want to spend the rest of the day at the library reading microfilm. That was probably where I would find what information there was to be found.

I stared at the two files.

Having just finished breakfast, it was too early to break for lunch.

Talk to the adults first. She most likely met the guy in her everyday life. I scanned the notes I had taken, did a quick online search, then sighed, brushed the croissant crumbs off my desk, and headed out. My destination was Tiffany's school.

Not that they advertised it that way, but it was a middling Catholic school, aimed more for the kids who would become administrative assistants or fast food managers, not the ones who went to Yale or medical school. It was out past Lakeside Shopping Center in the suburbs, a neighborhood I'd never been to. And wouldn't have gone to except for the case. The houses were tidy, most of them red or yellow brick ranches. Probably built after the war and into the sixties, GI Bill houses and white-flight houses. The safe suburbs; a good place to raise kids.

The school itself—Mother Mary of Grace—harkened to the same era. It was a yellow brick box, nothing notable about its design; it seemed a box that could have come out of a box, a small grass yard in front and a much larger mostly concrete yard in the back with stone benches and tables and a very small track. According to the website, it had originally been an all girls' school, but had become co-ed sometime in the nineties.

I parked a few blocks away, near enough to a convenience store that my car, if noted, would probably be linked to it. I could have parked in the school lot, but it's a habit to be discreet. This way no one would see an unfamiliar car pull in and mark my getting out of it. Besides, it was a beautiful spring morning and the croissant needed to be burned off.

I hadn't called ahead. It might mean I was out of luck, but I prefer that to getting a prepared speech. The suicide of a student was probably a touchy subject, especially if her blackmailer was another student. If they threw me out, I'd at least know they didn't want me to investigate.

However, they didn't throw me out; they made me wait in the principal's office.

As I had entered, a polite guard asked if he could help me. I said I needed to talk to someone about a student matter. He clearly assumed I was a parent—I like to think I'm not old enough yet to be considered a grandparent—and led me here. Slowly, as he was about old enough to be a great-grandparent, and probably this job was more to help him eke out a retirement than to truly provide security.

Even though I knew I was an adult—old enough to be slotted into the parent profile—school did not bring up happy memories. I was smart; I did well in class, enough to be a ticket out of here on a college scholarship that I had no chance of getting otherwise. But I had flunked everything else. Or maybe arriving at that suburban school after growing up out in the bayous, barefoot and free, eating alligator like it was an average meal, I was doomed to be the outsider, the one the kids could make fun of as a bonding ritual. Even when I did well, when I found friends, the nagging shadow of being a lesbian made me feel like a fake, a failure. If they really knew me…knew who I was, they would hate me. That was my refrain for so much of high school. I couldn't be who I was and had no idea of who to pretend to be. My pious Aunt Greta, even worn-down Uncle Claude, would have thrown me out if they knew. The teenage years are fraught enough—Tiffany proved that—having to navigate knowing I liked women and knowing I could tell no one made it a hell.

The yellow brick was the same, why didn't they ever change it? Couldn't we at least have red brick? I'd gone to public school; Aunt Greta only sent her real children to Catholic school.

Let it go, Micky, I told myself. *You survived those years. Now you need to concentrate on surviving these years*. Finding a life I wanted and not just the one I found myself in.

It was fifteen minutes before the principal, Melvin Freidman, MEd, ushered me into his office.

Two minutes later, I was ushered back out. All I found out was they were all sad about Tiffany's "unfortunate death," but he couldn't help me. He barely knew her, and even so, student files were confidential. I didn't argue. They might be confidential to me, but as she was under eighteen, her parents still had a right to see those files. If I needed to, I could sic Mrs. Stevens on him.

The guard smiled at me as I exited. Just as I hit the door, a bell rang and the chaos of several hundred teenagers exploded in the hallways. I was lucky in my timing. A stream of them ran around me down the stairs, charging off with the vigor of youth to wherever they were going, presumably lunch.

It seemed the convenience store was a popular destination, so I found myself jostled and passed by the streaming kids as I walked to my car. One advantage of being an adult was that my lunch time wasn't controlled by a bell. Or a nun with a ruler, although I'd seen none of them in my brief visit to the office.

I was mulling what to do about the students swarming around my car, one older boy perched on the fender, when I felt a hand on my shoulder.

"Excuse me," a voice said. An adult voice.

I turned to face a woman who was probably in her mid-thirties, dressed in a conservative gray pantsuit, clothes that seemed too sensible for her face. She was tall, we were almost eye to eye, and at five-ten, I mostly have to look down at women. Her hair was ginger, shading into blond, clearly from time on beaches and in the sun. Her face told the same story, with laugh lines radiating from her eyes, and paler skin around the eyes from sunglasses. Her shoulders were broad and looked like she either worked out or led an active live. Her hair had been pulled into a bun, to go with the pantsuit, but strands were escaping as if they had a life of their own.

"Yes?" I said.

"Shondra told me you were asking about Tiffany. The principal's secretary," she clarified.

"Yes, I am."

"Why?" she asked. "I mean, why are you here? Are you from the police?"

Her tone didn't seem hostile or defensive, instead I felt she wanted to talk to me but also wanted to know I had a legitimate reason for being here.

"I'm a private detective," I said. "I've been hired by her family to look into the circumstances of why she did what she did."

"Her mother, right?"

I nodded. I wanted her to be honest with me, so I hoped honesty from me would help. "You knew the family?"

She glanced around at the kids still passing by this way. "Let's take a walk." She led me down a quiet street away from both the school and convenience store.

"By the way," she said, "I'm Cindy Lee. I'm a teacher here. Oh, I know, not what a teacher from All Things Catholic in the 'Burbs schoolteacher should look like."

"Seems to me teachers come in all sizes and shapes."

"I'm finishing up an MSW. Social work. You know, to better save the world. This job helps pay the rent until I can move on."

"I'm Michele Knight, but my friends call me Micky." I pulled out my license. She looked at it long enough to read the major stuff.

"Really a private detective? I've had an interesting life, and you're the first one I've met."

"Not a bad thing. We're generally involved in things you'd prefer not to be involved in."

"Like this?"

I just nodded, and with a glance around to see we were out of earshot of the kids, asked, "How did you know Tiffany?"

"The obvious way. She was one of my students. I think what I noticed about her was how little she stood out—like she was the kind of average kid who only exists in average world—most kids have something—sometimes negative—that makes sure they're not average in some way."

"What do you mean?"

"Her grades were Bs and Cs, always passing comfortably, but not doing really well. She hung out with the 'beige' girls, not popular, but not rebels or geeks or Goths. The kind of kids the popular ones need to be popular, so they're not mean to them. But they're not included, either. Call me idealistic, but I felt there had to be something more to this kid than just showing up to school and going home to watch TV." She paused and we stopped walking, under a shade tree. We'd gone far enough and she needed to get back to school. Her life was ruled by bells as well.

"Was there?" I asked.

"Not that I ever found out. At least not until this."

"What do you know?"

"Mostly the rumors. The official line is that it was a tragic and accidental death. But the rumors are she killed herself over a boy."

"That's one way of putting it. The story I've gotten is she sent less-than-clothed pictures to someone—possibly one of her classmates. He was using them to blackmail her to have sex with him. It seems she felt so trapped and desperate she saw no way out except to kill herself."

"It's certain she did so?"

"Yes, she left a note. There were messages from him making it clear he was extorting her for sex, and the pictures exist."

She sighed. "I was afraid something like that happened. I'm not old, but everything happens so fast for these kids—all the social media takes off the filters. One stupid comment or angry retort, hanging out for the world to see."

"Who were her friends?"

"Oh, boy, let me think, she seemed to float around the edges of several groups."

"Afraid I might talk to them? Your name will never come up."

She gave a short—not funny—laugh. "Maybe. More that I don't want to land other kids into something they shouldn't be in."

"You think they can escape this?"

She watched a bird fly across the sky, finally answering, "No, I guess not. Much as we try, they can still fall off the edge. Okay, Janice

Watkins was the person I saw her hanging around with most. But I'd guess Sophia Gauthier was the one she'd talk to if she was going to talk. Janice was more popular, Sophia a science nerd."

"Hierarchies are so important, aren't they?"

"I keep thinking, that matters? Really? But to them it does. One slip down the cool kids ladder is a crisis."

"Where was Tiffany on the cool kid ladder?"

"Off to the side, would be my guess. She wasn't a cheerleader, not the type to run for class president. Was happy to hang out but just didn't have whatever it took to rate."

"Think she wanted to?"

"What kid doesn't? It seems so important in high school."

"What about boys? Any you can think of?"

She glanced at her watch. The end of lunch. "Also a hard one. This used to be a girls' school, then economics made it co-ed. So there are fewer boys than girls."

"Good for the boys, I'd guess."

"Except most of these boys are too nerdy to make the best use of it."

"Still scaring girls with frogs?"

"The high-tech version. Pictures of gross things on their phones. Brandon…some B-letter Cajun name, hung around with her crowd. Kevin Boudreaux. Gary Collier. Those are the only ones I can think of."

"She dating any of them?"

"I doubt it. They weren't considered dating material."

We started walking back.

"You think any of them will talk to me?"

"Probably. They all seem either numb, in shock, or still crying. I think they want to talk about it. Several have approached me, but we're supposed to refer them to the school counselor. And she's a gray-haired old lady."

"So am I."

"Not the way she is. You're wearing jeans. She probably never has. I can make you a list of all the names I can think of, phone numbers with some of them. Places they hang out."

"Please tell me I don't have to go to the mall."

"Bingo. Sorry."

"That's okay. I've survived worse. Thank you, this will be very helpful."

"I can ask—if you'd like—for them to talk to you."

"Yes, if you could. I promise to be discreet. And kind."

"Just see if you can make some sense of this."

"Why are you doing this?" I asked.

We turned the corner near the convenience store. "I used to be one of those beige girls, back in high school, when somebody liking me mattered the whole world. I got out, had a few good teachers along the way. Discovered a big world where high school seemed small and unimportant. I got the chance to travel, from backpacking Europe one summer during college, to a six-month trek down South America. Hiked Machu Picchu. A world lost hundreds of years ago. The slights of high school couldn't compare."

"But now you're back in high school."

We were at the school gate.

"Yes, but now I'm the teacher. The person who might convince those beige girls the world is far, far bigger than being third runner-up for homecoming queen. I pity them now, those popular girls and boys. It's the Peggy Lee song, 'Is That All There Is?' but they don't know that yet, and too many of them get to fifty before they figure out they should have kept going."

I nodded and thanked her. She gave me her phone number and we said good-bye.

I quickly hiked back to my car. I was beginning to itch; maybe I was allergic to the suburbs.

Besides, enough time had passed, and now I could call it lunch. To make up for the croissant, I contented myself with the turkey sandwich left over from yesterday. It needed to be eaten.

As I munched on the healthy whole wheat—chewy, okay, a little stale—bread, and turkey with mustard, I considered what I had learned.

Little that really mattered to the case. Teachers still care about their students—some of them. Kids are still caught in the small world of liking and being liked, fumbling, stumbling to adulthood. Most would make it, some wouldn't. A few of those would be lost the way Tiffany was lost, suicide, drugs, driving too fast, but too many would be adolescents trapped in adult bodies in an adult world, when all they could really manage was how many likes they had on social media.

It wasn't pleasant at the time—I knew I was queer and my home life didn't fit the standard pretty picture—but somehow knowing I'd never compete in the popular crowd games forced me to hope for something beyond that world. And maybe that little glimmer let me survive.

My reverie was broken by the ringing phone. It was Cindy Lee. Several of the kids were willing to meet me today after school, at a pizza place down the block. As luck would have it, they had all been scheduled for a science club meeting, but it had been canceled, so I seemed to be a better choice than going home.

With that sorted, all I had to occupy me was contemplating if the turkey sandwich had really been enough sustenance or whether I needed something more. I made it to needing more and was saved by the phone from having to decide if that should be an apple or something on the more chocolate side.

Lady Jane had gotten into the computer and phone. All I needed to do was hike down one flight, and this case would be cracked.

Chapter Eight

Edward Springhorn. "Call me Eddie," as his Facebook page said.

I thanked Lady Jane for her work. She said this was just the top layer, so to speak, mostly from the phone. Did I want them to pull any more data? I said yes, better to know more, and told her to put the bill in the mail—email in this case. I declined Timmy's offer of "rosemary-infused chai tea. It's delish," and headed back upstairs, taking the steps slowly.

Once at my desk, with a newly made cup of coffee in front of me—my idea of delish—I looked over the file she had handed me.

Tiffany, like most teenagers, had a secret life, one hidden from the adults around her. We all did it, keeping our tentative steps in a separate silo carefully sorted into closed boxes, the experiments with the forbidden—sex, booze, drugs.

There were a few pictures of her and some friends getting high on marijuana, some with beer cans around them. Tame compared to a needle hanging out of her arm.

And what for the most part were relatively innocent flirtations, all in hard-to-decipher text messages in made-up words. "Ur ht when u wk out." "No 'rents at home. Wann cum ovr?"

For the most part, the boys had been equally stumbling back.

But not, as I'm sure he liked to call himself, "Fast Eddie." He was easy to pick out in the pictures, clearly older than the others. A scruffy beard; big shoulders like he worked out or worked a manual-labor job; his hair, dark brown, was styled in the latest fashion, with the sides buzz cut, long on top. Although he was at most in his mid-twenties, his face was showing the middle-aged man he'd be. Chai tea was clearly not on his diet. His nose had a red tinge; the cheeks were bloated and starting to sag. Once he stopped working out, the fat would overtake the muscles, was so even now. My guess was at least a couple of beers every day, pizza alternating with hamburgers, and the only veggies the ones that came on the pizza if he didn't pick them off. Maybe he was a school mate who'd been held back a few years but just as likely one of the older guys who liked to hang around high schools, knowing that a few years and having a car or his own place made him seem like a catch to the young girls on the verge of being women. It was an old, sad story; older man takes advantage of younger girl.

I know I was delaying reporting back to Mrs. Susie Stevens, but I wanted to read the entire file, pull out things—like the beer and weed—that she probably didn't really want to know and give only what was most pertinent to what she had asked me to do.

Even then, I censored most of it. It wasn't pretty; Tiffany seemed clueless and lost. Even in the brief messages, she was torn between not wanting to lose his attention and reluctant to do what he was asking. He had the game down, albeit in crude fashion—first the mild flirting, just like the other boys, but he knew the next steps, a focused flattery—"ur so gdlk, u gotta hv men at ur tail," "ur serius 1 of the sexyish grls I er met." Then on to "I cant stp thinking abt u." "id lke to b w/u, hold you." Then, "can I get a pic?" "No, one only for me, just u no clthes."

First she sent him a picture of her under the pink rose sheets, only her shoulders bare, the rest left to imagination.

But that wasn't enough.

I jotted down a rough chronology. They'd met in fall, the end of the football season, late November, at some party. It was unclear who gave it and when. That was when the first flirting started. He mentioned traveling, a job (oh, how grown up) that required him to make deliveries along the coast to Florida and back. He called it delivering high-end goods. I wondered if they were the kind of goods you smoked or snorted to get high.

They met in person again over the Christmas holidays; he seemed to have even gotten a kiss under the mistletoe. "Ur lps r so soft, lk a woman, not a grl. Want more."

He was gone again but escalated the messages, asking for the nude picture until he got it. Once she bared her breasts for him, he knew he had her. She'd crossed the line, and he was cunning enough to pick the girls who would think it was their fault for giving in.

The one I'd found in her room was one of the last of the only-breasts ones. She made excuses, "cldnt get a pic, 'rents around," but always eventually gave in. First one nipple, then both breasts, then most skin revealed. A month before she died, she sent him one of her fully nude, shot in the full-length mirror of her closet door, the rose sheets in the background. The lighting was bad, it was clearly taken at night, and her facial expression was of doing a chore, not being sexy for her boyfriend.

After the first breast shots, he'd returned again, and it seemed this time there had been kissing and serious groping, maybe a hand job. Only enough to make him want more. "I need to have u. Pics not enough. Wanna be in ur pssy n ass. All the way now or u lose me. Ill get a hotel, the whole night."

How romantic.

She—finally—said no. Alas, not a firm no, but a "cant be out all night. 'rents will have a cow." She seemed to want a little more romance "cant we go to a movie and play a litt after."

He wanted sex. "u wanna be a woman or a ltl girl? stop teasing and give me what u promised." He was good at manipulation. And threats. "want me to send all those pics out? to all the boys on my list? all ur schl?"

She gave in, meeting him in his car for a blow job.

His tender response, "c, not so bad. u need to work on taking more in."

She didn't seem to agree, again making excuses for why she couldn't meet him. "cant get away, 'rents mking me visit grandma."

"dont be a bad girl, u no what happens to bad girls. pics all over school."

Her only reply was, "please dont." He kept hounding her, but she no longer texted back. My guess was that was when he started sending the notes. To make sure she knew she couldn't get away from him.

I got up for another cup of coffee. It would keep me awake tonight, but I doubted I'd sleep well anyway.

Her knight in shining armor turned out to be the dragon.

Why didn't she have enough sense to turn to an adult? For the same reason we all did at that age. We didn't want to admit we couldn't handle the situation, or we were so ashamed and lived in a black-and-white world and couldn't see that in ten years it wouldn't matter because ten years from seventeen seems so impossibly long that it might as well be the moon. All the future you can see is going to school the next day and the day after that.

I should call Mrs. Stevens and hand this off to her. Not the timeline I'd created, or the messages I'd used to create it. I didn't know Tiffany, and it was painful; it would break a mother's heart. I'd return the phone, computer, and flash drive and give her what information I had on Fast Eddie. Unless she asked—which I doubted—I'd keep most of the details to myself.

I made a separate file and put in it every sordid word and image from her phone and computer. That file would stay hidden deep in a drawer, separated from the official case file. I wasn't going to let Mrs. Stevens see any of it, even across my desk.

I made the call. She answered on the first ring. I told her I had information for her and offered to come out to her house in Metairie. I was too much of a coward to risk having her break down in my office and me being the only one available to deal with it. I was also too much of a coward to do it today, making an appointment for tomorrow morning.

That would also give me time to consider how to present this to her. And to come up with probes to see what she intended to do with the information.

I quelled my inner debate of whether or not to go down to the computer grannies and see if they wanted to do some hacking on this toad's life by calling Torbin; he'd be a distraction. Vigilante justice isn't my style, but Fast Eddie seemed to be begging for the karma train to catch him in the tunnel.

I needed to update Torbin on how useful his suggestion of online matchmaking had been. Four rings—almost voice mail—and he answered.

"I don't want any, and my mind is already made up as to who I'll vote for."

"Too bad, I have a sweet deal on a spectacular bridge out on the West Coast."

"Not a swamp? I'm disappointed."

"Swamps are all sold out. You missed a great deal."

"So what did I do to have your cheery voice brighten my day? It's been such a long time."

"Yeah, I know," I admitted. It had been a while since I'd picked up the phone to call him. But I skimmed over that and got to my point, "To thank you for your suggestion that women desperate enough to throw themselves on the internet might be good dating material." I then launched into a totally honest description of how completely awful my date had been.

His response was a bland, "It's only your first one. You can't condemn it after only one try."

"I think you owe me."

"I made a suggestion. You could have chosen to remain in your loveless rut swilling cheap Scotch."

"It's not cheap."

"Whatever. You could have come up with another plan or taken my suggestion. I think you owe me for having the temerity to suggest you do something besides work yourself to death."

"Okay, I'll buy the first drink if you buy the second."

"Agreed, but there has to be food involved. My stomach is no longer young enough to consume copious amounts of booze without something to soften the blow."

I proposed tonight. It would be nice to debrief after today, and I wasn't counting on the pizza place to be suitable supper, but Andy had already started dinner. I finally said, "How about the Saturday after next? I'll cook."

"Can't, have another obligation."

"Am I missing something going on? You're the second person to be already booked for that Saturday."

"Coincidence, I'm sure. We'll come up with a date and time. Have to go and help Andy with chopping onions."

After I hung up, I glanced at my watch. Time for another trip to Metairie.

CHAPTER NINE

The traffic back out there was the most annoying thing about the trip. The second most annoying thing was that it was for nothing. I already had the information I needed, and quite frankly, as much as I wanted to know. I doubted that Tiffany's school friends could tell me anything else that would be useful.

I pulled into the lot at Uncle Poppo's Pizza-Pie. Its appeal seemed to be how close it was to the school. It was in a strip mall that probably dated from the sixties and even then hadn't been built for high-end establishments. Boxy, yellow brick with big greasy plate glass windows, the kind that looked like they leaked when it rained. It was a quarter after three; the kids would be there around three thirty.

I sighed and got out of my car. Maybe Uncle Poppo's was one of those hidden gems and the pizza would be good. I could order one to go and that would be supper. And breakfast. *Cheer the fuck up, Micky*, I told myself. I needed to be witty and bright for the kids, or at least my most professional self. They had to be upset at the early death of someone they knew, they had agreed to give me their time, and I needed to respect that. I wouldn't let on I already knew who had pushed Tiffany to the edge. Maybe they would have some kind stories of her as a friend, ones I could give to Mrs. Stevens to help soften the blow.

The place was empty, only a table of three old guys nursing beers that were probably how most of their afternoons were spent. I headed for a large, circular booth at the back. I wasn't sure how many kids would show up.

It was a couple of minutes before the lone waiter ambled over to where I was. Slow afternoon meant everything moved slowly.

"I'm meeting some people," I said, to justify taking up all the space. I ordered a large everything pizza—that should cover all the bases—and two pitchers of soft drinks, one regular and one diet.

I was just pouring my drink—I opted for the diet, less for my girlish figure than my guess that it would be the less popular choice, when a group of kids came in. They didn't look old enough to be on the cusp of adulthood, high school seniors. But maybe I had looked that young and only thought I was older because it was how I wanted to be.

One of the boys spotted me and headed my way. The second boy hurried to follow, the two girls hung back, letting the boys take the first step. Or maybe they were mature enough to not be the fools who rushed in.

"Hi, I'm Kevin," the first one said, sticking out his hand, an awkward reach across the table. "It is true you're a lady detective?"

Bless his heart. I kept my face neutral. Lady detective went out in a previous lifetime.

I returned his handshake, a long stretch. I understood he was trying to be grown-up. "I am a licensed private detective," I said as I stood up to avoid any more far-reaching handshakes.

"I'm Brandon, the brains of the outfit," the second boy said, also sticking his hand out.

"Maybe once a month," Kevin said, "when I'm asleep."

I cut off Brandon's reply by asking the girls their names. Polite and professional didn't extend to listening to adolescent boy banter meant to show off.

"Janice," one said, also opting for a handshake.

"Sophia," the second one said, staying behind the others and giving only a vague wave in my direction.

I let them choose their seats. The two boys took the center, Janice sliding in beside them and Sophia perched on the outside, a gap between her and Janice. I took the other outside seat, closer to them than the shy Sophia. This allowed me to be able to watch them as they poured their drinks, diet for the girls and regular for the boys. Must things be so stereotypical?

Beige, Cindy Lee had called Tiffany. These kids were beige as well. Not in a bad way, not fully formed enough to be their adult selves. Or maybe I could only see the surface they dared show.

Kevin seemed more the leader, although I doubted any of the others would call him that. He was a little taller, his clothes were slightly better; he seemed a little more at ease. It might disappear in a year. His mouth was a bit large for his face, but other than that he was a forgettable (well, to me, maybe girls his age disagreed) young boy. Brown hair, brown eyes, a little shorter than me, about five-nine, the body of neither a gym rat nor a couch potato. He wore neat khakis and a navy polo shirt.

The second boy, Brandon, was several inches shorter than Kevin, maybe five-five. He might have a growth spurt in his future, but linebacker didn't look like a career option for him. He wore jeans that were loose and not a great fit, especially in the age of skinny jeans, with a T-shirt that probably needed a laundry date in the near future and a ratty zip-up sweatshirt over that. They were all dark colors, although different darks, as if he just grabbed what was handy. His hair was dark brown, almost black and straight, no styling, and either he was trying to grow it or was in need of a haircut. He wore glasses, gold framed and too round for his round face. Girls would call him cute, soft skin, little sign of a beard, some of the baby fat still there. I suspected he had Star Wars action figures in his room at home.

Janice was dressed in the girl version of Kevin's outfit, which meant she was better clad than he was. Girls have to be. She had on a white shirt with pink pinstripes, a round collar to make it clearly a girl's shirt, a dusty rose skirt that was a deeper shade of the pink in her shirt with matching shoes. She wore a touch of makeup and her hair was light brown, in an easy ponytail that she probably spent fifteen minutes getting just the right casualness. Either this was who she was, or she was doing a good job at hiding. Or maybe trying on different people until she found one she wanted to become.

Sophia had dark, thick hair, the kind the other girls envied, but she left it loose, and clearly little time had been spent fussing with it. She wore black jeans and a white button-down shirt. Plain, simple, as if she couldn't bother with decisions on how to dress. Or just didn't get how to fit in. Or maybe it was class, her family didn't have the money for matching pink shirts and skirts. She seemed the one who had been Tiffany's friend, although it seemed an odd pairing, while the others had connections with each other as well. Of the four of them, she was the most interesting. But, I suspected, the one I'd get the least from.

"Thank you for agreeing to talk to me," I said.

"Sorry we're late," Brandon said, almost cutting me off. "We had to get out of the school clothes."

Kevin rolled his eyes. The girls kept their faces neutral. Clearly they all wanted to act like they got to wear clothes of their choosing and not uniforms that labeled them still in school. Brandon was gauche to bring it up and spill their secret.

"Can I see your badge?" Brandon interjected. He seemed to want to control the conversation. Or at least get the attention.

"Why?" Kevin argued. "This isn't the movies."

"I want to see it."

I pulled out my license, not badge, and handed it to him, but Kevin took it first, examined it, and only then handed it to Brandon. So this was how it was going to go, Kevin and Brandon in an awkward adolescent fight for male dominance.

Brandon barely looked at it before handing it back to me. "Had to check," he said, just enough of a smile on his lips to indicate he'd won.

The pizza arrived and the boys grabbed two slices each, while the girls daintily took one. I also took one, more to take part than hunger. From the grease and smell, Uncle Poppo's didn't appear to be the solution to my dinner dilemma.

I started again, "I really appreciate you taking time to talk to me…"

"No problem," Kevin said for the group.

"We're happy to," Brandon added.

I'd have to be careful how I controlled the interview. I wanted to both let the group dynamics play out, but also get something from each of them.

"Tell me how each of you knew Tiffany," I said, nodding at Kevin to start.

The direct question put him on the spot. "Um…in class, I guess. You know, we just sort of hung around. Did some class things together."

I waited a beat, but that seemed to be all he had to say. "How about you?" with a nod at Brandon.

"Same. Class. First one together was in eighth grade, both science and English. We had just moved here that year and Tiffany was nice to me. Lent me some of the extra reading books for our English class."

"What kind of books?"

"I don't really remember. That was a while ago. Mostly boring stuff they made us read."

I'd been hoping that Tiffany would turn out to be an avid reader, something to give to her mother. But I remembered her room and the few books there.

Brandon's lack of memory and his clipped answer made me

wonder if he was hiding something. Then I reminded myself these were high school kids, not devious adults with something to hide, and no crime had been committed. The point of this interview wasn't for me to find information, but to let these kids feel like they were helping, and maybe that would help them cope with Tiffany's death. All I needed to do was be kind, ask reasonable questions, and make it last long enough for the pizza to disappear.

I timed my next question with both boys having just taken a bite. "What was Tiffany like?"

Janice and Sophia looked at each other, then back at me. Both started to speak.

"She was nice," from Janice.

"She didn't look where she was going," from Sophia. That got her another look from Janice.

"What was nice about her?" I asked.

"She helped with things," Janice said quickly as if she needed to fill the silence and not let anything negative be said about her dead friend.

"Like what?"

Kevin answered, "She sometimes let me copy her homework when I was too busy to do it."

I didn't point out that proved Sophia's point. They could both be failed for cheating, with Tiffany solving Kevin's problem by creating a bigger one of her own.

Brandon added, "She was nice to me when we first moved here. My dad was stationed in Afghanistan, so it was just me and my mom. We moved here to be closer to family, but I didn't have any friends here."

This speech got an eye roll from Kevin, making me suspect that Brandon pulled out the soldier dad on more regular occasions than high school kids wanted to deal with. It did explain his arrogant nerd demeanor, moving to a new school, a little short and young looking for his age, awkward social skills, and in a family that had to be going through a hard time.

Brandon continued, loosening up either from the caffeine, sugar, pizza grease, or the attention, "Kevin wouldn't have been lucky enough to meet me if it hadn't been for Tiffany." This got a snort from Kevin, but Brandon ignored it. "She invited us both to her fifteenth birthday, and that was how we both learned we liked to play World of Doom. I got to the first level two months before Kevin did."

"Only because you played it every day," Kevin interjected.

"So did you, you just forgot after you lost," Brandon retorted.

"Tell me more about Tiffany," I cut in. "Sophia, what did you mean when you said she didn't look where she was going?"

But again, it was Brandon who answered. "She was texting one day while crossing the street. Stepped in front of a bike and caused him to wreck."

"He was on the football team," Kevin added. "We all suffered for her stupidity."

"How?" I asked.

This got me another eye roll from Kevin. "We were the people she hung around with. He's popular, so he trash-talked us all. Brandon was running for chief dog-catcher—"

"Student council," Brandon said.

"And they decided they weren't going to let him win. No one really cared about the election except for that stupid thing," Kevin finished.

"Is that what you meant, Sophia?" I asked.

She nodded and mumbled in a way that meant it really wasn't, but that she wasn't going to argue it. She got a second slice of pizza and took a bite.

I asked a few more questions, but most of what I got in response was what TV show she liked, what music she listened to and, generational divide, I'd heard of none of them.

The pizza was gone; the boys had finished it off.

One last question, "Did she ever mention someone named Edward or Eddie Springhorn?"

Their reactions proved they were not devious adults.

"Don't know that name." Janice, for once, took the lead.

"He was dating Tiffany," I said, using the polite term for what he was doing. Still none of them admitted knowing who he was.

"She didn't tell us everything," Brandon said, more defensively than necessary.

They were lying; I knew they were lying, but it didn't matter. Maybe their parents had told them to stay away from him, and they were worried I would tell.

I thanked them for their time and stuffed enough money in the bill to leave a more-than-decent tip—the few dollars it would cost me wasn't worth the wait it would take for change.

As we walked to the door, Brandon said, "You're going to need to talk to us again, right? Smart kids like us could be really helpful."

"You have helped a lot," I said. "I'll have to see where the case leads me." But I dutifully took their names and phone numbers, with them all telling me it was better to text than call.

I assured them I would. In the unlikely event I ever needed to talk to them again.

Chapter Ten

A cloudy day. Perfect for the task in front of me, going to Metairie and telling Mrs. Susie Stevens the identity of the lout who harassed her daughter into despair.

I'd made our appointment at ten, mainly to both give me time to prepare and, more importantly, let the rush-hour traffic abate.

The overly clipped lawn seemed grayed by the drizzle, as if it was closer to winter than summer. Or maybe that was just the way I saw it.

She opened the door as I came up the walk, clearly looking for me.

As I entered, she hurriedly said, "Would you like coffee or tea?" as if the proprieties needed to be adhered to no matter what.

"No, thank you," I said. I had done my job; I wanted to get it over with.

She led me to the formal living room, sitting so close to the edge of her chair, I worried she might fall off.

I sat opposite her, also close to the edge of the chair, although I made sure my butt was securely settled. It wouldn't do for us both to slide off.

Her face was neutral, or holding a mask of no emotion, but her posture, from the chair to her hands, twining and untwining of her fingers, showed otherwise.

"I've found the identity of the person who threatened to send out the photo," I said needlessly.

"Who is it?" she asked, her voice a brittle whisper.

"His name is Edward Springhorn."

"I've never heard that name before."

Of course, Fast Eddie wasn't the type you brought home to meet the 'rents—parents.

After the computer grannies had given me what they'd found on the computer and phone, I'd done my usual homework. Eddie wasn't trying to hide, so he'd been easy to find. "He's twenty-four years old." Far too old, in my opinion to be messing with high school girls. But my opinion wasn't needed here. "He lives in Kenner, a local boy. I have a list here of his email address and social media information." I handed her the sheet of paper with that on it.

She scanned the page, then looked up at me. "What about his address? Where he works?"

This was the conversation I didn't want to have. "Mrs. Stevens, this boy is an unspeakable lout. You have every right to hate him. But breaking the law to get revenge isn't going to bring your daughter back. When we talked, you said you wanted to post online about him, warn others off. You don't need his address or workplace for that."

"You think he doesn't deserve it?"

"What I think doesn't matter. What about the rest of your life? Your son? If you do something illegal—as unfair as that may be—you could end up in prison, losing more than you've already lost."

"You don't understand." It was almost a shout, as if the emotions couldn't be held in check anymore.

"No, I don't," I admitted. "But I can't ethically help you do something that is both illegal and will likely only make things worse for you."

"But you have the information?"

I gave a bare nod. Of course I had the information. I even had his Social Security number because Eddie was only fast, not smart.

"My husband asked me to make sure I got it."

Ex-husband, but I didn't go there. "Why?"

"He says we can sue him."

"Yes, but keep in mind you might not win. It could force you to spend years dealing with him and cost a lot of money."

"I know all that," she said dismissively, her voice back in control, the emotions as contained again as the lawn. "But my husband knows lawyers, we can make his life a living hell, force him to hire a lawyer, take time off only to cancel at the last possible minute. It won't cost us much."

I hesitated.

"We're not going to do anything stupid. We had a long conversation with my brother-in-law, he's a lawyer, about what we could and couldn't do. We intend to do everything we legally can to make him pay. But that's all."

I handed her the second sheet with his home address and workplace (AOK Trucking—maybe it was legit). He lived in one of those hastily thrown-up apartment complexes out near the airport, the kind that would never be expensive because no one would pay to live next to the sound of roaring planes.

"Thank you," she said, but her eyes were fixed on the page as if the intensity of her glare alone could get to him.

I heard a back door open and a voice call, "Mom? Where are you?"

She seemed startled, not expecting anyone. Before she could react, he skidded into the room.

"Oh, there you are," he said, a hidden touch of relief in his voice.

The son. Now I wish I'd opted for coffee. He was tall, still gangly and growing. His nose was a little big, his mouth slightly too wide, but they saved him from being conventionally handsome and gave him an interesting face instead. His hair was brown, close to the shade of his mother's under her blond highlights. He was dressed in a way that was both neat and casual, as if he found a way to meet his mother's need for an orderly world but do it his way, with a purple (LSU color) polo shirt, tucked in, light khaki pants, and polished brown loafers.

"Alan, I wasn't expecting you just yet."

"Traffic was light, so I made good time."

"I'm just finishing up here. Give me a minute." She stood, clearly indicating I should as well, still holding the piece of paper in her hand, her knuckles white from how tightly she gripped it.

There would be no introductions. She ushered me out the door, saying on the threshold, "Thank you so much for all your help."

Well, I hadn't planned on bringing up the bill in any case.

The son's car was a cute little blue Mazda Miata. I suspected that the insurance father had picked the safest sporty car—and vetoed red—for his son. Alan? Was that what she called him?—had seemed worried about her, perhaps scared that one suicide could lead to another. I'd give him points for being willing to come home from Baton Rouge on a weekday to check up on his mother. Maybe Mrs. Stevens had talked to her ex-husband about going after Fast Eddie, but it seemed that her college-aged son was being kept out of the loop. She had avoided introducing us, a huge breach of courtesy for as proper a Southern lady as she was.

The case is over. Like I had predicted, no happy ending. Fast Eddie might be dogged by lawsuits and legal trouble, but in the end revenge takes time and effort and doesn't free you. But I doubted anything could ever free Mrs. Susie Stevens.

Less than an hour had passed since I stepped in her door to again hitting the parish line back into New Orleans.

Deciding I might as well work on the other case I'd taken, I swung into the French Quarter—the parking would be an expense I'd pass on to my client—and headed to the Historic New Orleans Collection on Chartres Street. Mr. Douglas Townson had the kind of expectations only money can buy. If I wanted to take some of that money, I'd need to at least have something to show before he called, which I suspected would be any day now.

Four hours later, with a short break for a lunch of coffee and beignets—everything else in the area would either take longer or be too expensive—I had probably about most of what I was going to find.

My eyes were tired from staring at the microfilm. I'd culled through most of the papers from the time. The story had gotten reasonable play, although not front page like I suspected they thought they deserved. I did find out enough to suspect the family story was tidied up.

The murder took place near the intersection of Marais and Conti. In 1906 that would have been in the downscale area of Storyville. Called a "vice district," it existed from 1897 to 1917. Services ranged from the putative high-class establishments along Basin St. to the low-rent cribs in other parts of the district.

Respectable, happily married gentlemen did not meet their demise in that part of town unless they had business there. The newspaper report was bland, not hinting at anything, but they may have figured that the location was enough to give it away. Frederick Townson had been stabbed multiple times and had bled to death. His body had been found by an early-morning delivery man. That also brought up questions. The area had not only the brothels, everything from huge mansions to one-room "cribs," but bars and restaurants to serve the other needs of the customers. The police report noted that Townson had last been seen leaving his hotel the previous evening. Had he partied all night and only met his demise on the way home in the early hours? Or had he been left there unnoticed for a good part of the night?

Those bare details hinted at why the police hadn't made it much of a priority. A man in that part of town was up to no good, and when trouble found him, he might be considered to have been looking for it. Unless his great-grandson was wrong about his wealth, he seemed more like a man who would frequent the upscale places on Basin, not in this area for the fifty-cent jobs. (Yes, I had to do some web surfing on Storyville.) A respectable gentleman in a very unrespectable part of an already unrespectable area of town.

He clearly wasn't the upright man he claimed to be, or else the constables were afraid that investigating would uncover something worse than murder, that he liked it kinky (yes, they did kinky back then). Or the reality that it was a random meeting of two strangers, and the people who lived in the area were unlikely to admit to having seen or heard anything, even if they were standing two feet away.

This, of course, was not the answer my client wanted.

The Historic New Orleans Collection has a good run of newspapers including the *Times-Picayune* going back a long stretch, far more than I needed. They did suggest the main branch of the New Orleans Public Library if I wanted to look more at public records—which, quite frankly, I didn't. But I would, because it added more hours to bill to Mr. Townson and part him from money I could probably put to much better use than he could. It wasn't likely I'd find much else.

As I walked back to my car, I called a friend who is an archivist to see if she thought plowing through the records in the main library would be worth the time and if she had any idea of where else I might search. I had to settle for leaving a message.

My phone rang as I was driving home. I assumed it was my archivist friend and she could wait the ten blocks until I was safely parked. Being in the French Quarter, roadwork, tourists, and people who underestimate their ability to imbibe and steer a car/bike/their feet are reasons to not phone and drive.

I parked in front of my house before pulling my phone out.

My phone rang again in my hand; the same number, one that looked familiar, but I couldn't place it. I answered.

"He's here," a woman's voice said to my answering.

"Wait, who?"

"Him, the name you gave me."

Susie Stevens. She was speaking in a harsh whisper, making it hard to recognize her voice.

"At your house?"

"Yes."

"Inside?"

"No, outside."

"Maybe you should call the police."

"No, I can't do that."

"Your husband?"

"He's…out of town."

A lie. But I let it pass. "Is he threatening you?"

"No, he says he wants to talk."

"What is he doing at your house?" That was the real question.

"You've got to help me. I can't deal with him alone."

I sighed, not into the phone, mind you. I said, "I'll get there as fast as I can," and hung up, pausing only long enough to run into my house to get my gun, a jacket to cover it, and a second phone. Trick of the trade: carry two phones; that way if one gets taken, you have a backup. Fast Eddie might be packing and he might be smart enough to take away my phone, but he probably wasn't smart enough to look for a second one.

My fervent hope was that he'd be gone by the time I got there. I kept to my promise that I'd be there as soon as I could, but even if traffic was kind, that was fifteen minutes. Patience didn't seem to be Eddie's virtue. I avoided the interstate and took the back roads to evade the evening rush hour, taking Bienville up to City Park Avenue, which turned into Metairie Road—it seems every time a road crosses a boundary, the name has to change—and from there squirreled around to Mrs. Stevens' house.

I was out of luck. The hulking black truck sloppily parked, its wheels over the curb and onto her perfect lawn, told me Eddie was still around.

I spotted him, just as parked as his truck, lounging on her front steps, fiddling with his phone. I wondered if he was texting another young girl while waiting out Mrs. Stevens. Eddie wasn't smart, but he seemed to have enough animal cunning to know when he spooked his prey and he understood he had Mrs. Stevens cornered in her house.

He'd aged a few more pizzas and six-packs from the picture I'd found of him online, getting old while he was still young, a little more bloated, the waist starting to strain at his pants, the eyes more lost in the face.

I drove past and around the corner before parking. I wanted to be out of the car and able to watch him before he realized I wasn't just someone coming home.

My phone rang again. Mrs. Stevens. I cut off the call and immediately texted. "Just got here." Then I turned my phone—both of them—to vibrate.

Time to be my best butch, bad-ass dyke. I was betting that Eddie was a bully and, like most bullies, only wanted to play with those he could beat.

I adjusted my jacket to make sure my gun was well hidden—I fervently didn't want to have to even think about using it.

Using a deliberate but not hurried walk, I turned the corner.

Eddie looked up at me but then dismissed me—woman, too old to bother with. I would take that as Eddie clearly liked them on the very young side.

I turned up Mrs. Stevens' walk and called, "Edward Springhorn?"

He glanced up from his phone.

"Who wants to know?"

"I do. You're trespassing. You need to move on."

"I need to talk to someone 'bout a misunderstanding." He smirked. Yes, he actually smirked at me. Some gray-haired lady wasn't going to boss him around.

I pulled out my license, flashed it in front of his face, far too quickly for him to see anything other than it was something official in a fancy leather case. "How many times do I have to ask you, Eddie?"

"My friends call me Ed." Smirk gone, petulant now.

"Good, Eddie, because I'm not a friend. I'm the detective who had to read through all those nasty texts you sent to Tiffany Stevens. I'm here because I'm the only one professional enough to verbally"—I made it three words—"warn you to get the fuck out of here instead of making sure you and your truck have a little accident on the way to lockup."

"What the—?"

"Get the fuck out of here, Eddie, and don't come back to this neighborhood unless you're picking up garbage."

He stood up, his face turning a shade of red that told me he'd have blood pressure problems by the time he was thirty. His jaw worked, grinding his teeth. "Let me see that license."

"You've seen it. Get out of here."

"Who do you work for?"

"Better be careful. We're watching you. That delivery truck might be stopped unexpectedly. Or we might just notice that you're texting someone a little too young. Statutory rape can put you away for a long time."

"You can't tell me what to do." Eddie didn't want to be run off by a woman—misogynistic bastard that he was—but he was blustering, his eyes not looking at me, darting quickly across the lawn to his truck.

"I just did. This is private property. Get off it and get out of here."

The jaw worked again, and his face was red enough that he might be having blood pressure problems now. Then he lunged at me, veering at the last minute to slam me with his shoulder as he passed, muttering, "Sorry," to pretend it was an accident.

I shot out my foot, catching his ankle, jerking up and back hard enough to trip him.

"Sorry," I said clearly. "Only trying to keep from falling."

He landed hard, smashing half onto the walk and half onto Mrs. Stevens' no-longer-neat flower bed.

"Fuck you, you fucking cunt." He jumped up, the adrenaline of anger moving him faster than his lumbering body should have. He faced me, his hands bunched into fists.

I'd probably win, I know how to fight, have trained in karate long and hard enough to protect myself. But Eddie was big and young, and one lucky blow could do a lot of damage.

I pulled my gun and did my best TV lawman stance. "Don't do it. You're on private property, you're been told to leave. The property owner called me to get you out of here. Come at me and I have a blank check to shoot you." I dropped the gun barrel slightly. "At this range, you'll spend the rest of your life dribbling piss down your leg. And texting is all you'll be able to do."

Some people never learn. He lunged at me.

I fired. But aimed at the lawn about twenty feet to the side, hoping the bullet went safely into the dirt.

The retort of the gun was—finally—enough to make him stop in mid-step. Then back up half a step.

He stared at me long enough I could feel the weight of the gun.

Then he spun around, a stream of variations of "fucking cunt" over his shoulder until he was in his truck and peeled away. He was driving so recklessly I waited for the sound of a crash, but heard only one squeal of brakes and a car horn.

I tucked my gun back into my jacket and headed up the walk to Mrs. Stevens' door. I had a few questions for her.

CHAPTER ELEVEN

She didn't seem eager to let me in, only opening the door a few inches to my knock and asking, "Is he gone?"

"We need to talk," I told her, wedging my foot in the door.

I heard her sigh and the door inched open enough for me to slip in, a clue as to how welcome I was.

"Is he gone?" she repeated.

"For now."

"Did you have to pull a gun?"

Oh, now the proper Southern lady shows up. "It was that or a knock-down physical brawl on your front lawn. That would have really ruined your flowers."

She was smart enough to look abashed, seeming to realize I'd just done her a big favor. "I'm sorry. I just worry that the neighbors might…"

"You have more worries than the neighbors right now." I walked around her, going to the room we'd met in this morning and taking the same chair.

She followed, also taking her chair from the morning, although this time sitting as far back in it as she could, as if the distance between us would keep this away from her.

I was silent long enough for her to be uncomfortable, her eyes darting from point to point on the floor, anywhere but my face. Finally, I asked, "What prompted Eddie to pay you a visit?"

Another dart of eyes across the room, then she said, "I'm not sure."

"I just got rid of him for you, not something you hired me to do, risking getting my face punched in. You need to tell me everything that might possibly have anything to do with him coming here. Who did you call?"

Her eyes jerked to my face, but only briefly before going back to the restless scanning of her immaculate floor. "I had to do something. I couldn't just let him…get away with it."

"I thought you said you were going to sue him."

"Yes, we are, but that takes time. He doesn't have the right to…go around like nothing happened."

"What did you do?"

"I called his work, told them what kind of person he was. That was all. I don't know how he found out about it."

I tried to keep the exasperation out of my voice. "Because his work did what most workplaces would do when someone they don't know calls out of the blue and accuses one of their employees of something. They talked to that worker. Think about it. Someone you don't know, never heard of, calls you about your son and makes accusations. He denies them. Who do you believe?"

"But that's my son!" Now she looked at me, like I was suggesting an outrage.

"Maybe Eddie works for his dad. Or a relative." I hadn't researched who owned the trucking company; there didn't seem to be a need. I had to admit that Eddie looked like the kind of guy who needed a favor to get a job. I doubted he'd be hired on his sterling résumé.

"What? Why didn't you check that out?"

"Because you hired me to find out who he was, not do a complete background check. And the last we talked, you misled me into thinking you and your husband were going to grind him through the legal system. You forgot to tell me you were going to call his workplace and try to get him fired the second I walked out the door."

Her eyes were still looking at the floor, but her expression showed I'd hit the mark. "I didn't think he'd come here."

"The guy is an arrogant, stupid thug. You called his work, trying to get him in trouble, possibly fired."

"I thought they would want to know."

"I doubt it." This woman needed some serious reality checking. "They want to know that he doesn't wreck their truck and delivers whatever he needs to deliver on time and in one piece. They might be interested if he uses drugs, but only because they're worried about him wrecking the truck. For all we know, they're the same kind of asshole jerks he is."

"Why on earth would she have anything to do with someone like that?" Mrs. Stevens wailed the question, then started crying.

This is not what I do well, but I had enough sense to go to the kitchen, get a glass of water—such neatly organized cupboards, the glasses were easy to find—and a wad of paper towels in lieu of finding any tissues.

Back in the sitting room, I handed her the water and towels. She drank half the glass before wiping her face.

In a gentle tone, I said, "She did what girls throughout time have done when they're young and on the edge of exploring the world. She responded to attention, to someone telling her what she desperately wanted to hear, that she was becoming an attractive woman."

Mrs. Stevens sniffed, a slight nod of her head.

"And she ran into someone like him, older, with enough wiles and experience to know how to flatter those young girls, to tell them exactly what they want to hear. Eddie was probably worse than most, more cynical, manipulative, crude, willing to do anything to get what he wanted."

"The pictures," she sniffed again, then took another gulp of water as if it could wash this away.

"Yes, the pictures," I agreed. "I think she was figuring out what was going on, that she shouldn't have anything more to do with him."

"She was smart, she would have known better quickly."

"Yes, she was," I said. I didn't know that was true, but I was willing to tell her what she wanted to hear. Maybe we all do it. I understood why Douglas Townson's family cleaned up the story of their grandfather's murder. Grief has to be tempered with what can be borne. His murder would have been hard enough; to also lose the man they thought they knew would have compounded the grief. Mrs. Stevens did not—and perhaps could not—need to know how naïve her daughter had been, and how far it had gone.

I continued, "I know this is terribly hard for you, to think he could do what he did to your daughter, ruin your life, and still be walking around free, but men like him don't escape. I can promise you that. Life will get him and it will get him hard, he'll go to jail, lose his job, never have a relationship or a son at LSU."

"How can you be sure?" she asked.

"Experience. He doesn't have the self-control, the ability to sacrifice for the future, to plan, to think. He is scum, and scum stays with scum. A bar fight, a drunken crash, ending up in jail. It's going to happen."

She nodded. Maybe she believed me, or maybe she just desperately wanted to.

"You need to let that happen. Do something with your son, hike the Rockies or go to Europe over summer break. Remember your daughter as the wonderful girl she was. Let life take care of Eddie."

"We were, Tiffany and I and Alan, going to celebrate her graduating high school by going on a cruise this summer. She was so happy planning it." Mrs. Stevens started crying again.

"Maybe you should go on that cruise for her. Take her memories, believe she's somewhere watching, with you."

Another gulp of water and the towels across her face, "I don't know if I can do that."

I am so not a grief counselor. Facing Eddie had been easier than this. Taking a breath, I plunged ahead, hoping I was helping more than I was harming. "That's okay. Do something else for you and your family. Don't confuse revenge with healing."

She again looked at me, a stray tear sliding down her face. "I guess it was stupid of me to call his work and think they would even care."

"Not stupid"—well, yes, it kind of was, but I didn't need to rub that in—"you have a right to be furious. It's understandable. No one wants to wait for justice. But you have to be smarter and better than he is."

Another sniffle. "Yes, I guess."

"Your son clearly cares about you. You need each other now." I'd learned a few things from listening to Cordelia deal with patients—remind them of others around them, help them identify support. Who knew it would come in handy? "Be strong enough to help him get through it."

She sat up and finished the water. "You're right. I need to think about those of us still here. I really appreciate you coming out here. I was so scared, I didn't know what else to do."

"It's not legal for him to harass you. If he shows up again, you can call the police."

"Just not you?"

"You can call me, but I'm just one person, and at the end of the day, don't have the authority they have. I can't arrest him. And I'm a woman. He hates women, doesn't see them as people. Next time if it's just you and me—two women—he might let his anger make decisions and get violent. He's more likely to think twice about that with a big guy in a uniform."

She nodded, although I doubted Mrs. Stevens was much into feminism. Maybe this and the divorce would give her a nudge. "You're right. It might be a good idea for me to go away for a while. Alan urged me to come up to Baton Rouge with him, that we could see the sights."

"Sounds like a good plan," I said, not that I could think of any sights worth seeing in Red Stick, but then I'm a biased New Orleanian.

She stood up. "I promise not to do anything that will bring him here again."

I also stood, trying not to be too hasty about it. I didn't want her to know how much I wanted to get out of here and leave her to the social workers.

"Another good plan."

"Thank you for everything you've done." The polite Southern lady was back as she walked me to the door.

I didn't quite trot down her lawn, but I was tempted. And while it was unlikely, I couldn't be sure Eddie wasn't still lurking. My money was on him being in his favorite watering hole on the third beer by now and mouthing off to anyone listening how much he'd been taken advantage of by women and how much he hated them.

No sign of his truck or him. Dusk was just coming, the lingering light from the lengthening days. A favorite watering hole sounded like a good idea, although mine would not be anything like the ones Eddie favored.

CHAPTER TWELVE

Brandon looked at the text message again, as if it would disappear. "Need hlp with the comp. Cum ov, stay 4 party." He considered deleting it or pretending he'd left his phone somewhere and hadn't gotten the message until later. That would save him making a decision.

His mother wouldn't approve. If she found out, he'd be in trouble. But like Kevin said, he was getting too old to worry about his mother's approval. He knew it was probably mostly for the computer help, but it was cool to be invited.

His mother would approve of him trying to keep his grades up; he would tell her he was doing a study project with Kevin. She was working late tonight anyway.

He was smart enough to hide his computer stuff in his school backpack with a couple of textbooks thrown in. It was heavy, but that was okay. It wasn't like he was carrying it around school all day.

He was even clever enough to do the dishes, just a few bowls and spoons left over from breakfast. That would help convince her he really was being good.

The dishes done, the note to his mother written, Brandon headed out the door, texting as he walked to the bus stop. "On my way. C U soon."

He was happy they included him, and he wouldn't be so stupid this time. Kevin had egged him on, had probably been as stupid the first time he'd gone to one of the parties, without anyone handing him a beer, then vodka, then that awful-tasting whiskey like Kevin had done to him. Kevin wanted to make Brandon look as stupid as he had looked.

He'd gotten sick, hustled outside to throw up on the lawn since both bathrooms were being used. It wasn't his fault he'd landed in dog shit; gotten it all over his jeans, the ones he'd tried to hide from his mother. He wouldn't have been so scared if he hadn't still been a little bit drunk, worried she would be able to tell what he'd been up to just by the dog shit on his jeans. Okay, maybe worried some of the throw-up got on them, too. But he'd been drunk when he stuffed them behind the dryer. And then had forgotten.

But the guys were probably used to this kind of stuff. Brandon was sure that Kevin had been worse because even though they were friends, Kevin wasn't as smart as Brandon. Kevin was the one who had lit the firecracker and held it to show how tough he was, only to mess up and not get rid of it quick enough. Kevin claimed he had thrown it, but it went off too soon. Yeah, right, he still had a big burned spot on his hand, one his mother had to take him to the doctor for. He got grounded for a month after that.

Brandon had never been grounded. He'd never been stupid enough to risk burning his hands off like Kevin had.

And he knew how to set up computers and do cool stuff with them because his dad had taught him before being sent to Afghanistan. He was pretty sure he could fix whatever they needed him to.

He wouldn't drink as much this time, wouldn't be so stupid, wouldn't listen to Kevin. He'd stick to beer, saying he preferred that. Brandon was almost grown up, after all, and he needed to act like it.

As he got on the bus, another text came in. "U on ur way?"

"On the bus," he texted back.

"Good. Will pik u up at stop."

"Thks!" he started to write, then took the exclamation point off. Too girly. "thks," he sent. Men were to the point, no wasted time or emotion.

A ding told him another text had come in. But he quickly closed it before it fully loaded. It was a picture, and not one he could look at on the bus with people around him. Brandon smiled. This was another way they treated him like he was one of them, including him in seeing the pics they sent around.

His phone dinged again, but he didn't open it. An old lady was sitting next to him. He wasn't stupid enough to risk her seeing anything.

He waited until the bus let him off. He took a quick look at the picture. *Nice*, he thought, trying to keep his smile to himself. He didn't want anyone to see his expression. He looked up, but no truck yet.

The next text wasn't another picture. Just words. "We need to tlk about Tif."

He looked up again to see the black truck pulling up next to him.

Chapter Thirteen

I doubted the kind of bar Fast Eddie would go to would have good Scotch. And mostly gay men. I had strongly considered staying at home, popcorn and mindless TV, but the confrontation with him was unsettling. Even though I knew it wasn't rational, if he could show up at Mrs. Stevens' with no warning, he could show up at my house. I wouldn't very well be able to call myself to solve the situation. And I'd had the advantage of surprise; Eddie would be prepared this time. No, not rational. Unless he'd speed-read my license when I'd flipped it in front of him, he had no idea of who I was. Even if he did, my name would only lead him back to my office. He'd have to get through hordes of chai latte–swilling customers—such a rough bunch—to be able to get to me.

Or maybe I just wanted an excuse to sit at the far end of the bar, drink a well-aged single malt, and contemplate life with people and music around me, so I could pretend I had a social life.

As I had predicted/feared, Douglas Townson had left a message on my voice mail asking for progress. I'd phone him tomorrow—after I spent a few hours at the New Orleans Public Library. I'd call later in the afternoon and hope he didn't work weekends and I'd only have to leave a voice mail.

I hoped Mrs. Stevens was ensconced in a nice hotel in Baton Rouge, maybe at dinner with her son.

We learn—slowly—to carry our losses. We never get over them. When I was a teenager, just coming out, struggling for a place I could belong, I was tall enough to get into the bars, the gay bars of the Quarter and Marigny. No, not ideal, but they were the one place I could feel safe from being hated. I couldn't afford much more than a beer or two, but some of the bartenders and patrons became familiar faces, a welcoming smile, a few even friends. But a plague came, and the plague wasn't kind to those kind men. A cough, a spot that looked like a bruise, then we visited them in the hospice and then went to their funerals. These were the mostly men, a few women, who told me I would be okay; I'd find a place or make my own, but I could do it. By a few kind words, a laugh, a hug, they saved me. So many of them gone too early.

We carry our losses.

I didn't know how Mrs. Stevens would ever be able to carry the loss of her daughter. I'd tried the best I could with my words, but they were small and frail against the torn hole in her heart. Maybe her son would be her anchor, a heavy load for a college boy. Tragedy doesn't respect age—he would grow up quickly.

I signed the bartender for another. Now I could buy the good stuff and tip decently as if paying back for those days when I couldn't. None of the bartenders were the same, but a few patrons were occasionally around. We'd smile, chat briefly, happy we were still here, a shared history that survived.

The case of Fast Eddie was over. I wondered if I'd ever find out what happened next, what the husband—ex, whose name I didn't even know, would do with his lawyers.

I took a sip of my new drink, the familiar burn welcome. I didn't need to know. It wasn't my loss to carry. I let the music beat catch me, watching the strangers take over my thoughts, a few sips every song, after song. But even the music can't last all night.

I finished the last dregs of my drink, left a nice tip, and gave my bar stool to someone else. Time to go home to the home that often didn't feel like a home. Torbin kept telling me if I couldn't get a girlfriend, I should at least get a cat.

I probably should. A living thing to welcome me. Maybe next weekend I'd check out the shelter. But getting a new cat would mean I'd never get back the cats I'd lost in the breakup. It was hard to take that step. I'm not good at the emotional, moving on, taking care of myself kind of stuff. Single malt was the best I could do.

It was a boisterous evening in the French Quarter, people enjoying the mild temperatures, wandering around with their drinks in hand. I wasn't part of them, walking home, leaving the party I wasn't invited to behind.

I kept glimpsing big, stumbling men who looked like Fast Eddie until I looked closely and saw only tourists or college boys out for a good time.

My unease increased as I left the crowds behind, walking the quieter residential streets of the lower Quarter, the ones that would take me home. Mostly I liked being able to walk from my house to restaurants and bars. It saved me from worrying about my sobriety level.

But I couldn't get rid of the look on his face, the cold, naked hate. Fast Eddie didn't seem like a forgive-and-forget kind of guy. I had to assume that if we ever crossed paths again—something I hoped would never come to pass—that he would have a stew of resentment goading him on. The last thing I wanted was a random encounter on a deserted street.

I hurried my steps.

Most of what I do as a private investigator is boring and mundane, trolling through databases and records, waiting for a call back, having a polite conversation with someone about a minor detail. I go to the shooting range once a month because if I'm going to carry a gun, I damn well need to know how to use it. And to understand why it's so much better to never have to use a gun.

I heard footsteps behind me.

I quickly turned the corner, heading up Ursulines, varying my zigzag route home. If the footsteps also turned the corner, it would be time to truly let my paranoia run free.

The street was quiet. I turned again onto Dauphine. It, too, was a quiet residential street in this part of the Quarter. I considered going up to Rampart, but it was a mess of road construction and had only a trickle of its usual busy traffic.

Four more blocks and I'd be home.

I turned onto Barracks. Just as I was passing the small park, I heard running footsteps behind me. I glanced back only long enough to see two figures running my way. I took off. They were either running from something, in which case I might want to run from it as well, or they were running to catch up with me, and since they hadn't called my name and offered to buy me a drink, they didn't seem on the friendly side.

Barely looking for cars at the intersection of Barracks and Burgundy, I sprinted across it. More time at the gym, I thought as I pounded up the block. After this, I'd spend more time doing cardio workouts.

The footsteps were gaining on me. I chanced a glimpse back and it wasn't a pretty sight; two figures in hoodies, far too close to me. They were probably both sober and younger. The downside to looking back was that it took my eyes off what was in front of me long enough for my toe to hit a patch of the sidewalk that had bulged up.

I stumbled.

A hand caught my arm. Another one caught my shoulder.

"Hey, don't fall."

"You will"—I gasped for breath—"die for this."

My cousin Torbin and his partner Andy.

"We couldn't resist. We spotted you, then you picked up your pace, so we ran up here to cut you off," Andy said, laughing between—I was gratified to note—heavy breaths.

"A slow death," I panted out. "Left in a swamp with the snakes and mosquitoes."

"Not a chance," Torbin replied. "The cousins once got me to go hunting frog legs at night. Never again will I darken the door of anything with that many bugs."

"I'm at the age when I might have a heart attack from being scared like this."

"Any day now you'll be sitting on the porch barely able to get out of your rocking chair and shouting to the urchins to stay off your lawn."

"I don't have a porch or a lawn."

"Metaphorically speaking."

We started walking again. They lived just down the block from me.

To change the subject—and to make them talk so I could catch my breath—I asked, "What have you been up to?"

"The usual French Quarter frolic, dinner with some friends," Torbin answered.

"Anyone I know?"

"Nope, I doubt it," Torbin said quickly enough for me to know he was probably having dinner with someone I did know well enough to give him hell for being in their company. "And you? What were you up to?"

"Just stretching my legs. Spent most of the day behind my desk." If he wasn't going to be honest with me, I saw no reason to be honest with him. Plus I was still mulling over what had happened today and wasn't sure I was up to talking about it.

We crossed Rampart holding hands because the road was so torn up, no one wanted to disappear into a pothole and never be heard from again.

"Just a walk after dark?" Torbin queried. "No stopping along the way?"

Andy was either smart or rude enough to be engrossed in his phone.

We're the lavender sheep, bonded by being queer in a family that wasn't welcoming. He had earned the right to worry about me. But that didn't mean I appreciated it.

"Only stopped at the gay bars."

"Have you eaten?"

"Yes, of course," I said. He didn't specify when. "And only two drinks. Total."

"Sixty-four-ounce daiquiris could count as one drink."

"Not in this case," I said. "Two slowly sipped single malts."

He nodded. My speech and gait were steady enough to back me up.

"And if you're so worried about me, maybe you should dump your friends that I probably don't know and spend some time with your favorite cousin. I actually can behave when out in public."

Torbin was quiet for a moment—a rarity for him—which told me my guess about the friends was correct. Then he said, "Soon, I promise. This time of year is always busy. We should make plans. I keep thinking because we live half a block away, we'll see each other all the time."

We stopped in front of my house.

We used to see each other all the time. But it had slipped away when my routine changed from being with someone to being by myself. Torbin and Cordelia had often made the plans to come over after work or meet for drinks after a hard day.

That was gone.

"Seems we should," I agreed. "Maybe we need to start sharing calendars."

"I'll call you in the next few days and we'll set something up."

"Maybe every second Tuesday we should meet halfway between your house and mine," I suggested.

"Good idea. Something to make sure we get together more often." He gave me a hug.

"That would be good," Andy agreed, his phone put away. We also hugged. They waited long enough to see me in my door.

Then I watched them as they walked the half block to their house, holding hands. It's easy to go out when you have someone to go out with.

The rest of the evening was something thrown in the microwave for dinner, mindless TV. And one more single malt before calling it a night.

The next day was an exciting one of having to take my car out to the 'burbs (again!) for the usual routine maintenance. I chose to wait in hopes it would speed things up. My other option was to rent a car, and there was nothing pressing enough to require me to risk driving an automatic in the insanity of the NOLA 'burbs instead of my manual car.

It took about three hours. I spent most of it in the waiting room on my phone trying to look like I was taking care of important business. Like checking the weather. Deleting spam email. I waited until lunch on East Coast time and called Douglas Townson back. He was out of the office and I had to—(yes!)—settle for leaving a message.

Two messages came into my dating inbox. One asking if I was butch or femme? Since it was written as *U btch or femme*, I decided the sender wasn't interested in a listing of the ways my characteristics could be a mix of both. My answer was *Neither, a bit of both*, which got no reply. The second asked how tall I was. At least it was in grammatical English. I answered, *five feet, ten inches*. That got an immediate reply. *That's too tall. I'm only looking for women between five-five and five-seven. Are you trans? Most women over five-eight are trans in my experience.* Because I was bored and didn't have anything else to do, I answered her. *No, not trans. Why would that matter? Just tall.* She replied, *Very tall for a woman. Sure you're not trans?* I replied, *I am tall. Maybe I should check. You could be right.* She answered, *So you are trans. I hate it when people aren't up front and honest in their ads*. I guess she had disabled sarcasm-font on her phone. I glanced at her ad, she made no mention of a specific height. She did say no trans. I didn't bother to reply. Silence seemed to be a wiser option than telling her she was a fucking bigoted idiot. That also meant I'd managed one smart thing today, so I was off the hook for the next twenty-four hours.

I closed the dating app. Maybe that was also wise and I could stretch it to forty-eight hours.

Since I was already out on the long, commercial stretch of Veterans Highway, I did the other errands that could only be done out there. (Oh, Target, why must you be so far away?) After Katrina almost all the car dealers had moved out of New Orleans. Since my Mazda was still under warranty, I had little choice but to go out there.

After unloading everything and putting it away, that was enough of a day for me. Dinner was real, cooked food (the payoff of the errands), a coconut cashew curry. And a few beers.

The real advantage of going to the main library on a Saturday was that parking was much kinder. It's located near City Hall and the Civil Court, so on weekdays parking is a shoot-to-kill sport.

Today I was right in front of the library. I'd even been a good girl and allowed myself only one cup of coffee instead of my usual weekend lingering of two or three cups. Of course, I intended to bill Mr. Douglas Townson for every second I was here. I wasn't optimistic, but would do an exhaustive search both for the billable hours and to be able to give him a long list of every scrap of paper I'd looked at so he would know I'd found what could be found. I suspected, without that lengthy list, he might be the type to argue over the bill, not understanding that he was paying me to do the searching, not for the results.

It wasn't very crowded, a few homeless people, a few developers looking over city plans to see what they could scoop up.

Why do librarians all look like lesbians? With same sex-marriage available these days, even a wedding ring doesn't help. Tempting as it was to flirt, it probably wasn't safe. I might be hitting on Mrs. Three Kids in the Suburbs.

A woman who was either a butch dyke or a too busy to mess with her hair mom came over to ask me if I needed help.

As a kid I'd always loved libraries, and now I found a reason to love them all over again. I knew I was going after the proverbial needle in a haystack, but the archivist who helped me restored my faith to order and filing. She guided me through the digging it took—maybe I was a better option than the other patrons, the scurvy developers looking at city maps, the runny-nosed teenagers looking for a shortcut to an A, or maybe I was just more charming—but she found the police record of the murder, court records for several names listed in the police report—with no arrest, there was no court proceedings for the murder—and newspapers I'd probably already perused at the New Orleans Historic Collection.

"Happy hunting." She waved at me as I made my way to the microfilm machines. Maybe she was flirting.

The police record confirmed what I'd surmised from the newspaper articles. No, it didn't spell out my theories, but the terse language left a lot of space to read between the lines. The involved officers weren't treating this the way Townson's story spun it: the heinous murder of an upstanding and innocent citizen.

I jotted down some of the telling lines, the laconic "no witnesses, no one says they saw anything" and "body found at 7:15 am by barkeep taking out trash" and "no mention at hotel of evening plans, no one admitted to being in his company." Mr. Townson had come to Storyville for the reasons most men came there, and the police were kind—or smart—enough to leave out that detail.

I jotted down the other names mentioned in the report.

Robert Byrnes, the barkeep who had found him, the police judged as too in his cups to have been the murderer. Evidently Robert, or Rob, as they called him, was well known to the constabulary for his frequent spells in the jail to sober up. The three witnesses who saw nothing were Mr. Michael Fordeaux, Mr. Gregory Herring, and Mrs. Consuela Taite-Carsen. The report also listed four houses of ill repute, three residential houses, two bars, and one coffeehouse/restaurant on the block.

The kind of block where a man shouldn't lie in the streets until 7:15 in the morning before someone notices him. Even if he was a rich man looking for what he'd find in Storyville.

I again found my friendly archivist and got street maps of the area back then. It was in the back part of Storyville, one that likely catered to the dock worker, the seaman, the ones who couldn't afford anything fancy. It was several blocks back and in from the train station that had been there at the time.

It was easy to see how Frederick Townson got killed. He was a posh-looking dude out of place in this part of town. Any thief would have jumped him. He fought back and the thief killed him. What nagged at me was why was he there? Douglas had indicated that he often came to New Orleans on buying trips. It didn't seem likely he'd gotten lost. Surely if he was looking for the nice houses on Basin Street, he would have turned back long before he reached this location. Maybe he had a taste for the low life. But even so, there were ways for gentlemen to make discreet inquiries—or to consult the infamous Blue Books that listed what was available—to find what he was looking for. He shouldn't have been wandering the streets. Nor did that adequately explain the police report. A rich man looking for a little on the side wasn't enough to shock back then. He was rich and powerful; the police should have been diligently searching for his killer rather than merely noting no one saw anything and leaving it at that.

Maybe he had pissed the police off. Accused them of taking bribes or been robbed before and not appreciated how they treated him.

My back was stiff. A look at my watch told me I had been sitting here for over three hours. No wonder I was creaky. Not to mention hungry.

However, the downside to the easy parking was that most of the nearby food options that were fast and easy closed over the weekend. I decided to push through for another hour or two. Maybe I could find a few court cases to indicate Rob Byrnes had a habit of rolling customers and make a case that he was the likely murderer.

Another two hours convinced me that Rob would be a hard sell as the murderer. He was variously listed as Robt. Burns, Robert Bryns, Robin Byrns, and Robert Byrnes, the latter being the most frequent, with an address a few digits' variation, but always in that block. The arrest was almost invariably drunk and disorderly.

Lunch. And another, kinder sitting position.

I managed food, but it was standing, as the best option was a food truck near Tulane Hospital, around the corner from the library.

The food was good, the weather was nice, and standing wasn't bad after all the sitting. I debated going back; all I'd probably get were more drunk and disorderlies on Mr. Byrnes.

But I was here, and Mr. Townson was paying by the hour. I trudged back to the library.

Trying another tack, I did a search for Mr. Frederick Townson. At first look, he appeared to be as his grandson portrayed. He had a plantation upriver, on the Westbank, and did well with cotton and sugar cane. In the one picture I found, he was expensively dressed, a fat watch chain, presumably gold, hanging at his waist. But as I dug deeper, the cracks began to appear. There was a property deed in his name with an address on Burgundy Street in the French Quarter. Over a hundred years ago, the French Quarter was run down, not the real estate jewel it is now. It was common practice for the rich men to keep their mistresses, especially the ones who were considered mixed race, in the so-called "back" of the Quarter, up on Dauphine and Burgundy Streets.

If Frederick was indeed keeping a mistress on the side, what was he doing in Storyville? I sighed. Too bad I couldn't get access to his bank account. *Follow the money* is a tried and true adage in my business.

As closing loomed, I did one final search for any court records on him, at least the ones the database would have.

Another crack. No, a fissure. A Mr. Frederick Townson was arrested in Shreveport in 1902 on charges of assaulting a woman, a lady of the night, the report made clear. He paid a fine and was let go. The police report called it a business dispute. One of the cops was clever enough—or unschooled enough to put in the report, "Victim alleges 'he tried to make me do something no one should do' and she fought him." His version was, "She tried to take my wallet and we had a struggle."

It was closing time. I hastily made a copy, returned the microfilm, and thanked the archivist for her help.

The days were getting longer, summer approaching, but now it was the balmy days of spring, a perfect day for idling outside. I enjoyed it for the brief walk to my car.

I was headed home but took a detour instead, heading up to the lake, stopping for a frozen daiquiri on the way. A small one. I found a relatively uncrowded place to park and sat on the levee, sipping my drink, watching the waves roll in, the sailboats in the distance, and then the sun as it set.

Then home to leftover curry and a few more beers.

That was my exciting Saturday night.

CHAPTER FOURTEEN

If the library was open on Sunday, I would have gone. Other than the usual chores, home had little to distract me. As a small business owner, I rely on what comes through my doors to set the rhythm of my days. I was finished with the case Mrs. Susie Stevens had brought me. I could spend a few more hours doing a paper dive on Frederick Townson, but it wasn't likely I'd ever find who killed him, and it seemed that additional research would only dredge up more things his great-grandson would not want to know. Medical records with "pox" in red letters on it. I was skating at the edge of not getting paid—beyond the handsome retainer—as it was. "Your great-grandpa was a serial philanderer and seemed to like it rough," is not the ticket to a bonus.

But the sad reality was I had little else to do other than the hated filing and billing or chores that I had so far put off successfully, and I didn't want to mar my winning streak. (I needed to prune the vines growing over the absent next door neighbor wall, but I needed to be zen enough to do the job and not toss the entire heap back on their side. Zen was not on the horizon at the moment.)

I did what any reasonable Southern girl would do, decided I'd think about it tomorrow, because after all tomorrow was another day, and settled myself in with a good book, accompanied by coffee in the morning and wine in the evening.

By the morning spring had fled. It was a blustery, rainy day, chilly in the way only places with a damp, persistent wet of constant high humidity can be. I had to shrug on a jacket.

As predicted, the piles of filing and billing had not vanished overnight nor been done by fairies. They were waiting for me when I got to my office around ten. Even most of a pot of coffee didn't up the energy level much above file one piece of paper and play two games of solitaire on the computer.

I was almost to the point of violating one of life's lessons, be careful what you ask for, as you may get it, and hoping for an interesting case, something challenging, anything, to walk through my door.

I edged too close to that wish.

The phone rang. I picked it up to hear, "I shouldn't be doing this, but you may want legal counsel."

I heard footsteps coming up the stairs.

"What?" I said. My caller was one of my oldest friends, Danielle Clayton, now one of the top prosecutors in the DA's office.

There was a banging on my door, immediately followed by it being thrown open.

Joanne Ranson, another friend and a NOPD cop, stood there with two other men, also clearly cops I didn't know. She looked so far from happy I had to doubt joy existed in the world.

I put the phone down. I suspected that Joanne was going to explain it all to me. I could only hope it wouldn't be in handcuffs.

She strode across the room until she was leaning over my desk.

"Did you murder Edward David Springhorn?" she demanded.

"Who?" Then it filtered in. I considered him Fast Eddie and had forgotten his real name.

Joanne said nothing, making me fill the silence.

"Wait, he's dead?"

She still stared at me.

"And you think I did it?" I stood up. I didn't want her looming over me.

"Tell me about your relationship with Edward Springhorn," she asked.

"There was no relationship. I knew him only in passing in reference to a case." The surprise was wearing off and I was able to regain a semblance of my professional cool.

"What case?"

"Cases are confidential," I replied.

"This is a murder investigation," she replied. One of the other cops was taking notes in the background.

"Look, sit down. Let me get you some coffee," I said, stalling for time.

Joanne let out a barely perceptible sigh. She probably hoped her unexpected arrival and questions might trip me up, but that moment had passed.

I busied myself with making another pot of coffee, pulling extra chairs around my desk, and finding passably clean mugs. I suspected I was going to need the coffee more than they would.

But it wasn't just busywork; it gave me time to think. The only person who had seen my fight with Eddie was Susie Stevens. Well, the only person who had seen it and knew who I was and where to find me. Maybe Eddie, in his towering rage, had mouthed off, but I hadn't told him my name, and it was doubtful in the brief glance I'd given him of my license that he'd seen enough to lodge in his lizard brain.

Which pretty much left Susie Stevens. She was smart enough to know she had to be a suspect. And evidently cunning enough to mention the fight I'd had with him. But had she done it to give herself time to get rid of evidence? Or had she panicked and grasped any way out to get them away from questioning her? Or had she just been a good girl and completely honest with the cops? There was no way of knowing; I could count on Joanne not revealing anything.

"I need to take possession of your gun," she said as I placed a cup of coffee in front of her.

I considered replying, "Et tu, Brute?" but thought better of it. I took my gun out of my desk drawer and handed it to the cop who held his hand out for it.

He placed it in an evidence bag, taken from the bulky briefcase he was carrying. They'd come prepared. I wanted to think Joanne knew me well enough to know I wasn't the killer and she was doing her best to get evidence proving that.

And if I had killed him, well, she'd get that evidence, too.

"Can you tell me what's going on?" I asked.

"We need to ask you some questions. Where were you last night?"

I waited before answering, trying to game her or one of the other cops into giving me more. But she was too good to fall for it. "I was home reading a book."

"With anyone?"

"No, just me."

"What book?" one of the other cops asked. It was clear I wasn't going to get introductions.

"*Holy Rollers*, by…I've forgotten the author's name."

"What's it about?" he asked.

"About a gang of thieves who plan to rob a hypocritical, homophobic megachurch. And all the things that can go wrong with their plans."

"Any good?"

"Lots of fun if you like wryly sardonic caper novels with gay and lesbian protagonists." Joanne had been inching her way out of the closet at work, but there was still enough bigotry around—both for women and queers—for her to be cagey about who knew. I wasn't making it easier on her by talking openly about gay subjects, but she wasn't making this easier on me, either. Since I worked for myself, I could be as out of the closet as I wanted. I added, "I downloaded it online around ten a.m."

"Did you call anyone? Talk to anyone?"

"Some email, but no actual phone calls. That's so 1990s. Oh, I downloaded some more books after I finished the one I was reading. I think about nine p.m."

"What books?" the other cop asked.

Joanne interjected, "Tell us about Edward Springhorn." She wasn't interested in my reading habits. Or was worried that I'd say *The Joy of Lesbian Sex*.

"You probably know more than I do."

Silence. She wasn't going to tell me anything.

"I was hired by a client. She wanted me to find the person threatening to send out private pictures of her daughter." I paused again, but they were too well trained to say anything. It was up to me to talk. "Her daughter had sent pictures to someone she thought liked her. Less than fully dressed pictures. But he used them to coerce her into having sex with him. When she refused, he threatened to send the pictures out to people in her school."

"Go on," was all Joanne said.

"She killed herself, the girl. The mother hired me to find out who sent the texts."

They didn't react. I had watched closely enough that I'd see even a blink. No reaction meant they already knew, had already reacted.

Which meant they knew everything I was going to tell them. "I tracked them back to Edward Springhorn. I gave that information to the mother. I talked to her about what she planned to do, and she said she and her ex-husband were going to pursue legal channels. They had the resources and they guessed that Edward did not, so it would make his life difficult."

I paused, but they were still silent, so I continued, "The mother, understandably grieving and upset, made the mistake of calling his workplace. The workplace passed that on to Eddie—Edward—and he showed up at her house. She called me and I came out and told him to leave. He grumbled, but he did so. That was my only encounter with him."

Then I was silent.

"That's all?" Joanne said, after a long pause.

"Yes, pretty much."

"We have a witness that says you argued heatedly and you fired your gun at him."

"Mrs. Stevens was inside her house. She could have only glimpsed us at an angle through a window and unlikely she heard everything we said. As I already told you, he wasn't happy about being told to leave, in my opinion, less so because it was two women, my client Mrs. Stevens and myself, doing the ordering. I did pull my gun, but my only intent was to equalize the power between us and prevent him from attacking me. He threatened to, took a step toward me. I fired a warning shot off into the lawn. Some grass may have been hurt. I wanted him to leave with as little fuss as possible."

"You did fire your gun?" Joanne asked.

"Yes, but not at him, off to the side, into the ground."

"Just that once?"

"Yes."

One of the cops asked, "Did you lie and tell him you were the police?"

"I told him I was a detective, which I am, and showed him my license. He may have been unsophisticated enough to not recognize it as a private detective license, but he did see it."

"Are you being honest about this?" he asked.

"I have no reason to lie," I answered. "I did not murder him."

"What did you think of him?" Joanne asked.

I glanced at them, weighing my answer. "A turd from a slime ball. He preyed on young girls, high school–aged, and manipulated them into sex. He was ugly and brutish about it. I considered asking some of the people I hire to do computer research if they wouldn't mind doing a little hacking in his direction. But I didn't even do that."

"Why?" the so far silent cop asked.

"It's not legal."

Joanne raised an eyebrow at me.

"Plus, I'm old enough to know life isn't going to be kind to people like Eddie Springhorn. I guessed he'd be in jail in a few years and was content to leave it at that. I didn't think it would go this far this fast."

"Could Susie Stevens have killed him?"

Again I weighted my answer. It was tempting to return the favor of her pointing the finger at me. "I don't know. She was grieving for her daughter and has good reason to blame him. But…my instinct says she's a woman who plays by the rules. As she told me, their plan was to make his life a legal hell. Maybe if they'd lost and he won, and she felt there would be no justice from any of the systems she trusted. Plus she has another child, a son, and they seemed close. She didn't seem to have the kind of hot temper that would abandon him even for revenge."

"What about the son?" Joanne asked.

"He goes to LSU and seems close to his mother. But that's all I know, I barely got a glimpse of him."

"He's close enough to have come down here," the formerly silent cop said.

"I'm sure you've considered this," I said, as politely as I could, since I wasn't sure they actually had, "Tiffany was not likely to be the first girl he tried this with. Plus men who manipulate girls just barely old enough to consent to sex don't tend to be fine, upstanding citizens otherwise."

"We are pursuing all leads," Joanna said. She stood up.

"Can you tell me what happened?" I asked.

"What do you think happened?" the second cop asked me.

Ah, if I said he was shot in the parlor, they'd want to know how I could know something only the murderer could know. Sorry, sunshine, that's an old trick. "Clearly he didn't do what I guessed he'd do, lose his temper and get into a bar fight that ended badly. If that was the case, you'd know who did it and have multiple witnesses. Since you're here, that didn't happen. As you took my gun, I assume he was shot. Plus with you willing to consider me or Mrs. Stevens as prime suspects, it's not likely either of us would have risked going after him with a knife or a baseball bat, given how much bigger he was than both of us. So I'd have to surmise that he was shot with a handgun someplace where no one was around, probably late last night/early morning, and his body wasn't immediately found, leading to a wider range of suspects. Is that close?"

The looks they exchanged told me it was right on the money.

Joanne didn't roll her eyes at the cop who'd asked the question—she's too professional for that—but she came close.

"Don't leave town," that cop told me.

"I have to cancel my trip to the Spanish wine region? Those tickets are non-refundable."

He shot me a worried glance, but Joanne shut it down. "She's not going to Spain any time soon. We'll be in touch if we have more questions."

With that, they left.

I called Danny back but only got voice mail. I told her I wasn't in handcuffs yet. I trusted she'd call back to get the details. I also wanted to see if she'd give me a clue as to why and how Joanne was involved with this. Given that I was a suspect, she shouldn't be investigating.

I debated calling Mrs. Susie Stevens and demanding to know why she had dumped me in it without warning. But other than venting my anger, it would be little good; it might even give the cops evidence I was more involved than I claimed. My gun would come back clean. I could provide some proof of my whereabouts with the sent emails and purchased e-books. Yeah, I'd crossed Fast—and Dead—Eddie's path in a less-than-pleasant encounter, but my money was that with a little digging they'd find much juicier suspects than me.

I started looking through what I'd dug up on him, then reminded myself this wasn't my case and I needed to leave it to the police.

Fast Eddie had lived up to his nickname. He'd gotten what he deserved fast.

Chapter Fifteen

To avoid the temptation of looking at the file for Fast Eddie, I left my office to focus on the other paying case I had and headed for the public library. Yes, it was likely all I'd find would be more sordid dirt on Mr. Frederick Townson, but at least no one could accuse me of murdering him, since I had the strong alibi of not being born yet.

Being a weekday, parking was not kind. At least I could expense the cost, if not the long walk, to my client.

My friendly archivist was again there. This time I got her name, Cindy Espinosa, so I could connect with her, as she would know what I was looking for. Even archives have their specialties. If need be, I'd come back every day this week and have a complete tally of every time Rob Byrnes got carted off to jail for being drunk, if that was what it took to keep me as far away as possible from the murder of Fast Eddie.

I continued searching on Mr. Frederick Townson himself, but the Shreveport arrest was the only one that came up. Even then, while the timing was right, in 1903, it was possible that it was another Frederick Townson. It wasn't like there was Social Security numbers back then to match up. If that was him, though, it was telling. Men of his rank and riches rarely went to prison. I found the usual blather of newspaper articles, his donations to his church, the marriage of his two sons and one daughter, all into seemingly appropriate families, both sons to daughters of fellow planters and the daughter to the son of the owner of a shipping company.

I went back to the police reports and my now good friend, Robt. Byrnes. Thirteen and counting on the drunk and disorderlies, but little else to link him to the murder other than to prove that he was probably so drunk he couldn't have managed to swat a fly. I did searches on several of his known associates, Mr. Gregory Herring and Mr. Michael

Fordeaux, but other than them being described as "artistic" and "not the manly sort," there was little else of interest. Mr. Fordeaux seemed to have left with a circus as part of an "astounding and wondrous dog who can count and read" act, and Mr. Herring began writing for the penny dreadfuls.

I again opted for the food trucks for lunch, although the weather wasn't the kind to make me linger in the small park near the library. Even with the drizzle, it was a welcome change to see daylight.

As I headed back from lunch, I considered that at least I'd be able to tell Douglas I'd done an exhaustive search. The real point being to exhaust myself so I wouldn't think about the murder of Fast Eddie. Or worry about more visits from the cops.

Cindy, my friendly archivist, came up to me just as I was sitting down.

"Hey, this might be of interest. We've only recently been able to process it and add it to the catalogue." She placed a thick binder in front of me. "It's a copy, of course, but could be great source material. The handwriting might be hard to read."

"What is this?" I asked, trying to smile like I really wanted to read everything there was about Storyville. This seemed more than an afternoon's work, more than a week's, even, and I doubted that Douglas would want to pay for that level of exhaustion, nor would I want to go bleary eyed over it.

"It's the diary of a policeman who worked the Storyville beat from 1905 to 1911. I haven't read it through, so can't promise what's in it, but it might give you more insight than the court records."

I returned her smile. "Thanks, this might be very helpful." I didn't need to read the entire thing, I consoled myself, just glance around the pertinent dates and scan for murder of Townson.

The writing was cramped and at times, scribbled, but after some practice, I could read most of it. I skimmed through the first part, his moving here from Philadelphia to make a better life for his family, the heat, etc.

A passage caught my eye:

> *I must do my utmost to spare my dearest Alibe from the horrors of what I see whilst I work the streets of this pestilential city. Yes, she is strong and would not flinch, but we have agreed that she can continue to work at the school until we are blessed with children of our own. I want*

her to be able to look at all her pupils, even the paupers, and imagine for them a felicitous future, one of virtue and productive work, instead of knowing that some proportion of them will fall and be the ones I encounter, the weak, the vile, the avaricious, the depraved. I live too much in their world; I will not take them home with me.

Much of it was mundane, the weather, what they ate, stories of her pupils and the insane politics of the city. His entries on his police work were mostly typical crime, done by the desperate and stupid, drunken bar fights, burglars who robbed the house next door and wore the stolen shoes the next day.

Then an entry from January 3, 1906, said:

This is a sad day. I was called in the early hours of the morning to Marais Street, below Canal. One of the women who had fallen into working in that area was found dead in the small room where she spent much of her life. Her ending was a brutal one, beaten, bruised, strangled, and her body violated, left more unclothed than not, with intimate articles of clothing blocking her mouth, preventing her from crying out. She was young, perhaps even pretty with the animation of life. I have seen the dead before; it is part of my professional life, but her death disturbed me as others have not. Women of her ilk often fall prey to that which snatches life away, liquor, diseases, the wear of how they spend their days, but she was too young for any of those. A wicked man sought his pleasure with her and instead took her life. Even if she grabbed his wallet, there was no need for this level of brutality.

I spent the day asking all in the area who knew the girl, who might wish her harm. But they knew little or admitted little if they did. Only one woman talked to me, the proprietress of the coffee shop nearby. She was polite, but I felt little trust from her, and little belief that I would do more than the shuffling of papers. She did not know the name of the girl beyond Annie, had seen her only recently come to the location. She had seen a man, a bit of a swell she called him, around midnight on the street outside. It was little to go on, and she may be right that only papers will mark the death of this young girl. I will, of course, search for the killer, but he may be on a ship sailing for a foreign land by now.

I started to read more carefully, but then reminded myself this was a murder that happened over a century ago. If the police couldn't solve it, I certainly couldn't. I needed to concentrate on what I was hired to do.

The afternoon was wearing on. I skipped to the date of Mr. Frederick Townson's murder, May 3, 1906.

My dearest Alibe is working hard for the finish of the school year, her pupils a trial and a joy. I worry for her that she cares so much for the children of strangers, but also happy as it shows how she will care for ours, a mother both loving and demanding. I worry for her too, with each murder of a woman close to her in age. Of course, these women aren't respectable married women as she is, and are in parts of the city she'll never set foot in, but I cannot imagine a life without her to come home to. Her laugh and merriment at the follies of the world are a light in my life.

I needed them today, as it has been a long one. Only now with her asleep for the school day am I able to put pen to this journal.

The heat is in the air, the edge of oppressive summer looming. I was called this morning for another murder, this one bizarre in the extreme. The body was left in the street, near the corner of Conti and Marais. I was only called at the comfortable hour of 7 a.m., itself a worry. A body in the street should not go so long unnoticed. But this time it was not one of the fallen women of the area, but a well-dressed gentleman of middle years but with the appearance of vigorous health, hair and teeth intact, limbs well fleshed.

His death was one of violence, his head bleeding against the rough sidewalk, likely the mortal blow, but with the marks of a fresh and furious beating, with several wounds from a knife, others a blunt object. Most shocking of all was that in his mouth had been shoved soiled woman's intimate apparel.

Unlike the unfortunate women, several of them left unclaimed, to be buried as paupers, this man, no matter what his proclivities, would be someone missed, with the attendant hue and cry for his killer to be caught.

Alas, that might be an unlikely outcome. I and several of my fellows have spent the day and into the night searching for the information that might lead us to his killer. The denizens of the area are not the friends of the police, and whilst some have tried to help with the murders of the young women, those of their own, so to speak, no one admitted to seeing this man, even lying in the street as he was. He could be a ghost of the night for all the notice anyone had of him or how he came to his unfortunate end.

I remind myself it is early in the investigation. Perhaps learning his identity will lead us in a productive direction. There may be gambling debts and his body was dropped in this area of town to obscure the time and place of his murder.

The night is late. I must go to bed.

A glance at my watch told me that my day, too, was about to end. The library would close in about fifteen minutes. I went to find my new best friend Cindy and ask her if I could arrange to come back in the next day or two (didn't want to overcommit with the police possibly questioning me about Fast Eddie's murder) and continue with this material.

She was very helpful, happy, it seemed that someone was delving into the stacks of history kept here.

At least with copies of the diary, I could give Mr. Douglas Townson a far clearer account of his great-grandfather's murder. I was assuming it was him, although he hadn't been clearly identified yet. How many swell gentlemen would be offed on the same day in the same location?

As I headed for my car, I debated my options. I could be super industrious and go back to the office and write this all up. But I could also just make a note of the pertinent passages, get them copied (and expensed to the current Mr. Townson). I hate paperwork. Plus if the police wanted to question me again, my office was one place they might look.

The other place they might look would be my house, the second of the major options of where to go and what to do.

I was hungry, and it would be after five p.m. in this part of the world by the time I got anywhere.

I headed for my new favorite local bar, a mix of dive and

gay—well, really genderqueer, as just about anyone, save straight suburbanites, would feel welcome here. It was on Rampart, the lower part of the Quarter, relentlessly gentrifying, but some of the old sordid was stubbornly hanging on. Riley & Finnegan. The only clue to the name was they served a mean corned beef sandwich and had a nice collection of Irish whiskey. And the main barkeep was a wise woman named Mary Buchanan. She was good at talking when customers wanted to talk and at being quiet when they needed to stare into the amber liquid and contemplate life.

It was also close enough to my house to walk there, although I didn't this time. I parked my car in the Tremé, across Rampart but not near my house. If Joanne came by, she would not see my car parked nearby.

Monday was a slow night, only a few regulars there. I took a table in the back. My goal was to not contemplate life, but just enjoy the corned beef and some beer and watch the queer, dive world go by.

Mary came over to say hi and take my order. After she brought my beer back, we chatted about how the streetcar construction was affecting the business. "It'll be great to have the line going along here," she said, "but hell to pay until then. Dust, dirt and noise. I bike in, but it's impossible to park around here. Glad you give us so much business."

I smiled and nodded. I didn't think I was a great customer, maybe in here a few times a month, mostly a quick drink after work, to occasionally meet Torbin or other friends, or just pass the time, as I was doing now. Mostly the latter.

I had just finished my corned beef sandwich, down to the last fry and pickle, when a large group of young people came in. They were loud, but in a happy way. It was hard to tell which were the boys and which were the girls, not that it mattered, unless you were their gynecologist or wanted to date them and had a specific genital preference. Neither an option, in my case.

One of them looked familiar.

What was the nice polo shirt college boy doing here?

I finished my beer. Maybe it was time to go.

Or maybe it was time to hang about. I could be a good girl and stay away from both Mrs. Susie Stevens and Fast Eddie's murder, but was it my fault when I was sitting around and her son and his friends happened to choose the same bar as me? Of all the genderqueer joints in the world, he happened to pick this one.

I was hidden in the back, too old to be noticed by them. Plus I'd probably see nothing more interesting than what drink he ordered. It wasn't like I'd overhear a confession to murder.

The neat, collegiate look was gone. He was in tight black jeans and a white T-shirt designed to show off his developed muscles, with his hair gelled in the current hipster style. Most of his friends were dressed similarly, hip, queer, jeans and T-shirts. The same kind of stuff I'd worn back when I was in my twenties.

I guessed he was here for the same reason I was, it was a cool place to hang out if you didn't walk the straight and narrow.

The louder parts of their conversation carried to my table, but it seemed mostly to be a discussion of where to go next and where they'd gone last.

Mary brought my second beer.

"New group in here?" I said with a nod at them.

"Not really, they're here about once a week."

"Know who they are?" She gave me a look. I'd never asked questions about the other patrons before. I added, "One of them looks like the son of a friend of mine." That was close enough.

"Mostly college kids, UNO, LSU. The ones old enough to drink. Yes, we do check ID when they look that young. A nice bunch, they come here usually after volunteering at the NO/AIDS office on Frenchmen."

"Thanks," I said. I didn't want to appear too curious. I doubted Mary would be happy with me playing detective in her bar.

Time to finish my beer and go home.

I'd just taken my third sip when he turned in my direction and clearly recognized me. He headed toward me.

I feigned a blank expression, like I took so many cases out in the suburbs I couldn't possibly remember them all.

"Hi," he said as he sat down, not even asking if he could.

"Hi," I answered. "Sorry, only interested in woman of the appropriate age."

"Don't you recognize me?" he asked.

"Should I?"

"You're the detective my mother hired."

Okay, I had choices here. I could continue to play dumb, like I had no clue of what he was talking about, or I could admit I knew, but cut it off. Or I could let him talk.

"The police questioned her," he added.

Decision made. I was curious.

"About what?"

"I'm not sure. About a murder. They think she did it."

"Did she?"

"No way! How can you ask that? You know her. You have to help her."

"Whoa, I'm a private detective. This is a police investigation. I can't interfere with it."

"But…she's really upset. She's never been questioned by the police before."

"Have they interviewed you?"

"Me? Why would they do that?"

Time for an injection of reality. Maybe he was this naïve. "Who's more likely to go after the scumball? The mother or the brother?"

"Wait, what are you talking about?"

"What do you know?" I countered. I had assumed his mother let him in on what was happening, at least a general outline, if not the gritty details. He could be playing dumb, as if he didn't know, as a cover-up.

Or maybe he really didn't know.

"She said you were a private detective working on something for her. I assumed it was about the divorce. Then yesterday, the police show up and demand to question her. I asked them what it was about and they said a murder investigation. They wouldn't let me stay in the room while they talked to her, but she was really upset when they left, almost not making sense, saying they thought she killed him.

"I had to give her a stiff shot of bourbon and drive her across the lake to stay with my aunt, her sister. Then I called my dad to make sure he was okay, and he was fine. Who do the police think she killed?"

I so should have gotten out of here an hour ago. If he really didn't know, I shouldn't be the one to tell him. If he did, but was pretending otherwise, he could be using me as a cover.

"Look," I said into his expectant silence, "there's very little I can tell you."

"But you know," he said.

"I know some things," I admitted, "but I can't really talk to you about them."

"My mother is falling apart. My dad is flying out to Las Vegas about now with his new girlfriend. I have to help her."

"Then talk to her and find out what's going on."

"It's about my sister, isn't it?"

"You need to talk to your mother," I repeated.

"You said who was more likely to go after the scumball, the mother or the brother? What did you mean by that?"

"I'm sorry, I thought you already knew," I said. Yes, indeed, I had planted my foot in it with that one. I continued, "What your mother hired me to do is confidential. If she gives me permission to talk to you, I can, but without that, I can't."

He pulled out his phone.

I prayed the cell towers were down. At two beers I was either not sober enough or not drunk enough to get into this.

"Hey, Mom, it's Alan." He explained the situation to her.

Then handed me the phone.

Not even waiting for her to speak, I said, "Look, Mrs. Stevens, I'm very sorry for this mess, but there is little I can do to help at this point. It's a police investigation and I can't get involved."

"I fully understand that," she said. Her speech was slightly slurred and she sounded mellow. Valium had probably been added to the bourbon. "I know I need to tell Alan what's going on, but I just haven't had a chance. Maybe it would be better this way."

"I really don't feel…"

"Please do this favor for me," she added, her voice beseeching.

I couldn't curse her out as a manipulative bitch in front of her son. "Favor" meant I couldn't even add it to the bill. Annoyingly, she had a point. He and I were sitting here talking about it. For her to tell him, he'd have to drive a hour or so across Lake Pontchartrain—I couldn't see this conversation taking place over the phone—that was a long time to wait, and he probably wasn't as sober as he should be for that drive. Plus, it wasn't my daughter who was dead, and it would be easier for me to go through it all than for her, even with a lot of Valium and bourbon.

"Okay, Mrs. Stevens," I agreed. "I'll do this for you, with your permission to discuss the entirety of the case you hired me for. There may be some things I'll need to follow up with you about"—that would be what she told the cops that had them racing to my door—"so we may need to talk again."

She agreed, not exactly enthusiastically, but I had no way of knowing if that was the bourbon or the prospect of seeing me again. In any case, I was taking care of a major problem for her, letting her son in on why the police might be looking at his mother for murder. And giving him a heads-up that he might be considered a suspect as well.

If I was going to step in it, I might as well get something out of it as well—maybe this would tell me if they were involved. If I thought they did do it, I'd leave them to the cops. I handed him his phone back. A nice iPhone, I noted.

"Did you sister ever mention someone named Edward to you? Someone she was dating?"

He looked puzzled, thought for a moment, then said, "Yeah, but that was forever ago. She said she met a nice guy, that was his name, and maybe we'd go out together sometime. When I asked again, she said it hadn't worked out."

"You never met him?"

"No."

"She never said anything more about him?"

"No."

"Or having troubles with someone?"

"No. Where is this going?"

I held up my hand to Mary for two more beers. We'd need them.

"What do you know about what happened with your sister?"

"I got a phone call. My dad. He never calls me, so I knew it was serious. Tiff was missing; they wanted to know if I had seen her. I hadn't, but I drove home. It wasn't like her to go missing. By the time I got home, they had found her car and the note. A few hours later they found her body. Everyone was upset, crying, me, too, I suppose..."

I gently interjected, "Do you know what was in the note? Why she killed herself?" I didn't need the blow-by-blow details, indeed, didn't want to be shown the enormous pain of the family. There were therapists for that, and I'm not good at it. I wanted to find out what he knew, what the family dynamic was like. And which one of them knew who Eddie Springhorn was and what he had done.

"I never saw the note. The police found it in the car. But I was told she was upset about a breakup with someone, thought she had done something that had messed up everything. I think something like, 'I can't fix this and I can't face it.'"

"What else do you know?"

"About her death? She took the keys to Mom's car without permission and drove off after school but before Mom was home from doing coffee with her garden friends in the neighborhood. They called me a couple of hours later. Dad had called in his connections and gotten the police to look for her. I kept thinking she'd show up at any minute, it would all be okay, even after they found the car and the note, that it was just some teenage acting out, a cry for attention. I made all sorts of plans to be a better older brother, to take her to football games, have her spend the weekend with me, but…"

He started to cry.

I handed him the napkin from under my beer. Not classy, but it was all I had. I keep tissues in my office.

I gave him a moment, then said, "I'm sorry, this won't be easy. Your sister met Eddie Springhorn, a man several years older. Bluntly, Eddie was pond scum, good at wooing young high school girls and manipulating them for sex. He conned your sister into sending him pictures of her without her clothes on and then used them to coerce her into having sex with him. She refused, and he threatened to send the pictures to people at her high school."

"That was all?" he said.

"He was persistent and not at all nice about it; that seems to have been his MO. She may have felt too ashamed to tell anyone and too afraid of him."

"That's why she killed herself?"

"It seems to be what may have pushed her over the edge," I carefully said. "There is no way to know for sure. Adolescence is a time of hormonal changes, new surges of emotions that can amplify despair." But I needed to get away from the messy stuff. "Your mother knew about what had happened, but she didn't know who the boy was. She hired me to find out. That's what led to Edward Springhorn."

"He was the guy that did this to my sister? How much time would I get if I beat the crap out of him?" He slammed his beer mug on the table, hard enough that his friends looked at us with worried expressions.

"Someone already got there. Edward was murdered."

"And they think my mother might have killed him?" His expression was outraged.

"They have to investigate everyone."

"But she didn't even know him. He was just a name."

I sighed. "She was angry and made the hasty decision to call his workplace. They presumably reacted the way most workplaces would do, told him some crazy lady was calling and making accusations about him. He came to your house and tried to speak to your mother. She called me; I came over and, after some arguing, convinced him to leave. So his workplace could have told the police about her, he might have had something about her. The police came and talked to me as well."

"This isn't real, is it? My sister, and now my mother being accused of murder. You have to help me prove she didn't do it." He was either a very good actor (I'd have to check and see if he was majoring in drama) or he was genuinely stunned. And, I might add, not thinking very clearly.

"I'm only a private detective; I can't interfere with a murder investigation. Leave it to the police. Eddie Springhorn is the kind of man who makes enemies. Unless your mother did it, she'll be fine."

"That's the problem. She might have."

Not enough vodka and valium in the world for this.

I took a gulp of my beer. And another. Still not enough.

"Look, you'd be better talking to a lawyer. If you say anything incriminating—"

"No, listen, I don't know anything, I just know this all doesn't make sense."

"Then why say your mother might have done it?"

"She's been not herself lately."

I stared at him. Another drink of beer. "That's it? Not herself?"

"No…well, yes. But…" Now he took a sip of his beer.

"Is there a gun in the house?"

"Of course. Dad has a collection of hunting rifles. Tried to teach me to hunt. I hated it. Soft furry creatures covered in blood. I threw up the first time—"

"A handgun."

"Like a pistol?"

Either this kid had a career ahead of him in the movies, or he wasn't the murderer. He had no clue about guns, and anyone who had just shot Fast Eddie had to at least know how to pull a trigger.

"Yes, like a pistol."

"Yeah, I think so. They kept it in their bedroom, for protection, you know."

"Did your mother know how to shoot it?"

"I guess so. You just pull the trigger, right?"

Um, not quite. That remained unsaid. "Did you ever go to a shooting range? Had she been trained on how to use it?"

"Maybe? Not that I remember. I think it was mostly for my dad. He may have taken it with him when he left. Now, he knows how to use a gun."

Ah, yes, the hunting dad. "Are you sure?"

"No, I'd have to check. But he said something about the guns being his. He took all his hunting rifles, moved the whole case out. I guess I just assumed he took that one, too."

"Can you check?"

"Sure. When I get back to the house tonight."

I took another sip of beer. The last one. That wasn't going to help this night get any better. Having him check on the gun was getting into cop territory, but they had gotten my name with questioning Susie Stevens. They had a chance to check for the gun then.

"If you find it, don't handle it," I said.

"Why?"

So touchingly naïve. "Fingerprints. If yours aren't already on the gun, don't put them there."

"Maybe I should wipe it down."

"No. Don't tamper with the evidence."

"But—"

"No. Just no. You're not smarter and better equipped than the cops. It's a gun your parents kept in the bedroom, it doesn't prove anything if their fingerprints are on it. Wipe it clean and it'll make it look like someone is trying to hide evidence."

"Oh. Okay." He took another sip of his beer. I envied him the still half-full glass. Then he said, "But you will help me, won't you?"

I should have said, "Frankly, my dear, I don't give a damn," and walked out. Instead, I said, "I will not help you tamper with evidence or cover up a crime. Put your college-educated hat on. Even if your mother—or father—killed Eddie, no jury in this state would give them more than a slap on the wrist. Eddie was scum, and most juries here will put him in the category of he-needed-killing."

"But I have to do something!" He started crying. Into his beer. What a waste.

"Doing something is fine. Doing something stupid is…well, stupid." I pushed my crumpled-up napkin (one finger only—it was soggy from previous use) back to him.

"So what should I do? I can't let my parents go to jail."

As quietly as I could, I sighed. "It's too late for that. If they had anything to do with killing him, then the consequences are already coming at them. You can't stop that, and you end up being accessory after the fact and go to jail as well."

"So what do I do?"

"Why do you think your mother may have done it?"

"She's been so weird lately."

"She's grieving. A mother who lost her only daughter. What else?"

"In the last few days, she's been angry."

"She just found out who the bastard was; that might well cause an eruption of anger."

"Yeah, I guess. But…I overheard her say, 'I'll kill him for this.' I thought she was talking about my dad going off to Vegas with his new girlfriend. Like he didn't want to have to deal with things here anymore."

"Who did she say this to?"

"No one. She'd been on the phone, put it down and then said that."

"Who was she talking to?"

"I don't know."

"Could it have been your father? Him telling her about the Vegas trip?"

"Maybe."

"Who else might it have been?"

"I don't know. You, maybe."

I had told Mrs. Stevens about Eddie in person. I tried to remember if there was a phone call between us in the time frame. However, people say "I'll kill" all the time without really meaning they'll kill someone. "What else?"

"What else?" he repeated.

"What else makes you think your mother might have killed him?"

"I'm not sure."

I left a silence.

He finally filled it. "Just a feeling, I guess. I mean, I want to kill the guy. So she probably did, too."

"Did you?"

"Did I what?"

"Kill him?"

"No! You can't think that. I didn't even know he existed until right now."

Yeah, so you say. And you're doing a good job of acting like it. My gut said he was real, this wasn't an act. But the gut is good at digesting food, not always so good at knowing who's being honest.

"You didn't do it, but you're telling someone you don't know very well your mother might have done it?"

"What are you suggesting?"

"What I said earlier. Think about what you're doing. You could be a confused kid—young man—who's spilling this out because you don't have anywhere else to turn. Or you could be carefully planting insinuations and making claims that make you appear innocent."

"What?" He stood up, fight or flight. But he was too rational—or stunned—to do either.

"Please sit down," I said to stop him from hovering over me. And attracting attention. "My best guess—and I'm pretty good at these things—is that you're exactly who you say you are and you're being honest—maybe too honest—with me."

He sat down. Finished his beer. "So why accuse me of lying?"

"Because the cops will. This is a murder investigation. They will follow any and every lead. Don't lie, but you might not want to share any feelings with them."

"So what do I do?"

I almost said buy me another beer. "First do no harm. Don't look for evidence you don't want to find. If your mother tells you she did it, encourage her to turn herself in. After she's hired a good lawyer. For right now, go back with your friends, get a good night's sleep. This will look better in the morning. Eddie wasn't a nice person, and it's likely one of his not-nice friends did him in. In a day or two the police will find the evidence clearing your mother of any involvement. The woman you know isn't a killer; it's not likely she turned into one."

"Oh, okay."

He stood up again, this time slowly, the fight or flight drained from him, turning back to his friends. Then over his shoulder to me, "How do I call you? You know, if I find out something."

I thought to say, you don't. Instead I handed him one of my cards.

I left a generous tip for Mary and left as quickly as I could without actually running out.

A big glass of Scotch was waiting for me at home.

CHAPTER SIXTEEN

Hey, Kevin," Brandon said as he caught up with him in the hallway.

"What do you want?" Kevin didn't look his way.

"I didn't see you."

"What are you talking about?"

"You know. If anyone asks, I didn't see you there."

"Of course you didn't. I wasn't there."

"You didn't see me there, either, did you?" Brandon reached out to touch his shoulder.

"I. Wasn't. There." Kevin jerked away and strode down the hallway.

Brandon started to follow, then thought better of it. Kevin was in a bad mood. He didn't like Brandon bringing up the things they did out of school, like there were two different Kevins and he needed to keep them completely separated.

Brandon wouldn't have mentioned it, but it was important.

He headed for his next class. Maybe Kevin was worried because he'd get in more trouble than Brandon would. His parents wanted Kevin to go to college and be an engineer. Brandon's mother only wanted him to clean up his room. Well, he'd probably go to college, but Brandon knew he was good enough with computers he'd be fine if he didn't. He could start a tech company and make lots of money. Kevin wouldn't brush him off then.

And if Kevin hadn't seen him there—hadn't been there—then no one would ever know.

CHAPTER SEVENTEEN

At first I didn't really believe him. I thought it was some stupid joke. Didn't think he might really go through with it. He seemed so nice and all that I believed him when he said he was misunderstood, people didn't know him, thought he was low class. But I'm the stupid one here. It seemed like it was real, like he really liked me. He didn't seem pushy. Not at first. No, I was stupid enough to send him that picture in my sexy bra.

Then he asked for one with a strap down, then unhooked, just barely hiding. There didn't seem much difference, so I didn't say no when he asked for more.

Now he wants even more. Telling me it's too late to say no.

Now I don't know what to do. But I have to do something.

Chapter Eighteen

What day was it?

I had no clue.

After coming home from the bar, I decided to not think about the conversation with Alan. It wasn't my case anymore; it was a police matter now, and I needed to stay as far away as I could.

Mixing Scotch and beer—even single malt and high-end craft beer—isn't a good idea. But it had been very effective in helping me to not think about Mrs. Susie Stevens and the mess her life had become. Even if she was innocent, it was a mess. If she wasn't—well, it was a far bigger mess, and all the king's horses and all the king's men couldn't fix it.

It also helped me not think about the mess my life was. Maybe that was the more important reason. Middle-aged, single, failed in the one long relationship I'd had. A few missteps and terrible decisions in trying to find love again—I'd blinded myself to what I should have seen. Maybe that's human; we do it all the time, see love when it's smoke. I'm a detective, a good one, but am carrying a lot of weight with both the house mortgage and the business one, a now constant worry of what would happen if the Douglas Townson cases didn't come along. Was this what I wanted? Work every case I could, even if I didn't want to, just to be able to come home to a house whose only company was a decent bottle of Scotch?

Coffee.

No, shower, then coffee.

It was a hasty one, just enough to wash away yesterday's grime, not any sins.

After the first few sips, the caffeine brought forth the rational part of my brain. Eddie had been killed by one of his scummy friends, the kind with anger-control issues. Sometime today, Joanne would call me to tell me that I—as well as Mrs. Stevens—was all in the clear.

Why had Alan approached me in the bar? He couldn't have known I was there. So it had to be an accidental meeting. Unless he'd followed me. I'd been worried about someone with the size and bulk of Fast Eddie, not the more slender Alan.

He was a college kid, not a practiced con man.

I smeared cream cheese on a bagel. I needed to stop worrying about this.

I knew for a fact I had not killed Eddie. That was all I needed to know.

It was awfully convenient for Dad and the new girlfriend to suddenly go off to Vegas. Unless they already had it planned long before Eddie's murder.

Not my case, not my monkeys, not my circus.

I resolutely skimmed the headlines to distract myself while finishing my bagel and coffee.

It was far enough into the morning that rush hour was long over and therefore safe to drive to my office.

Another pot of coffee, two aspirin, and sitting at my desk seemed likely to be the big accomplishment of the day.

There were no phone messages. Nothing from Alan saying he'd found the gun, what should he do with it. The good news. No new cases or inquires, nothing to keep me occupied. The bad news.

I could do billing or filing.

Five minutes in decided me that today was not a billing or filing day.

I sighed, big and loud. I couldn't just sit here staring at the walls. I had no business going anywhere near Fast Eddie's murder.

Back to the library to dig up more dirt on Frederick Townson. I could call it working on a case and pretend I might actually get paid for the character assassination.

Parking was not kind. It was too early for people to leave for lunch and late enough that everyone who needed to be in the vicinity was here. But the longest walk to the library at least helped stretch my legs. After I was done with this, I'd go to the gym. Maybe the shooting range after that. Oh, wait, I hadn't gotten my gun back.

I found Cindy, my archivist, and she set me up.

I backtracked to the parts I had skipped before. The diarist—I flipped to look up his name: Samuel Albertus Braud—was a decent writer, and I'd gotten used to his handwriting enough that it wasn't too hard to read.

And I had a hunch. One I wanted to be wrong.

Even though it was late, Luke Summit, my most trusted deputy, found me at home. He was apologetic and wise enough to bring me outside before telling me of the reason for the late summons.

"Sir, we've found another body. A young woman. In her accommodations on Marais Street." He pitched his voice low, so only I could hear.

Even so, my dear Alibe knew that all was not well. I kissed her good-bye, told her to go to bed without me, and made sure the door locked tightly when I left.

As we traveled there, Mr. Summit filled me in. She had been treated in a manner similar to the other woman. Beaten, unspeakably assaulted, her intimates shoved so deeply into the throat that they alone would have suffocated her, even had her injuries not been enough to end her short life.

On seeing her, my heart broke. She was indeed young, a comely honey blonde, the flush of youth still on her face, stark contrast to her staring eyes, the horror of her demise etched in them.

She had only lately come to the area, wasn't well known, struggling to survive in the back area.

No mother raised her daughter for such a fate. She should have been at home, in front of a warm fire, her father and brothers looking out for her, instead of this wretched fate.

The denizens of the area were little help, although this time I felt they were appalled enough that had they known anything, they would have told.

There had been sounds, but there always are sounds in this part of the city, darkness lends itself to the vices enjoyed here, the grunts and moans of coupling and drunken debauchery are loud.

The two women running the coffee shop on the corner, Miss Augustine Lamoureaux and Miss Roxanne Beaudoin, had the most to tell. The woman, who called herself Mistress Laurel, came, on occasion, into their shop. They had first seen her a few months ago. She wasn't friendly as many of the women of the neighborhood were, came in, got her coffee and soup, ate and left. Miss Lamoureaux called her shy; Miss Beaudoin said proud.

"Or both," Miss Lamoureaux said. She could add little other than the woman liked a little milk and sugar in her coffee and was especially fond of the chicken soup.

It was difficult; I wished I could have separated the two women, but Miss Beaudoin kept her hand firmly entwined with Miss Lamoureaux's arm.

What kind of work did she do, I asked.

They did not look at me as they answered, saying they weren't sure, they thought she did laundry or some such.

One of the rougher constables poked Miss Lamoureaux with his nightstick and demanded they stop lying. They knew what kind of girl she was.

I kept my anger in check; no wonder these women wouldn't talk to us. I told him that I would do the questioning and that these women were to be treated as civilly as those he passed in Audubon Park.

He goggled at me but was cowed enough not to retort.

I told them I needed to know as much as possible about the unfortunate young woman. It was likely she was killed because of how she made her way in life. This was murder; we needed to dispense with the rules of polite society and say the things that cannot be said.

Miss Lamoureaux finally spoke. The woman had arrived several months ago, heavy with child, alone and with little save a small valise and a meager number of crumpled dollar bills. They fed her, but even that kindness did little to loosen her tongue as to how she came to be in such straits. She shared a crib about the corner, one that served those who weren't choosy, several woman rotated, of all colors. Even in her condition, she found trade; indeed, it appeared that some men had an appetite for women in her condition.

I managed to keep the revulsion from my face as I listened.

Within a month, she had her child, but gave it up to the foundling home.

Miss Laurel continued to ply her trade, seeking out the more adventurous clients, if the rumors were true, for the greater price these services procured.

Miss Lamoureaux emphasized that this was only secondhand, common gossip and might not be factual, as if she did not want to further besmirch the woman in death.

And she never mentioned her background, family? I asked.

Both women shook their heads. Her secrets would go with her to the grave.

"It's obvious, isn't it?" Miss Beaudoin spoke. "It's why all too many of the women are here. Taken advantage of, then left to fall from whatever place she had when her body changed beyond denial."

"Thare's right, just blame the poor lads for girls what can't keep their legs closed," the rough fellow interjected.

I could not allow this to pass. I told him if I needed his opinion, I would ask for it. If he didn't hear me asking, he should not speak.

He was not happy to be remonstrated before his fellow officers as well as the witnesses. But I cannot have this behavior when investigating a crime this heinous. It is hard enough to get anyone to talk to the police; with men like him on the force, it is understandable why.

I gave Miss Lamoureaux my card.

We continued questioning of those in the area, but found little. One stable boy mentioned seeing a "toff" head that way, but he was more interested in the horses drawing his carriage than any description of the man.

That was the sum of the paltry information we could find.

As we left, Officer Smith, as I learned he was named, took to lecture me on how to best deal with "these people," telling me not to trust any of them, all the men in the area were thieves, the women in the trade, no matter them claiming to be respectable (he even spat in the street to emphasize his point) owners of a coffee shop, they all did it.

I merely asked him for proof of his assertions, which led to another volley of his opinions, and he seemed to have no idea of what the difference was. This was not a promising attribute in an officer of the law.

As quickly as I could, I severed my path from his and vowed to ask he be reassigned to another detective. After he was gone I asked Luke if it was true, were all women there in the trade?

"No, sir," he replied. "I've know Miss Lamoureaux and Miss Beaudoin for well over a year now. They are what they seem, hardworking shop girls, making their honest way in the world."

"You like them?" I asked.

"I respect them. They have helped many a girl in the area, from soup to a place to stay. Decent women are the ones who offer kindness where it is most needed."

Our paths parted and I made my way home alone. I have learned to trust Luke and his views. He is an observant, gentle soul.

I looked up from my reading. Over two hours had passed. I made notes, the time, the location of the murder. And the stable boy mentioning a "toff."

I have the advantage of Samuel Braud and the history he had yet to live. The arrest in Shreveport, the now two murders here in Storyville. My ugly hunch was that Mr. Townson liked it rough, murderously rough, and the violence he created caught him in the end. That was hardly the solution that Douglas Townson wanted. But I had already cashed his retainer check, and I was curious to see how much evidence I could find from this great a distance.

In the meantime, my stomach was interested in something resembling lunch. And my brain could use another cup of coffee. I picked up a sandwich and the largest to-go cup of coffee at a local PJ's, then found a bench in Duncan Park, right next to the library, to munch and muse.

There were no messages on my phone.

Impatiently, I called Joanne on her work number. This was official business. I got her voice mail. I left a message asking when I could get my gun back.

I also called Danny, same result, voice mail and a less formal message to call me back. She wouldn't reveal anything about an ongoing investigation, but I might be able to read something from her voice and tone. I wanted to know what the hell Joanne was up to, and Danny was my only possible source.

That left me with only caffeine and turkey on sourdough for consolation.

And a lot of questions. Either Joanne was being an asshole—possible, but not probable—and leaving me hanging, or they still had no clear suspects. Which meant that my theory of it being one of Eddie's scum friends with anger-management issues and therefore easy to solve might not be the case. Of course, he could have so many scum friends that it was hard to sort out.

Even if that was the case, they should have been able to eliminate Mrs. Stevens—and me—by now. Certainly me, even if not her.

The caffeine only seemed to make more worries course through my brain. Business was slow, and my bills never were. It should still pick up once people recovered from the excesses of Mardi Gras, and that should be any day now. Buying my office building still seemed the right decision, but a mortgage is a heavier lift than rent.

I was tired of coming home to an empty house. Maybe I needed to get a cat. Two, so they could keep each other company.

Why wasn't Joanne calling me back?

I finished the last bite of my sandwich. *Maybe she's arresting Eddie's killer right now and too busy to be fooling with the phone.*

I finished my coffee on the way back to the library. It, at least, was a place where not having a gun would be safe.

As before, I skipped through the diary. Then reminded myself not to fit the facts to my theory, but let them lead.

There was another murder, again a young woman working in Storyville, or "the District," as they called it, the same gruesome details, her underwear used as a gag, beaten and presumably raped; the delicate language of the time called it "repugnant violations," with few details. Certainly a horrific death.

They occurred about every two to three months. The intervals of Mr. Townson's buying trips? Maybe, but I had nothing to tie him to being here at those times. I could guess that he was killed because one of the women fought back violently and viciously, aware of the previous murders and knowing she was about to become the next victim. But other than the arrest up north and the location of his murder, both circumstantial at best, I had no proof.

Well, the great-grandson was a prick, and this rotten apple may not have fallen far from the tree.

Not compelling evidence to call great-granddad a murderer.

My eyes were bleary and my back aching. Besides reading Samuel Braud's diary, I'd also looked into transport from Townson's plantation to New Orleans. That required having some idea of where his plantation was. Which took me to property deeds. The actual land was sold into many pieces, but it had been located on the west bank of the river, about thirty miles this side of Baton Rouge. There was a train that ran from Baton Rouge to New Orleans, a distance of about ninety miles. I wasn't sure how long it would take—that would require finding train schedules from the era—but trains were a fairly efficient means of travel, so probably two to three hours. But he'd have to get to Baton Rouge, and that would be thirty miles via horse or early automobile, probably another couple of hours, plus taking a ferry across the river. At best, that was five hours one way. Probably closer to seven or eight. Not the quick day trip I could take.

He also might have been able to take the river down. Still, that would have been several hours at best, depending on schedules.

My best guess was that Mr. Frederick Townson didn't just jaunt down to New Orleans on a whim. It was at least an overnight trip.

I packed up my notes and returned the material. The library was about to close. Even if it wasn't, I was frustrated. There seemed little way for me to know much more than I knew now. I could keep reading Samuel Braud's diary, but I already knew he'd never find the killer. Nor would he link Townson to the killings of the young women. Even someone as upper crust and rich as Townson would go down for crimes like these.

As I headed back to my car, I checked my phone—I had politely turned it down in the library.

Voice mail. Yes!

Joanne leaving a message saying she'd give me my gun back when they were done with it. A terse enough message that it didn't invite a follow-up call to inquire about how long that would take.

Danny leaving a message that she couldn't really talk, given the circumstances. But once it was cleared up, we could have a nice long chat. The question was would it be as a friend or would it be as a prosecutor to a suspect.

A call from Alan. He hadn't found the gun. But maybe his mother had moved it. Should he ask her? He'd ask his dad, but he was still in Vegas and… I hit delete without listening to the rest. Either his mother had moved the gun, the cops had taken it, or his dad had it. That certainly narrowed things down.

The third—and final call—was from a voice I didn't recognize. "Hey, I've got some info for you. It might be important. Give me a call." No number other than the one saved on my caller ID. Local, but not one I recognized.

I had a message from the stupid dating service Torbin had talked me into. I was about to hit delete sight unseen, but curiosity made me open it. Expecting a torrent of abuse from Ms. Hummer, instead I found a note from a different woman saying she'd liked my profile, was in town, and wanted to know if I'd be willing to meet her for a drink or coffee, this evening if that was open. She was free today, but out of town for a few days after.

At least I'll accomplish something today. Scare off another date, I said to myself.

I looked at myself in the rearview mirror. Not as dressed up as I might have liked, but a decent pair of jeans, gray V-neck T-shirt that had no obvious stains. Good enough. I'd taken a shower this morning, so should get points for being clean.

It would have to do unless I wanted to be an asshole and cancel after just having said yes.

We'd agreed on a coffee place in the Lower Garden District. It was a few doors down from my gym, which meant I could cheat and park in their lot.

I was about five minutes late. CBD rush-hour traffic is always a crapshoot. I would have preferred to be early; occupational habit, I like to check things out and have a chance to observe the other person. But I barely had time to turn into the sidewalk gate before I heard, "Are you Micky?"

"Brenda?" I'd checked the name before I got out of my car.

She was sitting outside, a place she could watch the world go by. Early to mid thirties, a bit young for me, short blond hair, spiked up in the fashionable style. Eye color a shade between brown and gray. Hazel maybe? A face a little too long to be considered pretty, maybe strong. It might depend on the person behind it. She was dressed in white slacks and a sky-blue shirt, men's-style oxford.

"Nice to meet you," I said as I sat down. I had to sit facing the front of the coffee shop, with my back to the entrance and the street. Also, professional habit, I preferred to see who was coming and going.

But you're not on a job and it doesn't matter, I told myself.

She reached out and shook my hand. Strong grasp. Too strong? Or maybe she just worked out and was a strong woman.

"Can I get you some coffee?" I offered, seeing she had nothing in front of her. "Or tea?"

"Coffee would be great. A little milk and sugar."

I went into the shop and got two cups, fumbling with the milk and sugar since I don't take it. But I had offered.

At least it was just milk and sugar and not a double cream latte with mocha caramel foam.

Since this was only coffee and my stomach was grumbling, I added a croissant and a cinnamon roll to the order.

Just as I was returning to the table, a car backfired. I jerked, but not enough to spill anything.

But my date jumped under the table, pulling her chair in front of her like a barricade.

"It's just a car," I said, as I slowly sat down.

She didn't move.

"Are you okay?" I asked, wondering what weirdness I had stumbled into.

She still didn't move.

"Are you okay?" I repeated. Another minute of no answer and I was out of here. I'll stay for my friends being weird, but if it takes more time to deal with your weirdness than we've known each other, that's a big, red warning sign.

Her eyes darted up at me, then around and she slowly got up. "Yeah, this is New Orleans and it was just a car," said more to herself than to me.

She righted the chair, stood next to it as if deciding whether to sit or run, then abruptly collapsed into it as if exhausted.

"I'm sorry," she said slowly. "Not the best first impression. You must be wondering what the hell that was about."

I was polite enough to merely say, "It's a city, you never know when an idiot might start something."

"So, I just got out of the Army," she said. Then in a rush, as if she couldn't stop speaking, her story came out. She'd been stationed in Afghanistan, military police, what she'd seen, friends injured and killed, the people there injured and killed. Was a smile a friendly gesture or a trap? A car bomb got the truck in front of her. One she almost was on, but she had to tie her bootlace, so she ended up in the second truck.

One of her friends, a man she'd just had breakfast with, blown in half, still alive and asking about his legs. She wasn't hurt, she was fine. How she couldn't sleep, how any noise, anything could make her jump like she was back there and another bomb was about to go off.

"But I didn't get hurt. I don't understand," she said, finally winding down.

I'd already finished my coffee and eaten the croissant. I could listen and eat, and there was no point in letting it go to waste. She hadn't touched hers. I'd made the executive decision to leave the roll for her since there didn't seem much chance to break in and ask which she'd like.

"There are a lot of places we get hurt. Not all of them are visible," I told her.

"My family keeps telling me to get over it. I'm a hero. They never expected it from the girl."

"You are brave, just not invulnerable. It takes bravery to go someplace where we know we can be broken."

She looked at me, sadness in her eyes. "You think I'm broken?"

"I think you're wounded and you need to heal. There is no dishonor in that."

"Yeah, I guess that's a good way of looking at it."

I did what I was supposed to do, learned from my social worker friends, asked her about support, what she was doing to help. She had good answers, was hooked into the VA, had been seeing a therapist for the last few months, meeting with a support group of female vets. "In fact, they were the ones who encouraged me to do this. Said I needed to meet people. It's ironic," she said. "I wasn't supposed to join. My brother was supposed to carry on the military tradition. Army, every generation."

"Why didn't he do it?" I asked.

She nibbled at the cinnamon roll. Then took a sip of the coffee that had to be getting cold. "Oh, he did. He's just a rat-assed bastard and after a few months decided he didn't like it. So he started screwing up every way he could. Sloppy uniform, late, not pulling his weight. When they said he was going overseas, he upped the ante. AWOL. Drugs. Guess he decided prison was better than being shot at."

"So, it was up to you to carry on the tradition?"

"I didn't really care about tradition. Kinda knew it didn't count, me not being a man. And that gay thing didn't help either. Thing is I went, I served. Honorable discharge. Pulled a soldier out of that burning truck and helped with another. Come back here and my mom starts talking about how we need to visit my rat-ass brother. How hard he has it in jail. One of my uncles telling me it's men who have it hard nowadays. To my face he said, 'Women and queers are coddled 'cause the government is so afraid of not being politically correct.' I moved down here to New Orleans even though it pissed my mother off. Rat-ass brother's wife moved here as well."

"Are you close to her?"

"Not really. See each other once in a while, hang out with her kid mostly. She still defends him. Really defending her choice to marry him. Thinks he'll come out of prison a changed man, ready to take care of her and his family."

"Maybe, but mostly people don't change without some major force pushing them."

"I think he's holding on to that marriage so he can have a place to land here in the city when he comes out and not up in bumfuck northeast Louisiana. Nothing up there except flies and heat. Once he has something better, he's going to dump her and that lump of a kid as fast as he can."

"He sounds like a lovely person. That's in sarcasm font," I added to be obvious. Not everyone gets sarcasm. "What about you? What are you going to do?"

"Going to UNO, trying to put my life back together. Not make a fool of myself out in public."

"You haven't made a fool of yourself. You've been real. That's not a bad thing. Much better than polite chitchat. What are you studying at UNO?"

"Isn't that polite chitchat?"

"I wouldn't call what you're going to do with the rest of your life polite chitchat."

"Business. I want to eventually open a pet store. I like being around animals; they calm me. People are trouble." She suddenly looked down at her phone. "Shit. Sorry. My mother texting to remind me to send a package to my brother for his birthday. Like he'd ever send me anything, even when I was overseas."

"He older or younger?"

"Older, of course. Hit on all my high school girl friends. Grabbed one where he shouldn't have, she walloped him, and he acted like she was wrong. Never used her name after that. Just called her 'the bitch.' My mom and dad just laughed it off, said boys will be boys."

"That's a toxic attitude."

"Oh, yeah, he and his pals are charmers, all right. Macho guys working on cars all day but never really fixing anything, just an excuse to hang out and drink beer. Catcall any woman who walks by like they own us."

"They bother you?"

"As much as everyone else. Everyone else female. Brother laughing while his friends are making comments about my breasts. What kind of brother does that?"

"His name isn't Fast Eddie, is it?"

"No, Braddock. Braddock Brendan Beaujeaux. Why?"

"I just stumbled across that kind of man, and his name was Edward."

"I think one of his friends was named Ed."

"What happened to him?"

"Far as I know, he stayed pissing around at that little auto repair shop outside Monroe."

Stop looking for clues. There are none here. There were enough sexist men that there could easily be two—or more—named Edward in the whole state of Louisiana. Even the surrounding ten blocks.

"Do you want some more coffee?" I asked. "I need to take a bathroom break."

"No, I'm good."

"I'll be right back."

But when I came back she was gone, a note tucked under her coffee cup.

Sorry, I screwed up. This was meeting for coffee, not all my crap. You're a nice person. Thanks for listening. And buying me coffee.

I was upset, and enough of a coward to be relieved. There were too many things between us to be much more than friends. I liked to think it was more age, education, and worldview, not the baggage from her being in the military.

I sent her an email from my phone. *Hey, don't be too hard on yourself. I think I'm too old to be a girlfriend, but I could be a friend. I meant it when I said you were honest, and that's more important than being polite.*

That would have to do. I left a tip and headed back to my car.

Chapter Nineteen

When I got home, after making a sandwich out of the tail end of bread, cheese, and tomatoes, I did my duty and called Alan.

He answered on the first ring.

I also poured a couple of fingers of Scotch.

"I couldn't find the gun," he said.

I didn't tell him he'd told me that in his message.

"I really looked in a lot of places, but I couldn't find it."

Really, you couldn't find the gun?

Before he could tell me again, I broke in, "Okay, so calm down. It probably means your dad took it. So it's not a big deal."

"What if he didn't?"

"Who else would?" Well, the police, but I wasn't going to put that thought in his head.

"The real killer? To frame my mom?"

"Whoa! You've been watching too many TV shows."

"No, I read detective novels."

"Whatever. In fiction, they have to tell an interesting story. In real life it's the same sad one over and over. Another loser like Eddie decided he didn't like Eddie and killed him. There is no big conspiracy afoot to frame your mother by sneaking into your burglar-alarmed home and stealing the gun."

"Oh. Are you sure?"

"Yes. Now, go find a nice, engrossing book. And stop worrying about the gun."

"I'll try…" he said slowly.

I should have ended the call there. But I had to be the nice guy. "You're worried about your mom, aren't you?"

He started crying.

I took a sip of Scotch. Not drinking wasn't going to help him. Drinking was going to help me. It was a logical decision.

Another sip. Then I said, "I know this is hard. But you're going to be okay and your mom is going to be okay. It'll take time. But you'll be okay." Maybe he would; it sounded like the thing to say.

He blew his nose. "I'm sorry." Then blew his nose again.

"It's okay," I said. Not original, but I don't think that mattered. His sister killed herself, Dad had exited to Vegas, and Mom was falling apart. By default, I seemed to be the adult he could turn to. Oh, lucky me. I felt for him; I just didn't think I could do much. Except repeat "It's going to be okay" while he blew his nose.

At least the Scotch was helping me.

"I'm just so scared for her," he said between sniffles. "What if she goes to jail?"

"She's not going to jail. She needs a few days to pull herself together, then it's going to be okay." No, it wouldn't, but this was no time for harsh reality. Nothing would bring his sister back or heal the hole in his mother's life. He could be one son, not a son and a daughter.

"I hope so." He sniffed again. "I'm sorry to fall apart. My friends look like deer in headlights when I mention this."

"It's outside their experience; what they know how to deal with. Look, who do you talk to about things?" *Who can I foist you off on?* "Is there a teacher, a counselor, a pastor?"

"I talk to my mom. The church we go to isn't very gay friendly; I only go to please my parents."

"Anyone in school? A professor?" Anyone but me.

"No, not really. Could we meet again at Riley and Finnegan? I'll buy you a beer?"

A beer? A useful bribe for college students. I'd cost more than a beer. That was my rational thought. My words were, "Sure, that sounds good."

"This weekend? Friday or Saturday? I need to go to classes."

"Okay, text me when you'll be in town, and we can work something out."

That was enough to reassure him and get him off the phone.

One half sip of Scotch later my phone rang again.

The number was the one from earlier. I finished swallowing while I debated whether or not to answer it.

Oh, curiosity. "Hello?" I said.

"Hey, I got some really good info for you."

"Who is this?"

"Oh, sorry. Brandon."

Young. Young enough to be unaware that I might know more than a few Brandons. As politely as I could (the Scotch helps) I said, "I'm sorry, which Brandon are you?"

"The one from the school. You met us at the pizza place."

I considered claiming to have met a number of Brandons at a number of pizza places, in an attempt to teach him the value of giving more complete information than he was giving, but the Scotch had mellowed me. I chose not to be a jerk. "Oh, yes, of course. Thanks for calling. What info do you have?"

"Can we meet to talk about it?"

No, absolutely not. That case is over. "I don't want to waste your time." Or mine. "Can you give me some idea of what this is over the phone?"

"It's better not. Can be tapped. We should meet."

I did not sigh. I just wanted to. "Okay, let me look at my schedule."

I looked at my schedule, just in case I'd booked a three-week trip to Spain and couldn't meet until after that. Alas, it looked like all I had was a haircut. An hour tops. Indeed, my schedule looked more bare than not.

He suggested tomorrow. I put him off to the next day because my pride didn't want to admit I had so little going on. Same after-school time, same after-school pizza place.

Another Scotch, and the day passed.

Chapter Twenty

For reasons known only to my body, I woke shortly after the sun started shining. Maybe because it was a pretty day, humidity on the lower side, clear perfectly cerulean blue sky. I sipped my coffee on the back patio, contemplating what I'd do with this perfect day.

Sitting in my office and tending to paperwork wasn't calling my name.

I could work on the one official case I had. Or call it work and see if either the library or courthouse where Mr. Frederick Townson lived had any records. A long shot—oh, so long as to be hitting a needle in a haystack at one hundred yards—but it was an excuse to take a drive on a pretty day, and that was all I needed.

His former property looked like it was near the boundary between Iberville Parish and Ascension Parish. Iberville looked easier to get to, with both the courthouse and main library in Plaquemine. I'd manage enough searching to claim I'd done due diligence, have a good lunch at some local place, and drive back before dark. A perfect day, one I could claim was actual work.

Even with my earlier than usual hour, traffic was annoyingly busy. However, most people were coming into the city and I was going out. Once I passed the airport and took 310 to the Westbank, the cars thinned. I took the river road. It wasn't the fastest, but that wasn't the point of today. I drove through small towns, many of them looking like time—and wealth, even comfort—had passed them by.

It took me about two hours to reach my destination. It was a pretty town, old tin-roofed houses, lots of green space. Even the ubiquitous bail bond place next to the courthouse looked respectable. The kind of place people like me left as soon as we could. This was not liberal country and not the kind of place that welcomed gays or lesbians. Parking was easy; although a big lot was reserved for employees only, another even bigger lot was close by.

I found my way to the records office.

First I did a property search. Mr. Frederick Townson had inherited his land from his father, Charleston Townson IV. I didn't bother to check back, presumably Chuck had gotten it from I through III. I was right on my map reading, most of it was in Iberville Parish with a toehold in Ascension. The property was sold in 1907 to Herbert Gallier. No more Townsons. Presumably by his widow. Then I switched to birth and death records. He was born in 1867, which meant he was thirty-nine when he died. There had been a Charles V, but a check of death records revealed he had died at age ten of yellow fever. Further searching revealed that Frederick was the third son, another had been killed at age twelve in a riding accident. No vaccinations, no public health, no doctor close by. Life is ever fragile, was even more so back then. Frederick seemed to be the only son, of four total, who made it to adulthood. He also had three sisters. They seemed to be of hardier stock, as I could find no death certificates for them, only the record of their birth. Presumably they had married and moved away.

Interesting as this was, it really had no bearing on the case. It was late enough in the morning for me to call it lunchtime. I thanked the helpful clerk and exited to find food. I left my car in the parking lot and found a po-boy place a few blocks away (admittedly using my phone).

With an oyster po-boy sticking to my ribs, I retrieved my car and headed to the library.

Proving my point that it's hard to tell lesbians from librarians. My bias might be showing. It could be hard to tell smart, practical women from lesbians. So much overlap. The woman in front of me was fifty-ish, short salt-and-pepper hair, pants, and practical shoes. Oh, and a wedding ring. Maybe to another woman, but not likely to display it in this part of the world. I asked for copies of the local papers from around 1900 to 1907. She was very helpful and got me set up with what they had. There was an ongoing digitalization project, so some of it was searchable, from 1900 to 1905. I looked for the name of Townson.

Oh, yes, they were an important local family. I found marriage announcements of both his oldest niece and his youngest sister—the niece was sixteen, the sister a spinsterish twenty-two. Awards and events, blah, blah, blah.

A trip by Mr. Townson on a new riverboat up to St. Louis. I noted the date, the last week of September in 1903. Another trip noted for one of the first gatherings of sugar cane industry in Natchez, via train. Again I noted the date.

A lot of information on crops and how much was bought and sold. Yawn. In my lunch walk, I had noted there was no handy coffee shop to grab a cup to go.

I was falling asleep.

One final task. Check the papers around the time he was murdered. See what they said.

Spring of 1906? I was blanking on the date. May? March? This wasn't the Sunday *New York Times*; I could skim through a couple of months.

Mr. Frederick Townson took another trip in the middle of March that year, this time to Memphis to investigate the purchase of a motor car. Yep, that's what the newspaper said. When he came back in the end of March, they interviewed him about the new cars. He said he was still considering but felt it could never replace the horse, that wheels required easy surfaces, unlike hooves.

His wife had another baby, a girl. That was a smaller story than the one about his car adventure. A much smaller story.

Then at the end of May, front page, large headline: *Prominent Planter Murdered in New Orleans*. Then followed a sanitized version of his death. He was "put upon by vagabonds" and "fought back valiantly as any man with family who love and depend on him," but "in the end, it was for naught, the brutes overcame him in their lust for his purse and fine watch." No mention of where the murder took place other than the general New Orleans. It then went on to list his many awards and accomplishments, named his three sons, also mentioned two daughters and a distraught wife, whose only name was Mrs. Frederick Townson. And ended with "police are diligently searching for the foul fiends who would destroy such a family."

I rubbed my eyes and considered leaving it at that. But I was here, would likely never be here again, and I might as well read another month.

The story of his murder stayed on the front page for a few weeks, but as nothing came of the investigation, it gradually got supplanted by more important things like the price of cotton and sugar cane.

His body was brought back and the funeral held a week after the murder. Another front-page headline, with a list of who's who at the funeral. The last sentence of the last paragraph said, "Two of his sisters were unable to attend due to other pressing duties."

Interesting. I did a quick search on the digital pages. One sister married and moved to Lafayette, according to her marriage announcement. Certainly close enough to return for a funeral. I couldn't find the notice for the other sister and wasn't willing to go back to the courthouse to look for marriage licenses. But still odd that two of his three sisters did not attend his funeral. Maybe they were both pregnant, and that was called "other pressing duties."

I read a little further and was rewarded with a note about the missing sister coming to help her sister-in-law, still only named as the Mrs., with running of the plantation. She, it turned out, lived in Baton Rouge. Still no way to know why she skipped his funeral, but it hinted at the kind of man he was. His sisters were willing to overstep the polite conventions of the time to not pay him any last respects.

I looked at my watch. It would be closing time here shortly. I made a few copies of the more pertinent articles, ones Mr. Douglas might like, such as the big funeral headline. And a few for myself just in case I wanted to refer to them again.

I noted down where the plantation had been and found it on the current map. So many years had passed, nothing could remain that would tell me anything about Frederick Townson, but still I drove the back roads out to as close as I could get, stopping at the side to gaze at it in the setting sun. Desolate, fields that were no longer tilled, taken over by the slow creep of nature. Off in the distance a house, but even from here I could see it was derelict, crumbling, also being reclaimed by nature. After his death and his widow's remarriage, it had been sold, but, fanciful in the gloom, I wondered if his taint remained, an evil, vile man, and he left enough of it behind to haunt his land, driving owners away as if they knew they walked where a murderer had walked. A cloud covered the setting sun and a chill ran down my back. I started my car and drove away, one eye in the rearview mirror for ghosts.

I took the faster way back, not wanting to linger on the back roads after dark, catching the Sunshine Bridge and then up to I-10 just as the sun disappeared from the sky.

As I drove the all-too-familiar road—lot of records in Baton Rouge, and this is the way there—I debated how many of these hours I dared to charge to Douglas Townson. He'd only hired me for the quixotic task of trying to solve a hundred-year-old murder, not to dig up his great-grandfather's sordid life. See what the retainer covered, I decided, and then I'd deal with any extra hours, whether to charge them to him or just call it that I was damned if his ugly secrets would stay buried.

Chapter Twenty-one

My body was not so eager this morning, blissfully sleeping in as the sun climbed in the sky. It was close to 8:30 when I woke, having forgotten to set the alarm clock. I managed a quick shower, considered a bagel, then realized I didn't have any. Maybe there was a granola bar at the office.

I headed there automatically. I could sit at my desk, pretend to work and sort out my day.

No granola bars. My stomach rumbled. I vowed that I would run by the grocery store after meeting…what was his name? The schoolkid? Braydon? Bartok? What music was I listening to last night? Beethoven? Brahms? Ah. Brandon.

That left me with the debate of whether or not to break my rule and get something at the downstairs coffee shop or to hoof it to somewhere a few blocks away.

The phone rang.

Joanne. "We need you to show where you fired the bullets into the lawn."

"You what?" Not enough coffee yet.

She repeated it slowly. "Your bullet in the lawn."

"Umm, yeah. About fifteen-twenty feet to the right—facing the house—from the walkway."

"Why don't you come show us?"

Not what I wanted to do. Needless to say, I didn't mention that. "Now?"

"Meet us there in an hour."

The silver lining was it gave me an excuse to go downstairs and get a maple syrup pecan croissant—the plainest one they had. I scarfed that while chugging the coffee. Decided that if need be I could hit up

Mrs. S for the bathroom and made another travel mug to go. It was not possible to have too much caffeine this morning.

Fifty-five minutes later, I was again parked outside Mrs. Stevens' tidy suburban house. A few blades of grass were starting to grow slightly taller than their compatriots. Revolt in the lawn.

Of course I only noticed this because no one else was here and I had nothing better to do than scrutinize the blades of grass between checking my phone every few seconds for a message that said "never mind." I twice checked my calendar to make sure it wasn't April first.

When the police tell you to meet them somewhere, you can't ditch it when they're a few minutes late. Not even half an hour late, as it was now.

Presumably they're saving damsels in distress. Or dudes in distress.

Another five minutes ticked by.

Suddenly two cars pulled up behind mine, one marked as the Jefferson Parish Sherriff Office—JPSO, and the other not, but clearly a cop car, and the street was no longer a quiet bastion of suburban bliss.

I got out to greet them. My "hi" was answered with a nod from Joanne and a grunt from the deputy. The others were taking some gear out of the unmarked car. I was guessing that both NOPD and the Jefferson Parish folks were now involved since this case seemed to straddle the two jurisdictions.

"Show us where you think it hit."

It felt like such a blur—I didn't say that. The quickness of violence, little chance to think, only to react and hope I'd made the right decision. "I was about here," I said as I came up the walk. "And fired…around here." I lifted my hand as if I had a gun in it, trying to recapture the angle. I had deliberately aimed yards away to lessen the possibility of anything the bullet hit coming back at me. I'd call it us, if they asked, but really me. But I also made sure the bullet would hit the ground and not skitter someplace it shouldn't.

"Hold that," one of the crime scene techs said to me. Without asking he wound a string around my wrist, then walked it out at the angle I indicated until it touched the ground. A nice pristine patch of grass.

From there he started walking slowly, still using the string as a guide, carefully examining the lawn first on one side of the initial point and then the other.

My arm was starting to get tired.

He walked another few feet.

I wasn't really sure this was the exact place and angle I had been when I fired the gun; it was just my best guess. I tried to recall the scene. I had been looking at Fast Eddie, looking for any hint he would strike and I'd have to do more than fire my gun safely into the dirt. Only because I heard what sounded like a bullet hitting ground—and that had been what I was intending to do—did I assume it had hit somewhere in the lawn.

My arm was starting to tremble.

Maybe it had gone farther than I thought, through the hedge and into the next yard. Maybe I'd hit a bird and it had flown away injured. Or killed and carried away by a cat. No, I was pretty sure I hadn't hit anything. The truth was I mostly fired my gun at the range with heavy-duty earmuffs on, and I had no idea what a bullet hitting dirt or a hedge would sound like.

My arm dropped. I couldn't hold it up anymore. The tech looked back at me, disappointed. I shrugged and rubbed my shoulder.

"I'm sorry," I said, not really sorry. "I was worried about getting punched. I may have hit closer to the hedge."

"Grid search," Joanne called. She, both techs, and the JPSO deputy lined up along the walkway and then slowly moved across the yard.

I took the string off my wrist.

They were almost to the hedge at the property line when one of the techs said, "This might be it."

It was only about twenty feet off from where I had pointed.

How long can it take to dig a bullet out? Well, first they had to measure everything, then take pictures of the measurement, switching cameras from NOPD and JPSO. Slowly, I might add. If this kept up much longer, I was going to need a place to deposit the pass-through coffee. There were no lights on or movement in the house—and you'd think two cop cars parked outside your house would have generated movement—meaning Mrs. Stevens didn't seem to be home and was therefore unlikely to let me use her bathroom, which I'm sure she called a powder room.

I was checking my phone (only thirty-seven times so far) for the important message I knew had to be about to arrive to demand my presence elsewhere, when Joanne came over to me.

"We're having trouble finding the bullet," she said in her carefully controlled neutral voice that told me she wasn't just chatting me up because she was as bored as I was.

"Maybe it went to China. Or hit a stone in the ground and ricocheted elsewhere."

"These guys are usually pretty good at finding bullets," she responded.

"Look, I fired the gun. Once. There is a bullet there somewhere, but maybe not somewhere to be found."

"You didn't like Edward Springhorn, did you?"

"No, why would I? He was a scumbag who sexually coerced young girls, making their lives a misery."

"You think Tiffany wasn't his only conquest?"

"He was too practiced at it. You know that."

"The kind of guy the world would be better off without. As long as he's around, there'll be another victim."

"A lot of girls got lucky when he kicked the bucket."

"So you could say someone did a favor when they killed him?"

I didn't like where this conversation was going. "Inadvertent. My money is on one of his pond slime friends getting into a fight over drugs, or booze. No one was doing anyone any favors here."

"You've been under a lot of stress lately."

"We all have. No more for me than anyone else."

"Break up of a long-term relationship, fall into a messy rebound, carrying two mortgages with a downturn in business. That'd be a lot of stress for anyone."

"I'm doing okay," I said tersely. And didn't add *this is none of your fucking business.*

"Are you?"

She left a silence. I finally blundered in and filled it. "Yes, I'm fine. I didn't kill Fast Eddie, if that's what you're angling at."

"I wouldn't blame you if you had. He threatened you. He was clearly a violent man. It could have been self-defense."

"But it wasn't. I did not kill him. I was nowhere near when he died. After our encounter here on the lawn, I wanted nothing more to do with him and hoped to never see him again."

"You're not helping yourself if you wait until we have all the evidence," she said.

I stared at her. I had to literally count to ten to stop myself from yelling "what the fuck are you talking about?" Even then, the best I could manage was, "There is no fucking evidence to find because I fucking did not kill him. Ballistics will clear me. Do your goddamn tests."

"That's the problem; the bullet we found in him is too damaged to test. Your gun was recently fired. We can't find the bullet here. In fact, it looks more like someone was digging around in the lawn than a bullet trajectory."

"And that's enough to accuse me of murder?" I packed a steamer trunk of sarcasm in my tone.

"No. But someone saw your car near where he was killed."

"What!?" I stopped, swallowed coffee even though it was cold and the last thing my bladder needed. Anything to break this chain. "That's not possible. And besides, I drive the most nondescript car on the planet."

"A gray Mazda with a St. Charles Athletic Club parking sticker on it?"

I stared to her. Finally said, "Not mine. Or someone stole my car."

A SUV came down the street, then jerked to a stop beside us. Mrs. Susie Stevens jumped out, leaving her vehicle running, the door open.

"What is going on here? What are you doing on my property?"

"We're looking for evidence," the JPSO deputy said, he was closest to her.

"Evidence? For what? Haven't you people done enough to us?"

"They need to find the bullet I fired into your lawn," I said.

She stared at me as if she'd never seen me. "What bullet?" she said, looking from me to the deputies, to Joanne, her eyes never landing on anyone.

"You called me to come help you deal with him. When he showed up here. He almost punched me and I fired a shot to warn him off. It went into your lawn."

"You shot my lawn?"

"I was trying to protect you," I told her. Protect me, really, but she was next in line.

"I don't remember a shot," she said, the eyes still roaming.

How much Xanax was she on? "Do you remember when he came here? After you called his work? He threatened you and you called me."

"Shoulda called us," the JPSO deputy put in.

I agreed with him, but continued. "He was here. I came and told him to leave. You must have heard the argument."

"I don't remember," she said. "Please, you all need to leave. You can't just barge in here. I've answered all the questions I'm going to answer."

"You need to tell the truth about what happened," I told her.

She didn't look at me, turned her back to us all, and strode to her door, leaving her SUV haphazardly parked halfway into the street.

I started to follow, but Joanne grabbed my arm. I could only repeat, "You need to tell the truth."

She kept her back turned. We stared at her as she fumbled with her keys until she finally opened her door, slamming it behind her. No lights came on in the house.

"Damn her," I muttered under my breath. Make me a more likely suspect and it would make her less of one.

"Do you want to talk?" Joanne asked softly.

"No. There is nothing to talk about. Unless you want to discuss why she's lying. To save herself? So zoned out on anxiety meds she can't remember? Take your pick."

"We need to close down here," the deputy said. Then with a look at Joanne, "Unless you want to get a search warrant. If there was a bullet in that hole, we'd found it by now."

"No, let's leave," she said, letting go of my arm.

I started to protest, to say there had to be a bullet, to proclaim my innocence. But no words would change anything. I marched back to my car, intent on getting out of here.

Before they arrested me.

More practically, I had to make a coffee relief stop, which required me to hit the suburban strip with its legions of McBurger Things. Between Joanne and the stupidity of drivers who didn't seem to understand that the white lines in the road meant something, I found myself gripping the steering wheel tightly with both hands lest a finger put itself in the locked and upright position.

I like to think I'm ethical enough to actually buy something when I stop to pee, but the truth is it gives me an upstanding excuse to order unhealthy crap like a chocolate shake, probably made out of nothing resembling milk. The day hadn't even hit noon yet, and disgustingly unhealthy was as close to a consolation prize as I could find.

As I sat in my car and slurped, I considered what to do next.

Not be somewhere easily found came to mind. I turned off my cell phone. The cops can do GPS tracking—or maybe I was getting paranoid—in any case, a turned-off phone meant all calls would go to voice mail. Just in case Joanne called to ask me to come down to the station. I needed to lean on Mrs. Susie Stevens, but that would have to wait. Both she and the cops were probably expecting me to be circling back there even now, and I wanted to avoid letting them be right. I'd give her a day or so to think she'd gotten away with her lack of recall. The question was why she had suddenly developed a convenient memory problem. Did she kill Fast Eddie and wanted to pin the blame on me? To protect her son? Her ex? If so, was it because she knew they killed him or because she thought they did? Or was she was truly so bewildered and medicated, she was having trouble remembering? Did she think I had done it? If she or her son or ex did it, then she had to know I hadn't. So why not dump the blame on one of his low-life friends instead of me? What had I done to her to deserve this? Maybe she was desperate, lost in this new world of criminal suspicion—that doesn't happen in the safe suburbs—and didn't know what to do other than protect herself.

Fuck. This was taking me around in circles.

Joanne had said my car had been seen near where he was killed. Since I didn't know where that was, I couldn't say for sure it wasn't a stupid coincidence. But I doubted that I traveled anywhere near the same locations he did.

I glanced at the faded sticker for the gym parking lot. A nasty feeling crept up my spine. Someone would have had to be standing very close to my windshield to have made out the name. A few years of New Orleans sun made it hard to read in daylight. What were the chances a helpful citizen just happened to notice it in the dark? Far easier for someone to scout out my car and take note of anything that might identify it. I deliberately avoided bumper stickers, Saints flags, etc., keeping my car as plain as could be. I only put the sticker on the windshield because I needed it for the parking lot. Torbin hung a Muses shoe from his rearview mirror, claiming, "This is New Orleans, we don't do dice." Now, that would be noticed. My faded sticker? Not so much.

And the missing bullet? Had it been removed already? The cops did say it looked more like someone was digging there.

I burped. I was going to regret this fake milkshake later. Like many things in my life.

I headed back into traffic, wanting to get away from suburban insanity before the frenzy of lunch hit.

I decided the library was the safest place to be. Joanne wouldn't think to look for me there, and it gave me a plausible excuse for turning the phone off.

I could hang there until I went to meet…I hoped I remembered his name before I got there.

Either I'd blacked out and murdered Fast Eddie, or someone was trying to frame me. Driving back from suburban hell to CBD chaos and thinking that thought upped my screaming at drivers all the vile things I hoped happened to their testicles for their utter inability to use a turn signal unless they forgot they had one blinking and kept going straight.

"Fuck this," I muttered, as I finally parked close enough to the library to gaze at it in the distance. I needed to calm down, stop feeling sorry for myself, and think this through.

Entering the long-ago world of Samuel and his beloved Alibe Braud might help.

At least it would keep me off the streets.

CHAPTER TWENTY-TWO

The library seemed a kinder, gentler place than the cold, cruel (okay, reasonably temperate) world outside. A hushed calm, Cindy, my favorite archivist, happy to lend a hand. And an excuse to not be at home or my office or even have my cell phone on.

As for being arrested, I'd think about that tomorrow. Another day and all that.

There was a single candle burning when I arrived home, so late as to be closer to morning than night.

"You needn't have waited up," I told Alibe, quickly kissing her on the cheek, the haste to avoid that she might catch the lingering stench of death. "We have electricity, you needn't consign yourself to a flickering candle."

"There is no reason to waste it; all I need is to keep the dark out, and the candle is enough."

I had gone to the washbasin to wash my face and hands, as if mere water could erase the taint of what I had seen. Looking up at her, the water still dripping on my face, I saw the lines of care etched on her face.

"You needn't worry on me. I'm with other officers of the law, well protected." Better protected than even you, but I did not say that. The woman I had seen tonight was younger than my dear Alibe.

"I know. I suppose it's silly of me. But I can't sleep, I might as well be up so when you come home, I can rest with you."

"What worries you?" I asked, wiping the water from

my face and hands. "I am with armed men, as well as armed myself. My badge protects me."

"I know. But you're on the streets few respectable people tread. One bullet, one knife. And to be selfish, I worry about what would happen to me without you. I have little to sustain me beyond my marriage to you."

I am a man and have made my way in the world as such, with opportunities both of education and work enough to keep myself. The world of a woman is not something I had much considered. Of course, I pitied the women of the District, wondered what had led them to such a life, the choices they had made. But little considered the choices they had. Could the death of a husband so callously bring to fruition the worries I beheld on my wife's face?

"I will not let that happen," I said, wrapping my arms around her. "For my own sake, I am careful on my behalf. I will be doubly more for your sake."

She relaxed in my embrace. But I still felt the tension in her back. We both knew my words alone were no protection, a guttering candle against the darkness.

I woke before her in the morn, my thoughts still on the night, the young girl dead too soon, and what Alibe had said, her care of what would happen to her if I were to be killed or disabled.

I made the coffee and toast, something she usually did. Even with armed men about me, there were so many ways to fall into mortality; a spooked horse, a careless driver of the new automobiles, yellow jack, or the other miasmas that could fell a grown man in his prime. I had considered little of what would happen to Alibe—and children if we were blessed with them—should I not be here. Her father and mother might take her in, but he is not in good health and has little beyond the meager farm from which to provide. He was never fond of me, with my big-city ways, but happy enough that I would be the one responsible for his daughter's keeping. Her older brother, meant to take the farm, had lost his arm from falling off a horse, and does little to support his wife and children, save a litany of saloon jobs where he drinks more than he serves. Perhaps as a widow, the school would keep her on—they only allowed her to continue after she married because they were so short of teachers. But the paltry sum they pay her could do little more than provide the most shabby of living circumstances.

I brought the coffee and toast to her in bed. Her worrying in the night had possibly been more taxing than what I had done. I, at least, have action and purpose, and deal only with tragedies that are not part of my life.

She woke, surprised at the coffee before her. Then alarmed that she had neglected her duty.

I kissed her gently on the forehead. "You are the greatest part of my heart. I do not want you to worry or fret on my behalf, on things that may never be. Together we will devise a plan. I would not be a man if I did not care for the woman I love the most, even beyond the grave."

She smiled. "You are right, I must not worry about events that aren't real. I will try to do better as your wife."

I wished to reassure her that she was everything I wanted in a wife—brave, strong, smart, resilient, funny—and foolish enough to love me—but the day called. She had to ready for school, and I had to finish my coffee and toast as well. There would be time to talk later.

I started skimming at that point. As interesting as Samuel Braud was, the tales of a robber caught, a slow ride on the streetcar, the searing heat of the summer held little interest. I wanted to see if any more women were killed, but after the death of Frederic Townson, the ones I found were the ones to be expected, sadly. A fight with a husband, a boyfriend, the all-too-common ways women are still killed.

Tellingly, once he was dead, no more women were murdered with their undergarments jammed in their throats. Still not proof, but there would be no trial, no beyond all reasonable doubt. Everything I had found said that Frederick Townson was a murderer, one who may have been killed by a random thief, or perhaps one of his victims had fought back. I liked the latter theory but had even less evidence for that than for his being a vicious serial killer.

I glanced at my watch.

No wonder I was hungry. The hour resembling lunch had long passed.

Maybe I'd have to settle for a slice when I met with…Brandon.

It seemed wrong, going out to the Metairie suburbs twice in one day.

Save for that being the last place Joanne would look for me.

I turned on my phone just long enough to make sure there were no messages calling this meeting off. Then I turned it off again, as in forgetting to turn it on after the library.

The drive out there was a combination of the after-school idiocy and the early rush-hour stupidity. Streets have one-way signs for a reason, people.

Brandon had arrived before me. He was ensconced in a booth with a large everything pizza in front of him, two slices already missing and a pitcher of soda close at hand.

"Who else is joining us?" I asked as I sat down.

He gave me a look like I was some sort of idiot.

"It's just us. I told you that."

"You going to eat all of that?"

"I planned to take part of it home. I hope you don't mind."

I started to ask why would I mind, until I noticed him nudging the bill in my direction.

Don't argue with a teenage kid over twenty bucks, I decided, hiding my annoyance by picking up the grease-stained check and taking it to the register.

I also got a plate for myself. If I was paying for it, I would be eating some of it. I didn't want my stomach rumbling while we talked.

He gave me a side-eye as I took two slices, but didn't say anything.

After a few minutes of eating, I finally said, "So, you said you had information for me."

"Yeah," he said, at least polite enough to finish chewing before he replied. "Real important. Cheap at just the price of a pizza."

"I'd like to be the judge of that," I said.

"So what else will you give me?"

I gave him my best WTF look.

It took him a few moments, but he finally got the message. "I mean, this is stuff you need to know."

"Maybe the police should know it as well," I said, putting my phone on the table. The last thing I needed was some pimply-faced kid acting like he could outbluff me.

He swallowed, not pizza, but a gulp of nervousness. Amateur. Worse, young, immature amateur. Here in this greasy pizza place, I was safe enough to be annoyed. Give him a gun and he'd be my worst nightmare. Like Fast Eddie. I had been honest when I told Joanne I wanted nothing more to do with him. Men just young enough to still think they'll live forever and adolescent enough to think of consequences as nothing beyond today or tomorrow are the ones who scare me the most.

But over greasy pizza, Braydon, Braddock, oh, yeah, Brandon was just annoying.

"So what do you have? If it's truly good, maybe I will throw in something extra." I'd won the round, no need to rub it in his face.

In a low voice, his idea of conspirators, he said, "Eddie Springhorn has been murdered."

I waited for him to continue. Long enough for me to realize that was it.

"Yeah, I know," in a voice that indicated "no more pizza for you."

He stared to me. "No one else knew. I had to tell the kids at school."

"Really? What did you tell them?"

"Just that he was dead. Got shot."

"How'd you know he was shot?"

"That's just what I heard."

"From who?"

"A friend of his."

"The friend who shot him?"

"No, no! Not that kind of friend. A friend who would hear something like that. Someone close to his friends who would know what had happened."

Well, that was an interesting reaction. It meant he either knew more than he was saying—not likely—or that he knew a lot less but wanted to act like he knew more. I could push, but it would only expose how little he knew, and there was no point in that except for my ego winning over a kid who should be doing his homework.

I tried a different tack. "Did any of your school friends know him?"

"Yeah, maybe. He hung around. Think Kevin did. How did you find out?" His question was almost accusing, as if I'd deliberately cheated him out of a second large everything pizza.

"I read the papers. Have friends on the police force." I didn't elaborate that some of those friends were threatening to arrest me, so I was more involved in the murder than I wanted to be.

Deprived of his big revelation, he seemed to have no follow-up.

"So tell me about the friend who told you?" I asked. Mostly because

I had another slice to go and didn't want to sit here silently staring at him. He had asked for this meeting, after all. Time to introduce him to the life concept of *be careful what you ask for, you might get it.*

"Um…a friend of mine told me."

"A school friend?"

"Yes…no. A different school. Not this school."

"Who is it?" And another bite closer to freedom.

"I don't really know. A text message. Only know his screen name."

"How did you know it was legit?"

"He's dead, isn't he?"

"How would this friend-on-screen-only know?" I didn't really care, but Brandon was being skittish about it. I was buying the pizza, so I got to ask the questions.

"I don't know. He just did." He took a big mouthful, followed by a large gulp of soda and then another mouthful.

"Set up a meeting with this friend for him to tell me how he found out, and that would be worth my while." I made the offer knowing it wouldn't happen. Brandon had probably been nerd-boying alone at home, caught it on the news, and wanted to act like a big deal by knowing something others didn't. It had probably worked with his schoolmates, who would never abandon their social media flavor of the week to follow any real news. He made up a mysterious friend as his special connection. It had worked so well on his classmates, he thought it would work on me.

Another gulp and mouthful before he finally mumbled, "Not sure he's into that. May be out of town. But I'll see what I can do."

"Okay, let me know." I got up, went to the counter, snagged two to-go boxes, took what remained of the half of the pizza I considered mine and left him with the final slice from his half.

I waved as I headed out the door.

He was still eating.

Much as my pizza victory was fun, it still didn't give me a place to go.

The phone remained off. I'd turn it on around midnight. That might be safe.

CHAPTER TWENTY-THREE

Brandon was hungry. He had counted on having leftover pizza, and one slice wasn't enough to satisfy him. He told his mother not to worry about dinner; he'd take care of it. But only the tail end of the kind of bread he liked was left, along with that grainy, healthy stuff his mother ate. Yeah, he'd forgotten to put bread on the grocery list, but his mother knew he only liked one kind. She had eyes; she could see when it was only down to the heel ends.

Kevin had blown him off when he suggested they go out and get something. Kevin now had his older sister's car. It was nothing more than a beat-up old Honda Civic, but he acted like it was a Corvette, and no one could ride in it except the chosen few. Kevin had claimed he had to run to the grocery store, but Brandon knew it was a lie. Kevin wanted to act like he was popular, not a nerd. But he was, and cruising by the girls in a drab gray dinged-up car wasn't going to change that. He'd be much better off hanging out with Brandon. Even with Eddie gone, nothing had really changed, just the players, and if Kevin wanted to play, he needed to be nice to Brandon.

It wasn't like he'd suggested going out for steak or anything like that. Just a burger and fries. Kevin had a job, and Brandon would pay him back once he got paid for the computer stuff he was doing. Eddie hadn't paid other than the party invites, but Steve would. He had already asked Brandon to keep doing the computer stuff he'd been doing.

But for now he was hungry, and there was nothing in the house to eat. Next time he'd order two pizzas to make sure he had enough. That old-lady detective wasn't smart enough to know how much Brandon could help her. She should be buying him pizza every week. Maybe if Steve didn't pay him soon enough, he could sell the stuff to her.

He texted Kevin again. This time he reminded Kevin about some things Kevin didn't want anyone else to know. Yeah, he'd seen some stuff on Eddie's computer.

A few minutes later a text came back: "bring burger/fries for U. 1/2 hour."

CHAPTER TWENTY-FOUR

I parked in front of my house, not even turning the car off while contemplating what to do next. I was even paranoid enough to scan the neighborhood for anything that could be an unmarked car.

Necessity required me to run in long enough to go to the bathroom and toss the leftover pizza in the fridge. It wasn't good enough to be anything more than desperate food. Which gave me an excuse to head out and have a few beers until I was hungry again.

I left my car where it was parked. It wasn't like moving it a few blocks would make much difference. Plus, Joanne knew well enough that I could walk to all sorts of places in the French Quarter and Marigny from here. My car left here gave no clue to which of those places I was going to.

I considered being unpredictable and going someplace I'd never gone before, but in the end the comfort of the familiar won out and I was back at Riley & Finnegan again.

They have good beer and decent food.

My first beer was just in front of me when a noisy group entered. Alan, Mrs. Stevens' son, was one of them.

Then I noticed another familiar face. The Goth girl from the school friends Brandon had assembled. Gay Goth? Was that a thing? Was wearing all black even considered Goth? Or acting like you'd just moved here from Brooklyn? I couldn't keep up anymore. The butch and femme of my youth seemed so quaintly simple.

Now I had a moral dilemma. Did I rat her out as underage? If I did, they'd leave and I'd lose any chance to talk to Alan. If I didn't and, not likely, but if someone decided this was the night to do random ID checks, Mary could get in a lot of trouble. I got it; I had done the same when I was too young to legally go (but tall enough to look like I was). But what had I just been musing about youth? Not thinking through the consequences. I certainly hadn't back then, although at least that was when the drinking age was eighteen and bars were more likely to be raided as gay than underage. (This was the South, after all.) Still, this was a safe place for all the young queer folks to hang out, bathrooms had signs that said "Whatever—just don't pee on the toilet," and Mary was likely to run a tab or even give you a bar T-shirt for free if you needed it.

But I did want to chat with Alan.

I made a moral compromise. After a sip of my beer—my first—I got up and headed toward them, desperately trying to remember her name from our one encounter.

"Sophia," I said, hoping I was right.

She looked up at me. At least I'd hit close enough to her name for her to react to it in this noisy bar. Then stared as she recognized me. Looked a little panicked even. Was it just that I knew her as a high school kid who shouldn't be in this bar? Was that worth the expression I saw on her face? Was she selling drugs? If so, she needed to be much better about being cool.

But I'm not a cop, and my only interest was making sure she drank beverages of the non-adult kind here where she could lose Mary her license.

"What are you doing here?" she blurted out.

"I live around here. Come here often. Am a good friend of Mary."

Her eyes darted around the bar. "Yeah, well, good to see you here." She started to sidle away.

I put a hand on her arm. "I am a good friend of Mary's, and I'd hate to see her lose this place because of being busted for serving alcohol to underage kids. So I need to see you drinking only soft drinks or soda water. Got it?"

"Did my parents hire you?"

"What?" Then I answered, "No, I have no clue who your parents are."

"Yeah, right. So why are you here?" The fear had given way to anger. They're always so close together.

I repeated, "I live close by, I come in here often. Ask Mary." Or ask any of the other bartenders, I almost added, but that was more true than I wanted it to be. I didn't want to think I came here so often every single employee could pour my drink of choice before I even asked for it. Then I added, "Look, I'm queer, too. It wasn't always easy when I was young. I don't care about that. Just stick to drinking what's legal."

Alan had seen me and joined us. Sophia used that as her excuse to pull away. I let her.

"How do you two know each other?" I asked, before considering the obvious. Sophia was a friend of Tiffany's.

But he answered as if it was a reasonable question. "She and my sister are—were—friends. I think we kind of recognized each other, you know, gaydar. So I've tried to help her get through when I could."

"She seemed worried about her parents," I said. I was slowly moving back to my table and away from the crowd.

"Oh, yeah. You know that big church out near the lake?"

I nodded as if I did.

"Her father and mother run it. He's even got a local radio show. One of those hellfire and brimstone ones. Sof needs to hang on until she's old enough to get out of there. They want her to go to some Bible college in the hinterlands of Mississippi. A dry county, no less. They don't know their only daughter is a queer, and they won't be happy when they find out."

We were close enough to my table for me to snag another sip of beer.

I reminded myself I could not solve Sophia's problems. I was a private detective, not a social worker. Besides, I had enough of my own.

I motioned Alan to join me. He did so easily, as if he liked talking to me.

"How's your mother doing?" I asked ever so innocently.

"I don't know. Sometimes she seems okay, but too okay, if you know what I mean. Like too chipper, like she's faking it."

I only nodded, leaving a silence for him to fill.

"And other times, she seems like she's falling apart, like she's lost in some wilderness."

To hide the venal purpose behind my questions, I asked, "How are you doing?"

I signed Mary for a beer for him.

"I don't know," he answered. "The days pass. Sometimes things seem okay, then I remember my life's a shit storm and then it's not okay. You know what I mean?"

Now was not the time to tell Alan that constantly saying "you know what I mean" was a bad habit. Again I nodded. Then said, "You'll be okay. It'll take time, and it'll never be what it should have been. You've got a big, wide life in front of you."

"You think?" he asked slowly.

"I know," I answered as I paid for his beer.

He took a long sip. "But it's still a shit storm at the moment."

"Are you worried about your mother?"

"Yeah."

"How about your father?"

"Yeah, I guess. But he's off with his new girlfriend. She's nice, I like her and all, so he's got someone to help him through all this. My mom doesn't have anyone, and I don't have anyone."

I did not sigh. I did not point out that his self-pity wasn't helping, nor was his Prince Right fantasy solving everything a realistic one.

"Yeah, it's nice to have someone love you and to come home to, but that's outside you. You need to find what's inside you, the places you're strong. That's what gets you through. No one can give that to you, even the love of your life. What about your friends here? Other friends? Teachers? Preachers—the good ones? What about the things you care about?"

He took another sip of his beer. The hair on his chin was a bare wisp, as if it, too, was struggling into adulthood.

"You can be strong for your mother, and that can help you find the strength in yourself."

"Yeah, I guess. What do I do for her?"

"Do you think she did it?"

"Did it? You mean killed him?"

"Yes. Is it possible?"

"No, no way. I can't see her taking a gun and hunting him down. Just no."

"Could she hire someone to?"

He hesitated. "No, I don't think so. Not enough money. It's tight now with the divorce."

"Did you tell she about the cops coming back out to her house?"

He looked puzzled. Then worried. "What for? Do they think she did it?"

"They were looking for the bullet I fired when I scared him off."

"Why would they do that?" He seemed genuinely confused.

"Your mother didn't mention this?"

"No, she didn't."

"She seemed really upset to find the police back at her house. She told them to leave."

"Well, that seems to be her right, isn't it?"

"Yes, it is. The problem is they left before they found the bullet."

"Why does the bullet matter?"

"You know they can tell if your gun was fired recently?"

"Really?"

"Yes. The problem for me is that the cops took my gun—this is a murder investigation, after all."

"Yeah, they took guns from us, too. We haven't gotten them back yet."

"And they can tell I fired it. They're wondering if I fired it into the lawn or if I might have fired it at him. So I need to prove it was fired into the lawn."

"Oh, but you did, didn't you?"

"Yes, of course I did."

"Wasn't my mom there? She must have heard the shot."

"I would think so. But that day she was so upset, she told the cops she couldn't remember. My guess is that she was too stressed out to talk to them any more then, so blew them off. She probably thought they'd find the bullet and she wouldn't need to talk to them."

"Oh. Yeah, that makes sense."

Not really, but it was his mother, and I had to soft sell this as much as possible. I continued, "I don't want to upset your mother any more than necessary, but it would help if you could talk to her. She can just send a statement to the investigating officers, doesn't even need to talk to them, just to let them know that I did fire my gun as a warning to protect her."

"Yeah, I can do that." He finished his beer and got up.

Mine was getting warm. I'd had no time to drink it.

"That would really help me," I told him. I walked him back to the bar and bought a pitcher of beer—and one of soda—for his table. I hoped it was subtle enough of a bribe.

I ordered another beer for me and a burger and fries. They did good ones here, and it would make me full enough that the leftover pizza could go where it belonged, into the garbage.

As I was walking home—yes, walking, not stumbling, I'd had only three beers, including the first half-drunk one—my phone chimed. A text message.

Not from a number I recognized. "Brandon gave me #. Can give you info on Eddie. Tell me what it's worth and we'll talk."

I sighed. Young, amateur. It was from Brandon, and he wanted a whole pizza for himself. I almost sent that as a return text but decided he needed to wait. In the age of instant communications, waiting was the hardest part.

CHAPTER TWENTY-FIVE

It couldn't be this easy. Like a switch had gone off.

She looked again at her phone. Nothing.

He's dead. Ghosts can't text.

She remembered his staring face.

The blood.

The taunting message still on her phone, demanding she come see him.

Be careful what you ask for, she thought. *You might get it.*

She started laughing, then buried her face in her pillow so no one would hear.

The laughing turned to crying.

Chapter Twenty-six

I'd let Alan have time to speak to his mother. Then I'd talk to her. Pour ginseng down her throat to help with her memory problems. Her lack of recall could put me in jail.

It would also give me an excuse to go back to F&R again this evening on the pretext that I might run into him. And the more realistic hope that I'd get to drink uninterrupted beer.

I had been considering going out to the suburbs this morning, so that left me with no plans that required being away from my office.

I still hadn't answered the text message from last night. Maybe I could demand he meet me for brunch; that would rule out going back to the same dismal pizza place.

It was a beautiful, spring day, a mix of dramatic clouds and sun.

Take a walk, Micky. There was no pressing reason I needed to go to my office. I could walk into the Quarter, hit a coffee shop I liked.

And contemplate how to avoid being charged for murder.

The walk was pleasant, the coffee good. Maybe the caffeine would give me inspiration.

I hadn't killed Eddie.

Someone had.

Someone who was trying to make it look like I'd done it. The bullet was missing, and Mrs. Stevens had conveniently forgotten about firing the gun. Someone claimed seeing a car the same make and model as mine with the sticker of the gym I went to on its windshield.

The cops knew my gun had been fired. They also knew I'd had a fight with Fast Eddie.

Because, honest me, I'd fucking told them.

Only the caffeine and the clouds made this morning better.

I started to cross Burgundy Street, then quickly stepped back when I realized a car was far too close for me to do that. I hadn't been paying attention.

It was a late-model Subaru.

A brief glimpse of the driver, through the reflections of the car windows.

No, she doesn't live here anymore.

It can't be her, only an image of memory brought to mind by a hint of resemblance.

The license was out of state.

Then it turned the corner.

I started to run after the car.

Then stopped myself halfway down the block.

It couldn't be her.

And even if it was…

I trudged back home.

I wondered at how all my friends—all our former circle of friends—were so coincidentally not available the same weekend.

Don't be that kind of jackass ex where you demand all your friends pick either you or her.

Or maybe they already had.

The day didn't seem so sunny anymore.

Yes, they could see her; we'd all been friends. I could be pissed about that, but I couldn't be justifiably and fairly pissed off because I'd want them to remain my friends if the situation were reversed.

But no one had said anything. Just "we're busy" that weekend. The entire weekend. Yeah, our schedules were crazy, but that Torbin, Andy, Joanne, Alex, Danny, and Elly were all busy on the same weekend was a bit much.

If that was Cordelia.

If she was here.

If they were meeting her.

Maybe I was seeing ghosts of my past and it was all a big fluke that they were all unavailable at the same time.

Fuck, just fuck. Once those demons of doubt get in, they're hard to get out.

The past should stay the past. It never does.

Life went on. I grabbed my phone and jabbed in a text message: "Meet at the same place at the same time."

That would call his bluff.

I got in my car and drove to my office. Getting arrested might improve my morning.

One of the coffee shop guys was outside. Yes, I should know who's who, but too many man buns and hipster beards. He was handing out coupons for one free croissant with two cups of coffee. To be fair, he tried to hand me one as if I might be an actual customer.

I smiled as politely as I could, dodged around him, and headed up the stairs.

The computer grannies were in.

I sicced them on Brandon and his text message games, giving them the number he had used to text me and the first number he had called me on. I asked them to trace them back as far as they could.

Lady Jane nodded, said they were a little shorthanded, as one of them was off at a wedding—her grandson and his boyfriend—so it might be a day or two.

I had hoped to have it by this afternoon for our meeting, but that was only to stomp down a teenage boy, and I really should be better than that.

Then I ran up the stairs, as if motion could help dispel the mess this day was becoming.

The usual scan of email showed nothing. Then, defiantly, I checked the dating website. It was, after all, past time for me to move on with my life.

There was a message waiting. *Hey, you looked interesting. I like a woman who can manage a complete sentence. Would you like to meet for coffee or something?* I checked out her profile. Liked reading and good coffee. I messaged her back saying that sounded good.

A few more moments of trying to waste time online convinced me that today was not a day to sit behind the desk.

I left the office again, went back home, threw on gym clothes, then stuffed another change of clothes in my gym bag and headed back out.

After a good hard cardio workout on the elliptical and a scrubbing shower (fortunately in the middle of the day, so I wasn't forced to share the space with twenty-year-olds whose expressions clearly indicate they think gravity won't happen to them), I was back in my car.

I looked at my watch. A little early to head out to the greasy pizza place. Plus I was hungry and wanted decent food.

Feeling foolish, I got out of my car again, leaving it in the gym parking lot—if I was going to get arrested on the basis of a parking sticker, I wanted to get as much mileage out of it as possible—and headed to a sushi joint just down from the gym. It was enough after lunchtime that there were tables available.

Once I was finished eating—fried oysters and raw salmon are two of my favorite food groups—it was still a little early, but that could work to my advantage. Even if Brandon had conned some friend to act the part, he'd probably still be lurking about. Cruising around early might catch him unawares.

Back in my car again, and with a sigh, I headed out to Metairie.

This time I didn't park in the lot but just around the corner. I could see the front and had a view along the side street. Most likely he was coming from school, and this was the most direct route.

So predictable. I didn't even have to wait long. He was plodding up the street, his face buried in his phone. I could have been standing directly in front of him and he might not have noticed me.

He continued into the pizza joint, still not looking up from his phone. I waited another ten minutes, but no one else entered. Or left.

I wondered what his story would be. And how many pizzas I'd be paying for.

Two seemed to be the answer. As I was entering, the waiter gave him a to-go box and put an everything pizza in front of him. As well as a pitcher of soda.

"So, I didn't expect to see you here," I said as I slid into the booth opposite him. The wafting pizza smell was wasted on my full stomach.

"My friend couldn't make it."

"He could have messaged me and let me know. Would have saved me the drive out here."

"No, he couldn't come here, but we can text him the questions. He doesn't want to be seen in public."

Okay, someone who watched a lot of bad TV might think that a plausible story.

"Why not? What's he got to hide?"

"Nothing…except he has information that might be important. And dangerous in the wrong hands."

I am so good. I did not even crack the hint of a smile at his cliché.

"What information does he have? Who killed Eddie Springhorn?"

Brandon ignored my question by taking a large bite of the pizza.

When he finally finished eating, he said, "We have to work out a deal."

"What kind of deal?"

"What the information is worth to you?"

"About two pizzas' worth," I shot back.

He looked at me as he took another bite, then tried to talk about the food, "No…this is better—"

I cut in, mostly to avoid seeing masticated pepperoni. "No, so far you've told me nothing that's close to what it's cost me. Yeah, your information is much cheaper than the pizza they serve here. So I need to know just what the information is and why it's so important before we can think about any deal. I'm not coughing up a dime to find out stuff I can read in the newspaper."

He finally swallowed. "This is better than that."

"Yeah? What is it?"

"If I tell you, then you'll know." Then he looked at his phone and said, "Let me text my friend and see what he says." He jabbed at the phone with his thumbs, carefully keeping the screen out of my view.

I went to the counter and asked for a sparkling water. No such thing. I settled for a root beer.

When I sat back down he looked up from his phone and said, "It's five hundred up front or nothing."

This time I did laugh. Stood up. "It's nothing." I started to walk away.

"Wait," he called.

Somehow I knew he would. "It's nothing. Deal's been negotiated. That's the outcome."

"But what about the pizza?"

"What about it?"

"Who's going to pay for it?"

"Guess you are." I kept walking.

"But I don't have any money," trailed after me.

I took a few more steps. I made it to the door before turning around.

The counter guy was glaring at Brandon, who was looking down at his phone as if that would offer escape.

He looked up at my footsteps. He smirked. I stopped and the smirk disappeared.

I probably should have just walked out then. People who don't think about consequences are the most dangerous of all.

But instead I came back to the table.

"How about two fifty?" he said as I slid in the seat.

"How about two pizzas?" I said. "Or nothing."

He finally seemed to realize the corner he'd backed himself into.

"I don't know if my friend will go for it," he said, again looking at his phone.

"Then you need to get your friend to cover the pizzas."

He seemed to be thinking. That included taking another bite of the unpaid-for pizza.

"Okay, but if it's useful, maybe more?" he finally said after swallowing.

"Maybe," I said. Silently adding, "and maybe not." To play along I asked, "What does your friend know about Eddie?" I took out my wallet, peeled out two twenty dollar bills—he'd ordered the kitchen-sink pizzas—and took them to the guy at the counter.

When I came back, he read off his phone, "Eddie liked to party."

"Yeah, I knew that."

"Drugs, illegal stuff," he read. Or pretended to.

"Knew that, too. Also coerced underage girls into sexual favors by conning them into sending him nude pictures like he was their boyfriend."

Brandon blushed. Oh, not much of one, but enough to recognize that he knew all about that and had impure thoughts on the subject.

"Can he tell me who any of the other girls were?"

Brandon didn't look at me, but read from the phone, "No, no, he can't. Knows Eddie did it, but doesn't know the names."

Problem was he didn't seem to actually send any question before he answered it. My guess was Brandon did know who some of them were but was too embarrassed or too complicit to admit it. If you're going to lie, you have to be consistent in your lies.

I continued to play along. "How many pictures did Eddie show you?"

"None, I didn't see any," he answered too quickly, then said, "Oh, you meant to ask my friend. Let me text him now." He stared down at the phone, screen still held away from my view, and took a long time texting.

You weasel, I thought. His too quick—and too guilty—answer made it clear he had seen a few. Fast Eddie probably used them as a bonding ritual, show the boys the titty pictures, so they could all laugh and enjoy the show together. I'd peg Brandon as a third-tier outer circle. Other than fawning attention, he could offer Eddie little. No money, no drug connections. Too young, nerdy, and pudgy to bring any girls into the fold. And needing to pretend he was more important and knew more than he really did.

However, even that little might help me. Or at least give me some names to hand to the police.

"Where did Eddie have his parties?" I asked.

He looked up at me, then down at his phone. He typed something on it. Waited as if for an answer.

"Not sure," he finally said.

"You never got invited?"

"Of course I did," he answered. Then, "But there were different places. Some friends' houses, parents out of town, that kind of stuff. No regular place."

I stifled a sigh. Maybe he was telling the truth. Maybe he'd never been to one and didn't want to admit to being that uncool. Or maybe he was lying to avoid giving the answer.

"Yeah? Give me a few. Or just the one you went to."

His slight blush returned. Bingo, he had been there. My money was on a regular place. Fast Eddie was too old to hang in places the parents might come home to. And too wild.

He again looked at his phone.

I reached across the table and grabbed it out of his hand. The only thing on the screen was a brightly colored game.

His face first was the wide-open mouth of surprise, then he reacted, jumping up and reaching for it. But my arms are longer.

The counter guy looked at us.

"Game over, pal," I told him. "You get your phone back when you give me some answers."

He sat back and looked down as if out of habit, but no phone was there. Then back at me. The slight smirk appeared, much as he tried to hide it. "What will you give me?"

"What you've already got."

"What I know is worth more than a pizza or two."

"This is the fourth pizza you've cadged from me."

"Four? Whatta you mean?"

"I recall you eating pizza when we met here with your friends. That was one. Then the one you got the last time, and now these two. Four."

"I had to share the first ones, that didn't count."

As if I needed reminding, his focus on a pizza or two made it clear I was not dealing with an adult, but a boy firmly in the hormonal imbalance of the teenage years, a socially awkward one at that. He was just sly enough to recognize that the most likely little info he had was his only leverage, and once it was gone, so was the free pizza. I had to decide whether I wanted to get that info as easily and quickly as possible or if I wanted to engage in the trivial jockeying of ego—mine over his.

Be a fucking adult. As boring as it is. A lot of guys have been jerks, from hitting on me, catcalling, mansplaining, telling me to smile, telling me I wasn't pretty enough or too mannish. Taking all that out on this one nerd boy wasn't worth it. Nor, at the end of the day, who I wanted to be.

"I need to know about Eddie. His friends, where he'd hang out, who he might have taken advantage of. Anything you can tell me, okay?" I pulled three twenty dollar bills out of my wallet and placed his phone on top of them, but kept the entire package firmly under one hand and as far away from him as I could. "Tell me what you know."

He bit his lip. Then admitted, "It wasn't like I was a good friend of his."

"But you did go to at least a few of the parties."

"Yeah, but nothing much happened. I mean, mostly drinking beer and stuff."

"What kind of stuff?"

"You know, watching movies, playing computer games. Nothing really exciting, just hanging out."

"Who was there?"

"I don't really know."

"You spoke to no one? Heard no names? Even first names?"

"Well…Steve, but I don't know his last name. Someone called Ace, but I doubt that was his name."

"So, it was Eddie, Steve, Ace, and you?"

"Well, no, there were a bunch of people, but I didn't know most of them."

"What about the ones you did know? What can you tell me about them?"

"They liked to drink beer. Play games. Fool around, you know, joking and stuff."

"So you really don't know much?" I said, slipping one of the bills out of the pile and stuffing it back in my wallet.

"Some. Not everything, though. I didn't know Eddie was doing the stuff with pictures."

A little too much protesting for me to believe. And something else. Envy? Dejection?

I took a guess. "Did he give you a hard time?"

Brandon looked up at me, then down again as if trying to hide in the phone he didn't have. Still not looking up, he answered, "No, it was fine."

"He kidded you for being too young, right? A nerd? Told you about the pictures, but wouldn't show them to you. Rubbed it in your face that he could get girls—"

"No! That's not true. He was nice to me. He liked me."

Still no eye contact. His jaw was clenched and red was creeping up his neck. I'd hit a raw nerve.

"I believe you," I lied. "You're a smart man. He probably liked your sense of humor." More lies, but Brandon was the kind of not cool enough, not well-off enough, not good-looking enough that guys like Eddie used as punching bags. Of course Brandon wanted to hang out with the cool boys. And of course they'd used him.

I didn't push. "How'd you meet Eddie?"

"Through some friends."

"Which friends?"

"A teacher. She knew him."

"A teacher at your school?"

"Yeah." With a look of "where else?"

"What class?"

"Chemistry."

"What's her name?"

"I can't tell you that."

"Why not?"

"She asked me not to."

"Why?"

Another look that told me this was a dumb question. "Because he got killed. And the stuff with Tiffany. She could get in trouble if that came out."

Like I couldn't figure out who it was from what he'd already told me. "Why should that matter? It's not criminal to know people."

"I think they were going out, and she dumped him when she found out about the pictures."

"How did she find out?"

"When it came out about Tiffany. Think she read it in the paper."

"Did you tell her?"

Again, the look up then back down. "No, not me."

"Who?"

"I can't tell you that, either. Just a friend who knew them both."

"One of your school friends?"

The look away. "No, nothing to do with school."

Yep, one of his friends. Given that he didn't seem to have too many, I could probably figure that out as well. "Was it Kevin?"

He looked at me, then down again, then took a bite of pizza, but didn't really chew. A gulp of soda, then finally chewed it for far longer than it should have taken. Finally, "No, why would you think that?"

"Or Janice or Sophia. Had to be someone you know and the teacher knows and who would know Tiffany."

He took another bite of pizza. After a thorough chew he said, "Well, maybe, but I can't tell you."

Another topic I'd come back to if I needed. "When did you start going to the parties?"

"I don't remember. I guess in the fall, right after school started."

"Where was it?"

"A fishing camp on the lake. Out on Highway 90."

"How'd you get there?" Brandon didn't have a car, and that wasn't someplace you took a bus to.

"Eddie gave me a ride."

"Eddie picked you up and gave you a ride?" That didn't sound like the Eddie I knew.

"Yeah. We had to go early."

"Why?"

"He needed me to get internet out there," then added, "To set up the computer games and stuff."

Just in case I might have thought it was to surf for porn. No, just innocent computer games.

"How much computer stuff did you do for him?"

His face brightened. "I'm good at computers. I know the best games and am really fast at setting things up." He then launched into a detailed account of what he had to do to get internet access set up at the remote fishing camp.

I nodded at the appropriate places and acted like I had a clue about what he was saying and also—harder—that it was interesting.

When I finally felt I could break in, I said, "Wow, you really know a lot about computers." The truth was I didn't know enough to judge. But if I had to put money on a bet between him and the computer grannies, my money would be on the grannies. Oh, he wasn't stupid, but he came off more as the kind of boy who stayed home and played computer games and learned what he needed to know to do what he wanted to do. But he also was one of the boys who desperately needed something he was good at, that he could be the best at. If flattery got my questions answered, I had no compunctions about using it.

He smiled.

I continued, "So, Eddie needed you to help out with setting up all the games and computer stuff for the parties?"

"Yeah. He and his friends had no clue. They'd have been sitting watching TV if it wasn't for me."

"Did all the parties take place there?"

"In the fall, yeah, but around Thanksgiving they moved," he said.

"Where?"

"Out by the airport. A garage out there. One of his friends worked there, so we could use it after it closed."

"Did he need you to set up the internet out there as well?"

"That had internet, but he needed me to set up the games and stuff."

"What kind of stuff?"

He shrugged, feigning modesty. "Like a couple of TVs, so people could watch in different rooms."

"How often did the parties take place?"

"Usually the weekends."

"And you went to most of them?"

He ate another bite of the now-cold pizza before answering, "Yeah, some, but only the ones when they needed me to set stuff up. So no, not all of them."

A lie. But which one? That he went to most of them and saw things that he didn't want to admit to? Or that he was only used for computer set up and dumped as quickly as possible afterward?

I was getting tired of the smell of stale pizza grease. I put the twenty I'd stuffed in my pocket back on the table.

"Tell me where the place by the airport is."

He looked at the money and his phone.

Then gave me the address.

As I headed back to my car, I considered what I'd gotten for my money. That Eddie was involved with a teacher at Tiffany's school who found out in a humiliating way that he was two-timing her with her students—nothing like a woman scorned. That Brandon and possibly his friend Kevin were at the parties. I doubted they were innocently watching movies the entire time. Had they seen the pictures? Was that why he was so evasive?

And I had the name and address of an auto body shop out beyond the airport.

I got in my car. Time to get out of the suburbs.

Now my dilemma was to follow up on these on my own or hand them over to the police. In normal circumstances, I'd be speed-dialing Joanne right now. But as a suspect, anything I passed on would be viewed with suspicion.

And even without the suspicion, I only had a few hints of clues from a kid who probably couldn't shave yet. Only I'd seen his evasiveness, the places where he'd lied or omitted information, and much of what I'd gotten was less from what he said than how he said it.

I sighed. Big sigh. The cops weren't likely to believe me and, even if they did, were not likely to think it important.

And they were very possibly right.

Just before crossing the line back into Orleans Parish, I turned away.

Maybe Mrs. Stevens was home and we could have a friendly chat.

The fates were either smiling on me or toying with me. She was unloading groceries from her SUV.

"Let me give you a hand," I said as I came up behind her.

She gasped, startled, dropped the bag, and apples rolled down the driveway.

I bent to pick them up.

"What are you doing here?" she demanded.

"Since I was so good about helping you with your problems, I thought you might be willing to help me with mine. Like the cops think I might have killed Eddie, and one of their big pieces of evidence is that my gun was fired, but they can't find the bullet in your lawn."

"I didn't take it," she said, her words clipped.

I dumped the apples back into her bag. She didn't even thank me.

"No, but you were here and you witnessed it. I get you don't want anything else to do with the police, but you know I did fire a warning shot here in front of your house. I need you to tell the truth to the police."

"I don't want to talk to them."

"I understand. I don't want to talk to them either. But if they can't find the bullet, you're the only proof I have that my gun was only fired here as a warning."

"I don't know that."

I stared at her.

"Yes, I heard the shot, but you were fighting with him. Maybe you kept fighting. Maybe you killed him."

Bitch.

"No, I wasn't fighting with him. You," I repeated for emphasis, "you were fighting with him. I intervened on your behalf. I have no fight with him and no reason to kill him."

"Are you saying I did?"

I kept my voice as calm and reasonable as I could. She was still a grieving mother. "Certainly more than I do. He's a scumbag. He hurt you and your family, took despicable advantage of your daughter. I wouldn't blame you for shooting him. If I were you—"

"Get out of here! Get off my lawn. How dare you say these things?"

"Because I came out here to help you and now you're lying to the police—yes, omission is a lie—to make it look like I killed him."

"I don't know who you are. I don't know you didn't kill him. I want you gone!"

She was veering into hysteria.

I wanted to scream back at her. But doing so would only make me look like what I was being accused of—someone out of control, willing to harass a mother who had just lost her daughter to get what I wanted, enough anger issues to have gone after Fast Eddie because he pissed me off.

Literally biting my tongue, I spun away from her and strode to my car and drove five blocks away before stopping to put on my seat belt.

Chapter Twenty-seven

Two aspirin and at least a gallon of coffee. That was the minimum it would take to make me feel human—well, functional.

I'd said fuck everything and just taken the entire weekend off from work, thinking about work, thinking about anything else, with long workouts at the gym (and now sore muscles), catching up on my to-be-read pile, a frenzy in the kitchen with the freezer now stuffed with pizza dough and bread, plus a few containers of healthy chicken soup. Maybe if I could just defrost it I would eat a more healthy diet. Maybe. And hanging out at any reasonable bar (no tourist ones, no karaoke) where I was likely to see no one I didn't want to see. Stayed out too late last night.

Now it was a brutal Monday morning and I was paying the price for too much activity, too much alcohol, and too little of any of the trendy self-care.

It had taken me three cups to get out of my house.

Although I'd made it to my office, that was likely to be the sum accomplishment of my day. I was staring at a blank computer screen because I hadn't bothered to turn it on yet.

After the debacle with Mrs. Stevens, I'd come home, parked my car, and made the rounds of my favorite and, to be honest, not-so-favorite bars in the vicinity. A location, I should add, with a high concentration of watering holes.

I took three aspirin.

I had drunk away my sorrow and anger, and this hangover was testament to how much of each I had.

Mrs. Susie Stevens had decided she was going to lie to the police by claiming a faulty memory about whether I'd fired my gun or not. It was a devious strategy. She wasn't really lying, as no one could call her on her loss of memory. It made it seem like she knew I hadn't fired the gun but wasn't going to say that because I'd helped her find out about her daughter. She got to appear loyal while putting me front and center in the list of possible murder suspects.

The things I'd learned from Brandon yesterday. As I'd suspected, he hadn't given any of the proverbial smoking guns. A few names, a few people to talk to who might give me a few more names. A few more details about Fast Eddie, and maybe in that haystack I'd find the needle that would lead to his real killer.

Or at least prove that it wasn't me.

The glimpse of someone who looked like Cordelia. Driving the kind of car she'd drive. Could she really be in town?

Of course, planes fly in every day. Major highways lead here.

The phone rang.

Maybe I needed another aspirin.

Answer it I did not.

The machine brayed, "Hi, I'd like an update on my case. Haven't heard from you. Give me a call today and let me know. Want to know what my money's being spent on. I'll be in town next week. I'll plan to come by."

Then he hung up.

Maybe the whole bottle of aspirin.

He'd left no name or info about the case, but I recognized the arrogant tones of Douglas Townson.

What update did I have for him? *Your granddad was probably a sexual sadist and killer, certainly liked to visit the rougher parts of Storyville. He was most likely somewhere he shouldn't have been doing something he shouldn't have been doing and was too much of a sociopath to think he'd taste the dish he was serving*. Did one of the women—and her friends—take him on when he tried to kill her? Or was it a common robbery turned violent? A rival planter who took the opportunity to dump him to make it look like a robbery?

At this distance, there was no way for me to solve it. I doubted Douglas Townson would be willing to pay top dollar to find out what I had uncovered.

Nor was it likely I'd find who had killed Fast Eddie. The best I could hope for was to turn up enough to muddy the waters so thoroughly I became one of many who might have done it, and eventually the police would shrug their shoulders and move on to the next crime.

That left me with no clear direction for my day, other than getting rid of my throbbing headache.

More coffee.

Track down who the chemistry teacher was. The easy way would be to call the friendly teacher, Ms. Lee, but for all I knew the cops had tapped my phone. I could probably count on them at least pulling my phone records to see who I was calling. And if I could avoid it, I didn't want to put her in the position of deciding whether or not to rat out a colleague. They might be best friends, and a call on my part would tip her off that her secret affair wasn't so secret.

It only took me about an hour, and that mostly because of the continued intake of coffee, which required an outflow of the used-up coffee, and every trip to the bathroom included staring out the window for several minutes, doing a few rounds of a word game after sitting back at my desk before continuing the search.

It confirmed my assessment that Brandon knew a lot about what he wanted to know and found useful but didn't have a truly comprehensive grasp of information technology. He seemed to have little knowledge of how much data was accessible and how easily the few details he had given led me to her identity. My guess was that he thought, or rather, didn't really think about it and assumed that only school people would have access to the teachers.

For one, he had said "her." That alone considerably narrowed it down.

Enid Emily Gardner. Graduated from LSU eight years ago. Education major, chemistry minor. Liked knitting scarves. Yeah, she hadn't locked down her Facebook account.

I try not to judge people on looks, but nature hadn't been kind to her. A weak chin, lumpy nose, flat, stringy hair. Small eyes a little too close together behind thick glasses.

She was about five years older than Eddie. Assumptions are dangerous things, but from her looks and list of activities on social media, it didn't sound like she had an active dating life. Maybe the kind of wallflower who would be so desperate for attention, she could get taken in—at least for a while—by someone like Fast Eddie.

She'd be at school now, and that would not be a good time to try to talk to her.

Fortunately, the all-knowing, all-seeing internet had coughed up her home address. I do pay the bucks to access the main databases that have information not as readily accessible to most people. To be fair to her, that is where I found her address.

I wanted to do none of this. To bury my head in the proverbial sand, ignore life by reading articles that had nothing to do with anything relevant until it was reasonable enough in the day to move on to cocktails.

Joanne thought I'd possibly killed Fast Eddie. That stung. Of course, the prospect I'd be arrested, maybe go to trial, and the mess and cost of hiring a lawyer to defend me was also a worry. But the rift that had seeped into our friendship—and how it might affect my other friends. Could they really be close to something they suspected might be a murderer?

All compelling reasons for me to do my utmost to clear my name.

Get the fuck out of your office and at least do something.

Car. Drive.

To the address for the auto place Brandon had given me.

It was in the no-man's-land beyond the airport. I know the main arteries—I-10, Airline Highway, Veterans, but only until they reach the airport. Once you pass that, it's uncharted territory for me. I had to take Veterans, an annoying stretch of chain joints, stoplights, and the worst of suburban driving. A few blocks after passing the airport turn I found the first of several side streets I needed to take to get there. It was in a cul-de-sac that ended at a field surrounding the airport. I drove by twice, mainly because I didn't realize the road dead-ended and I couldn't do the block.

I had hoped to be able to park somewhere nondescript and observe, but the best I could do was go back before the corner and pull over. There was little traffic here; the only people who traveled these roads had a destination in mind. It made me conspicuous. I pulled out a map to make it look like I was a lost soul who was trying to figure out where I'd taken a wrong turn.

I could only see an oblique view of the body shop, no way to watch who was there or who was coming and going.

"Can I help you?" caught me unawares.

I stared at the frumpy woman at my car window.

I rolled it down.

"I seem to be lost," I said.

"Figured. No one comes this way 'less they work here or missed the airport turn. Where you tryin' to go?"

A quick look at the map and I picked a random street several blocks away.

"Why you going there?" she asked.

I had found the neighborhood busybody. Good if I wanted info, not good if I wanted to be discreet.

"Work for a property firm. Looking at some possible investment properties out here," I lied.

She laughed. Coffee and tobacco stained teeth on full display.

"What's funny?" I asked.

"Out here, in this dirty dog hind leg of a place? Only investment here is where to dump bodies or brew meth."

"Looks like some thriving business out here. Close to the airport."

"Yeah, right. Close means the planes roaring overhead day and night. What's your real reason for coming out here? Looking for drugs?"

"No, no, I'm really out here to scope out land. You've read about the new airport expansion, right?"

She narrowed her eyes. The airport was, indeed supposed to expand.

"So now is the time to buy. You know of anything for sale around here?" I wasn't so much pumping her for information as trying to ask her the questions so she'd stop asking me questions, forcing me into even more elaborate lies.

"I got a bridge I can sell you," she said with more display of the browning teeth. But she added, "Right price, anyone around here would sell."

"You own any of these businesses?"

"Naw." She shook her head. "I manage that apartment over there." She pointed to a building that had looked cheap when it was new, two stories, probably one or two small bedrooms, everything bottom of the line. No one was going to pay high rent to live in the shadow of planes.

To make the point one was overhead, the throb of the engines drowning out her words.

"I'm sorry, what did you say?"

"Said it ain't such a bad place to live. Too unruly, I get to throw 'em out. No drugs, not in the place I run. Not even the sniff of pot."

"But you thought I was here for drugs?"

"Not at my place," she said. "But I can't control what else goes on 'round here."

"Like what?" I didn't really care. I wanted to talk long enough to not appear to be blowing her off. Maybe I could work it around to the body shop, but it was a long block away from her apartment fiefdom.

"Down there." She pointed in a vague direction.

I used her vagueness. "Like that car place?"

"Oh, yeah, them, they're the worst. All them places on that block."

"Really? How?" I asked, keeping my voice the same tone, not wanting to show more interest than in any of the rest of them.

"Big black trucks in and out all hours of the night. Once the planes stop, you can hear anything. They think no one is watching, but I am. Parties too often. Who would party in a body shop?"

"How do you know it's drugs?" I asked, just enough skepticism in my voice to goad her into elaborating.

"What else could it be?"

So much for elaboration.

"Sex. Close to an airport. Easy to get that kind of stuff in. Maybe that's what the parties are for."

"Out here? No one's coming for sex out here. Nothing sexy about this place. Has to be drugs."

"Maybe they need the money to do deals for after-hours body work."

"Naw. The noise changes. In the day, you hear their machines and stuff. At night, none of that. Just big trucks, a few cars. In for a few minutes, then they leave. Almost every night."

"What about the parties? How often are they? You smell any weed from them?"

"Not so often, maybe every week or so. Weird nights like a Tuesday sometimes. Goes to all hours. Loud music, until we called the cops on them. Then they quieted down right good."

"What kind of people go to them?"

She looked at me as if wondering why I was asking such questions.

"I mean, why would anyone come out here?"

"My point exactly. Don't know who goes. Same type black trucks, 'cept they all come 'round the same time instead of in and out through the night."

"Any kite flyers hanging around?"

"There? Naw. Some of these other blocks, you might find 'em. Not in my place. We throw 'em out at the first sign."

"If no one is high, how do you know it's drugs?"

"Late one night, saw a cop car drive in. Left a few minutes later and parked right under my window. Watched him open an envelope and count money. Gotta be drugs."

"Well, you might be right. But I bet things will change with the new airport expansion."

"You gonna be buying stuff 'round here?"

I hedged. "Possible. Not my call. I just do the footwork."

"You let me know if you're gonna buy my place." She handed me a worn, cheap business card. "Kinda gettin' old to find a new place."

I took the card. My lies gave me no choice. "I will let you know if I know anything."

At least that wasn't a lie. I would tell her. But I wouldn't know anything.

I drove away. In the rearview mirror, I could see her watching me. I kept driving, leaving the neighborhood. I'd found few answers and plenty of other questions. If she was right, and they were dealing drugs out of Fast Eddie's party place, that might add a whole long list of suspects.

I cruised around the neighborhood a bit, staying safely away from where the neighborhood watch might see me. Mostly to get a lay of the land, what streets dead-ended and which were an escape. If I wanted more answers I'd have to come back here. If I needed to get out fast, I'd need to know where the exits were.

After that, and getting tired of the constant roar of airplanes, I headed back to civilization.

But stopped on the way. First for a late lunch of mostly grease and fat at a Burger Thing. The lizard brain that lusted after calories to survive a famine was happy. The rest of me would pay for it later, but I was hungry and it was convenient.

From there I drove to the address of the chemistry teacher. It was around the time school would let out. I was hoping I could catch her when she got home. Of course, if she decided to run errands or go to the gym, I was shit out of luck. I'd give her until I needed a bathroom break, including enough time to safely get to the bathroom. Knowing my bladder, I calculated that to be about half an hour.

She also lived in an apartment building, still soulless in my opinion, but much nicer than that one by the airport. Cookie cutter, but not the basic box shape of the other, with balconies tastefully shielded from too much contact with your neighbors, large enough for a grill and a few chairs. I parked in one of the spots marked for visitors, where I could see her unit.

Fifteen minutes later, a used Prius pulled into the parking spot reserved for it.

I watched her get out. She opened the back and dug for some bags.

I got out and approached her.

"Ms. Gardner?"

She whirled around at me—surprise, yes, but more than that. Maybe she was the nervous type. Or maybe she had something to be afraid of.

I flashed my license at her. "I just need to ask you a few questions."

"Let me see that," she said, still guarded.

I handed it to her. She had a right to see it. Her reaction was curious. One of the things that works for me in this business is that I'm a woman; people don't usually feel threatened. We were in clear view of anyone in about ten different apartments and yelling distance of about fifty.

After reading my license at least twice, she said, "Who are you and what do you want?"

Not the question I'd expected after she'd just scrutinized a document with my name and occupation on it. Maybe Eddie had gotten her involved in meth making and she had reasons to be nervous. Or his murder had scared her.

I didn't want to step on to any land mines, so I quelled my sarcastic impulse to ask if she'd like to read my license again.

I did reach and take it back from her, though. They're a pain to get and a pain to replace.

"My name is Michele Knight and I'm a licensed private investigator here in Louisiana. I've been hired to look into—"

"I don't know what you want, but I know nothing about it. Please leave me alone."

"If you don't know what I want, how do you know you don't know anything about it?" I asked. Pointing out her contradiction took her aback. But not enough to make her talk.

"It doesn't matter. I'm not talking to you."

"What are you so afraid of?"

She stared at me. Watery gray eyes behind thick glasses. Her mouth open, emphasizing her weak chin. No, not a pretty woman, not the kind men would notice. I was hoping there was some other spark in her, a fierce intelligence, a searching curiosity, but at the moment, she was so closed down, I could see nothing save her outward appearance. Wearing a pink dress that tried to look stylish but didn't hang right on her gawky frame, medium height, taken down an inch or so by a hunched back and sloping shoulders. Lank brown hair, growing long past the last haircut. A nose slightly too big for her face, as if emphasizing the narrow, receding chin.

She turned her back to me, again digging in her car for her school supplies.

"I'm not afraid of anything," she mumbled.

"Except having a conversation with me," I pointed out. "I'm not the police, I can't arrest you."

"I knew that."

Okay, wrong guess. She wasn't doing anything illegal. Or illegal enough that being put in jail was her primary concern.

"You worried that whoever killed Eddie might come for you?"

She turned, almost dropping her canvas bag of books save the white-knuckled grip she had on it. "How do you know about that?"

"That he was killed? It's been on the news."

"No, not that. Why do you think he has anything to do with me?"

I considered saying, *because of your reaction*. But that was too close to blaming the victim.

"I've been hired to investigate some of his activities. Your name came up."

"Came up? How?"

"Anything you say to me will be confidential." *Unless you confess to murdering him.* "As I won't bring up your name or identity to anyone, I have to do the same for the other people I talk to."

"I can't imagine how my name came up. I don't know him."

"Look, you can answer my questions truthfully, or you can keep lying and make me suspicious. This is a murder investigation. Of course you knew him. You dated him until you discovered what a lout he truly was."

"You can't know that," she gasped.

"I'm not the bad guy," I said. "I'm not here to hurt you. I can even help you, if you let me. If I can find out, others can find out. You're safer talking to me."

"I'm not safe talking to anyone."

"You're not safe being silent, either," I pointed out.

She started to cry.

I reached into her car, took the other bag there, and said, "Let's go inside and talk."

She merely nodded and led the way to her door, still saying

nothing as she found her keys and opened it. The inside echoed the outside. Maybe it came furnished, but everything matched in a bland, designer way, as if bought in a set from a store that aimed for the middle of the middle class, beige and cream, a splash of a trendy red as the latest accent color.

She dropped her bag amidst all this beige-ness, finally speaking only to excuse herself to go to the bathroom.

I looked around the room: open concept with the living area flowing into the kitchen. Also, nicely done, the requisite granite countertops, a neutral color with stainless steel appliances. Other than a few chemistry books on the built-in bookshelves, cream colored and only capable of holding a paltry number of books, more to display pictures or knickknacks, the inside matched the outside—it could have been any place, with no clear view of the person who actually lived here.

She returned, her nose pink from blowing.

"How did you find out?" she demanded.

"I asked questions. I got answers. No one named your name, but enough bits and pieces fell together to lead me to you." That was as much as I was going to answer. "How did you meet Eddie?"

She flopped down on the couch. I copied her, sitting just across on the perfectly matched love seat.

Something in her changed; no, not a spark, but giving up. As if this was a battle and she had lost. The words tumbled out. She'd been convinced to go out with some of her old high school friends, a reunion of sorts. But it turned out they wanted to go to a singles bar; if they got lucky, the reunion was history. Two of her friends had peeled off, leaving her stuck with the other "ugly" woman, too heavy to be considered attractive. At least in the shallow world of straight bars. They'd finished their drinks. "More than I'm used to," she explained, when Eddie approached them. He flirted with them both, bought another round—or two—of drinks. Offered to walk them to their cars. Got serious in his flirting in the parking lot. Enid—yes, she went by that. I would have ditched it for her middle name of Emily—"won" because she didn't have a roommate. Not that anything happened then, she assured me. He called the next day, and they met for dinner and a movie. He told her he really liked smart women, was bored with the bimbos. (Okay, warning sign, if he calls another woman a bimbo, he's not very likely to be an enlightened man who actually likes women.) He came home with her that night and they dated for about six weeks.

"Why'd you break up with him?" I'd heard Brandon's more than secondhand version; I wanted to hear hers.

She started crying again.

"I found one of those pictures on his phone."

"What kind of pictures?" Again, I wanted to see what she'd say.

"You know, of another woman."

"Maybe his sister?"

"No," she said, wiping her face with her sleeve. "It was a girly shot."

"A naked woman?"

She nodded, then hurried to explain. "I thought we were dating seriously, that he shouldn't be looking at other women. Not like that. I asked him to get rid of them."

"Them? He had more than just one?"

"Yes, but I didn't know that then. I told him if he wanted to keep seeing me, he needed to get rid of them…it."

Yeah, that was her reaction to knowing he had titty shots of too-young girls. Maybe she thought she could reform him.

"He laughed at me. And…told me I was the ugliest girl he'd ever…slept with."

Oh, Eddie, such a white knight. She had clearly amended his "ever fucked" to the more polite "slept with."

"I don't get it," she said. "He was over here almost every night, he really liked having sex with me. Said I had a great body."

I kept my eyes focused on her face. This was not the time to assess her body. Maybe she did. Or maybe it was another one of his lies.

"If that doesn't keep a man satisfied, what the hell does?" She let out another sob. "Two or three times a night. I did everything he asked. Oral sex riding in his car. We even tried anal once, but it hurt. We stopped right after he came."

No, I did not want to know this. But I let her keep talking. She was as close as I'd gotten to anyone who knew Eddie.

"Why would he do that to me?" she wailed.

I considered pointing out it was because she let him, both the painful sex and what she really meant, pretending to like her to get sex. It almost never works.

"So, he broke up with you?" I asked, handing her a tissue from a tastefully beige box next to the couch.

"He said he needed those pictures to get horny enough to have sex with me. But that's not true, he came here, I'd cook dinner, then we'd have sex. He wasn't looking at those pictures the whole time."

"When did you realize he had more than just one?"

Another sob. "He showed them to me. Made me look at them. Said we could do porn together, but he wasn't giving them up."

"How many did he show you?"

And another sob. "I don't know, some, a few. He just flashed them at me."

"When did you see the one of Tiffany?"

She rocked back in the couch. "I never saw her."

Too quick a denial. If she truly hadn't seen a picture from one of the students at her school—with the suicide, she had to know who Tiffany was—she would have been shocked or upset or disbelieving. Not this quick dismissal.

"Did you kill him?" Even if she did, she'd deny it, but I wanted to see her reaction.

Another wail, "No! I loved him! I didn't kill him. The last thing I wanted was him to be dead!"

"Even after he treated you that way? All the other women he'd been interested in?" I asked.

"We could have worked it out. I know he was better than that. Just not educated enough and he hung out with the wrong people. They led him astray. Under it all, he was a nice guy!"

Oh, wow, she was living in a pink-colored fantasy world. This would probably take years of therapy to get over. Since I didn't have years, I just said, "You might be right. Who do you think could have killed him?"

"Why do you want to know?"

"You loved Eddie, you can't want his killer to go free. If you talk to me, I can help. I can work with the police, keep you out of it. Tell me what you know."

"I know if I talk, they'll kill me. I hate that they killed him, but I don't want to die."

Ah, clarity. She loved him, but not enough to do anything about his killer.

"Why would they come after you?"

That brought another bout of crying and me handing her a few more tissues.

Finally, she said, "It's the drugs."

"What drugs?"

"I knew we could work it out, that we were meant to be together. He just needed to understand how much I loved him."

"What happened?" I needed to keep her talking, despite her crying.

"I went to see him. He didn't like me to come to his place; it's not as nice as mine."

"Where did he live?" Certainly the police had tossed his apartment, but I could talk to some of the neighbors, especially the ones who wouldn't talk to the police.

"A place out by the airport." She didn't know the address, but described it. No, not the "no drugs" one near the body shop, but one probably just like it a few blocks away.

"So you went to his place?"

"Yes, just to talk to him. I knocked and he called to come on in, the door was open, so I did. But I guess he wasn't expecting me. He started yelling, told me I had to leave, he was meeting a business partner and it wasn't a good time. I could tell he wanted to talk to me, but it needed to be a different time."

"How did you know that?"

"He told me. Said I was right, we needed to talk. We could work things out, but we could do it later."

"How did drugs get involved?"

"I saw something on his table that looked like white powder all wrapped up in plastic wrap. Like those ones you see on the news when they did a drug bust. I told him if he needed money, I could help. But he said, no, it wasn't what it looked like and he'd explain later."

"So what happened next?"

"He walked me out. Just as we got down the stairs, a man showed up. I guess the one he was expecting. He was so gallant, told him we met at the door and I hadn't even been inside."

Must keep face neutral. Oh, yeah, gallant. Saving his ass by claiming he hadn't been sloppy enough to let his latest sex toy walk into a drug deal. That was for him, not for you.

"He even walked me to my car, making his friend wait."

"Did you get a name of the friend?"

"No, Eddie was in too much of a hurry to introduce us. Oh, but he did call him Steve. I think. Something like that."

"What did he look like?" She was no longer questioning my questions. While it worked for me, that wasn't a good sign. It meant she wasn't looking where she was going. Yeah, I was safe, but she had no way to really know that.

"Oh, I don't know. I was so focused on Eddie. So happy that I was right and he wanted to see me again."

"Was he taller than you?" After asking about twenty questions—taller, shorter, heavy or not, the best I could get out of her was that "Steve," if that was his name, was taller than most girls, but not so tall for a guy, sandy or light brown or dark blond hair, no idea of eye color, not too heavy, but a beer gut, wearing black jeans and a black T-shirt. Oh, he didn't smell nice, like he was a day or two beyond needing a shower. Eddie always smelled nice. He showered regularly. Thanks, I really wanted to know that.

Then she started to cry again. More tissues. Close to emptying the box.

That was the last time she saw Eddie.

Once she stopped crying—a good five minutes' worth; yes, I looked at my watch while she was blowing her nose—I asked, "Have you talked to the police about this?"

"No! I'm not stupid. If I talk to them, then whoever killed Eddie will have a reason to kill me. As long as I'm silent and leave them alone, I'm safe."

I went back and forth with her. As long as there was a risk she could talk, they had a reason to kill her. If she talked to the police, she was actually safer. Killing her would only add another murder charge.

She was adamant that her safety was in her silence. That choice left her living her beige life, no change in routine, not having to risk being pried from her rose-colored illusion that Eddie had loved her.

I did try my best to convince her there was no safety in her inaction, but she claimed Eddie wouldn't have told them who she was, so the only way they could know was if she went to the police.

I left a card; maybe she would change her mind, although I held little hope. She wanted to keep the Eddie who had loved her. Going to the police would force her to see the real Eddie, and that would blow her romantic fantasy to tiny pieces.

Although I had gotten more unwanted info on Eddie's sex life—and bathing habits—I had found he lived close to the body shop where he partied, that someone possibly named Steve was involved both at the body shop and in Eddie's drug deals. And Eddie had let his nice girl ex see enough to know he was doing drug deals. I had no faith he had gallantly protected Enid, refusing to give out her name, no matter what. If they had asked—and they had ways of asking that made it hard to refuse—he had answered.

The only argument in her favor was that she was still alive. If they really wanted to close loose ends, she would be dead by now.

I headed home, breathing a sigh of relief when crossing the Orleans Parish line.

But that was the only relief available. I could wash my hands of Enid Gardner; she was an adult, she got to make her choices. But she'd made a bargain with the devil of her ego, and it wasn't a good one.

The police should have stumbled over her by now. It wasn't a good sign they hadn't. Either they were still in the dark—people don't always talk to the police as forthcomingly as they should—or the cops felt they had their murderer.

Inferences, he said, she said, but no real evidence, only a list of people who might have killed Eddie that didn't include me. Possible suspects? His drug buddies? Sure, but nothing other than men who dealt drugs were usually not upstanding citizens. A scorned girlfriend? Yeah, on paper she might look good, but I doubted she'd killed him, still too wrapped up in her fantasy. Slam her into reality and then she could do it. But that hadn't happened yet. Unless she'd had one brief moment of clarity, long enough to pull the trigger before slipping back into her dream world—one that didn't include her firing a gun.

Eddie was a messy man, and he'd left a mess behind him.

I really wanted to just hand this all over to the police. But again, I had no real evidence. *I talked to people, this is what they said.* Yeah, right, that's going to be convincing. Even if I was just a private citizen, they would be polite not to roll their eyes. As a suspect, no way. It would all come off as self-interest.

Which it was. But if there was such a thing, it was honest self-interest. I had not killed Eddie, but at the moment, I was the only one who knew that for sure.

Well, me and his real killer.

The next step—and one I did not want to take—was to stake out the body shop/drug dealing den. If I could get a few pictures of something shady enough to interest the police—more than the gossip of the local self-appointed neighborhood watch person or the ex-girlfriend living in la-la land—maybe I could get them to look more closely into Eddie's unsavory friends.

I took the slower, but less trafficked, side roads. One more left-hand turn from the right lane might be enough to send me over the edge.

I went home, not bothering going back to the office. Probably all that waited for me there was another message from Douglas Townson demanding I solve a hundred-year-old murder case.

I'd be doing well to make the current one unsolvable.

Chapter Twenty-eight

Admittedly, this was a shot in the dark.

Literally in the dark.

I'd come home, had some fruit to make up for the grease-and-more-grease lunch, then lay down to take a nap, although it was more tossing and turning than any real sleep.

Now the clock on my dashboard read 1:48 a.m.

I don't stake out criminals, well, not real criminals. I mostly look for missing people, and sometimes the reason they're missing isn't so savory: missed child support payments, running away from the boredom of two kids and a picket fence for a new life with a Vegas showgirl, that sort of stuff. Some want to be found, others don't.

But not drug lords or murderers. That's for the cops, the FBI, the ones with ten cars of backup.

Yet here I was, gliding past the airport, on my way to see what I could see at Steve's auto place. I had no idea if it was his or not. I'd done a brief internet search but got little more than the name—ACD Auto, guess ABC was already taken—the address and hours. No owner listed or even employees. I could find no internet ads, nothing on social media, nothing promotional. Maybe they had enough business. Or maybe they didn't need a lot of auto body work. Or maybe they just weren't up on the tech stuff.

There was little traffic at this hour, making it a quick trip of about twenty minutes from my house. I hoped for as quick a trip back.

Much as I would have preferred to stay in my car—all the better for quick getaways—a strange car in this area would cause suspicion. I was going to have to walk in. Yeah, that would be suspicious, too, but my hope was to not be seen; much harder to do with a car.

I had planned my route from my earlier driving around the area. This little tab of land was hemmed in by the airport, the interstate, and several drainage canals. A number of the streets were dead ends.

Still no traffic as I turned off Veterans Highway. It was cloudy, a chance of rain. The temperature wasn't hot yet, not the kind of hot we get. We were still in the perfect part of spring, but summer was approaching and even now, at this time of night, I hardly needed the light jacket I was wearing.

I parked a few blocks away, near a much busier auto place, one that had multiple cars around, spilling onto the street. From there I could walk. I was in black jeans, a black T-shirt, a dark navy jacket—yes, fashion faux pas, but the only other black jacket I had was a leather one, and I didn't want it messed up. Plus a small black messenger bag with my cameras, night goggles, and a recorder. I wasn't expecting to get much audio, but you never know.

I sat in my car for a few minutes, listening and watching. If there were dogs or guards, better to find out before I started walking. Again, it was a quiet, still night, made even quieter by the silence from the airport, the dead-of-night lull between the taking off and landing of planes.

I really wanted to turn back around and go to bed. There were too many drainage canals around here, perfect for dumping dead bodies.

But I got out of my car, carefully closing the door so it made no sound. I didn't lock it, both to avoid the blinking of lights and because if I needed to get away in a hurry, that second might make a difference. Plus there was nothing to steal.

You'll probably spend half an hour watching an empty building, I told myself.

The air was moist, our usual humidity and the closeness of the canals, the ground still wet from recent rains. I walked on the side of the road, keeping my footfalls as quiet as possible. I hoped to pass as a service worker, home from a late shift, walking from the bus stop. Although in about half a block, there would be no homes to go to.

My plan was to approach from the back, cutting along the drainage canal to the dead end.

As far as I could tell, no one else was about. The few sounds were distant, from the interstate, or sounds that belonged in the night, an insect buzz, the croak of frogs.

The shuffle of my footsteps.

I stopped to make sure it was only mine.

No, no sound. Save for the beating of my heart.

I started walking again, alert for any noise, any shadow not fixed in place.

It was a long two blocks to the canal. Less light here, but the bank had been mowed recently. I carefully made my way through the grass, looking out for both men and snakes.

But the most threatening thing was a small pile of garbage, plastic bottles, beer cans.

I finally made the corner near the auto shop.

Again, I stopped.

The night noises had changed. There was the faint pulse of a music beat. I edged closer to the corner. It could be a parked car, a couple seeking a secluded place.

There were no homes or apartments back in this area, making my excuse of being someone heading home implausible. My best defense was to remain hidden in the shadows.

Joanne still had my gun, otherwise it would have been part of my equipment. Not that I planned to need it—I never planned on needing it, I was in the wrong business if I did—but for some people, it's the only argument they understand. Even so, I missed the weight under my arm.

I edged closer to the corner. Over the music a voice, male, I couldn't make out the words, but it sounded like a shouted joke, as it was followed by laughter and other shouts. All the voices were male.

I slunk behind the nearest building. Only then did I risk peering around the corner. Several trucks, most of them dark except one that looked to be red, were parked outside ACD Auto. A few faint glimmers of light showed from around windows covered with what appeared to be taped-up garbage bags. Maybe it was to keep Ms. Noisy Neighbor from calling the cops on them again. Or maybe they really didn't want anyone looking in.

After listening for a few minutes, I risked sliding around the corner, keeping close to the building. It was next to ACD Auto. Maybe I could find an uncovered window between the two buildings.

As I got closer, the music and the voices got louder. They weren't noisy enough to hear them all down the block, that might attract too much attention, but at this distance, enough for me to know it was a party. This was a weeknight, not the typical time or place for some guys hanging out after work.

This argued for the partygoers being the kind of men who didn't need to be up and on the job by nine. They could be, as I was pretending to be, workers for the partiers, waiters, bartenders, and this was their after-work hour. But this hardly seemed like the kind of place they'd pick.

My guess was that Brandon had told the truth. Eddie, and now his friends, were giving the kind of get-together that needed a lot of privacy. Porn, drugs, a wild time they wanted to keep hidden.

And they had done a good job of it. Other than the soft sounds of music and voices, and a few vehicles around, there was little sign of what was going on here. Anyone driving by with windows closed and a radio going would miss it.

The two buildings had a high chain link gate between them. And the windows down that side showed only thin slashes of light. Also covered. Maybe they thought if no light showed, then no one would notice the party going on. But that struck me as a bit much. This was a dead-end road. The only people coming here would be the ones for ACD or the now-closed building beside it.

This was frustrating. I knew something was going on, but there seemed little way to know exactly what. I was leery of creeping closer and attempting to peer through the small slivers of light. If I could see in, they could see out. Not likely they'd be looking, but I'd prefer not to take that chance.

Maybe it was time to go back to my car and think this through again.

Then I heard the sound of a motor.

Coming this way.

I hid back into the shadows, slowly moving away until I was past the chain link gate, by the other building. Their trash cans were at the far end, and I didn't want to risk moving fast enough to get to them. Movement catches the eye.

I pressed into a doorway, hoping it could help block me.

The glow of headlights appeared at the corner, then turned this way, flooding the street. As best I could, I pulled my jacket up around my face. If they were looking, they could see me.

The truck roared to a stop in front of ACD, but the engine kept running. And the lights stayed on.

I barely allowed myself to breathe.

The body shop door opened. A wave of sound, thumping music and voices followed it. A brief crack of light, then the door was quickly closed, the sound and brightness gone. Again, it was just the beams from the truck throwing harsh shadows down the street.

Do not look this way, please do not look this way, I silently pleaded.

Against the glare of the beams I could make out little. Someone had come out, he—I was guessing, it was only a bare outline against the bright lights—was near the driver's window talking. I strained to hear him.

"You're late."

The driver replied, but I couldn't hear it.

"Fuck you, that's not a good excuse." The tone was joking, but the words still carried their meaning.

Again, a reply from the driver I couldn't make out.

"Don't let it happen again," the other man said. "Did you get rid of it?"

A muffled reply.

"In the canal? That's too close."

Something that sounded cajoling.

"Yeah, well, we'll just have to hope they won't look."

Again a reassuring murmur, a mumbled, "Don't worry."

The building door opened again. Two more people came out. One appeared drunk, the second one had a hand on his arm, seemingly guiding him.

No, wait, her. For a brief moment, she was not hidden by her companion, and the outline revealed breasts. And not the kind of figure that could possibly be man boobs. But that was all, she and her companion got in the truck.

"Keep the merchandise safe," the outside man said to the truck driver.

At best she was a working girl, here to make some money, and they were treating her the way men had always treated sex workers, like a commodity.

Or maybe the coercion for sex hadn't stopped with Eddie.

I had no time to think about that, as the truck engine revved and it started coming my way.

Was that another person coming out the building door? Short? With a reflection from glasses?

I couldn't stay where I was. The truck clearly intended to turn around in the wide part of the road right beyond me.

That left only one option.

Run.

Like hell.

I tore out of the door, sprinting for the canal. I heard a shouted, "What the fuck?" behind me and the roar of the truck.

No way my feet could outrun an engine.

The light flooded the street, getting closer.

And closer. I was clearly outlined in them.

My one advantage was that I was off and running before they even knew I was there.

If they reacted quickly they would catch me.

If they were drunk and slow—

I leapt over the curb onto the grass verge of the canal, tearing away as fast as I could. The light dimmed as I moved out of it, taking the turn to run along the canal. But I had to put a lot more distance between me and them to be safe. Like about twenty miles.

I had to trust there were no unseen holes or roots in this dim grass. I couldn't risk slowing down.

"Hey, you, there, stop!" someone yelled from the truck.

I kept running.

The lights turned toward me. They were driving up the grass bank.

For a moment they got brighter.

Then the truck stopped. They weren't going to risk it. Maybe there was enough space for it to get by, but the sloping bank, a few trees, and the soggy ground make it difficult.

It squealed back in reverse, then roared away in the other direction.

They weren't giving up but would try to catch me at the next road that ran into the canal.

I could try doubling back in the hope they wouldn't think I'd go back the way I'd come, but there was little back here and I could too easily find myself backed against the fence ringing the airport. I could probably climb it, but risk being caught by airport security—and I had to assume I would be caught; no modern airport was without twenty-four-hour security these days. Although that might be preferable to floating facedown in a drainage ditch. They might shoot first and ask questions later, and even if the latter, it would be a lot of questions for which I had few good answers and a lot of time in faded green interview rooms, if not a cell. Plus, they'd find my name as a suspect in a murder, and that would really make it a bad time.

Safely through the grass, I was almost at the next dead-end road. I could hear the truck coming around the corner.

Keep running, you don't have any other choice.

I hate jogging, so I'm not a treadmill person at the gym. Yeah, I'm in shape for a woman my age, but not in sprinting shape.

Maybe the adrenaline would make up for that.

I kept running, cutting across the next road, just as the headlights swung around the corner.

Maybe if I was lucky, I'd just made it out of range.

But the truck was coming this way.

I was starting to gasp for breath. I cut off from the open grass next to the canal and into the weeds and bushes. They could too easily see me out in the open.

But I had to slow down to clamber through them.

Glancing back, I could see the lights coming closer, flooding the road.

I wasn't far enough away.

I dived beneath a patch of scruffy brush, glad for our year-round growing season. Even in this part of spring, everything was a leafy green. With what I hoped were enough leaves to hide me.

The truck slowed at the end of the road. I didn't dare look but could tell from the engine noise and the illumination from the headlights it was turning to throw the beams first down the canal from the way I'd come…

Then moving to light where I was now hiding.

There is a reason we wear black clothes to do things like this. I kept my jacket up, covering my face to my eyes, mussing my hair down my forehead. Maybe as I got more gray in it, I'd have to consider dying it to make sure the lighter color wouldn't give me away in situations like this.

The beam roved over the grass in front of me, tires on gravel and the light shifted, to the bushes hiding me. Stayed there.

I didn't dare breath for fear it would move a telltale leaf.

"Where the fuck is he?" mumbled from the truck. A male voice.

No one answered.

One chit in my favor; they thought I was a man. Probably only got a glimpse of a figure in black. I'm tall, shaggy hair, but it can turn into a curly nest if I don't keep it a reasonable length. So short enough to be boy length.

"Gotta be hidden in the bushes," the voice said. "Go look."

Shit.

A mumbled reply.

The truck voice again, "There are no snakes. Maybe only small ones. Don't be a pussy."

I tensed my legs. If the truck door opened, running was my only option.

"I can't drive on the fuckin' grass, there are holes."

Another reply from within.

"Fuck it, man. You got an excuse for everything. I'm not scared of no snake."

The driver's door opened and he got out.

I held still.

He took a few steps in my direction.

"See, no snakes," he shouted back to his companions. He was still on the grass.

As quietly as I could, I felt the ground. A pebble, a stone, some cut glass, a clump of dirt.

He took another step.

Outlined in the light, I could only see that he was medium height, medium build, hair short, no big muscles or large stomach.

Another step.

I tossed the clump of dirt, the darkest and heaviest thing I'd found toward the canal.

It made a small rustle in the bushes.

He stopped.

I shook the pebble and stone together. Not sounds a hiding human would make, not footsteps or breathing, what he expected to hear. Maybe the rattle of a snake.

He took another step.

I shook them again, this time more agitated. Then let out a short hiss of air.

"What the fuck." He stopped.

Took a step back.

Pulled out a gun.

He-man, beat up on a little bitty snake with a gun.

A car horn off in the distance.

He cocked an ear to it. Put the gun away, seemed to realize a shot would be heard.

Ms. Snake lives to hiss another day.

Took another step back, then turned and walked back to the truck.

Slowly back to the truck.

My body was aching from the hunched crouch I was in. I didn't dare move until they were well gone.

He was in no hurry, lingering outside, listening. Playing the same waiting game I was.

He knew the figure he'd seen running couldn't be far away.

At this time of night, this was a quiet, desolate place. Footsteps, a car motor, would be heard.

We waited.

My leg started to cramp.

I pressed my thumb into the muscle.

He got back in the truck, but the light remained on the bushes I was hiding behind.

Another minute.

I pressed harder with my thumb. I couldn't move the leg without risking being seen.

From the truck, "Quiet, I'm listenin'."

If he were smart, he'd pretend to drive away, pull behind a building, and listen from there. Let me think they'd given up.

Another chit in my favor. He wasn't that smart.

I let out another small hiss of breath. This one of pain.

Then the driver's door slammed and the engine whined into reverse. The lights arced away.

I listened as it slowly drove off. I couldn't risk raising my head enough to see, my only visual cue the fading of the light until it was only the dark of the night.

Even in the darkness, I still counted to sixty, as slowly as my cramping leg would let me. Listening to the motor of the truck. They were leaving but at a crawl, still searching.

I slowly, very slowly raised my head.

I couldn't see the truck.

If they were smart they would have let one of them out, backtracking quietly on foot while the truck moved on.

I had to hope they weren't that smart.

Carefully, I eased my leg to another position.

It did little to ease the cramp, only made it start to cramp in another place.

The truck had stopped. I couldn't see it, couldn't hear it. Had they stopped and given up? Or just waiting?

Cat and mouse, with me very much the mouse.

I couldn't stay here. The bushes were just thick enough to shield me from one side. If/when they came around to the street on the other side, I'd have to go to the far side of the bushes to hope to be hidden.

I was hemmed in by the fence around the airport and the flood wall on the canal, leaving me only two directions to run.

Still no sound of the truck. Maybe they'd given up and gone back to the party.

Or maybe they were doing what I was doing, playing the waiting game.

A lot of the businesses out here were places like scrap yards or body shops, lots of machinery littered around. Most of them had fences. I could probably get over them, but could I get over them without being seen? Plus, they might have security, from alarms to dogs. If I picked the wrong one, a screaming alarm would be a dead giveaway.

I risked changing positions, still unsure of what to do.

Truck engine. It was on the move again.

Lights coming down the street behind me.

They were doing what I was afraid they would do, circle the block, check out the far street.

I tried to hide in the bush, to keep protection on both sides, but it wasn't thick enough.

Damn. And double damn. They were smarter than I'd hoped for. I could see the light of a cell phone on the near block. They'd left Mr. Scared of Snakes behind.

However, he was stupid enough to be on his cell phone, not realizing what a bright beacon its screen was.

At least I could see where he was.

Dark clothes. Slow movement. I'd have to count on them.

He didn't have the strong beams of the truck to stab between the leaves. I'd have to count on him being too afraid of snakes to get close. If I could stay black against a black bush, he might not see me.

I could clearly hear the truck coming down the other road now, lights brighter, engine louder. I edged around the bush, keeping it between me and the strong beams of the truck.

If Mr. Scared of Snakes had a decent flashlight, he would see me.

He was close enough I could see he was texting.

The truck swung around, pointing its lights at me. At the bushes in front of me.

Some of the light bled through, casting stripes of light and shadow around me.

Mr. SoS kept texting.

And he kept walking my way.

I tried to crabwalk to a thicker part of the bushes, away from the shafts of light.

"Hey, you see anything?" This from the texter. He was keeping his voice down, a quiet whisper, but close enough I could hear it. It wasn't Mr. Scared of Snakes, but the other voice, the one I'd heard. The one smart enough to go around to both sides.

If he looked up from his phone—and I had to assume he was smart enough to do so—he could very easily see me.

I did not move. As shallow a breath as I could take, not blinking, jacket pulled up to just under my eyes.

I kept watching him. I had to see when he saw me.

I also had to assume these were the guys who had killed Eddie and they would kill me if they needed to.

Closer. He whispered into his phone, "Keep looking."

I could still track his every step by the cell phone glow.

Smart, but not smart enough to realize how far that small screen can carry. He solved one problem—how to communicate—but hadn't thought through how much it would give away his position.

Or maybe he had and, with his gun, he wasn't worried about it. He was the hunter.

Ah, but why whisper as if not to be heard? The slow, stealthy tread?

Nice and clever, but all this thinking was doing little to get me out of this situation.

Okay, he didn't want me to know he was here but wasn't smart enough to remember how annoyed he was at the movies when the person three rows down kept checking his cell phone screen, that bright point in the dark theater.

He probably also didn't realize how much that bright screen was ruining his night vision. As close as he was now, less than ten feet, he should have been able to make out my dark outline against the black bushes. But he was still scanning, looking left and right. Then back to the cell phone.

That mistake, that one mistake, gave me the opening I needed.

I lunged at him, aiming a shoulder at his midsection, taking him by surprise. I was silent, no yelling, a moving shadow.

He saw me just as he felt me, a solid slam into him.

Then one hand striking a blow to his solar plexus, the other to his nose. I don't know how well I connected, but it was enough to hear a huffing grunt of pain.

I deliberately knocked the cell phone from his hand. Then, in the moment of surprise, felt quickly for the gun.

Idiot, he had it tucked into the front of his waistband, the perfect place to blow off his balls. I grabbed, thought for a second of keeping it, then did the sensible thing, throwing it as far as I could into the bushes. It was likely to be a hot gun, and the less time I had it in my hands—my still-gloved hands—the better.

A final kick to the back of his knee to take him to the ground, then I ran away as fast as I could, giving the cell phone an extra kick as I passed it.

I heard another gasping groan—I had at least hit him hard enough in the solar plexus to keep him down, and a tinny voice from the phone, "Hey, man, what's going on?"

Keep running.

My feet pounding on the pavement, my breath starting to sound ragged in my ears.

Behind me, a shout. He had gotten his wind back. He was smart enough to call the truck to cut me off. I had to assume that's what they'd do.

This was a long block and it turned into a T. Damn.

Two directions to go. One would lead me to the airport fence, the other in the direction of my car. Fewer options than I liked.

At the corner, a shape loomed off the side of the road. A big panel truck.

I ducked behind it, then crawled under, hunched up against the tire.

A glow of headlights.

Bright.

Brighter.

Brighter.

Passing me.

Turning down the road I'd just run on, to meet up with his friend.

I took a hasty glance from behind my tire, the lights facing away from me. Balancing quiet and haste, I hunched down and trotted along the road, trying to keep my footfalls light, finding my next hiding place behind another truck.

I could hear the strident, angry voices. "At least two of them," came through loud and clear.

Naw, dude, just a girl, an old lady girl at that.

Slamming of the truck doors and the roar of its engine.

The lights again, driving slowly by. Prowling.

I waited until the engine sound indicated they had turned a corner, then I moved again, to the next hiding place, this time behind a reeking dumpster.

I could hear the truck turn around taking the block, coming back around. I hunched down, barely breathing as the lights glided by.

I had about two more blocks to get to my car. Two long blocks. Long blocks with few, if any, places to hide. I took a quick glance at my watch. Almost four in the morning. That meant about another hour for me to make it to my car. Once it got light—if they were still looking—I would be too easy to find.

I stayed where I was—the goddamn stench of the dumpster—for another pass of the truck. I'd attacked him—taken his gun—he had to find me now. They were still prowling, the truck's engine whining down the block.

Then either inspiration or desperation hit.

A little stealthy—and, to be honest, squeamish—dumpster diving. A couple of plastic bags that looked like they were stuffed with clothes, hiding my camera bag in the least disgusting of them. I took my jacket off and tied it around my waist, brushed my hair back. And the final touch, a beer can in a paper bag. Oh, and gross, but found a cigarette butt and put it in my mouth.

I think I'm up to date on all my immunizations.

Then I started shuffling down the road, approximating a drunken weaving, my shoulders hunched down as far as I could to make me seem shorter, the jacket emphasizing my female hips.

A faint glow of lights behind me.

Closer.

I didn't vary my shuffle. Or try to hide.

The engine growling behind me.

Lights bright, surrounding me.

Slowing beside me. The window down.

"Hey, what're you doing here?"

Now, only now, did I look in their direction.

The driver. Young but scruffy, he would be old fast. A short haircut that needed to be kept short and hadn't been. The eyes were brown, a dull brown, too many drugs had altered what he saw, and there was no light in them anymore. His skin had a pasty sheen, again drugs. And the teeth were showing the signs of meth.

I pitched my voice high, as female as I could make it. "You got any smokes?"

"I asked you what you're doin' here?"

"Quiet here. People don't bother me. I could really use a ciggie. You sure you don't got any?"

"You seen anyone else around?"

"Like you?"

"No, not like us. On foot. Some guys."

By the faint glow of the dashboard, I could make out the second person, the scared of snakes guy. Pudgier, probably a lot of time with the munchies. But also the pasty, pale skin, hair slicked to the point of looking greasy. Not even looking at me, his eyes, also a dull dark color, on his phone. Another addiction.

"Couple guys, big ones, run past me a little while ago. Didn't even stop when I asked for a cigarette."

"Where'd they go?"

"That way." I pointed vaguely in the direction to the interstate. "At least I think. Heard a car take off."

"Which way?"

"I don' know. Just heard a squeal, you know, didn't see. Maybe you got some spare change? Could use some food."

"Fuck off, you skank."

The truck slammed into gear and roared off, as if it could catch a fictional car. But not so fast that I couldn't read the license plate number.

I remained in my disguise in case they came back, although I picked up the pace. They might be frustrated enough to take out their anger on a homeless woman.

Only when I got to my car did I get rid of the bags—as close to a garbage bin as I could get—fishing out my camera case and putting my jacket back on.

But even then I didn't leave, just got in, quietly closing the door, then slid the seat down so I wasn't visible. In case I dozed off, I set the alarm on my cell—making sure no one was around to notice the light—for about an hour.

Chapter Twenty-nine

Of course I didn't sleep, instead let my brain ramble and hit on everything I possibly could worry about from hurricanes to whether I could wash these clothes enough to get rid of the smell of sweat, dirt, the dumpster, whatever I'd rolled in under the trucks, and then back again.

I waited until the day was clearly breaking, not just the first gloaming. People would be stirring, cars around; I could slip away as someone going to work, instead of driving in the deadest part of night when the lights of the only other vehicle on the road would be too obvious.

I was exhausted and wanted nothing more than to sleep.

But I also needed to think.

The pasty-faced twins seemed like so much better suspects than anyone else. My problem was how to point the police in their direction.

I discovered the interstate entrance out in this part of the world; I'd never had occasion to use it before, hoping that it was still just early enough for traffic not to be too crazy.

For once, my good deeds were rewarded, with only a few idiotic merges to get past.

I did the painful but expedient move of going to my office instead of home, with its all-too-tempting bed. I had a shower there and a few generic changes of clothes in the storage closet.

And coffee.

The shower helped clear my head. And the coffee, especially the second cup. And the third.

I went through what I'd done last night and decided, while not exactly clean and dainty, I'd pretty much stayed within the law. No breaking and entering on my part; the closest was my attacking the skinny guy, but that was clearly self-defense in my book. Plus, since I doubted they'd gone to the police about it, I wasn't going to mention it unless I had to.

The big takeaway was overhearing them talking about throwing a gun in the canal. Odds were it was the gun that killed Eddie, and that meant the police needed to find it as soon as possible.

Which meant I'd need to come up with some way of telling them so they'd believe me.

Before she thought I was a murderer, Joanne and I used to be friends. I'd have to risk there was enough of that left that she would believe me now.

I dialed her number.

"Ranson," she answered on the first ring.

I had expected—hoped—to leave a message and for it to be several hours before I actually had to talk to her.

"Kind of early in the morning for you," she continued.

Damn caller ID. Not only did it identify me, but it robbed me of my preferred option—just hanging up.

"Can we talk?"

"Sure," she answered.

"Somewhere besides on the phone."

"Should I come to your office?" she offered.

"No." I didn't want to be cornered here. "I'm out of coffee," I lied. I named a coffee shop on Esplanade Ave., about equal distance from where we each were.

She agreed. "Half an hour?" she said.

"Yes. Come alone."

I put the phone down before she had a chance to respond.

I quickly made notes: the gun in the canal, the truck license plate, what Eddie's girlfriend had told me. It seemed so small, only a few scribbles.

A glance at my watch told me it was time to go.

Joanne, of course, was already there.

She had staked out an outside table, one off to the side, reading the paper, her sunglasses hiding her eyes even though the day was a mix of clouds with little sun, none at the moment.

I sat down.

She put a cup of coffee in front of me.

"Black, right?" she asked.

I nodded, nonplussed by the common gesture of courtesy.

I took a sip, biding time.

"You wanted to talk," she prompted.

"I've been investigating," I started.

"This is a murder inquiry." Her eyes were hidden, only a slight downturn of the mouth indicated her displeasure.

"Yeah, well, my client is wrongly accused of murder, and I have to clear her name."

"The client would be you?" She took a sip of her coffee, keeping her face unreadable.

"Yes, that would be the case." I was at her mercy now. I laid it all out, starting with what Brandon told me—I didn't give his name; he was a kid, maybe a confused, over-his-head kid, but still, he didn't need the police knocking at his door when he could only tell them what he'd told me. From there to the girlfriend.

"Wait, Eddie had a real girlfriend?" Joanne interrupted.

That was the first sign I'd found what the police hadn't. Yeah, she hadn't wanted to go to the police, but there was no way to avoid it at this point—and it would make her safer.

I went from the girlfriend to the garage to as short a version as I could of what I'd done out there.

I noticed that Joanne wrote down the license plate number.

She took another sip of her coffee, then said, "Well, they don't sound like law-abiding citizens, but having a party late at night is hardly a crime. Not enough to do much with. We can dredge the canal for the gun, but unless the water hasn't worn away the fingerprints, it's not very helpful. Any half-rate defense attorney would claim you planted it there."

I told the less abbreviated version of my night's adventures. That they'd seen me and obsessively hunted for me. The meth mouth. They had guns, almost fired one into the bushes where I was.

Joanne was silent when I finished. Another sip of her coffee. "Homeless dumpster diving, huh?"

"Yeah, I took one of the longest showers of my life before I came here."

"I appreciate the effort."

Another sip of her coffee. Her face, and what she was thinking, hidden.

"Damn it, Joanne! Do you really think I offed some two-bit punk? Or is this about me going out with Alex when you two were split up?"

She was too controlled to slam her coffee down on the table, but it was close.

"Sorry, you're way too professional and ethical to let something like that in any way influence your investigation. I'm sure you've already thoroughly looked into all the other suspects—so many of them, and they all had perfect, unbreakable alibis—before you settled on me." The words were said, but the font was definitely sarcasm.

Her hand tightened around the coffee cup, then she pulled away, realizing a paper cup and hot coffee would not be a good combination to crush.

"Damn you, Knight." It was a harsh whisper. "It's more complicated than that."

"Oh, I get it, the JP cops decided the dyke did it and you kept your mouth shut."

A crack, enough of a grimace to let me know something had hit. She gripped the edge of the table, her knuckles white.

Same harsh whisper. "Did you sleep with her?"

I'd hit a live wire. I told the truth. "Joanne, it doesn't matter. She chose you."

"It matters to me."

"Then you need to ask her."

"I have."

Ah, that was the snake in the grass. Joanne didn't trust Alex's answer.

"She chose you," I repeated. We had been friends for a long time, close friends once, an affair a long time ago when we were both single, too combustible to be compatible. But our friendship had held for long after that. Only recently had we drifted away, life pulling us apart, but maybe also not wanting to walk around the messy places we'd made. Like this one.

First it was innocent, mostly, wanting to go to a concert and not wanting to go alone. Alex invited me. I said yes. Then we both realized we were, at least technically, single. Went out a few more times, mostly talked. Should we, shouldn't we? Both aware we were in the messy aftermath. Loneliness—and alcohol—moved things along. But even then only to fooling around, somewhere between second and third base in high school terms. I had not stayed the night, not slept naked beside her through to the sunrise.

In the end, Alex had decided she couldn't throw away all the years she had built with Joanne and gave it another try. One that, so far, was working.

The kind and decent part of me was happy for them, happy the years mattered and two people I cared about found the love that bound them together. The not-so-decent part of me? They were together and I was alone. Did I resent that? It wasn't the ache of losing someone I thought I could have a life with; we hadn't gotten that far. But I hadn't been the chosen one. Even if it was the right decision for all of us, it still rankled that part of me that wasn't as perfect as I wanted to be.

I had let that bleed over into our friendship, being busy when they invited me over with our other friends. But the invitations were few, and then none. Maybe Joanne hadn't wanted me around, either. Out of sight, out of mind. Almost.

Could we repair it?

Did we want to?

Maybe, at least for now, I just needed to settle for not going to jail for murder.

"No, I did not sleep with her," I said. The truth was too messy for yes-and-no clarity, but we hadn't spent the night together into the morning light, and I would take that as my definition. It worked for both of us; she heard what she needed to hear and I told the real truth. Alex had chosen to stay with Joanne.

"Would you lie to me?" she asked, her hands still gripping the table.

"Of course," I said. "But I'm not. Not about Alex. Not about the murder."

Joanne nodded. Took a sip of her coffee. At least brought the cup to her lips, but I didn't see her swallow. Time to compose herself.

Putting her cup down, she said, "Look, this is complicated. We have both Orleans and Jefferson Parish involved. They see the evidence one way, and I have to listen to them and hope they listen to me as well."

"Are you saying they think I did it? And you don't? And why are you involved?"

"To your last question, I'm a liaison with the Jefferson Parish cops. Eddie's murder happened out there, as well as your confrontation with him. Yeah, I shouldn't be in on this, but we have too few people to spare. As to the first two questions, I can't say. You know that. Could you have killed him in self-defense? Yes."

"I could have. But I didn't."

"Could you have killed him because he was a scumbag and needed killing? A serial rapist? I might have killed him for that."

"But I didn't. He was enough of a scumbag that life was going to take care of him."

"Even if I believe you—and I do—that's not good enough. The JP guys are going to go where the evidence leads them."

"Fine. I get that. There has to be evidence that leads away from me. Lean on Mrs. Stevens. Check some of the other neighbors. A gunshot in that neighborhood gets noticed. Do surveillance on the garage. Or raid it. Question the girlfriend. She needs police protection whether she knows it or not. Find the gun in the canal. It will not have my fingerprints on it."

"Okay, I'll do what I can. But you have to promise me you'll stay out of this. If those thugs point a finger at you for being out there, it'll taint any evidence we find. The further you stay away, the better for you."

"They think it was two men who tackled them. Not a middle-aged lady."

"If it comes down to you being arrested, we can argue self-defense. Edward Springhorn was not a nice guy. We found enough vile stuff on his computer that he'd have gone away for a long time. We haven't found his phone yet, but he probably used that more than anything else."

"I would prefer it not come to that."

"Me, too."

Her cell phone rang; she looked at the screen and answered, just long enough to say she was on her way.

"I have to go," she told me.

"Yeah, I guessed that."

We both stood up. She picked up her things.

I asked, "Is Cordelia in town?"

She looked at me, the eyes hidden, her face neutral, giving away nothing except the hint that there was something not to be given away.

"Why do you ask?" She busied herself with putting her phone away.

"Thought I saw someone that looked like her. None of you are available this upcoming weekend."

Joanne threw her half-drunk coffee into the trash can. Then said, "No, she's not in town. At least, not that I know of."

She started to walk away, saying, "I'll give you a call in a few days. Stay out of trouble and away from our investigation."

She kept walking.

I took my cup of coffee. I needed both the caffeine and the warmth.

I headed back to my office, mulling over our conversation. She said Cordelia was not in town. It had probably been as true as my saying I hadn't slept with Alex. She didn't say Cordelia hadn't been in town or if she was coming. Just not here right at the moment.

Maybe I had seen her. Maybe I hadn't.

Maybe I'd be cleared of murder. Maybe I'd have to claim self-defense.

Too many fucking maybes.

It was too early to spike my coffee with brandy.

I had to settle for the cooling comfort of caffeine. After finishing the cup Joanne bought me, I made another pot. At least this would be hot.

Two messages from Douglas Townson were blinking on my answering machine. The first was asking—not really asking, but asking in the kind of tone that made it an order—to call him back and the second was saying that he would be in town in the next few days. Asking—in the same tone—for a meeting.

After a slug of fresh coffee—and wishing for the brandy—I called him back, fervently hoping I could get away with leaving a message.

The worst of both worlds. A pleasant woman answered, told me Mr. Townson wanted to speak to me, then left on me hold long enough for me to finish the just-poured coffee and consider whether I wanted another cup or if I should go to the bathroom first.

The time on hold would be put on his bill.

Just as I was deciding that maybe I should take a bathroom break, "So, what do you have for me?" broke into my contemplation.

I recovered enough to answer smoothly, "As I said at the beginning, I didn't think I could solve a century-old murder, but I have stumbled over interesting information about your great-grandfather's excursions into New Orleans that might at least give you some idea of what may have happened."

"Really? Like what?"

"I'm still piecing things together. I'll need to do more research before I can have anything that I'd feel comfortable presenting to you." My first real out-and-out lie of the day.

"I'm going to be in New Orleans sometime next week. Do you think you can have it for me by then?"

"Next week, when?"

"Not sure yet. Can we meet and you show me what you have?"

I agreed. He was a paying customer. I suspected Mrs. Stevens might be slow, like never, to pay her bill and I couldn't very well bill myself, so money coming in was a necessary thing. I'd have something by then—even nothing more than I had now would do.

He hung up without even saying good-bye. Too busy, obviously.

Then I heeded the call of nature and went to the bathroom.

Then I started at my computer screen, wondering how soon I could call it lunch and have deciding on whether to get a sandwich or a salad to occupy my time.

Then I remembered the glint of glasses from someone at the garage. A figure outlined in the glare from the door. Short.

Brandon?

"You dumb fuck," I muttered. Eddie had hired him to do computer stuff. Had Eddie's friends continued the deal? Was he there helping them to set up their putative "movie" links and too dumb and naïve to realize he was in with drug dealers? Everyone, even stupid-as-shit drug dealers, needed internet access these days.

Another glance at my watch. Not even lunch. He'd be in school now.

Not your problem. You're not his mother or his guidance counselor.

Joanne had warned me to stay away, a suggestion I was happy to honor. Drug thugs with guns are not what I want to tangle with.

Go buy the kid one more pizza after school. Warn him away from having anything more to do with that garage and the people in it.

Come home and sleep well at night.

I texted him, asking to meet at the pizza place after school. Said I was buying. One more all-meat pizza to salve my conscience.

Lunch sounded like a taco truck by the library. I had told Douglas Townson I'd have stuff for him by next week, so I would dig as deep as I could.

Better in the archives than sitting here staring at my computer screen.

CHAPTER THIRTY

Brandon felt the vibration from his phone, but he didn't dare look at it. Ms. Lee was too near and she was known to confiscate phones from students paying more attention to them than learning. She'd grabbed Kevin's one day and texted his mother saying that he wanted to do more to help around the house, so could she teach him how to cook?

Brandon almost smiled at how much explaining Kevin had to do to get out of that one.

He also wasn't feeling good. Maybe getting sick.

Or maybe just too many late nights. He'd had four beers last night, more than he'd ever had. He wanted to keep up with Kevin and the others. But halfway through the fourth one, he didn't think he could take another sip without gagging. He'd been so proud of himself for getting through it without anyone catching on.

His mother had caught him coming in, but he'd claimed he just needed to take a walk. He told her he couldn't sleep and he thought a walk about the block would help. He was a good liar, he decided. She hadn't questioned him, just told him to go back to bed.

Now Ms. Lee couldn't tell that he was dying to see what was on his phone.

He told himself it was probably Kevin wanting to sneak off for burgers for lunch. Not what he was waiting for. Now that Brandon could pay, Kevin was happy to drive.

Finally class was over. He hurried off, needing to find a quiet place to look at his phone. He found it in the hallway near the principal's office. No one came here unless they had to.

Leaning on the wall, with a final look around to make sure no one—no one who would question him—was about, he looked down at his phone screen, scrolling for the messages. "We need 2 meet asap.

Aft. sch?" He typed back his reply, "Yes, gr8. Where?" The answer, "Next block. Red truck." He typed back "OK," but was puzzled. Why were they sending a truck? He'd never seen a red one before.

It didn't matter. They didn't have his experience. The one thing he had learned in computer games was how to win.

Another message came through. "Can we meet? Pizza place?" He was also puzzled by that one. He'd answer later. The bell for the next class was ringing, and he was on the wrong side of the building.

Chapter Thirty-one

She stared at the text message.

He was dead. He couldn't be sending her any more messages.

But there it was on her phone. "Suck me off or I show the pics," just like the last message he had sent. The same time. A different location. Of course a different one. The cops still had the first one taped off.

Three bullets. She'd watched them hit him, the sound, the blood. The look on his face. First surprise. Then anger. Finally fear. And then nothing.

But it was the same number. The same message.

The same nightmare.

Chapter Thirty-two

The musty smell of old books. Libraries give me the comfort of knowing I'll never run out of books to read. Indeed, the real frustration is I'll never get to read all the books I want to read, not even know about books that I would want to read.

I was back in front of Samuel Braud's diary, on a case that had nothing to do with the present murders and in about as safe and serene a place as I could find.

I would let the billable hours pile up. Even what I charged would be a pittance to the kind of money Douglas Townson earned. Better some of it trickle down to me.

I finished reading all of 1906 and into 1907.

He mentioned the murder of Townson Senior a few times, mostly recounting reports to his superiors in which he outlined everything the investigation had done and what it had turned up. The final report said it was likely to be unsolved and hinted that Townson's behavior might have been the cause of the murder. Women were still found murdered, especially "those kinds of women," but none choked on their undergarments. Those had stopped.

Lunch was indeed a taco truck parked out by City Hall, and it was a nice enough day to sit and eat in Duncan Park, a small respite of green between it and the library.

I went back to the library even though I doubted I would find anything more to tell Douglas Townson. The truth was I had come to like Samuel Braud and his beloved Alibe, as he called her. My curiosity wanted to finish reading his diary, to visit a century long before I was born, lived on streets I walked on today.

I didn't get a text back from Brandon until the middle of the afternoon, probably just as school was letting out. "Can't meet 2day.

Tomorrow?" I stared at it before replying, "OK," wondering if he was doing something with the garage boys tonight. Or maybe it was band practice. Brandon looked like the kind of guy who played the French horn. I didn't want to text a warning; it would be hard to explain in the brief format what was going on. Plus I didn't want to leave any record I was doing this. Joanne might view it as breaking my agreement that I wouldn't interfere. I viewed it as not letting a kid ruin his life because of adolescent stupidity.

I went back to reading Samuel's diary. He did what I'd done, searching for other similar murders to the woman in the District, in case the murderer had moved on. But, like I had, he found none similar enough to raise suspicions.

He solved other murders, mostly the usual ones, drunken brawls, domestic violence. Some of the people reappeared. Rob Byrnes—as he insisted was the proper spelling—continued his drunk and disorderly, but there was affection in his mentions as if Rob was a funny and polite drunkard, too fond of his wine, but with few other vices. Augustine Lamoureaux and her coffee shop partner Roxanne Beaudoin reappeared, from offering a kind cup of soup on a cold day, to giving him information, mostly on those who preyed on the weak, but, he acknowledged, claimed to know nothing when a posh gent said his wallet was stolen. Reading between the lines, I began to suspect that Augustine and Roxanne were more than just friends. That theory was bolstered when he found out from them that Teddy, the stable boy, was actually a stable girl—woman really. As Augustine said, "She loves horses and hates skirts. She works hard and is kind. Leave her alone." To his credit, Samuel Braud did. The Corner Coffee Café, as they called it, seemed to be the place where the queer people of the time gathered. It made sense. Storyville was not for the polite people, and it seemed to accept those no one else would. Even drunken Rob had a roommate, a fellow by the name of Brady. Oddly, I hoped they found love and some semblance of happiness in their long-ago lives.

Samuel mentioned the War, the first one, the Navy insisting the District be closed, if New Orleans was to be a naval base. In 1917 Storyville ended.

The people I had come to know through his diaries dispersed, and their names did not appear again. Instead, he told the love story of his life with Alibe (he several times mentioned it needed to be pronounced Ollybay and his last name Braud was Bro). She left teaching for the birth of their first children, a set of twin girls. *Praise the Good Lord, Mother and Children are well and healthy.* A blurring of the letters as if water—tears?—fell on them.

Another child, also a girl. And again his diary recorded joy, not disappointment in no son. Their fourth child was a boy. Again, happiness that both mother and child were well. *This is true courage, that my sex are not good at admitting, our shouts of battle are nothing to carrying of life at the risk of our own life and the pain and worry it takes to bring another being to the world.*

He continued as a policeman, rising in the ranks until, as he said, *I am higher than I ought to be, much higher than I want to be, but the money is good for our growing family, and that is more important than any fleeting wish on my part to be back on the street with Luke Summit. Paper will be my life, and the fellows can tell me jolly tales of their adventures with miscreants over a pint.*

In all they had seven children, five girls and two boys. All healthy and well.

When women got the right to vote, he insisted Alibe take advantage of it. *The laws affect her equally. Why should she not affect them as well?*

I started skipping through it, the stories of the children and their school, his tedious paperwork and meetings. Certainly a life well lived, but after the tenth A in grade school, my attention wandered. I skimmed over the kids growing up—they all did well in school, some of them even going to college, two of the girls and one boy. *Smart like their mother*, he wrote on accompanying his oldest daughter to Newcomb College.

After thirty years in the police force, he retired. They moved to a smaller cottage in the Garden District, closer to the river and away from the grand mansions of St. Charles. Their children were grown and away with children of their own. The oldest daughter had never married, had gone on to medical college and was a doctor in New York. Tried not to read much into that.

I glanced at my watch. It was close to closing time. Just for the sake of finishing what I started, I wanted to get to the end, to find out what had happened to Samuel Braud.

As I scanned the pages, I saw a familiar name.

Augustine Lamoureaux. The entry was from November of 1943. Another war had come to the world. A quick calculation put him in his mid-sixties. Almost forty years after I had first met them on these pages.

I often walk alone these days. Alibe accompanies me when she can, but her knees are not able to manage the long rambles that are my solace. I was revisiting my old haunts, streets I walked as a vigorous young man, thinking I could right so many wrongs of the world. I found myself on Basin Street, the houses of sin torn down, now to be houses for the impoverished, to give them a safe, comfortable place to live. I wonder at that concentration of desperation, but better minds than mine have thought this through, so the buildings go up. In this contemplative mood, I noticed a figure down the street, leaving from the cemetery. Decades at least had passed since I'd seen her, but her erect carriage, the fine-boned face, even as it aged, showed it to be no other than Augustine Lamoureaux.

"Miss Lamoureaux," I called. She turned, started, as if seeing a walking ghost.

"Mr. Braud," she said. She always pronounced my name correctly. "You still walk these streets?"

"I walk to keep walking," I said as I approached her. "I don't want my bones to get out of the habit of movement. At my age, they may not get started again. And you, Madame? Are you also visiting the old haunts?"

She smiled a sad smile. "No, I have no desire to live in the past, save for some fond memories. I was here visiting a friend in the only place I can visit her."

"Ah, yes, we are of the age we visit graves. I am sorry for your loss." It was a loss, I could see by her face a lingering sadness, one to long outlast the funeral.

"Thank you, Mr. Braud, that is kind of you."

"I do not mean to intrude on your grief, but I often wondered what happened to those who lived in the District. You, Miss Beaudoin, Teddy, the stable...hand, Rob Byrnes of the rosy cheeks, Michelle Gierden, who played the piano so beautifully, Josie, Alice, the others."

She was silent. I wondered if I had breached decorum by asking such questions. For all I knew, Miss Lamoureaux had moved on from her life in the District, shirked off its taint.

I turned to walk with her, to give her time to reply if she so chose. Or to let me know that the past was gone and we should talk of the weather, the winter chill from the river.

"So long ago," she said softly. "Do you want the good or the bad first?"

"Perhaps a mix, to soften the blows." I proffered my arm for her. After a moment's hesitation, she took it.

"Rob Byrnes sold one of his fanciful stories to one of those magazines he liked to read, the ones about crime and detectives. It did well and he sold more, enough to move to New York City and live there. He writes faithfully once a month—"

"He is still with us?"

"Yes, says the wine of his youth has preserved him into his dotage. And sends a check, claiming it is for all the coffee and soup we fed him when he had nothing." She stopped, opened her purse, and took from it a photograph. A well-dressed man amid the lights of Broadway. I barely recognized him other than the eyes, the same glint of humor. "He sent this to me last month. He is still writing his stories, living a comfortable life amidst the Bohemians of New York. He promises he will visit in the spring before it gets too hot."

"That is good news, I am happy for him. I had suspected it was his grave you were visiting." With one last look, I handed the photo back to her.

"Michelle Gierden is still playing the piano. The war gave her new chances to play with so many men overseas. She sends postcards. I saw her about five years ago when she last played here."

"Ah, that is good to know. I'd love to hear her play again."

"The last I heard, Teddy and Josie headed west to California. Neither of them were writers, a few postcards. Teddy found work with the horses they used in the movies. Someone needed to train them, and she was always good with the animals. Josie worked as an actress, small parts, in the crowds. I saw her in one years ago, keep looking for

her face in the crowd when I go to the cinema. But of course, she would no longer be the pretty young girl she was then. I believe Teddy found happiness, a little house by the sea, a place where all that mattered was her skill with horses. Teddy sent a postcard of the ocean, said that was her view and that Josie had married an auto mechanic and moved up the coast."

"Teddy was—is—good with horses." We spoke in the past tense, but like Rob, she could still be with us, enjoying her usual toddy in the evening. We both chose to leave it at that.

"The sad ones. Alice was caught in the yellow jack run that summer of 1906. One of the last to succumb. In her fever, she said to me, 'at least I'll be pretty in heaven.' She knew she would die young."

"I'm sorry," I said. "Her life was not going to be an easy one, no matter what."

"No, it wasn't. We called them the girls on the edge of summer, always ready to fall into the suffocating heat, the fevered miasmas that seemed to follow the rising of the temperature, the slow summers with no trade save the desperate or despicable. Everyone who could be gone from town had left. They held on to spring and hoped for the fall. So many of them were lost in the summer."

I could merely repeat, "No, they did not have easy lives."

"Thrown away, left to survive on their own. You were one of the few police to consider that a crime could be committed against those girls."

"Yes, the blasting, wet heat, inescapable, so miserable for us all. I regret I could do little more."

"Luke Summit, you trained him and his colleagues well. They also listened to us."

"I trained them to treat you and your friends as their allies. Not just the uptown gentlemen were the ones most hurt by misdeeds. You helped me solve crimes that would have otherwise gone unsolved."

"I helped with the ones who would prey on the weak and the fallen."

"Yes, I did notice you weren't forthcoming when the uptown men had their wallets taken."

"Perhaps they dropped them in a drunken stupor and chose to blame those they could get away with blaming."

"Perhaps. I see you and I will not agree on this."

"Perhaps the contents of the gentleman's wallet, plenty for his evening's pleasure, was enough to see a girl through the summer when few people came calling."

"Miss Lamoureaux, I have always admired you for your morals." At the look on her face I added, "No, I am not mocking you. The rich could fend for themselves; you took care of the poor. The soup, the coffee, the kindness, the blind eye to acts of desperate survival that hurt those who could best afford it. Perhaps not agree, but admire."

"Thank you, Mr. Braud. We tried to live as best we could, letting kindness and compassion be our guides."

"I'm guessing it was the case with Frederick Townson," I said.

She looked off in the distance, maybe seeing the buildings that had been torn down for progress, the people who once lived there.

"The murders stopped after he died," I said.

She looked at me but still said nothing.

"The young women working in the District. A brute horrifically violated them—"

"Yes, I remember. The youngest, the most desperate. He hunted them."

The rustle of movement intruded. It was closing time. I would have to return to read the rest. I could call it doing work for Douglas Townson, but it was for myself. I hastily packed up, not wanting to be one the dawdlers who forced the library staff to work late.

As I exited, I paused long enough to text Brandon, asking him to call me even as I was telling myself I was not the confused teenage boy whisperer. At least over the phone, I could give him some kind of heads-up to stay in and do his homework.

He didn't reply.

I headed for my car.

No groceries had been bought in the last few days, so I defaulted on stopping by Riley & Finnegan. Tomorrow—or next week—a greater intake of salad would begin.

Mary Buchanan was at the door. She tagged me as I walked in.

"Underage or not? They have IDs that say they're old enough, but they don't look it. Or I'm turning into a grumpy old lady."

"You could never be grumpy." I looked at the group she indicated. Alan, the young Goth girl, ah, Sophia and her friend from the pizza place, whose name I had no chance in hell of remembering.

Like it or not, I was going to have to be the teenage-don't-do-stupid-things whisperer.

I sauntered over to their table just as the waiter put their beers on it. Reaching over Sophia's shoulder, I snatched the one from in front of her.

She looked up, annoyed, then abashed.

I shook my head, then took a sip of the beer.

"Thanks for buying this for me. I know you weren't buying it for yourself since, no matter what your fake IDs claim, you're not old enough to drink."

Alan looked sheepish as he corralled the beer in front of the other girl, taking it for himself.

"You don't have a right to tell us what to do," Sophia said. She was dressed all in black, including black fingernails and black lipstick. Her hair was such a uniform black it probably had to be dyed. And a black *X* cross around her neck. Charming.

I took another sip of her beer. "In this case, yes, I do. If you want to break the drinking laws, do what I did, get the one legal person to buy a six-pack and head out to the levee and drink there. That way, Mary doesn't lose her license and get put out of business."

To prove I wasn't going to be nice and leave them alone, I pulled up a chair and sat down. And took another sip of her beer.

"I'm sorry," Alan said sheepishly. "We're just trying to…"

"Take care of Janice," Sophia finished for him.

Ah, Janice, that was her name.

"I'm fine," Janice interjected in a vehement enough tone to tell me she wasn't. But whether it was a crush who hadn't texted her back or something real was impossible to tell. She was more conventionally dressed: jeans that were ripped before they were sold, an upscale pink T-shirt, patterned with rhinestones and stitching that would not look good after a few washings. Pale pink nail polish, the kind her mother would approve of, although her lips were a deeper red than her age could carry. Her hair was brown but had blond highlights, but again ones her mother probably approved of. They might even have gone to the same hairdresser.

The figure I'd seen at the garage, the one led into the truck.

No, it can't be. I had nothing more than a vaguely female shape in the glare of the lights. Average height. Enough shape to be a woman, but not overly endowed. That could be just about any female in this bar. Including me.

And the other shadowy figure, the short one with the glint of glasses? Brandon still being the computer water boy? Eddie had liked to prey on the young and vulnerable, like Tiffany. He might have taught his meth-head friends his dirty tricks—or learned from them. Maybe they were still using Brandon.

Time to stir the shit. "What about your other friends, the ones I met at the pizza place?"

"What about them?" Sophia said, fuck-you dripping off her tone.

"Brandon and, uh…Kevin. Where are they?"

"Not here." Again Sophia answering. "What do you want?" she challenged.

"To sit here long enough to ensure you order an age-appropriate beverage." Still stirring, I continued, "Why are you so reluctant to talk about your friends? I met them, know who they are. Just asking a common question."

"They're straight, don't feel comfortable here," Alan said.

"They're clearly not here. Just wondering where they are."

"Why do you care?" Sophia shot back at me.

"Because you seem so bothered by me asking. Are they at the garage by the airport? The place Eddie used to party?"

"No! You can't know about that!" Janice burst out.

"Were you there a couple of nights ago?"

"No! Why would you think that!" she replied. "I've never been there!"

"Then how do you know about it?"

"I told her," Sophia said.

"Wait, what garage? What are you talking about?" from Alan.

"Eddie's former party place, now taken over by his cohorts," I explained. "How do you know about it?" I asked Sophia.

"Kevin told me. Said I could make a lot of money."

"How?" I asked.

She looked at Janice, got no response, and then looked back at me. "Said all I needed to do was show my tits. Let them take a few pics."

"Did you?"

"No!" with enough disgust in her voice to make me think she hadn't.

"Did you?" I turned to Janice, wondering what that look had been about.

"No. I told you, I've never been out there." She looked at me as if trying to convince me she was telling the truth; I held it long enough for her to look away.

"Why?" Sophia challenged. "You interested?"

"Alcohol isn't all you're underage for. No. I'm attracted to women, not adolescent girls." Reminding them of their age wasn't a crowd pleaser. To keep us on track, I asked, "What else did Kevin tell you?"

"Nothing. He saw I wasn't interested and shut it down."

Just as she was trying to shut down this conversation.

"Look, this is a murder investigation. Someone killed Eddie Springhorn. If you know anything about—"

"I heard it was you," Sophia threw out.

"Your sources aren't very good," I retorted. "Only very wrong. Eddie and I weren't best buds, but I didn't know him or hate him enough to kill him."

"Why do you think we know anything?" she said.

"What did Tiffany tell you about him?"

"Nothing—" Sophia.

"He was using her—" Janice.

Again, they exchanged a look. Janice hesitated, then said, "She told me what he was doing. If I'd known how desperate she was…those awful pictures…" She started crying.

Both Alan and Sophia tried to comfort her, Alan awkwardly patting her on the back, Sophia putting an arm around her shoulder and glaring at me. Ah, body language, it can speak so loud. Sophia had a major crush on Janice and was taking on the role of dragon-slayer knight. Janice, however, was leaning toward Alan. Everything about her screamed straight girl; even the hardcore lipstick lesbians didn't play the damsel in distress the way she was. But she was interested in Alan, and he was only trying to be nice and gay-boy supportive to his dead sister's young friends.

I went up to the bar, ordered a couple of sodas and a big order of cheese fries to let her cry herself out.

When I returned with the sodas, Sophia said firmly, "We can't talk about this anymore. It's too upsetting." Aided by Alan, who seemed lost amidst the teen girl angst, she resolutely kept to her word. I tried a few questions, but she always said, "We're not talking about that," and then launched into a discussion of TV shows I'd never heard of or boy bands I knew nothing about.

I had to settle for interjecting when she took a breath, "If you know anything, anything at all that might relate to Eddie's murder, you need to tell the police."

I got an eye roll and a bare nod that made me suspect adults were the last people they would go to with their problems.

I gave up, headed to the quiet end of the bar to get my burger and fries and talk with Mary about adult things like movies we'd both seen.

Later, as I walked back to my car, I contemplated what I'd learned. It boiled down to teenagers keeping secrets. But secrets about what? As Janice had blurted out, Tiffany had told her—them?—about what Eddie was doing, and they didn't see how troubled she was. Was that where the shame and guilt came from? It was, I had to admit, certainly enough. Had it ended there? There were other undercurrents I couldn't tease out. Sophia had a crush on Janice, Janice had one on Alan, and Alan was looking at the boys. Both Sophia and Janice had been vehement enough that I believed them when they claimed they had been nowhere near the garage. But it felt like shades of truth. If Eddie was true to form, he would have hit on all of Tiffany's friends. Sophia wouldn't have been interested, except to be with her friends. Janice might have, at least initially, been flattered by the attention of an older male, even if he was supposedly dating her friend. What girl/woman isn't at least intrigued by "I don't really love her, you're so much more beautiful, alluring, etc."

I'd had a second beer with my burger, and that was not nearly enough to wade through all this teenage Sturm and Drang.

I needed to keep to my promise to Joanne. Stay out of it.

When I got home, I considered another beer but found I was too tired. Time for bed and to deal with things in the morning light.

CHAPTER THIRTY-THREE

I started to get dressed to go to the office, but then realized it was a Saturday. Where had the days gone?

Oh, yes, a last-minute security job for a longtime client. They had a special event Thursday night and needed me for several days early in the mornings for setup and late at night to follow through, so my hours had been jerked around more than usual. The night of the event had gone well into the early hours of the morning—I was being paid well and couldn't complain. And the days had gone.

Brandon had texted at the last minute—just as I was parking in the pizza place lot—to let me know he couldn't make it. His excuse was his mother; she needed him to help with cleaning the hall closet. The details and the tone—disappointment—made me inclined to believe him. I'd tried to fit him in with my crazy days, but he had canceled once and vaguely replied once. I still needed to take care of that.

I suggested today, but he hadn't responded yet.

The huffiness of his last text made me wonder about the others. There had been no excuse like mothers or teacher, just that he couldn't make it. Was it because he was doing something he wanted to do? Like hang with the big boys at the garage and imagine he was a cool kid, too?

Or was he just in a hurry and didn't have time for a longer answer?

If the police were going to raid the garage, it would be soon. Evidently kids these days (get off my lawn!) don't actually talk on phones, only text. Or send pictures they shouldn't. I'd called twice, had to settle both times for leaving a vague voice mail. He promised via text that we would meet up this weekend. I had to hope it was soon enough.

Even though it was the weekend, I headed for my office. Home felt too empty, too easy to sink into doing nothing of use just to pass the time. I did not need to explore new games to play on my phone. The battery life was short enough as it was.

The coffee shop downstairs was busy. Raspberry crème lattes were the special today.

I'd make my own coffee in my office. Black, freshly ground beans.

While waiting for it to brew, I sat at my desk. Glanced at my calendar.

Shit. I'd agreed to do the coffee/drinks date this morning with the woman I'd met online.

In an hour.

A drink sounded like a nice idea. Bloody Mary, so it would be appropriate for the time of day.

I had checked her profile after her message She was about ten years older than I, in her mid-fifties, and the face in the photo matched her age, a little on the skinny side for my taste, but that was just crass looks. She lived in the Baton Rouge area, wrote in complete sentences, and didn't claim she liked moonlit walks on the beach or any other such meaningless clichés.

She suggested meeting at the Carousel Bar at the Monteleone. I had considered suggesting Riley & Finnegan—that was more my style. But I didn't want to start being seen there before noon, and a woman from Baton Rouge might not be up for a dive queer bar.

So back home it was. I changed from my too-big (but so comfortable) jeans to my decent black jeans, nice gray sweater, and a deep-purple suit jacket. I rarely had occasion to wear it, and this one seemed like it might fit. I glanced over myself in the mirror. Respectable, but still looking enough like me to be honest.

"In any case, it'll have to do," I told my image.

I really needed to get a cat. At least then I'd have an excuse to talk to myself.

The Monteleone is a hefty walk from my house. Imagine a rectangle. I live at the upper corner of one side and it's on the lower corner of the other side, with the French Quarter being the quadrangle. Given the parking zoo at that end of the Quarter, it was a toss-up whether driving or walking was faster. Walking, however, was cheaper, and I wouldn't get stuck in traffic.

Walk I did, dodging around tourists like the pro New Orleanian I am.

I got there just as the hour was ending. The bar was the usual tourist busy, no seats available at the carousel that gave the bar its name. I scanned for a woman looking like the picture I'd seen of her.

I finally found her in the far corner near the back bar.

She saw me, nodded a welcome, and indicated a saved chair.

I sat down. "Hi, I'm Michele."

"I'm Jacqueline," she replied, holding out her hand.

I shook it; it was a feminine handshake, almost limp. I wondered how many drinks before we would become Jackie and Micky. She already had one in front of her.

"Are you here on business?" I asked. "Or is this pleasure?"

"A bit of both," she answered, snapping her fingers for the barmaid.

At my look, she said, "I come here a lot. As a regular customer, I expect better service than some tourist who'll never be back."

Once she got the waiter's attention, she turned back to me. "And you? You live here? What do you do?"

I ordered a Bloody Mary—my preferred drink, a Sazerac, was a little too much alcohol for this time in the morning—then answered her questions, I lived here, I was a private detective. Those begot more questions, how long, how did I end up in that career.

I was halfway through my drink before realizing she was controlling the conversation, learning about me while revealing little about herself.

Instead of answering her next question, I said, "How about you? Where do you live? And what do you do?"

She answered the first question at length. Outside of Baton Rouge, in a "safe" location. A gated community. A nice big house, her dream home, with a pool and several fireplaces. It was filled with the finer things in life.

I almost asked what the finer things were, but I knew what the answer would be—the things money can buy.

No, I didn't expect her to be the love of my life—the new love of my life. But it would have been nice to have someone to do things with, dinner, movies, all the activities I hadn't done because they're not much fun when you do them alone.

I ordered a second drink.

She looked at her watch.

"Oh, the time has escaped me," she said, her tone telling me escape wasn't possible, the time was tightly corralled. She had allotted about an hour for me, and that hour was over. "I have another appointment I have to be going to."

I wondered if this was true, or if she was just a higher-class version of my first date. If I made the grade, she would have suggested lunch; if not, then another appointment appeared.

"Time has a way of escaping in New Orleans, doesn't it?" I agreed politely. In truth, the hour had been enough for me as well.

But my voice wasn't as hidden as I intended.

"I really do have an appointment, and I am sorry. I have enjoyed your company," she said. A smile. A genuine smile. "Perhaps we can get together again?" Politeness cracked, yearning slipped through.

I had been insulted when I thought she was blowing me off. Now I wished that was the case. I considered the polite no, saying yes but never setting a time. Like she wasn't even worth being honest with.

"Thank you, but it doesn't seem like we have enough in common in what we want out of life. I wish you well," I said.

She looked at me. Finally said, "Am I really worse than being lonely? It's not a kind world out there, not for women alone."

"No, you're not worse than being lonely. But I'm not lonely. I'm just being honest. I thought you deserved that."

"Thank you," she said, without looking at me, then got up and left.

I slowly sipped the last of my drink, watched the people around me. Maybe I was lonely, but her finer things weren't my finer things. Don't get me wrong, I truly love my washer and dryer; there is nothing so freeing as being able to do laundry at midnight in a stained T-shirt, being able to afford at least the middle-of-the-shelf Scotch, a reliable car. But they're nice, I appreciate them, I don't bend my life to chase them.

I finished my drink, paid the bill—she had left it for me—and walked home. Alone.

Halfway there my phone rang.

Joanne.

"Hey," I answered, hastening my steps to get to a quieter street. Good news or bad news, I didn't want to listen while walking by people on the street.

"I shouldn't be calling you, but I am," she opened.

"Thank you."

"There may not be much thanks when I'm done." Without giving me a chance to reply, she continued, "Yeah, you were right about the garage being a drug den. Meth, heroin with enough fentanyl to cut it with to cause more overdoses than we want to think about. They were stupid, like most crooks. Bought shiny new trucks in their own names.

A bunch of cash deposits to bank accounts. We've found porn on the computers, but it looks more like it was for personal use, no signs of distribution."

"But if they were doing it electronically, would that show?"

"The computer guys are still digging. I'm guessing so, but we'll have to see." She continued, "We did find a gun, the one thrown in the canal. Again, stupid. They didn't throw it very far and it was close to the water line, visible if anyone was looking for it."

"That's good news."

"Yes and no. It's not the murder weapon. Wrong type of gun. It looks to be a hot gun, serial number scratched off, probably used in crimes and they needed to get rid of it."

I crossed Rampart before answering. "That's not good news."

"It is for them. Not so much for you."

"But if Eddie was involved with them, drugs and money are big motives for offing someone. Eddie let his girlfriend see the drugs. That alone could be enough for them to think he was a too-loose end."

"Great theory. We've interviewed the girlfriend, and she's playing dumb. Has no idea what we're talking about."

"You don't believe her, do you?"

"She's not fooling even the JP cops. You did not hear me say that," Joanne added. "But knowing she's lying isn't getting us the truth. The one piece of good news for you is that we canvassed Mrs. Stevens' block and one neighbor thinks she heard a gunshot. But she can't remember which day or the time, and unfortunately 'doddering' is a word that could be easily used to describe her."

"Great," I said, pausing on my front steps. Today might be the day to go home and spend the rest of it watching mindless TV.

"It might be useful in leaning on Mrs. Stevens. If he tells her another neighbor remembers hearing a shot, it might jog her memory. She can't very well claim she didn't hear it from in front of her house when someone at the other end of the block heard it. Her 'I want to be left alone' ploy is wearing thin."

"You think she did it?"

"Honestly, no. But I think she's covering up something. She could pick up the phone to call his workplace, but she's not the type to confront him alone late at night in a dark parking lot."

I had to agree with that. Given that she called me to come help her when he was at her house in daylight. "My guess is she thinks—or knows—either her husband or son did it and is protecting them. If I'm the suspect, then they're not."

"Maybe. But the husband has a good alibi. Or a watertight alibi. They were out at a club, his new girlfriend was upset with the drink service and made a stink about it. They were arguing with the manager and the bartender when Eddie was being killed." She sighed, then added, "Obviously, if I thought you had anything to do with this, I wouldn't be telling you this."

"Thanks," I replied. "The problem is I don't see Alan, her son, as that kind of killer, either."

"You know him?"

I told Joanne about meeting him at Mary's bar. "I don't see that kind of anger in him."

"Interesting," she said. "The JP cops interviewed him, and all I got from that was he claimed to know nothing and was a student at LSU. Nothing about him being gay or knowing his sister's friends."

"It's not something he'd likely bring up to a burly suburban cop. I think he's worried either his mother or father might have done it. So either he's a great actor or he didn't do it."

"I trust your instincts on this, but it makes it puzzling. It wasn't a quick execution to shut someone up. It was personal."

"What do you mean?"

She was quiet, then said, "I can't give details, but think about it. Drug gang wants to shut up a loose end. How do they do it?"

"Quick bullet to the head. Dump the body someplace it's not likely to be found."

"Exactly. Now, how do you kill someone you hate, who took a picture of a young girl and used it to coerce her into sex?"

"Are you asking to see if I know the details of the murder?"

"No. I'm using you to bounce ideas off of. I need an intelligent conversation about this case. This is, by the way, totally off the record."

I smiled, a small one. Joanne had moved from neutral to believing I wasn't the murderer. It would be nicer to have actual evidence that cleared me, but this was a civilized step.

"If the murder was about how he used the young girls, then it probably had a sexual element to it. Cut off the genitals and stuff them in his mouth?"

"Not that gruesome, but there were more bullets fired at his groin than his chest."

"What if the drug dealers wanted to make it look like it was sexual? Or they were jealous of how much action he was getting?"

"Now you're complicating things. Do the kinds of morons who can't throw a gun at least into the middle of the canal strike you as the kind who would think of that?"

"No," I had to admit, thinking of the men chasing me. Even the smarter one was dumb.

"So, that takes us back to someone who hated Eddie for his scumbag ways."

"But Tiffany wasn't the only girl he used that way. He was too practiced at it to have started with her."

"We're looking, but so far not much has turned up. We've only found one computer. If we can find a laptop or his phone or tablet, that might help. We're still looking through the garage. Maybe it's there."

"Maybe his killer took it."

"Possible—shit, I have another call. Have to take it. Stay out of trouble."

I clicked my phone off. No wonder the cops were focused on someone who would go after Eddie for the things he'd done to women—girls really, not women enough to realize what a slimly manipulator he was. I flicked back over the list of people. Mrs. Stevens, Alan, her husband might have hired someone, but again that wouldn't have had this level of rage. But as I had told Joanne, Fast Eddie had to have left more victims than just Tiffany. There could be any number of people with reasons to want Fast Eddie gone from this earth.

Except for the timing. His murder was close to her suicide. Coincidence? Or cause?

I needed to go back and look at the dates of her death and his murder.

I entered my house.

Or maybe I needed to leave this alone. Let the police with their resources do the investigation. Obey Joanne's request to stay out. Except for her to toss around ideas with.

But it nagged at me.

Instead of staying home, I headed back to my office.

As I was going up the stairs, Lady Jane was entering the door for the computer grannies.

"Ah, Micky," she said on seeing me. "I have something for you. The deep data dive. Come grab it and save me walking up a flight to put it under your door."

"What are you doing here on the weekend?"

"It's quiet. And claiming important work to do gets me out of babysitting the terrible-twos grandbaby." She gave me a conspiratorial wink.

I followed her in and she picked up a folder from her desk, handing it to me.

"Highlights?" I asked.

"Low lights, more likely. A lot of text messages. Most of them about when or where to meet or minute-by-minute updates on being bored in class. We have everything you asked for. Can dig deeper if you'd like, but I doubt we'll find much else useful. Thought you should look at everything first."

I thanked her for the work, promised a check would soon make its way downstairs, and left her to her quiet weekend.

Interesting, but not overly helpful. I'd pass it on to Joanne when I got the chance. Maybe she would see something.

I went immediately to my computer and searched for news articles on both Tiffany's suicide and Eddie's murder. Half an hour later I had my answer. A week. Exactly a week. Tiffany had driven the car out to the levee on a Thursday evening, at dusk. Her body had been recovered the following morning. No way to know if she waited, perhaps a last sunset on the river, or if she gave herself no room to change her mind and, with a running leap, had thrown her life away. Eddie had been killed the following Thursday night. Again, I didn't have the exact time; only the murderer would know that. The police report would include estimated time of death for both of them. The same day and time of day was pushing the coincidence to the breaking point. When I talked to Joanne, maybe I'd mention that as well.

The office phone rang, but I ignored it. It was Saturday, I wasn't officially here, and my brain was trying to tease out this puzzle.

My instincts were dead on. It was Douglas Townson telling me he'd be here Monday afternoon and wanted an update on his case. He said he'd arrive at three p.m.

Arrogant asshole. No "I'm sorry, I can only make it around three, will that work for you?" Instead, "I can meet at three p.m. I'll see you then. Please have an extensive update for me."

I started again at the times, started to do a chart of the likely suspects, then put my pen down. Not my case. I really needed to stay out of it.

Instead I sighed, shoved the folder Lady Jane had given me into my briefcase. I needed to read it over before I handed it to Joanne in case there was any hacking that didn't quite toe the legal line.

I shut up my office and headed back to the library. It was open until five on Saturdays. I could at least have as extensive a report as possible for Mr. Douglas Townson See You at Three.

Chapter Thirty-four

I picked up where I had been reading last in Samuel Braud's diary.

"I'm guessing it was the case with Frederick Townson," I said.

She looked off in the distance, maybe seeing the buildings that had been torn down for progress, the people who once lived there.

"The murders stopped after he died," I said.

She looked at me but still said nothing.

"The young women working in the District. A brute horrifically violated them—"

"Yes, I remember. The youngest, the most desperate. He hunted them."

"Hunted them?"

"The girls had little protection other than their wits and those of us who listened for their screams. The police, all too often, cared little if a woman like that was beaten. But he picked the late hours, almost dawn, those who had just started and knew little of how best to protect themselves. Or those desperate enough to agree to...the less savory acts."

"Was he hunted in return?"

She stopped, taking her arm from mine. "If that was true, would I admit it to a policeman?"

"I have retired and am now just an ordinary citizen."

"Ordinary enough to let this pass?"

"It was the one major crime I did not solve. Nor will it ever be solved. This is only between us and goes not beyond this small patch of earth."

"He did murder those young girls. We knew. Not with the strength of what you police needed, but he would be seen about and a woman would die that horrific death. Only when he was in the District. Arriving in one suit, leaving in another after the bloody attack. Teddy followed him once to see him throw a sack into the garbage bin. She fished it out to find clothes stained red.

"And then Mary came running into the street, screaming, blood running down her legs from his butchery, but she was a sturdy farm girl and fought him off. We heard the terror and threw on what clothing we could."

"Did you kill him?" I asked quietly, keeping my voice as close to only the two of us as possible, even though there were few people on the street.

She shook her head.

"Then who?"

She paused for a thought, then said, "We all did."

"All?"

"Yes. Teddy saw him running down the street, so she threw a rope on him, just as she did with the horses. He fought and Rob lobbed a bottle—a full one, no less—at his head, taking him down. Then Roxanne, brave, strong, Roxanne, who wiped the blood off Victoria, his last victim, so she could be buried, hoisted a shovel and struck him. Then we all went after him, the rest of the girls on the street, Alice, Josie, Michelle Gierden, our piano player, Rob and Teddy, Roxanne.

"I kept watch but am as guilty as the rest. There was no need for me to strike a blow, otherwise I would have. But we needed someone to watch, to give warning."

"No one came by?"

"It was the darkest part of night, in the back of the District, away from the gleaming houses on Basin Street. No one came by."

"You left him in the street."

"We left him as his victims were left. You saw the crimes, what he did, Mr. Braud. Beaten to bloody pulp, violated in ways only fiends can imagine, left to choke on their most intimate garments."

"Who stuffed the clothing in his mouth?"

"Mary. She took what he had rammed into her mouth and shoved it in his, screaming, crying, hysterical in her anger. And fear. 'I cannot kill him enough,' she cried as she did the deed. She is long gone, took to drinking after. She drowned in the Basin Canal. We don't know if she fell or if she jumped. She could never get away from the nightmare that was real."

I nodded. "Save for what you and I know, this case will never be solved. It will go to our graves. Thank you, Miss Lamoureaux, for your honesty and letting me know what I suspected is indeed truth. Mr. Frederick Townson met justice."

We continued walking.

"Miss Beaudoin? Was it her you were visiting today?" I asked. The one name whose fate she had not told me.

The shadow of grief passed across her face, the tightening of the lips, eyes narrowed and looking into the distance.

"Yes, it was," she replied. "She passed two years ago today. I had to come visit her."

"This is no longer a good street."

"It never was a good street. I doubt it ever will be."

"What happened after the District was closed?"

"We moved to the Irish Channel, put our coffee shop on the first floor and lived on the second. The men at the docks, and their wives, gave us a steady living, enough to put a little aside. I'm comfortable and can afford the flowers I bring her. Especially with Rob's help."

"You must live not far from where we are," I said, giving her my address. "My wife is not able to get out as much as she'd like. Perhaps you'd be good enough to call on her?"

Her hand tightened at my elbow. "Thank you, Mr. Braud, but it would not be appropriate."

I glanced at her, the faintest olive sheen of her skin giving way her meaning.

"As a policeman, I saw some of the worse of humankind. And some of the best. One man, as dark as the night, was one of the bravest and kindest men I've known. The vice that runs through the heart of this country is how some of us are allotted a portion of liberty and happiness and others are

denied it. If you choose to come, you will be most welcome in our house. My wife is a big fan of Mrs. Roosevelt."

"Thank you again, Mr. Braud. You are right, there is kindness and decency where you least expect it."

We came to Canal Street and she took her leave of me, having other errands, but promising she would call on my wife within the week.

I continued on my walk, contemplating the past. Every day lived becomes a part of you. I wondered at my motives for inviting Miss Lamoureaux to come visit my wife. Perhaps I wanted Alibe to hear tales of me as a dashing—and kind—young policeman, the part of me I had tried to protect her from. But also a part of me I was proud of. Or maybe I wanted to relive those days through my wife's eyes, to recall a day when my bones didn't ache and creak, my eyes had vision that was clear and crisp. Or just to hold on to the precious few people who have passed through our lives and made a difference.

I looked up from the page, focusing my eyes to the far wall to give them a rest. I had my answer. The answer I thought I would never find, the one meant to go to their graves, except for recording it on paper he thought no one would read save himself. I skimmed the rest of the diary, but it only continued for two more years, until the death of his wife Alibe. His final words, *I love you more than life itself and know not how I will go on.*

Then the pages were blank. Augustine Lamoureaux had been only mentioned a few more times, seeing her in passing as she visited his wife. At her funeral, with Rob Byrnes, down from New York.

I stared at the blank page for several minutes. Considered looking for the death records for Samuel Braud and Augustine Lamoureaux.

No, I didn't need to know that. Let the last I knew of them be that fateful meeting on Basin Street, near where the District—Storyville—used to be.

Chapter Thirty-five

As I left the library, the late-afternoon sun warm on my face, my phone made its text noise. I looked down, didn't recognize the number, so ignored it. I was tired, and propping my feet up in an easy chair was calling.

But a trash truck was passing, and I'd have to wait until it moved on to get out.

Bored, I opened the text message.

"Can meet 2nite."

I texted back, "Brandon? Pizza place?"

"No, need to show you something. Out by garage."

"The police are out there," I texted back.

"No, not close enough for them to find. Need to show you. 9p."

"Okay," I reluctantly agreed. "Maybe 8?"

"No, has to be 9."

"Okay," I agreed. "Tell me the address."

"Don't have it. Will text around 9. Be in area."

"Give me more info," I texted back.

"No time. Gotta go."

I texted, "Give me the block, at least."

He didn't reply.

Frustrated, I started my car and pulled out, only to be caught behind the slow-moving garbage truck. The last thing I wanted to do was fight drunken Saturday-night traffic to head out past the airport. I was tempted to tell him to forget it—if he had anything, to show it to the police.

But he wouldn't do that. Somehow I knew. Innocent as his involvement with Eddie and his friends might have been, or at least started, he had been sucked over the line—peer pressure, the bottomless need to fit in, had pulled him along. He thought I was safe, that I would protect him. But we didn't live in a world of superheroes with right and wrong bright and clear. This might be a mess I couldn't help him clean up.

I would try. Maybe fail, but I would try.

I headed home, having little else to do. Tempting as a beer at Mary's place was, the last thing I needed was to be less than sober myself to face the drive through the drunken hordes.

That left me twitching at home, with little to do but wait.

And wait.

I spent a little time tidying up the case notes for Mr. Douglas Townson, for his demanded meeting at three p.m. on Monday. Maybe he'd give me a bonus for actually solving it. Maybe I'd buy myself a decent bottle of Scotch if I managed to be polite to him for the entire meeting.

Time ticked slowly away.

I pulled out the notes the computer grannies had given me and started reading through everything they'd pulled off Tiffany's phone, jump drive, and computer as well as the hack into Brandon's phone. I started with the computer, but in a divide between generations, there was little of interest on it except for school papers and pictures arranged in albums from beach trips to pet selfies. I quickly skipped over those, her smiling face still alive, still able to be happy.

Most of what she wanted hidden from her parents was on the phone. Pictures she didn't want the 'rents to see, like ones with beer cans prominently displayed, or on Bourbon Street with red and green drinks that probably weren't non-alcoholic. They also had printed screen shots of all the text messages. Interspersed with the ones from schoolmates about meeting before class or after class or before and after class were the crude texts from Eddie, a foul build from sweet and charming, or what passed for it to someone seventeen, to claiming love that twisted into abuse. It was sad to see how long Tiffany tried to be a nice girl, trying to see his increasingly crude demands as evidence he really liked her. How do we teach our girls to do anything other than tell these pieces of elephant shit to fuck off?

My eyes started to burn and I put the pages down. I needed to read through them all before I handed them off to Joanne. But that didn't mean I needed to do it right now. *I'll take them with me*, I bargained.

If I have to wait for Brandon, I can read a few more pages. Timeliness didn't seem to be his super power.

I made a quick toasted cheese sandwich, not so much because I was hungry, but it was going to be a long night and I needed something besides bile in my stomach. After eating, I even washed the dishes. Anything to keep me alert and moving while the time passed.

I gathered the few things I might need—night goggles, cell phone battery pack. Gun…no, the cops still had my gun. I considered guns like hammers, a tool I needed, nothing more. I had one hammer; I had one gun. Inconvenient when it was unexpectedly elsewhere. Which reminded me that Torbin and Andy had borrowed my hammer and hadn't returned it.

More out of something to do than any intent of going over there and asking for it back, I went to the front of the house and pulled back the blinds to see if they were home. They lived down the block, and depending on where they parked, I could see their car from my window. They were home. Or their car was. They shared one, since Andy mostly worked at home on computer projects.

As I was watching, I saw them come to the car, Torbin carrying a covered dish, probably his crawfish mac and cheese from the shape of it, and Andy a pitcher, probably of Cosmos, one of their signature drinks. They were nicely dressed. On their way to a dinner party, I guessed.

Then I remembered, this was the weekend no one was available.

Torbin and Andy had friends I didn't know; they could certainly be going out to see any number of them. But it was an odd coincidence that Joanne, Alex, Danny, and Elly were also busy tonight as well.

You'll regret this in the morning, I told myself.

Only if I get caught, the devil on my other shoulder argued.

I grabbed my already packed kit—oh, preparation—then came back to the window to watch until they started to pull away.

Lucky for me, they had to carefully arrange their dishes in the car, so I had plenty of time to prepare before they left.

Just as their taillights winked on, I put the key in my door lock, stepping on the top step in time to see them at the corner. I hurried to my car and jumped in. They were no longer in sight, but these were mostly one-way streets and I knew the routes they'd take.

Proving my point, I again saw their taillights as I came to the corner, turning the direction I had guessed. It wasn't hard, there was so much street construction these days only a few roads were even passable.

I hung back, just close enough to catch glimpses of their taillights on occasion as we wound through Tremé.

I had a couple of advantages on them—and reasons to think I could do this and not be detected. The main one was they had no reason to think they were being followed and therefore no reason to look for a tail. There is no foolproof way to avoid being spotted, but this is my bread and butter and I know a few tricks of the trade. Also, they drive a cherry red Mini Cooper Clubman with a rainbow stripe across the back window. Hello! I drive a ubiquitous gray Mazda 3 that looks like every other small car in its class. In glimpses from the rearview mirror, it would be hard to notice it was the same car, especially in the approaching twilight. I also threw on a ball cap and glasses without lenses, kept in the glove box for just such occasions.

Another plus was that Andy was clearly the driver, and his goal in life is to never ever get a ticket, so he drives like a mellow granny.

They headed uptown, through the CBD. I let several cars get between us. Cherry red is so easy to spot. I wondered if they were going to one of the new apartment buildings that have sprouted up in what was now known as the Downtown Development District. It's mushroomed with restaurants, condos, all the things rising young professionals crave.

But no, they kept going, leaving the trendy area behind to head up on the far less trendy Simon Bolivar Avenue, going past Martin Luther King Avenue, multicultural diversity in intersections. It's the quicker way uptown, unless you're the kind of person who isn't willing to drive through "bad" neighborhoods. It's never bothered me, as I think I'm more a bad person than a good one.

There were fewer cars here, but again, it's a known route. I just had to keep them close enough to know if they turned off.

They stayed on until Louisiana Avenue, turning toward the river.

I just managed to get through the yellow to keep behind them. But again, this road was an orgy of construction, so no one was going fast. I was one car behind them.

I didn't want to get too close, so let another car slip in between us, but cut off a truck that was aggressively nosing in. It was big enough it would block my view. Their car might have been a cherry red car, but it was a small cherry red car.

After crossing Magazine, they turned uptown on Constance, a narrow residential street.

I almost kept going straight, but at the final moment turned to follow them. There were no more cars between us, so I had to go slowly, at one point pulling to the side and turning off my lights to let distance build between us.

We crept uptown for several more blocks before they slowed, then parked.

I also pulled over, a not-quite-legal space too close to a fire hydrant. But I wasn't leaving my car.

Again I witnessed a slow dance of them getting out, taking the carefully packed dishes, juggling that with a gift bag that looked like a couple bottles of wine.

Lots of people drink wine, I reminded myself.

I found my binoculars and, with a glance around to make sure no one was walking the dog or taking any evening stroll to wonder why someone was sitting in a car watching, used them to get a closer look. I was just under a block away.

They walked to the house near the corner, a recently renovated Greek revival, a double with two doors and a neatly divided porch, work still being done on the landscaping, with the small front yard more dirt than plants. The solid wood doors both matched perfectly, with shiny brass clear even in the encroaching evening, too new to have had much time in New Orleans weather. A blue Subaru was parked in front.

The door opened.

Just the hand reaching out to help with their bundles answered my question.

It was her. Cordelia was in New Orleans again.

She came out on the porch to greet them, bobbling help with the packages to hug and kiss Andy and Torbin.

More gray in her hair? Or was I just noticing it, with so many memories of her when there was none? Slimmer, even skinny, in my opinion, but my opinion didn't count. Nicely dressed in navy slacks and an off-white V-neck shirt.

Laughing, talking easily.

Another woman joined them.

Average height, short hair, but a stylish cut that would have passed muster in the suburbs. No gray and just enough highlights to make me suspect it was the result of time at the salon, not genes.

The gift bag was opened; two bottles of wine and a set of bar tools. A housewarming gift.

I put the binoculars down. They receded to a group of strangers caught in the warm glow of light on a balmy spring evening. No, I could still recognize them all, but the distance helped.

Joanne and Alex came from around the corner and joined the group on the porch.

"They're your friends, too," I said softly. I could only hope they were still mine.

I would have left, but the one-way street gave me no option but to drive by the house. I'd have to wait until they went inside.

Or back up about twenty feet.

Another car was coming down the street.

I pulled the cap lower and slunk down in the seat.

"Oh, darkness, you are such a friend of mine," I muttered as it passed.

Danny and Elly. They didn't spot me, otherwise Danny would have been tapping at my window asking what the hell did I think I was doing.

I felt a buzz from my phone but didn't dare look at it. The light might show my face too clearly or be just enough of a pinpoint of new light to call attention to me sitting here.

The one advantage of the new arrivals was that the porch was becoming too crowded, so they moved inside.

Cordelia was the last one in, pausing for a moment, looking into the night. A wistful look on her face? Or was I just imagining it?

The door shut.

I gave it a full minute before starting my car and creeping down the block, still hunched low in my seat. I did not glance in the direction of the door or the soft porch light as I drove past.

After another two blocks, I pulled over again to check my phone. It was only a notice from my bank that they had automatically withdrawn my mortgage from my account.

A look at the time told me it was early to head out to the far 'burbs, but not enough time to go home. Or do much of anything else.

I considered stopping for coffee, but my bladder overruled that. Brandon didn't seem like the kind of host who would take into account female bathroom needs. The last thing I needed was being a long way from relief with a full bladder.

With not much else to do, I headed back downtown to catch I-10 out to where we were to meet.

I tried to just focus on the driving, to wonder what the hell Brandon was up to.

But she was back in town. No one had told me. Or no one wanted to tell me.

It had been a bad breakup, messy and terrible. She was fighting cancer, had moved to Houston for treatment. I had stayed here, clinging to my life, afraid to let it go and find I had nothing, nothing there and nothing to return to. The distance and time apart, through all those important days, took a heavy toll, one I blinded myself to. I curse myself for my choices and wonder what I could have done better.

I run a small business, essentially just me. To put everything on hold for a few uncertain months would have destroyed it, all my clients going elsewhere. It was a stark choice, and I couldn't help but think I'd made the wrong one.

She'd found someone who could be there when she needed them, not the dragging weekends I could manage.

They had left Houston, moved to the northeast where her sister lived—the one who had never approved of me—and I thought that was it. I would never see her again. Messy and terrible.

Maybe it was easier that way. Gone, just gone.

But she was here, seeing my friends.

Did they really think I wouldn't find out?

I caught Louisiana Avenue and took it, through its name changes, to Carrollton.

I took a hard look at who I was—who I'd become since then. Drinking more than I should, living in a cocoon of work and alcohol. I told myself it was fine, I didn't drink during the day, well, not much. I managed my affairs, kept up a busy work schedule for the most part, as if every hour needed to be filled. And the ones that didn't have the daily necessities stuffed into them blurred away in an alcoholic shade. How much of a friend had I been to my friends?

Enough that Joanne could wonder if I'd fallen far enough into a pit of despair to murder someone.

I hadn't exactly been putting out a welcome mat, claiming work or other obligations to hide my reluctance to go to places where it had so often been the two of us. I couldn't quite face that single face in the mirror—and the failure it represented—not with my coupled friends.

Much as I didn't like it—I wanted my anger clean and hot—there were good reasons no one had told me. I'd been too sarcastic, too distant, too…well, drunk to be easily approachable for even the common exchanges of friendship, a quiet meal where we talked about our days. In their shoes I would have avoided it until it was inevitable.

I turned left on Tulane, the only legal left turn in its entire length to get to the on-ramp for I-10. Traffic wasn't rush-hour busy, a small mercy, just weekend crazy.

I should have told Douglas Townson to go fuck himself. Did I really need the money that badly? I could have used the time to work on myself, to sing the song that I was strong, I would survive.

Yeah, right, like I was ready to do that.

And I could use the money. The two of us had split the cost of things. Now it was just me. Carrying the mortgage of both the house and my office building meant I had a high overhead. While the rent I took in from the coffee shop and the grannies covered a lot of it, it didn't cover it all, nor did it leave much of a surplus for things like painting the building or replacing the elderly heating/air system.

You can't go back and change anything, I reminded myself. My only starting place was now and tomorrow and all the days after that.

Did I want her back?

Did it matter?

It would be harder with her here, the chance glance, seeing her in the grocery store, strolling on the levee. Wondering if that was her when I saw a tall woman in the distance. With our circle of friends, we'd either have to carefully avoid each other or learn how to be together with everything changed.

I didn't like either of those options.

I didn't like the direction I was going; this was a night I needed to be home alone with my thoughts, not heading out to cater to an adolescent boy's whims.

But I was already cruising by the Causeway exit, closer to my destination than my home.

This was why I needed to take cases like Douglas Townson's, I told myself, so I could indulge in helping a young boy get out of the mess he'd gotten himself into. He was just the kind of kid no one noticed and therefore the kind of kid who would see or learn something. If Eddie let him get into his computer, there was no way to know what else Brandon might have had access to, all the info on the drug ring, or how extensive Eddie's sexual coercion went. Maybe Brandon's other high school friends.

Could that be a motive for murder? Yes, but the question was for whom. Brandon didn't seem to be carrying a torch for the other girls I'd met. Maybe his friend Kevin? What if Brandon had let Kevin know that someone he had a crush on—can you call it love at that age?—was being sexually blackmailed by Eddie? A dose of macho movies and misguided protective Southern gentleman could do it.

I kept driving.

This has to end it, I told myself. *Whatever Brandon knows—or thinks he knows—all I'm going to do is help him take the next step, most likely going to the police. Let them sort it out.*

As long as the sorting out didn't include arresting me for Eddie's murder.

Traffic thinned past the airport. I turned off at the last exit before the highway went over the swampy morass between the outer suburbs and the next town over.

I hesitated at Veterans Highway, unsure of which way to go.

I decided to stay close to the well-lit area until I had more information and pulled into the parking lot of one of those bargain dollar stores. It was still open, and I could look like I was waiting for someone.

Which I was.

I parked at the far end of the lot, away from the few late-night shoppers. I glanced at my watch. Not even eight thirty yet. To pass the time, I went into the store and bought a bottle of water and a packet of cashews.

I was hungry, I realized; the cheese sandwich was long ago. I was also thirsty but wanted to go easy on the water. Once this was over, it was a half-hour drive back to my house, and the last thing I would want to do on the way home was have to make a potty stop.

That took about ten minutes even with the slow line.

I was parked close enough to a streetlight to take out the file the grannies had given me. The sooner I read it, the sooner I could give it to Joanne. I started at the beginning to go through it thoroughly.

After about five minutes of scrolling through her text messages, I was glad I wasn't a high school kid today. Or maybe I was just old enough to know it's not as important as it feels at seventeen. Worrying about not getting a message quickly, worrying about responding too quickly, and most of these were about getting together after school or to work on homework.

"You're not going to remember any of it," I said softly, not when the years fly by and teach you what real loss and heartbreak are.

Texts from Eddie. Even the early "nice" ones sounded hollow, unctuous with an obvious undertone of what he really wanted. He had a slick cleverness, slowly building the demands into the flattery, making them seem like the same thing, he was so attracted to her because she was so beautiful, just the girl for him. Yeah, he called her girl the entire time, never woman; even that slight nod was too much for his misogynistic lizard brain.

His demands became more insistent, laced with blame, claiming she led him on, or if he was nice, that she was so attractive he couldn't help himself—not in those terms, "U so hot, makes me need u, got to have u, plse help me, baby."

He didn't text her for two days after she finally gave in, only her string of texts, first happy that "U made me a woman. So happy," to "R U OK? Plse answer. Lost ur phone?"

He finally replied, claimed he'd been busy, a quick sorry. And wanting to meet again.

The pattern repeated, like a tired old clichéd love song. He'd woo her, or at least make enough of an effort until she gave in, then blow her off for a day or two. Each time he'd go a little further, adding more threats to the flattery to get her to go along. Until it got to out-and-out blackmail.

Her last texts to him veered from beseeching to angry. "Hw could u do this to me?"

His were cruel: "Ur nothing but a nasty cunt. Leave me alone." His last to her was "Sending out the pics now. Might as well spread ur legs for evy boy who don't vomit at the site of u."

"What a creep," I muttered. If anyone needed murdering, it was him.

Her last text was, "I can't do this. Only one way out. Ur next, he'll do the same to u," to three different phone numbers. She sent it the afternoon she died.

I scribbled down the three numbers. I could have the grannies trace them.

Or let the police do it. Her warning might mean one of them was also blackmailed and reacted differently.

I glanced at my watch. It was a minute past nine.

I shuffled the papers into a neat stack and put them back in the folder. Something nagged at me—maybe just the foul taste in my mouth.

The three phone numbers.

I scrolled through the numbers on my phone.

Bingo.

One of them was to the number Brandon had first called me on.

I flipped to his file. Same phone number. A text from Tiffany. Should have mentioned that to the police.

I sighed. I had been going to impose my fifteen-minute rule on him. If he didn't contact me by 9:15, I was leaving. But this threw a new twist into things. I doubted Eddie was bi—and even if he was, he would probably go for someone less, shall we say, nerdy looking than Brandon. Eddie was physically attractive enough—for those who liked those sorts of rough looks—to easily pick up a gay boy on Bourbon Street.

He could've used Brandon's computer work against him as blackmail. Let the school and his friends know that Brandon had been helping with getting the porn out. That would be totally in character for Eddie. Blackmail meant he could get the work without having to pay Brandon.

At 9:16, my phone buzzed.

A text from Brandon. "Meet me 22 st. far end. Come alone."

I texted back, "Which end is the far one?" I almost added, "nice time to tell me to be alone. What do I do with the five other people with me?"

I pulled up the map on my phone. It was the last street before the airport. Maybe less than ten blocks long.

A drizzle started, just misty enough to cloud visibility.

A plane flew low overhead, coming in for a landing.

I looked back at my phone. No reply from Brandon.

Well, damn, I could check out both ends of the street.

I pulled out of the parking lot. Only three sips into my water bottle, so I should be good.

No one was about, not even a stray cat. This was a desolate area, large metal buildings with junked cars outside separated by empty lots, soggy with recent rain.

"Why the hell did you want to meet out here?" I muttered.

And kept driving.

I wondered if I could be walking into a trap.

Except that made no sense. Eddie was dead. Most of the rest of the drug gang were in custody. If any of them had escaped they should be in Mexico by now, not waiting near the scene of the crime to ambush me.

And they had no reason to ambush me. Yeah, I'd tipped off the cops, but they had no way to know that. I'd only talked to Joanne, and she wasn't going to mention my name as the tipster. What other reason?

Douglas Townson might hate that I'd uncovered his forebearer's hideous crimes, but he wasn't going to call up Brandon and have him lure me out here. And he didn't even know what I'd uncovered yet.

This felt like teenage melodrama. Maybe there was something to show me, a second hideout they used. Maybe he was trying to impress me with how brave he was, meeting out here in the dark.

Twenty-second Street was easy to find, the last one before the high fence around the airport. Other than the occasional roar of planes landing or taking off, there was utter silence. No one was here, only empty buildings. No other cars around, only the quiet swish of the rain.

I was at one end of Twenty-second and paused, but no one seemed to be here, no lights, no cars.

Let me try the other end before I get pissed with the games he's playing.

Desolate, the bright lights from the airfield making deep shadows on the far side of the street.

I followed the road until it dead-ended as the fence angled this way, taking the land for the green field around the runways.

Another plane roared overhead.

Also, dark. No cars. This wasn't just industrial, it was the butt-end of industrial.

I pulled over, taking out my phone to text Brandon.

A pinprick of light appeared, flashing by a window in the hulking warehouse on the corner. A cell phone screen? A flashlight? Hard to tell through the distance and mist.

"I'm here," I texted him.

I waited.

Looked at my watch. Two minutes had passed since I'd sent my text. Forever.

"You get five," I muttered, "then I truly am out of here."

I wondered what they were doing, at that dinner party. On to dessert by now or still lingering over the main course, content with a leisurely evening that made no demands on time. I didn't even know what her name was.

My phone buzzed, bringing me harshly back to my swanky Saturday night, out in a hellhole in the rain under landing planes.

"B wt u in a sec," a text read.

It wasn't Brandon's phone. Oh, wait, it was, the same number he'd used the last time. I hadn't added his name to it.

A snake slithered up my spine.

I grabbed the file the grannies had given me, quickly scrolling through the texts, using the glow from my phone to read.

It was the same number. Brandon was texting me from Eddie's phone, the one the police couldn't find.

Maybe it was time for me to drive away and hand this over to the cops.

Even stupid adolescent didn't explain why Brandon would have, keep, and use Eddie's phone.

Another text pinged, "On my way."

I scrabbled in the glove box and took out the Swiss army knife I kept there and shoved it into my sock. Not much of a weapon, but this was getting too weird, and anything was better than nothing.

Maybe this was it, his big reveal, showing me he had Eddie's phone. Compromised evidence. This was beyond stupid, and I didn't think I could fix it.

Again a faint glow, but this time it was walking toward me, coming from around the side of the warehouse. A young, short, slightly pudgy boy outlined by the cell phone light.

I got out of my car.

"What are you doing?" I asked as he approached. He was wearing a dark zip sweatshirt, the hood pulled up to keep the drizzle out. His pants were too long, the hems rolled up but even so dragged on the ground.

"I need to show you something," he said.

"That you took Eddie's phone? The one the police have been searching high and low for?"

He was close enough, still holding the phone as if it was an revelation, that I could see his expression of surprise. Shock.

He recovered enough to say, "What are you talking about? Why would I have Eddie's phone? I thought the police took it." He could do the words, but his tone and expression couldn't match them. A bad liar.

"They couldn't find it. They're still looking for it. Because you've been too dunderheaded to turn it over to them."

"I don't have Eddie's phone." His face was slack, again saying the words, but without the semblance of emotion that should go with them.

"You just texted me from his phone number," I pointed out.

"It's my phone now," he said, as if that made it all right.

"No, you need to turn it over to the police. It might help them find who Eddie's killer is," I argued.

"I know who Eddie's killer is," he said. Now emotion crept into his voice, smug, like he was the only kid in the class who knew the answer.

"You do?" But I couldn't tell if he was on the level or just a bragging kid. "Even more reason to go to the police."

"No, I need to show you something."

"You need to tell me how you got Eddie's phone." I tried to put as much adult authority in my voice as I could to attempt to jar him out of his adolescent fantasy.

The ones who are too young to know the consequences are the most dangerous. Another snake down my spine. I cursed myself. I had dismissed him as a naïve, nerdy schoolkid. And he was. But a layer under that was a boy desperately struggling to be a man and having few of the markers of success—sports, looks, popularity—to easily give it to him. Most boys like him—and girls, like I was at his age—took a side street, found a home with the rebels and the outcasts. Held on until we could escape those toxic years.

A few didn't. I should have seen it, his desperate neediness, his clumsy attempts at manipulation, to be in control. I hadn't let him, an unforgivable crime. Especially since I was a middle-aged woman. Enlightened feminist guys don't hang around with man like Eddie.

There was a bulge in his jacket that looked like a gun.

Keeping my voice steady, I said, "This isn't a computer game, Brandon. Real people, real consequences."

"I win, I always win," he said. The same smug tone.

The snakes on my spine stared hissing.

A crash from back in the warehouse, something falling?

His head jerked at the noise. "You need to come with me," he said, insistence rising in his voice.

"Who's in there?"

"No one."

"Who made the noise?"

His head spun back in that direction.

"Who else is here?" I said calmly. He was getting agitated and I didn't want to add to it. "You can tell me," I said. "No one can hear us out here."

He shook his head as if clearing it. "There is no one here. No one who counts."

"Who doesn't count?"

Then he laughed, "Just my friends from school. The buddies who always hang around with me unless they have something better to do."

"You're angry at them?"

"No," he snapped, "why say that?"

"Because you sound annoyed," I said. But I didn't want to get into his anger. It was too dangerous. "Why do you need me here?"

"You killed Eddie, don't you know?"

"But I didn't."

He took the gun out and pointed it at me.

Not good. His hand was steady and he looked comfortable with it, someone used to guns.

"You need to come with me." There was an edge to his voice, the anger honed to a fine point, almost gloating.

"What are you trying to accomplish?" I asked, buying time.

But there was nowhere to sell it in this desolate area, the drizzling mist muffling sound, blurring vision. No one would come out here until the morning; resisting him would get me shot here. Even as small as he was, he could drag my body into the canal, only yards away.

"You just need to come with me," he said, the gun still steady.

"Okay, I'll follow you," I said. *This is crazy*, I wanted to yell. I'd forgotten, or neglected to consider, all the crazy young boys, stung with teenage hurt, raging hormones, and raging humiliation, and the fury with which they lashed out. Little nerdy Brandon. Seventeen and probably hadn't even been kissed yet.

"No, you go first. I'm not stupid."

I didn't reply, because he was stupid. He might kill me—guns are good at that. But he couldn't walk away from this and go back to his life. He'd have a short moment of glory—rather, attention—then he'd rot in jail for more years than he could imagine. But he said he always won, and that was the only outcome he'd considered.

I walked in the direction he'd come from, slowly, from the dark, and to scan for anything that could help.

Another noise from within the warehouse.

"Damn it," he muttered. "Hurry up!"

"Where am I going?"

"To the door," he answered, as if I should know where the door was.

I guessed it was somewhere near the side he'd appeared from. The noise at least let me know someone was alive in there. I had wondered if he'd lured us all out there to kill off one by one everyone he thought had humiliated him.

"What are you going to do with us?"

"You'll see," he said, a grim satisfaction in his voice.

I came around the corner of the building and could just make out the outline of a door partway down the side.

Still no lights except a faint wisp from his phone screen behind me. He had turned it to flashlight mode to light his way.

"This the door?" I said as I approached it.

"Yeah, go in."

I entered an office area, vague shapes of desks, file cabinets, chairs in the dim light. I moved slowly in, my foot brushing a trash can near one of the desks.

"Now where?" I asked.

"Keep going," he said.

Not helpful, except it told me he had little empathy, no ability to consider I'd never been here before and couldn't know what he did.

I plodded my way to the far end of the room, only the glow from his phone giving any light back here. Guessing, I turned right.

"No, the other way," he said, as if I'd done something stupid.

Brandon had carefully thought this all out, that was clear. But he'd only planned to win. Even something as minor as my not knowing the way to go disrupted his plans.

Oh, baby cakes, welcome to the real world, I vowed, as I shuffled along in the dark, his cell phone light doing little to help me navigate the dim hallway. I was going to do everything I could to ruin his plans. Computer games only have a limited set of variables. Life is infinite.

It was a charcoal tunnel that got blacker as the tiny glow from the office windows was left behind. I had to assume there was a door at the end of the hallway; it was too black to see anything. I fumbled for a doorknob, my hand feeling in the dark.

Since Brandon didn't tell me not to, I opened the door.

Another dark void. This one felt bigger, the interior of the warehouse. There were no windows to let in even the faintest of lights from the airport.

I thought I heard shuffling, breathing, then a plane rumbled overhead and drowned out any other sound.

"Keep going," Brandon instructed.

I took several steps in the dark until my foot clunked against something solid. And painful.

"Keep going," he said, his voice growing agitated.

"I can't see and I don't know where to go," I answered. If his goal was to just shoot me, he would have done it by now.

He let out an annoyed sound, then stepped around me, too far away for me to tackle him.

A light blazed on, a single bulb hanging from the rafters. It cast hard shadows in the corners, but was daylight compared to the blackness before.

Three other people were in the room.

Sophia and—what was her name?—Janice had their hands tied together, wrist to wrist, forcing them to encircle one of the steel supporting beams. Tied to another beam with his hands behind him was Alan. He was slumped to the floor with blood trickling down his chin, but his eyes were open and he was watching.

"Where's Kevin?" I asked.

"I'll get him later," Brandon snarled, as if that was one part of his plan that hadn't worked right.

"What are you going to do?" I asked. "Kill us all?"

"No, you are," he said, with a triumphant smile. "You're going to shoot everyone here and then in a fit of remorse shoot yourself."

"You think I'm going to go along with that?" I mocked him.

He leveled the gun at me. "It doesn't matter what you do. They're dead, killed with the gun that killed Eddie, and then you're dead. Who's going to talk?"

"Are you crazy? You played a few computer games around forensics and you think you know enough to fool the cops?"

He had the gun, the only weapon I had was my brain. I hoped it was enough.

"It's not that hard," he retorted, but his face was getting red. "You're about to be arrested for his murder anyway." The smug smile came back as he pulled something from out of his jacket and tossed it to me.

A baggie containing a bullet.

"I was smart enough to dig it out of the lawn," he bragged.

"How did you…?" I started.

Sophia answered, "I told him. Alan told me, and I was talking about what a creep Eddie was. Brandi-bots here said he didn't seem so bad, so I told him about Eddie attacking Tiffany's mom."

"And I was smart enough to make the bullet go away so the cops couldn't find it," he said, gloating. "Plus your car was seen around the time Eddie was killed."

"So you lied and claimed to have seen it. They're already suspicious of that one. The gym sticker is faded from the sun as it is. A passer-by on a dark night notices it? Not likely. The cops aren't as stupid as you'd like them to be. If they haven't traced that call yet, they will."

Again, the look of uncertainty as I pushed against his perfectly laid plan.

The really sad thing is I was right. Joanne would know I would never do anything like this. Kill a scumbag like Eddie? Maybe, but not three innocent kids. The police would dig and dig again. He'd go to jail, we'd be dead; it would all be a sad, stupid waste. Unless I could stop him.

"Ever won a computer game straight through? No stopping and going back to the last saved version to avoid being killed by trolls? One mistake and you go to jail for the rest of your life."

"I'm not going to make any mistakes."

"Never got surprised by the trolls?" I taunted. "I told my two cop friends I was coming out here tonight, meeting you. Just in case. If I don't call them in about an hour to say I'm okay, then they're out here with sirens screaming. Think you can kill us all and clean everything up in that time?" I glanced at my watch. "Oh, make that a half hour."

"No! You're lying!"

Well, yes, I was, but he had no way of knowing that.

"End it now," I said, my voice as calm as I could make it. "If it stops here, you'll be okay. Claim Eddie threatened you. No DA is going to go to the mat for him. You'll get a slap on the wrist. Bragging rights, even, for how tough you are. But if you go through with this, you're going to spend the rest of your life in prison."

"No, you're lying!" he yelled again.

"It's the tape," Janice said.

I looked at her.

"Shut up!" he yelled.

"What tape?"

Sophia said, "Him sucking Eddie's dick. They got bored and drunk and turned on their little nerd. They made him suck their dicks."

"Shut up! Just shut up! You're lying!" He was sweating, and even the dim light showed the red of his face.

If he wasn't pointing a gun at us, I would have felt sorry for him. But I had more important things to worry about than his male psyche.

I quietly stepped away from them, opening us up so we'd be more-spread-out targets.

"No, she's not. I saw the tape," Alan said. "You throwing up, running out the door, tripping, them grabbing you and rolling you in dog shit. They filmed it all."

Again, keeping my voice calm and soothing, I said, "Brandon, that's a horrible thing to have happened to you. But it's not your fault. Men get assaulted, too, even strong men."

"No, you're lying! The video is fake! It didn't happen like that."

"If it's fake, then why does it matter? Why bring us here?" I asked. But I knew the answer. It wasn't fake. He'd been humiliated and degraded in a brutal way. First he'd lashed back at Eddie—who made the same mistake I'd made—thinking Brandon, pudgy little Brandon wouldn't do anything.

"Because you'll tell these lies about me. I'm not like that."

"No one thinks you're like that," I said.

But he kept going, not listening. "I'm from a long line of hunters and soldiers. We're men, real men. My dad's a soldier, fighting overseas."

"Your dad's in jail for going AWOL," Sophia said.

"Liar! He's got medals to prove it."

Worlds collide. "No, that's your aunt," I said. "His sister."

Brandon whirled on me. How many messed-up kids could there be with soldier fathers locked away? The toxic misogyny my date had described would produce a kid like this, caught between expectations of what men were and the short, round body nature had given him.

"She's a bitch!" he shouted.

Bingo.

I wondered if there was a kid in there who could be saved, who could find his way out of that noxious swamp of rigid, impossible expectations.

But that would be up to the psychologists. Right now I had to save the rest of us.

Every time he'd been distracted by one of them, I'd moved farther away.

Now he had to swivel his head back and forth.

He finally seemed to catch on.

"Hey, you move over there."

"Move where?" I asked. I took a step, pretended to stub my toe and stumble, enough to bend down and grab the knife, sending it sliding along the floor toward Sophia and Janice.

Then I spun around and jumped for the light switch, and everything was black.

I immediately threw myself on the floor, sliding away as far as I could.

As I expected, the gun fired, aiming for where I had just been.

"Stop it! Turn the light back on!" Brandon yelled.

But we weren't playing in his game anymore.

It's an old trick but I felt along the floor, finding a few discarded bolts and nails. I tossed them across the room to an empty place.

Brandon fired again.

Two bullets gone.

I hadn't had a chance to get a good look at his gun but had to assume it had at least ten shots. Eight bullets was more than enough for four of us.

Brandon turned on the light on his cell phone.

Guess he didn't like to be in the dark, either.

But this was a huge space, open in the middle, but with piles of large wooden crates and partly dismantled cars spanning the edges.

His light didn't go very far.

A plane roared overhead. Taking advantage of the deafening sound, I skittered back behind one of the cars, grabbing another handful of junk and tossing it behind him—and away from the others.

He fired again.

He was getting close to the light.

I picked up what felt like a wrench and threw it right at him, outlined in his light.

A good blow to the shoulder. He dropped his cell phone. "What the hell? That's not fair!"

There was an open tool kit beside the car. I grabbed what I could, screwdrivers, sockets, and threw them at him. He was trying to retrieve his phone, but the light gave me a target.

In frustration, he fired in my direction, but the bullet went wide.

Suddenly the door slammed and his muffled voice yelled, "You can't get out. You're locked in here. No one is getting out of here."

Footsteps running away.

I gave it a moment, then retrieved his cell phone, but I clicked his light off. Softly I said, "Did you get the knife?"

From the dark, "Yeah, working on it," from Sophia.

Janice said, "He has one of those guns, the kind that shoot a lot of bullets."

Well, that was cheery news.

I risked clicking his light on, going back to the outer wall. There had to be another way out of here. But other than the inner door to the office, there was only one big bay door at the far end, and it was securely padlocked. If I had a gun I could blow it away.

So I did the next best thing and called 9-1-1, using my phone. As I dialed, I went to the inner door.

Ah, yes, it could be locked from in here. Just a cheap doorknob lock, but it might slow him down enough…for a miracle.

He could be back any second, so I merely said, "Location is warehouse at the west end of Twenty-second street, Kenner, right by the airport. Hostages and an armed and dangerous suspect. Young, short and pudgy, glasses, black hoodie, jeans, about five-four, one-forty pounds. White. Name is Brandon Beaujeaux. Need help asap. Can't talk. He might hear. Murderer of Edward Springhorn."

Then I brought the waning light from his dying phone back to them to help free them.

Sophia had cut through the ropes on one of their wrists, freeing them from the pole.

We quickly cut though the rope on their other wrist, at least enough strands for them to work their way free.

"Hide," I told them. "Get under a car if you can. Go to the back wall."

I went to work on Alan.

"Prick tricked us," he muttered as I cut. "Said he was playing a prank and asked us to go along. Got us to tie each other up. Then started laughing like an idiot. Hit me when I said to let us go."

"The cops are on their way," I assured him.

Maybe Brandon would have second thoughts and, finally, be smart enough to get out of here instead of coming back.

The outer door slammed.

And maybe not.

I clicked the light off, sawing Alan's ropes furiously in the dark.

Footsteps in the hallway. The flickering beam from a flashlight licking through the door frame.

A thud as he hit the door, expecting it to open.

Alan was free.

"Hide in the cars," I instructed, pointing him in that direction.

Kicking and cursing at the door.

I felt my way in the opposite direction.

No, not to be a hero. Well, not much of one, but the more spread out we were, the more bullets he'd have to fire to kill us all. If need be, which I hoped it would not, I could distract him to fire over here. And hope these crates held things like engines or steel plates.

I crawled around several of them, worming my way back as close as I could to the outer wall. And as far away from the door as I could get.

My phone rang.

What the fuck?

I grabbed it out of my pocket, only wanting to shut it up. Brandon was making too much noise cursing and kicking at the door to have heard the initial ring.

Joanne.

Oh, fuck, yeah, the 9-1-1 call from this number and mentioning it was the Eddie Springhorn murder.

I swiped it on, then darkened the phone before answering.

She was already speaking, "—the hell is going on? Where are you?"

I cut her off and told her in a harsh whisper, "I can't talk. Teenage kid. Brandon Beaujeaux murdered Eddie and he's trying to get all the rest of us who might know something."

Gunfire erupted.

Brandon had finally figured out his kicks weren't working and he had something that would.

"Do not say a word, you'll give away my position," I said, then stuffed my phone into my pocket, leaving it on. If I didn't make it, it would be evidence.

The building reverberated as the door slammed open, hitting the wall hard.

Another second and the light came on.

Hidden as I was I couldn't see him, but I could hear his footsteps, get glimpses of his moving shadow.

"I know you're in here," he yelled. "All I need to do is open fire and you're dead."

I pulled the change I had gotten from my nuts and water. Two quarters, a dime, and three pennies.

I wondered how many times he would fall for the same old trick. Maybe enough to exhaust his ammo.

I carefully slid around the wooden box, just enough to get a clear shot into an empty area of the warehouse. I held still listening for his footsteps. He was nervously pacing. I waited until they sounded like they were walking away from me and then tossed the change as far as I could before skittering back to my hiding place.

They hit the back wall, metal on metal, making enough noise to capture his attention.

At the first sound, he opened fire, as if his finger was too close to the trigger and being startled was enough to make him shoot.

Some of the bullets hit a car, the ping of ricochets landing close to where I was.

After the deafening clatter, the silence was sudden.

"I'm not kidding," he yelled.

Then he let go another burst to prove his point.

I thought I heard sirens in the distance, but another plane flew overheard.

Even if the cops got here, they wouldn't storm in, not against an idiot with a machine gun and a death wish.

Again, I felt furious at the stupidity of this. His stupid choices, his stupid little ego. At my cynical worst, I could argue that Eddie got what he deserved—Brandon could kill the scumbag and that would be a rough justice. But now the four of us. And the first responders he might take out as well. An utterly stupid, useless waste.

"You'd better come out!" he yelled.

Yeah, right, like we're going to do that.

A paint can clattered against the back wall. Someone else had picked up my trick.

His jittery finger fired again.

And he'd fallen for it again.

I needed to have a better idea of where he was and what he was doing.

The problem being that if I could see him, he could see me.

I crept around the back side of the box, holding still, then took advantage of another plane overhead to crawl farther out.

Around another crate.

Then another.

I could see him in a sliver of light, only a brief glimpse, but enough to know where he was. He was still clinging to his script, that he was in control, pacing in the central, lit area, as if we would eventually come to him.

Hey, Cordelia, this is a Micky Knight welcome back to New Orleans. I hoped their dinner party had ended early, although past ones never had, and that Joanne was at home or well on her way there before calling me. She would at least have enough sense to go somewhere private, where no one would overhear me blown away by a machine gun.

Yes, that was a siren in the background.

Maybe he heard it, too.

He opened fire again, aiming where the girls had gone.

Please be under a car behind several cars, I silently pleaded. The sound was harsh, loud from the gun and the bullets hitting the metal wall, the cars, the steel posts.

And a small cry. Someone had been hit.

"You're dead. You're all dead," he said, satisfaction, even relief, at finally having a target.

"You're just a pussy-boy with a gun." Alan, from another part of the room.

Brandon spun in his direction and opened fire.

In the cacophony, I yanked a board free from one of the containers.

The firing stopped.

Silence.

"Missed me," Alan taunted.

Brandon fired again.

I stood up, slipped past the box, and heaved the board at Brandon's now-turned back.

Hit him square between the shoulders.

The gun jerked up, still firing, as he stumbled off balance.

"What the fuck!" he yelled, finally letting go of the trigger.

I slid back behind the containers, crawling on the floor.

Brandon may have been trained, but he was firing level from where he was holding the gun. If I were standing, he'd be firing right at my chest.

Which was why I was on my stomach, crawling on the floor.

Now he fired in my direction.

Or close to where I had been.

I could hear the bullets overhead, the splintering of wood from the containers, the thud as they hit the metal outer wall.

I kept crawling back to the far wall.

One of the crates cracked open from the bullets, the wood and its plastic-wrapped contents clattering to the ground.

A shaft of light hit a metal box on the wall.

I pulled myself to a crouching position and managed to grab one of the shattered boards.

Cupping my mouth and pitching my voice to the back wall to hide its direction, I shouted, "You're a lousy shot, Brandon!" then threw the board that way.

It hit the back wall and he opened fire.

How many fucking bullets does that gun have? I thought as I unfurled from my crouch to slide along the floor, heading for the circuit breaker box.

Ten feet, crawl, another two feet.

I was going to be so bruised. If I survived.

Another plane thundered overhead. I couldn't tell if the sirens were closer or not.

Five feet.

"Come out!" he yelled. His plan was not going well, desperation replacing gloating in his voice.

"To let you kill us? Fuck no!" That was Alan.

That distracted Brandon, and he fired toward his voice.

I pushed myself up from the floor.

Bruised and sore muscles.

Was at the circuit box. A tumbling of noise from the bullets' destruction covered the creaking open of the lid.

"Lights out," I muttered and spread my arms to cover both sides, then pushed.

Darkness.

"Lights out, Brandon, baby," I yelled before again diving to the floor.

The bullets whizzed overhead, grinding through the wooden boxes, destroying them. But he was aiming in my general direction, not at me, still far too close for comfort. Some of the shattered boards landed on my back, a nail scraping painfully into my leg.

I gritted my teeth and swore silently, creeping as quietly as I could to get behind the remaining intact crates. But the floor was now littered with debris, making it slow—and painful—going. Bruises, sore muscles, and splinters.

He turned his flashlight back on, so was easy to spot.

He went back to the light switch, uselessly flipping it back and forth.

"Turn the fucking light back on!" he yelled.

"Afraid of the dark?" Alan yelled.

Then the little boy screamed, "You're cheating!"

We weren't playing his game.

"You're not a winner!" I yelled at him, flattening myself on the floor as I finished.

I wasn't disappointed. A flurry of bullets spewed just above me. More wood shattering, turning to shards.

He swung wildly, letting the bullets fly in a circle.

But he was shooting high, higher as he became more erratic. He was doing damage, destroying anything that wasn't solid metal, the wooden containers and their auto parts groaning apart, piles of paper from somewhere, a pale ghostly white floating to the floor.

I kept inching around the crates, as one was damaged, to a whole one. But there were few of those left.

Another barrage of gunfire overhead. My shoulder was hit. But no, it came from behind me, had to be a ricochet. I couldn't tell if I was bleeding or just badly bruised. My jean jacket, a favorite, would never be the same.

Like the gunfire, the flashlight wavered erratically. He was having trouble controlling both.

Unless he was a secret jock—and maybe even if he was—his arms had to be getting tired.

As if to prove my point, he fired again, but this time lower, the bullets biting into the concrete. I could see the white dust swirl in his flashlight.

The cops had to be here by now, I calculated. Joanne would be smart enough to relay what she knew to them. But they had to be prepared to confront a man with a high-powered weapon.

How long? A few minutes?

When the next second could bring the final bullet.

He fired again, this time in the direction of the girls, also lower, either too tired to hold the gun up or having finally figured out we wouldn't be standing tall, ready for his next shot.

A yelp. Surprise? Pain?

He fired again.

No sound this time.

I crept around the box. I was behind him, but at least forty feet back, across a floor littered with debris.

Another round of firing.

But only a few bullets.

Followed by a click.

Out of ammo.

In the jiggling of the flashlight, I could see him frantically digging in his jacket.

I threw myself off the floor, screaming, "Now!" as I flung myself in his direction, running, jumping, ignoring the junk on the floor, caring only if I kept my balance and going forward. Hurt didn't matter.

I had only a few seconds.

He heard me and turned in my direction, madly trying to jam in another cartridge.

Almost tripping on a large piece of pipe, over it, nail in my foot, ignore it.

He dropped the flashlight, then scrabbled for it, then stopped, back at the gun, but without light to guide him.

Ten feet.

Five.

He lifted the gun.

I grabbed the barrel, shoving it aside, feeling it shuddering in my hand as bullets exploded out of it.

It didn't matter. Even if I was hit, the force of my momentum would drive me into him, my fist plowing into his face, my whole body slamming into his, taking him down.

We crashed onto the floor.

My fist again in his face.

The gun stopped firing.

I hit him again.

Yeah, I wanted to hurt him. But mostly I wanted to stop him. To make sure he was too hurt to fire that gun again.

I wrenched the gun out of his hand.

He yowled in pain.

I kicked the gun across the floor. Out of his reach.

I brought a knee hard into his groin.

Another grunt of pain and he tried to curl up, but I put my forearm across his neck, pinning him down, enough pressure to keep him from moving.

"You're hurting me," he muttered. His nose was bleeding.

"Too bad."

I didn't let go.

"It's safe," I yelled to the others. "I've got him pinned."

Footsteps, running.

Alan. He picked up the flashlight.

More footsteps, slow, halting.

"Back to the left on the wall, there's a circuit breaker box," I told him.

He trotted away, shining the light to the ceiling so it reflected enough to give us all a dim glow.

"Let me up, I'll behave," Brandon said.

I ignored him, looking where Sophia and Janice were coming from.

Janice was limping, blood running down her leg, her arm across Sophia's shoulder.

"I'm okay," she said.

"You will be," I promised her. Relief was too small a word for what I felt seeing them standing and moving. Okay considering what could have been.

"Please, I will behave," Brandon again pleaded. "Let me up."

"Fuck you," Sophia said for us all.

"Not a chance in hell. You're restrained until the cops arrest you," I explained. *Soon*, I hoped. It was a strain holding him like this, left knee in his chest, right arm across his neck with my other leg and arm to balance and hold me up enough to not choke him or break ribs.

The light came back on.

The warehouse looked like a tornado had ripped through it, debris everywhere, paper strewn across the floor, concrete dust hanging in the air.

"There are cops outside," I told them. "Go out slowly, with your hands up, announce who you are as you exit."

Janice was sagging against Sophia. I didn't know how long she'd been bleeding, and she needed medical attention.

Alan went to the other side of her, taking her arm over his shoulder.

Sophia let her go. "I'll stay here," she announced. Then she sat down on the floor, bracing her knees around Brandon's head, pinning him down.

"Girl power. I think he'll hate that," she said. She grabbed both his wrists, holding them together.

I gratefully took my arm from his throat so I could hold myself up with both arms.

For a few mere seconds, it was us and our ragged breathing; then a sea of uniforms and lights invaded the space.

As I had promised, I let Brandon up to be taken into custody.

"This isn't fair," were his parting words.

In relief and exhaustion, Sophia and I hugged each other. "I'm glad you're okay," I told her.

"Me too. I'm glad I'm okay," she answered. "I'm glad we're all okay."

We broke our hug.

I remembered the phone in my pocket.

It was still on.

"Well, I think I used just about all my minutes," I said into it. I had no idea if she was still on the line.

She was. "Probably the most interesting phone call I've had in a long time. I'm outside. We can hang up now."

I did and limped out of the building.

"We're all okay." I wondered if that was true. I should have been more suspicious, not treated Brandon like a schoolboy. But did I want to live in that world, wondering what lurked beneath even the most innocent face?

I welcomed the outside air, even the rain on my face. The place was surrounded with flashing red and blue lights, harshly jarring against the black night.

Joanne touched my arm.

"I'm sorry I ruined your party," I said.

"That's okay…wait, what are you talking about?" She tried to save it, but it was too late.

"You were all busy this weekend. You, Danny, Torbin. And…I saw her. Driving through the French Quarter. Put them together." As wrung out as I was, I wasn't going to admit to following Torbin and spying on them.

"Ah. That wasn't intended."

"That's what life is, so much unintended, isn't it? All we can do is climb into the next day."

We were silent until she said, "You need to be looked at. Your leg is bleeding and you've got cuts and scratches all over." She led me to a waiting ambulance.

I was too exhausted to argue. Or claim I was okay.

Chapter Thirty-six

Somehow I managed to drag myself to my office for my meeting with Mr. Douglas Townson.

Yeah, I was limping. Everything hurt. I was right about the bruises and sore muscles. Way too right. I'd required two stitches on my leg, a glancing ricochet, and three on my shoulder, also a rebound, thankfully. Maybe I could stitch the jacket back together; dark denim is so forgiving of blood stains. After being released from the hospital early Sunday morning, I had crawled into bed and only come out to take painkillers.

Over twenty-four hours of rest should be enough, right?

I kept telling my aching bones that.

My hands shook when I thought how close it had been. Half a second? How much can you split seconds and have them mean anything? My hand had hit the barrel, deflecting it just as he fired. If I had run into that barrage…my funeral would be closed casket.

But the days didn't stop coming, and I was still here.

Janice had been hit in the leg, also from a bullet that was flying around, but unlike me, it had hit her square. She would be okay. Physically.

She had gotten entangled in the mess, too. We'd ended up rooming together for a few hours until they let me go. She had dated Eddie a few times, only because she was intrigued by an older guy being interested in her. He managed to get his hand up her skirt and down her blouse—and get a picture of it. She thought she could get him to stop by telling him her uncle was a cop. She'd agreed to meet him one more time. Foolishly, out at the drug garage. They'd started arguing, then the door buzzer rang, three short, one long, like a code. Eddie stuffed her in an office, told her to not say anything. She saw him letting someone in but could only see Eddie, not the other person. He started yelling at whoever it was. Then gunshots. Silence. She waited for over an hour before finally peeking out. Eddie was dead, his crotch area a bloody mess.

She ran away and said nothing, too scared. Thought it might have been someone else like her, someone he'd blackmailed with pictures.

Eddie had showed her the tape of Brandon, showed her the pictures of Tiffany. She was scared of him and his friends and didn't know who had killed him. So she, conveniently, didn't think she needed to go to the police.

Brandon had taken over Eddie's phone and attempted to do what Eddie did, coerce sexual favors by threatening to send out pics. A few days after Eddie was killed, Janice got another threatening text from him. Or his phone.

But Brandon was not Eddie, not even the foul, rough version of the manly man he was. When Janice finally gave in, agreed to meet behind the football stadium and found Brandon there, she laughed.

Then told him she'd seen the video of him. Eddie had emailed her a copy. If he sent her pictures out, she'd send that out.

She walked away, thinking that would be that, but mad enough that she showed Sophia the video. And Sophia told Alan.

And nobody told their parents, a teacher, an adult. They wanted to be grown-ups who could handle the world.

Brandon begged her to destroy it, not tell anyone. Oh, and she should go to the prom with him to make it all okay. She again blew him off, throwing in his face that she'd shown it to Sophia and Alan, and no way was she going to the prom with him.

The fuse was lit.

No, that's not true—that fuse was lit a long time ago, when Brandon was born into a family with rigid, rancid ideas of men and women. It was just Janice's bad luck—with a few less-than-perfect choices—that she stumbled into his burning rage.

We all make bad choices at times. Mostly not too bad and mostly that don't spiral out of control into this madness.

I made a pot of coffee. Yes, it was the afternoon, but I needed the caffeine. Just to get up the stairs, let alone the meeting with Douglas Townson. But I wanted it over with and him out of my life.

None of us saw the boiling rage and insecurity. Alan, Sophia, and Janice had easily agreed to meet him, went along with his claim that he was playing a big joke on Kevin to make it look like they were hostages. What was truly happening was too bizarre to contemplate. Until it happened.

Alan said he wasn't being all that heroic by yelling at Brandon. He was behind three engine blocks. "If anything could stop bullets, it was that much metal." Sophia had crawled under a Jeep that was behind two other cars, but with so many bullets, they were lucky only Janice got hit in the leg.

Brandon's family was already on TV saying he was a good boy and they couldn't believe he'd done anything like that. In one clip I glimpsed the woman I'd dated—Brenda?—in the background. A scowl on her face—no one was smiling—but she seemed to not want to be there, to help excuse what he had done.

Joanne had called me last evening to check on me. And update me. The building had two security cameras inside. Some of the tools were expensive and they'd had problems with them wandering. One had been shot out, but the one over the door behind Brandon had been working. It was damning enough with all four of us as witnesses, but video sealed his case. They'd found his, formerly Eddie's phone, and that also showed Brandon had been using the pictures Eddie had taken the same way Eddie was using them. They'd even found the baggie with my missing bullet in it.

"That should clear me, right?" I'd said.

"All of this should clear you. Plus add a few more charges to the long list against him."

She'd offered to come over, but I said I was okay and only interesting in sleeping. Half-true. I was only interested in sleeping.

Mr. Townson, of course, was not on time. He kept me waiting until three thirty.

When he finally arrived, he started the meeting with, "So, what's my money bought me?" No greeting, let alone noticing my bruised face and hands.

"I found who murdered your grandfather."

He looked taken aback.

I laid out my case, piece of evidence by piece of evidence, damning bit by damning bit.

Uncharacteristically, he said nothing, the frown on his face deepening with each piece of paper.

Finally, when I showed him the last piece, Samuel Braud's diary, he said, "Well, this is not what I expected."

"That I'd solve it? Or what kind of man your grandfather was?"

"Great-grandfather," he amended, a subtle hint I'd proven my case. "Both, frankly."

I handed him the invoice. "This is the time and effort it took me to uncover all this information." I didn't expect him to pay it. I'd put every hour I'd spent on the case, even the ones I really didn't need to. I'd probably only get the advance.

He looked at it longer than he needed to.

"What happened to you?" he finally said.

He didn't care; he was stalling for time.

I told him, "A teenage boy was taught to look down at women. That resentment grew into rage and a sense of entitlement. He thought he was very smart, smart enough to get away with murder. He wasn't."

"You stopped him all by yourself?"

"No, I'm not that kind of hero. We stopped him, two young women and a young gay man. If you want to know more, you can read about it in the paper."

"You don't like me, do you?"

"I think you're going to weasel out of paying your bill because you don't like the results."

He stared at me. He was rich enough that people spoke softly to him. He wasn't expecting me to be any different.

"I don't much like the result. Finding out my great-grandfather was an alleged killer."

"An alleged sexually deviant serial killer."

"You can't expect me to pay full price for that."

"My expectations of you are pretty low," I agreed.

Another deep frown. "You'll keep this quiet, won't you? I don't want this public."

"Full price buys discretion."

He sighed. Twice.

I'm a woman, I'm supposed to play nice, not make it too hard. As with Brandon, there was a script running in his head of how women were supposed to be.

"Just think of me like a man," I said. "It'll make it much easier."

"You think I'm sexist?"

"You tell me. If I were a male private detective, would you be expecting me to lower your bill because even though I found everything you asked for, the information wasn't to your liking?"

"No one has more respect for women than I do."

We don't want respect, asshole, just equality. It doesn't matter whether it's a pedestal or a pit, we're still not human the way men are.

"Then respect my time and pay my bill," was all I managed to say. I looked at my watch, making sure he saw.

He sighed again, then looked at his watch, making sure I noticed it was much more expensive than mine. Then he slowly took out his checkbook, as if giving me a chance to change my mind, and finally wrote a check.

I remained silent.

He handed it to me. It was for the full amount.

I held out the case file, copies of the information to share with him.

"Shred it," he said and got up. He looked at his watch as if he had so many important things to do and left without saying good-bye.

I gave him fifteen minutes, then after a quick rinse of my coffeepot, locked up and headed out. Much as I wanted to go home and put my aching feet up, instead I went to the bank to deposit the check. I didn't want to give Mr. Townson much time to change his mind.

Then home, blessed home, empty, lonely home. But I was okay with solitude.

I was okay.

Two fingers of Scotch would make me even more okay.

I changed, sweatpants, T-shirt, bra off.

Just as I was taking a highball glass down, there was a knock at my door, followed by another insistent knock.

The initials WTF were crossing my brain as I crossed to the door.

Joanne stood outside, balancing a pizza box in one hand while about to knock again with the other. Behind her on the steps was a six-pack of the latest Abita seasonal beer. She had to put it down to knock.

"Thought you might need to eat," Joanne said. "Can I come in, or should we picnic on the steps?"

"Um…come in. Can't promise it's a clean house."

"I'm used to your dirt." She picked up the beer and followed me in.

The pizza smelled good.

I'm starving, I realized. I hadn't eaten much in the last few days, since I was too lazy to defrost anything—as well as be healthy—so all I had in the house was the tail end of a loaf of bread and some peanut butter. One meal a day, yeah, but it was a bridge too far for breakfast, lunch, and dinner.

She opened two beers and handed one to me.

I took a sip. "Did you really think I might have killed him?"

"It doesn't matter what I think," she answered. "I have to follow the evidence. But no, much as I could understand killing that scumbag, it didn't seem like a Micky Knight crime. If you'd done it, you would have been much smarter about it."

"Thanks, I think." I took another sip. Then busied myself with grabbing plates and putting a slice of pizza each on them. At least this was from a much better place than the one I'd met Brandon in.

"Tell me what happened," she said as we sat at the kitchen table.

"This part of the investigation?"

"No, the investigation is over. At least as far as you're concerned. Maybe testifying, but he'll probably plea bargain, use his youth to get a shorter sentence. I don't interview suspects over pizza and beer."

I told as best I could, Tiffany and how it led to finding Fast Eddie, ending with the shootout in the warehouse.

We were silent when I finished.

I held up my hand. A slight tremble. Softly, I said, "I'm okay, but my hand still shakes, I can still feel the recoil of the barrel. Half a second…"

"But that half a second didn't happen," Joanne said. "You're here. You need to be here."

"I'm doing okay," I said. I knew what she meant. I needed to be here living a life, not hiding in work, avoiding the hard questions, to keep building friendships instead of leaving them to lie fallow. That derelict house that had once been Frederick Townson's. Was that what I was letting my life become?

"That's what you tell yourself?" Joanne said. "You drink yourself to sleep with booze and get through the day on a stream of coffee. You call that okay?"

I took a sip of beer, then a bite of pizza. "I call it okay. Not great. Not where I'd like to be. Okay for today. That's the best I've got." But I didn't want to talk about myself. I asked, "Why didn't you tell me she was back in town? Why did you lie?"

Joanne followed my example, delaying answering with drinking and eating. "How did you know?"

"Answer my questions first."

She sighed. "Because it was someone else's job. I thought Torbin should tell you, but he thought Alex would be better, and Alex thought Danny should do it. So no one did it. I'm sorry. I wasn't sure she was really coming back or if it was just temporary, and used that as an excuse to tell myself I only needed to tell you if she was moving back here to stay."

"So, is she?"

"Nope. Your turn. How did you know?"

"I'm not stupid. Every one of you was busy at the same time, and no one would tell me what was going on."

"That was all?"

"Okay, I followed Torbin to the party."

She snorted into her beer. "Fuck. Of course. You're a goddamn good private eye. What were we thinking, we could hide it from you?" She started laughing, then shook her head. "You shouldn't have done that." But she couldn't help laughing. She took another sip of beer to stop it, then said, "What did you see?"

"You on the porch. Now answer my question."

"Yes, she's staying. She took what she called her dream job as the chief medical officer at a new community health care center, one that is working to become a leader in health care for the LGBTQ community."

"Is she happy?"

Joanne didn't answer immediately. Another sip of beer. "She seems happy and engaged in her work. We learned more than we wanted to know about scheduling, all the things that go into coordinating labs and insurance before the provider—they're all called providers now—can see a patient. She's happy to be back here." She paused long enough to open another beer. "As for the rest, I don't know."

"What's the new girlfriend like? Or are they married now? Since that's possible."

"You have to ask the difficult questions, don't you?"

"You don't have to choose sides," I said. "I'm not going to be—try not to be—the asshole who bitches because you include her. If it feels disloyal, you don't have to answer." I took a second piece of pizza—yeah, I was hungry—to indicate we could move on.

She took another sip, then said, "If you quote me on this I will deny it. Boring. Not someone I'd be friends with if she wasn't attached to someone I am friends with. Not bad, nice enough, but…boring. Suburbs, safe and comfortable."

"Everything I'm not."

"You are certainly not boring. And that's it, that's all you're going to get out of me."

I opened a second beer, I wasn't driving anywhere. Then I asked, "Why are you here? You thought I might have murdered someone, and now you're the one friend braving my closed door?"

"You've been a major jerk and an asshole—"

"Thanks, I appreciate the compliment."

"Shut up, I'm talking. Major jerk and asshole. You're also one of the brightest, funniest, and most compassionate people I know. You put yourself out for those kids; he probably would have killed them if you hadn't done what you'd done. It pisses me off when you do something that brave and kind, then throw it away with cheap alcohol."

"It's not cheap."

"Whatever. No, we're not perfect either, myself very much included."

"You've been a jerk and asshole, too."

"Yeah, guilty. Can we stop? Can we be friends?"

"We are friends. Not perfect ones, but friends. Beer and pizza. No, good beer and pizza, that's enough."

"You almost got yourself killed. You shouldn't be alone. You're just too pigheaded to realize that."

"I did realize that. I just didn't know who to call."

"Fucking call me. If you almost get killed, call me. Beer and pizza anytime that happens."

"Noted. Is it all right if I call you even if I wasn't almost killed?"

"Yeah, but you might have to split for the beer and pizza."

We finished the beer and the pizza. Joanne took a cab home.

As I lay down in bed, I noticed my hands weren't trembling. They were steady and calm. It might come back. What had Samuel Braud said in his diary? "Every day becomes part of who we are." It would be part of who I am.

Chapter Thirty-seven

Joanne was right. Brandon—and his mother—were working as hard as they could for a plea bargain. He could be out in as little as ten years with good behavior. And significant mental health counseling.

I saw Alan frequently at Riley & Finnegan. He was helping Mary Buchanan with her two rescue kitties, Sammy and Ms. M, taking them when Mary was out of town. He reported that his mother was doing as well as could be expected. She had lost a daughter. As annoyed as I was at how she treated me, she lived in a hell I could not comprehend.

Sophia was smart enough to not apply to any colleges below the Mason-Dixon Line. She'd be heading to NYU in the fall, getting as far away as she could from her toxic parents. Janice was going to LSU and wanted to be involved with the rape prevention group on campus.

And me? I was cooking up a storm for a dinner party tonight. Torbin, Andy, Danny, Elly, Alex, and Joanne were all coming. Torbin had offered to bring the good champagne if I would tell them all about my adventure. He had seen the news stories but had yet to hear my version. I had not said no.

Spring was becoming summer, not yet the oppressive heat of July and August, but sweaty days that were harbingers. Of course, now we had the modern conveniences, air-conditioning, to deal with them in a way Augustine Lamoureaux and her girls on the edge of summer did not. As much as things had changed—and they had—it was still bitter how close so many women lived to the edge. One jealous boyfriend, walking down the wrong street, saying the wrong thing, not being "feminine" enough, bad luck, combined with a few wrong choices—we all make them—and like Tiffany, we would fall forever over the edge.

I needed to move as far as I could away from the edge, to build the life I wanted. Someday I'd be at a party and Cordelia and her new partner would be there. I needed to be okay for that day. Not for her, but for me. And I needed it to be just a day, just a passing day. I'd redone my profile on the dating site, made plans to join a book group, to open the world as best I could. To be so much more than okay.

The doorbell rang.

"No one loves you if you're an asshole jerk," I reminded myself and went to open it.

About the Author

J.M. Redmann is the author of a mystery series featuring New Orleans private detective Michele "Micky" Knight. Her novel *Ill Will* made the American Library Association GLBT Roundtable's 2013 Over the Rainbow list. Her previous book, *Water Mark*, was also on the Over the Rainbow list and won a *Foreword* Magazine Gold First Place mystery award. Two of her earlier books, *The Intersection Of Law & Desire* and *Death Of A Dying Man*, have won Lambda Literary Awards; all but her first book have been nominated. *Law & Desire* was an Editor's Choice of the *San Francisco Chronicle* and a recommended book on NPR's *Fresh Air*.

Her books have been translated into Spanish, German, Dutch, Norwegian, and Hebrew. She is the co-editor with Greg Herren of three anthologies, *Night Shadows: Queer Horror*, *Women of the Mean Streets: Lesbian Noir*, and *Men of the Mean Streets: Gay Noir*.

Redmann lives in an historic neighborhood in New Orleans, at the edge of the area that flooded.

Visit her website at http://www.jmredmann.com.

Books Available From Bold Strokes Books

Escape in Time by Robyn Nyx. Working in the past is hell on your future. (978-1-62639-855-9)

Forget-Me-Not by Kris Bryant. Is love worth walking away from the only life you've ever dreamed of? (978-1-62639-865-8)

Highland Fling by Anna Larner. On vacation in the Scottish Highlands, Eve Eddison falls for the enigmatic forestry officer Moira Burns despite Eve's best friend's campaign to convince her that Moira will break her heart. (978-1-62639-853-5)

Phoenix Rising by Rebecca Harwell. As Storm's Quarry faces invasion from a powerful neighbor, a mysterious newcomer with powers equal to Nadya's challenges everything she believes about herself and her future. (978-1-62639-913-6)

Soul Survivor by I. Beacham. Sam and Joey have given up on hope, but when fate brings them together it gives them a chance to change each other's life and make dreams come true. (978-1-62639-882-5)

Strawberry Summer by Melissa Brayden. When Margaret Beringer's first love Courtney Carrington returns to their small town, she must grapple with their troubled past and fight the temptation for a very delicious future. (978-1-62639-867-2)

The Girl on the Edge of Summer by J.M. Redmann. Micky Knight accepts two cases, but neither is the easy investigation it appears. The past is never past—and young girls lead complicated, even dangerous lives. (978-1-62639-687-6)

Unknown Horizons by CJ Birch. The moment Lieutenant Alison Ash steps aboard the *Persephone*, she knows her life will never be the same. (978-1-62639-938-9)

The Sniper's Kiss by Justine Saracen. The power of a kiss: it can swell your heart with splendor, declare abject submission, and sometimes blow your brains out. (978-1-62639-839-9)

Divided Nation, United Hearts by Yolanda Wallace. In a nation torn in two by a most uncivil war, can love conquer the divide? (978-1-62639-847-4)

Fury's Bridge by Brey Willows. What if your life depended on someone who didn't believe in your existence? (978-1-62639-841-2)

Lightning Strikes by Cass Sellars. When Parker Duncan and Sydney Hyatt's one-night stand turns to more, both women must fight demons past and present to cling to the relationship neither of them thought she wanted. (978-1-62639-956-3)

Love in Disaster by Charlotte Greene. A professor and a celebrity chef are drawn together by chance, but can their attraction survive a natural disaster? (978-1-62639-885-6)

Secret Hearts by Radclyffe. Can two women from different worlds find common ground while fighting their secret desires? (978-1-62639-932-7)

Sins of Our Fathers by A. Rose Mathieu. Solving gruesome murder cases is only one of Elizabeth Campbell's challenges; another is her growing attraction to the female detective who is hell-bent on keeping her client in prison. (978-1-62639-873-3)

Troop 18 by Jessica L. Webb. Charged with uncovering the destructive secret that a troop of RCMP cadets has been hiding, Andy must put aside her worries about Kate and uncover the conspiracy before it's too late. (978-1-62639-934-1)

Worthy of Trust and Confidence by Kara A. McLeod. FBI Special Agent Ryan O'Connor is about to discover the hard way that when you can only handle one type of answer to a question, it really is better not to ask. (978-1-62639-889-4)

Amounting to Nothing by Karis Walsh. When mounted police officer Billie Mitchell steps in to save beautiful murder witness Merissa Karr, worlds collide on the rough city streets of Tacoma, Washington. (978-1-62639-728-6)

Becoming You by Michelle Grubb. Airlie Porter has a secret. A deep, dark, destructive secret that threatens to engulf her if she can't find the courage to face who she really is and who she really wants to be with. (978-1-62639-811-5)

Birthright by Missouri Vaun. When spies bring news that a swordswoman imprisoned in a neighboring kingdom bears the Royal mark, Princess Kathryn sets out to rescue Aiden, true heir to the Belstaff throne. (978-1-62639-485-8)

Crescent City Confidential by Aurora Rey. When romance and danger are in the air, writer Sam Torres learns the Big Easy is anything but. (978-1-62639-764-4)

Love Down Under by MJ Williamz. Wylie loves Amarina, but if Amarina isn't out, can their relationship last? (978-1-62639-726-2)

Privacy Glass by Missouri Vaun. Things heat up when Nash Wiley commandeers a limo and her best friend for a late drive out to the beach: Champagne on ice, seat belts optional, and privacy glass a must. (978-1-62639-705-7)

The Impasse by Franci McMahon. A horse-packing excursion into the Montana Wilderness becomes an adventure of terrifying proportions for Miles and ten women on an outfitter-led trip. (978-1-62639-781-1)

The Right Kind of Wrong by PJ Trebelhorn. Bartender Quinn Burke is happy with her life as a playgirl until she realizes she can't fight her feelings any longer for her best friend, bookstore owner Grace Everett. (978-1-62639-771-2)

Wishing on a Dream by Julie Cannon. Can two women change everything for the chance at love? (978-1-62639-762-0)

A Quiet Death by Cari Hunter. When the body of a young Pakistani girl is found out on the moors, the investigation leaves Detective Sanne Jensen facing an ordeal she may not survive. (978-1-62639-815-3)

Buried Heart by Laydin Michaels. When Drew Chambliss meets Cicely Jones, her buried past finds its way to the surface. Will they survive its discovery or will their chance at love turn to dust? (978-1-62639-801-6)

Escape: Exodus Book Three by Gun Brooke. Aboard the Exodus ship *Pathfinder*, President Thea Tylio still holds Caya Lindemay, a clairvoyant changer, in protective custody, which has devastating consequences endangering their relationship and the entire Exodus mission. (978-1-62639-635-7)

Genuine Gold by Ann Aptaker. New York, 1952. Outlaw Cantor Gold is thrown back into her honky-tonk Coney Island past, where crime and passion simmer in a neon glare. (978-1-62639-730-9)

Into Thin Air by Jeannie Levig. When her girlfriend disappears, Hannah Lewis discovers her world isn't as orderly as she thought it was. (978-1-62639-722-4)

Night Voice by CF Frizzell. When talk show host Sable finally acknowledges her risqué radio relationship with a mysterious caller, she welcomes a *real* relationship with local tradeswoman Riley Burke. (978-1-62639-813-9)

Raging at the Stars by Lesley Davis. When the unbelievable theories start revealing themselves as truths, can you trust in the ones who have conspired against you from the start? (978-1-62639-720-0)

She Wolf by Sheri Lewis Wohl. When the hunter becomes the hunted, more than love might be lost. (978-1-62639-741-5)

Smothered and Covered by Missouri Vaun. The last person Nash Wiley expects to bump into over a two a.m. breakfast at Waffle House is her college crush, decked out in a curve-hugging law enforcement uniform. (978-1-62639-704-0)

The Butterfly Whisperer by Lisa Moreau. Reunited after ten years, can Jordan and Sophie heal the past and rediscover love or will differing desires keep them apart? (978-1-62639-791-0)

The Devil's Due by Ali Vali. Cain and Emma Casey are awaiting the birth of their third child, but as always in Cain's world, there are new and old enemies to face in Katrina-ravaged New Orleans. (978-1-62639-591-6)

Widows of the Sun-Moon by Barbara Ann Wright. With immortality now out of their grasp, the gods of Calamity fight amongst themselves, egged on by the mad goddess they thought they'd left behind. (978-1-62639-777-4)

Arrested Hearts by Holly Stratimore. A reckless cop who hates her life and a health nut who is afraid to die might be a perfect combination for love. (978-1-62639-809-2)

Capturing Jessica by Jane Hardee. Hyperrealist sculptor Michael tries desperately to conceal the love she holds for best friend, Jess, unaware Jess's feelings for her are changing. (978-1-62639-836-8)

Counting to Zero by AJ Quinn. NSA agent Emma Thorpe and computer hacker Paxton James must learn to trust each other as they work to stop a threat clock that's rapidly counting down to zero. (978-1-62639-783-5)

One More Reason to Leave Orlando by Missouri Vaun. Nash Wiley thought a threesome sounded exotic and exciting, but as it turns out the reality of sleeping with two women at the same time is just really complicated. (978-1-62639-703-3)

Pathogen by Jessica L. Webb. Can Dr. Kate Morrison navigate a deadly virus and the threat of bioterrorism, as well as her new relationship with Sergeant Andy Wyles and her own troubled past? (978-1-62639-833-7)

Rainbow Gap by Lee Lynch. Jaudon Vickers and Berry Garland, polar opposites, dream and love in this tale of lesbian lives set in Central Florida against the tapestry of societal change and the Vietnam War. (978-1-62639-799-6)